# BLOOD & BONES: CAGE

Blood Fury MC®

Book 5

## JEANNE ST. JAMES

Jeanne
ST. JAMES

———

**Acknowledgements:**

Photographer: 6:12 Photography by Eric McKinney
Cover Artist: Golden Czermak at FuriousFotog
Cover Model: Jason D.
Editor: Proofreading by the Page
Beta readers: Andi Babcock, Sharon Abrams & Alexandra Swab
Blood Fury MC Logo: Jennifer Edwards

———

**www.jeannestjames.com**

**Sign up for my newsletter for insider information, author news, and new releases:
https://www.authorjeannestjames.com/**

## Character List

TO AVOID SPOILERS THIS LIST ONLY INCLUDES THE
CHARACTERS MENTIONED IN THE PREVIOUS
BOOKS

### <u>BFMC Members:</u>

**Trip Davis** – *President* – Son of Buck Davis, half-brother to Sig, mother is Tammy, Runs Buck You Recovery

**Sig Stevens** – *Vice President* – Son of Buck Davis, mother is Silvia, three years younger than Trip, helps run Buck You Recovery

**Judge Scott** (Judd) – *Sgt at Arms* - Father (Ox) was an Original, owns Justice Bail Bonds

**Deacon Edwards** – *Treasurer* – Judge's cousin, Skip Tracer/Bounty Hunter at Justice Bail Bonds

**Cage** (Chris Dietrich) – *Road Captain* – Dutch's youngest son, mechanic at Dutch's Garage

**Ozzy** (Thomas Oswald) – *Secretary* – *Original* – manages club-owned The Grove Inn.

**Rook** (Randy Dietrich) – Dutch's oldest son

**Dutch** (David Dietrich) – *Original* – Owns Dutch's Garage, sons: Cage & Rook

**Dodge** – Helps manage Crazy Pete's Bar

**Whip** – Mechanic at Dutch's Garage (formerly known as the prospect Sparky)

**Rev** (Mickey) – Mechanic at Dutch's Garage (formerly known as the prospect Mouse)
**Shade** – works at Tioga Pet Crematorium (formerly known as the prospect Shady)
**Easy** – works at Tioga Pet Crematorium
**Tater Tot** - *Prospect*
**Possum** - *Prospect*

**Stella** – *Trip's ol' lady* - Crazy Pete's daughter, owns Crazy Pete's Bar
**Autumn** (Red) – *Sig's ol' lady* – Accountant for the club's businesses
**Cassidy** (Cassie) – *Judge's ol' lady* – Manages club-owned Tioga Pet Crematorium
**Reese** – *Deacon's ol' lady* – Civil law attorney

## Former Originals:

**Buck Davis** – *President* – Deceased
**Razor Stevens** – *VP* - Deceased
**Ox** – *Sgt at Arms* – Deceased
**Crazy Pete** – *Treasurer* – Deceased
**Tin Man (Tinny)** – Deceased

## Others:

Reilly – Reese's sister, works at Dutch's Garage
Henry (Ry) – Judge's son
Daisy – Cassie's daughter
Jemma – Judge's sister
Syn Stevens – Sig's sister
Saylor – Rev's sister, Judge and Cassie's house mouse
Silvia Stevens – Sig's mother, Razor's former ol' lady
Tammy Davis – Trip's mother, Buck's former ol' lady

Bebe Dietrich – Cage & Rook's mother, Dutch's former ol' lady

Clyde Davis – Buck's father, Trip & Sig's grandfather, deceased

Lizzy/Billie/Angel – Sweet butts

Max Bryson – *Chief of Police* – Manning Grove PD, Bryson brother

Marc Bryson – *Corporal* – Manning Grove PD, Bryson brother

Matt Bryson – *Officer* – Manning Grove PD, Bryson brother

Adam Bryson – *Officer* – Manning Grove PD, Brysons' cousin, Teddy's husband

Leah Bryson – *Officer* – Manning Grove PD, Marc's wife

Tommy Dunn – *Officer* – Manning Grove PD

Teddy Bryson – Owner Manes on Main, Adam Bryson's husband

Amanda Bryson – Max's wife, owner Boneyard Bakery

Carly Bryson – Matt's wife, OB/GYN doctor

Levi Bryson – Adopted son of Matt & Carly Bryson (birth mother: Autumn)

# Prologue

## SAYING GOODBYE

CHRIS SCRAMBLED AROUND HIS ROOM, stuffing whatever he could find, whatever he couldn't live without, into a trash bag. His heart raced and his thoughts twisted.

He needed to hurry.

Before it was too late.

"Mom! I'm going with you, Mom!" He hiccuped when he tried to hold back a sob.

He didn't get a response.

Quickly glancing around his room, he made sure he didn't miss anything important. But his room was a mess. His clothes were scattered on the floor. His sheets a tangled ball in the middle of his unmade bed.

His closet door hung open because he couldn't close it anymore. He had stuffed it with so much crap. Stuff he thought was important, stuff he thought he needed to keep, but not important enough to pack.

Underwear!

He scrambled over the piles on the floor to get to his dresser and ripped open the top drawer.

Empty.

He scoured the discarded dirty clothes taking up most of

the floor space and found a few pairs not too holey or worn, throwing them into the black garbage bag. His eyes then landed on his most treasured possession propped in the corner next to his bed.

He rushed over to it, almost tumbling when his feet caught in a pair of dirty jeans on the way. Without a second thought, he shoved the last item into the bag and decided whatever else he'd need his mother could get him when they got to where they were going.

He had no idea where that was. He just knew they were leaving. And quickly.

His mother had had enough.

And he had no idea where his father was.

Probably at the garage. Or the warehouse. Or Crazy Pete's.

Or in some other woman's bed. He'd heard his mother yell at his father about that one too many times.

Something happened tonight, though.

Something she wouldn't explain.

When she had walked through the front door a little while ago, she shot him and his older brother a frown, shook her head and announced, "You two will end up just like him."

Right after that, she went into her bedroom. Chris had followed her, wondering why she was so mad.

What had their father done this time?

Or did Randy do something? He was always getting in trouble.

What he found was his mother packing a bag. Emptying her closet and drawers, and throwing everything that wouldn't fit into that bag onto the bed.

She didn't even hesitate when she spotted him standing in the doorway, clinging tightly to the frame. "Go get me the box of trash bags under the kitchen sink."

"What are you doing?"

"Do what I said."

He always did whatever his mother said because maybe, if he did, she'd give him a smile or a hug, or tell him she loved him.

She never did.

But he always hoped...

Maybe she would this time.

He'd taken off down the hall, found the open box of black garbage bags and ran back to his parents' bedroom.

By then she had so much stuff on the bed. Possibly everything she owned.

As he'd stepped closer, staring at the mountain, she snatched the box from his fingers.

"What are you doing, Mom?" His heart had been racing so badly, his chest became as tight as the drum he'd found in a dumpster a few weeks ago. The drum he wasn't allowed to play in the house, but only outside.

And even then, it still disappeared.

Randy said Mom had thrown it away, somewhere Chris wouldn't be able to find it, because him playing it gave her a headache.

His mother, with an unlit cigarette hanging out of her mouth, began to pull bags out of the box.

"Are you leaving?"

She didn't answer him, only kept stuffing bag after bag full.

"Randy!" she yelled. "Randy, get the fuck in here. Now!"

She was piling bags up on the floor, all of them full of her things.

"Yeah?" Chris's older brother came and stood in the doorway, his face unreadable.

His brother's eyes, the same dark brown as their father's, had swept the room. But he said nothing. He stood there casually, not caring that their mother was leaving and hadn't told them to pack, too.

"Start loading those bags there in my car," she'd jerked her chin toward the pile of full trash bags, "while I pack the rest of my shit."

"I can do it, Mom," Chris had volunteered quickly, even though at twelve, Randy was taller and stronger than him. "But I'm going with you."

"No, boy, you're staying here. Boys need to be with their father."

Boys needed to be with their mother, too. Didn't she know that? Even he knew that and he was only eight.

"But, Mom—"

"Get out of your brother's way," was all she said as she made sure Randy was doing what she told him. She turned back to the bed, shoving more clothes and other stuff into more bags.

His eyes landed on an empty trash bag that had fallen to the floor. He grabbed it and rushed back to his room and that was when he began to pack.

She was not leaving without him.

Now, with his own full bag, Chris stepped out into the hallway, no longer hearing any activity coming from his parents' room.

With the bag bouncing off his legs, he ran back there anyway to check.

Empty. His mother was gone, her bags were gone and he had no idea where Randy was.

"Wait, Mom!" he screamed. "I'm going with you!"

He rushed down the hallway, his stuffed-full garbage bag becoming heavier with each step. "Mom! Don't leave without me!"

He dropped the bag to the floor and began to drag it behind him so he could move faster. He had to catch her before she left.

He wasn't staying here.

He wasn't.

Another hiccup-sob surged up from his gut as he reached the front living room. She wasn't there, either.

Neither was Randy.

The front door was wide open and he could see his older brother standing outside on the porch, staring out at the street.

Alone. Quiet. With both hands on his hips.

Chris dragged the bag, which held everything important to him, through the door and out onto the porch, pushing past his brother who blocked the two steps to the yard.

"She's gone, kid." He turned his head and spat into what used to be a garden in front of their small house. Before the weeds choked the flowers the previous renter must have planted and had been left to die once his family moved in.

Chris kept going, the heavy bag thumping down each step, even though her car was gone.

Even though their mother was nowhere to be seen.

No sign of her anywhere.

"Why?" he screamed. His stomach ached painfully, like it had been hollowed out with an ice cream scoop. "*Why* would she leave us?"

She'd come back for them. She had to. They were her sons. What mother didn't want her own children?

"She's a fuckin' whore."

"No, she ain't! Dad's the whore!" he shouted at his brother.

"Dad ain't a whore, stupid. Dad didn't do nothin' Mom didn't do. Saw her suckin' dick plenty of times. And it wasn't Dad's."

*What?* Now Randy was just plain lying!

At the bottom of the steps, Chris dropped his bag on the narrow sidewalk and, with a roar, rushed his brother.

Before he could make it to the steps, Randy jumped down and tackled him. Chris fell backward and his head just missed the edge of the concrete.

"You're an asshole!" he screamed, grabbing Randy's hair and ripping on it.

A wild, flailing fist made contact with Chris's cheek and the pain caused him to lose his breath.

He growled and tried to roll his brother, but he was much smaller and couldn't get his weight behind him. Instead, he shoved his brother with both palms, knocking him off balance.

As soon as he rolled on top of Randy, he found himself once again on his back in the grass, unable to catch his breath. His brother was sitting on his chest, crushing his lungs and pinning his arms to the ground.

"Knock it off, you little shit. You made my fuckin' lip bleed."

"Good!" came out on a half-sob. He couldn't cry. Not in front of Randy. But he couldn't wipe the tears away while his asshole brother held him down. "Lemme go!"

"Only if you stop tryin' to fight me. I didn't do this to you. That bitch did. You think she gave two shits about you? She didn't. Her leavin' just proved it. She was just the twat used to squirt us out. That's it. Nothin' more."

"You're wrong." Why was Randy lying like that?

"Yeah, so wrong," Randy muttered and shook his head. "I'm gettin' off you. You try fightin' me again, I'm not gonna hold back. Dad will find you out in the yard when he gets home with your ass kicked. Then he'll kick it a second time for bein' a whiny-assed pussy."

Randy slowly lifted his weight and, when he was on his feet, his brother wiped the back of his hand across this mouth, smearing the blood. He spat into the grass next to Chris's head. Luckily, Chris twisted it away in time to keep from getting splattered.

"We don't need that bitch. What the fuck did she ever do for you?"

Chris laid in the grass, taking deep inhales since his brother was no longer crushing him. Anything to keep himself from crying.

With another shake of his head, Randy walked over to Chris's worn, dirty teddy bear that had tumbled out onto the dead grass, along with the rest of his things, when the bag spilled during the struggle. His brother picked up the stuffed animal, stared at it for a second, then came back to where Chris laid sprawled on the ground. He dropped it onto his chest. "I'll tell you what the fuck she's done. Nothin'. So, don't be such a fuckin' baby. We're better off without her."

Chris laid there, staring up at the late afternoon sky, and a hot tear slid from the corner of his eye. He heard his brother stomp back up the steps, go inside and slam the front door shut.

From inside the house, Chris heard a muffled shout of, "Fuck her!"

He grabbed his teddy bear, hugged it against his chest and curled into a ball around it. "She'll be back," he whispered, unable to stop the tears anymore. No longer caring who saw him cry.

Shortly after, the tears stopped.

And much later, he forgot what she looked like.

Because that night, when his father got home, he burned every damn photo of her in that house. Anything she left behind was burned, too. Then he told them never to mention her name again.

That rule wasn't difficult to follow because Chris never knew what her name was.

He'd only ever called her Mom.

## Chapter One

FUCKING MONDAYS.

Monday mornings were always the hardest.

Cage's hand slipped down his bare chest and under the tangled sheet to find another reason mornings were *hard*.

With one hand wrapped around his morning wood, he yawned. He needed to take a piss but that wouldn't happen any time soon. At least not until his current dilemma was resolved.

The toilet flushing in the small bathroom attached to his room in the club's bunkhouse had his eyes popping open and his heart skipping a beat.

*What the fuck?*

Who the fuck was in his bathroom?

He jackknifed up to a seated position and glanced around the room, trying to remember everything that happened last night at, or after, the club's pig roast.

They'd gone on a Sunday club run. Check.

They had a pig roast afterward since they had a lot of leftovers from the prior weekend's charity poker run. They'd raised a shit ton of scratch for the Kids Can Do Foundation. So, he stuffed his gut full of good grub. Check.

He'd played a couple rounds of pool with Ozzy and scored a Benjamin. Check.

Then he lost it to Dodge at darts. Unfortunate check.

Billie had been trying to drag him back into his room all night. She didn't succeed. Check.

Wait.

Or did she? Uncheck.

*Fuck.*

He scanned the floor for a female's clothing. No black combat boots or goth shit. No heavy makeup staining his pillow. *Thank fuck.* Check.

He usually ended up hurting after Billie got her hands on him. She was into some crazy shit. Currently, he wasn't sore, bleeding or bruised. Check. Check. Check.

He quickly continued to go through his night as he heard the water run in the sink.

Whiskey? Check.

Lots of whiskey? Check.

Too much whiskey? *Fuck.*

So much so, he didn't have a fucking clue who was going to pop out of his bathroom like a stripper coming out of a surprise birthday cake.

Did it really matter?

Probably not.

The only problem was, one of the bunkhouse rules was no women overnight. He didn't need Trip kicking his ass out of his room. He liked living here. It was cheap. He had his own crapper. He had full access to the stocked kitchen down the corridor. He could get drunk off his ass and just stumble his way back to his bed. And, best of all, plenty of pussy was always available.

He held his breath as the doorknob on the bathroom turned.

It was like spinning a roulette wheel. His dick could've been placed in anyone's box.

Well, female only, of course.

The door swung open and...

He blinked.

The woman smiled and tossed her long platinum-blonde hair over her shoulder.

Well, at least she wasn't fugly.

But he had no idea who she was. "Uh..."

Her smile widened as she climbed into bed with him. Naked.

He had to admit her body was banging.

Which was probably why he banged her. Even drunk he had good taste.

"We banged, right?"

"You don't remember?"

Cage weighed his options on answering that with a lie or not. "Last night's a little sketchy. We use a wrap?"

She combed her fingers through his hair, making him pull his head away and grimace. "Of course."

*Oh, thank fuck.* Last thing he wanted was to knock up some woman he didn't know. Or, *hell,* any fucking woman.

"Three."

He cocked an eyebrow. *Huh.* He guessed the amount of whiskey he drank, which robbed him of his memory, hadn't done anything to affect his studly performance.

"The last time I had to work a little harder."

*Damn,* he wished he remembered it now.

"If you're a little sore back there, that's why. I had to work you deep for a while to get everything up and running properly."

*Say what? Back where?* "Uh..." He clenched his ass checks, checking to see if anything felt different.

She laughed and slapped his bare chest. "I'm just kidding!" Her laughter faded away. "You really don't remember?"

He scratched at the whiskers on his chin. "Bits and pieces." *Total fucking lie.*

She pouted.

*Oh fuck.* "Look, you gotta go. You can't be in here."

"You invited me."

"Right. For…" *Whatever the fuck we did.* "For that, yeah. But we got rules."

The sweet butts knew the rule about scramming before sunrise. If they wanted to keep in good standing with the Fury, they followed the rules. Rules like any brother with an ol' lady was off-limits. No hard drugs. Their good-looking lady-friends were welcome as long as they were legal, open to anything, and could keep their fucking mouth shut.

Since he had no idea who this female was, it made sense this one didn't know the rules. But whoever invited her to the party last night should've told her.

Or he should've. *Fuck.*

"I gotta get to work and you gotta get outta here before you're spotted."

"I have to sneak out?"

"Sneak out. Crawl out. Evaporate. Don't care. Just do it."

She grabbed his hard dick over the tented sheet, causing his hips to jerk. "You don't want me to take care of this first?"

He pursed his lips as he considered her offer. "What time is it?" What did it matter if she left at seven or seven-fifteen? It would still give him enough time to get to the garage.

"Almost a quarter after eight."

*Oh fuck!* He surged from the bed, dislodging not only her hand but the rest of her body, too. As nice as it was. "You gotta go. I'm gonna be late for work." Not *gonna be*, he was.

"You work?"

He frowned. "Of course I fuckin' work."

"I thought you guys just rode your motorcycles and sold drugs or something."

He stared at her. "Who the fuck invited you here last night?"

"You did."

"No. To this property. It's by invitation only. Who invited you?"

Her over-plucked eyebrows pinned together. "Janie."

"Who the fuck is Janie?"

The naked twenty-something on his bed shrugged, making her really sweet tits jiggle. *Fuck*, they were so damn perky. "A chick I met at a party in Williamsport."

"Who the fuck invited her?"

Platinum Barbie shrugged again, put a fingertip to her lips and tilted her head. "I think..." She put that finger in the air. "Janie."

Cage gritted his teeth. "You just said Janie invited you."

"Oh, yeah, right. I don't know then."

*Christ.* It was clear he hadn't brought her back to his room for her smarts. "Don't matter. You gotta get your ass outta here."

"But—"

"No buts. Not a discussion. Get dressed, get out. Do it quick. Do it quiet. Just go."

She huffed.

"Takin' a fuckin' shower. Be gone before I get out. Don't steal shit. Don't touch shit. Just go."

"Don't you want my number?"

He paused only a step away from his bathroom. Did he? No. He couldn't remember how she was. She might have totally sucked and, if she did, he didn't want to get stuck doing her again when he was sober.

He learned that lesson before.

A couple times.

"All right... uh..." *Fuck*, he didn't know her name. "*You.*

See ya 'round." Thanks for the fucking memories. Or lack of them.

She wasn't moving. She sat there wearing nothing but a disappointed look.

"Only gonna take me about five minutes to shower, so..." So, she needed to move this along.

She smiled and perked up. "Oh, you want me to wait?"

*Damn it.* "No. Stick to the original plan. Be gone before I get out."

Again, the fucking exaggerated lower lip pout. It wasn't sexy, it was fucking annoying.

He shook his head and went into the bathroom.

Eight minutes later he stepped back out into his room. Once again, his heart skipped a beat.

Instead of one blonde, another one stood in her place.

"Jesus fuck," he muttered.

Reilly grinned and didn't even blush as she raked her eyes over his damp, naked body.

*Fuck it,* if she didn't care, he didn't, either.

"Do you know what time it is?" she had the nerve to ask.

"How'd you get here?" She didn't have her own cage and she'd been living temporarily at The Grove Inn. She certainly didn't hoof it there on foot.

She shrugged. "Ozzy."

"Why the fuck would Ozzy bring you here?"

"Because you never showed up to get me this morning."

*Damn,* it had been his morning to pick Reilly up from the motel and take her to work. They needed to get her a damn cage. And soon.

But she couldn't afford one yet and the stubborn woman was determined to do everything on her own. And right now, she was saving up for first and last month's rent on an apartment, along with a security deposit.

"So, why the fuck didn't you get Ozzy to drop you off at the garage?"

"He did. But as soon as I got there, Dutch was on a damn rampage and told me to find your ass... *or else.*" She growled the last part in a deep voice, but not even coming close to just how grumpy his father could sound.

*Jesus Christ.*

She grinned. "You were pretty fucked up last night."

He didn't need that reminder. His pounding head was a constant one. "Figured that out."

"Your head hurt?"

"No," he lied.

"I would have a wicked hangover if I was in your shoes."

"You don't wear my fuckin' shoes. You just gonna stand there while I get dressed?"

"Give me a good reason why I shouldn't."

He shook his head. *Whatever.* He dug through the piles of clothes thrown on the floor and draped over his dresser, and everywhere else, to find a half-decent pair of jeans and a T-shirt. Not that it mattered if they were clean, they would end up with grease on them by the end of the day, anyway.

Deacon's ol' lady's sister leaned back against the closed door as he dressed. She had her arms crossed over her chest, which pushed up her tits nicely, and a grin on her face as she watched his every move.

She was hot as fuck, but he also wasn't stupid.

Not always, anyway. Sometimes his decisions could be questionable.

Even so, both Judge and Deacon had given the "hands off" rule when it came to Reese's younger sister.

So far, so good.

And he wasn't going to be the first to break that rule.

Fuck no.

He lifted his head when he finished buckling his belt. "Where'd she go?"

"I pointed her toward the back door. She was cute. A little dumb, though."

"Musta fucked her brains out."

Reilly rolled her big green, *doesn't-miss-a-thing* eyes. "Sure you did."

Cage turned in a circle, searching for his cut. He followed where Reilly pointed and jerked his chin up in thanks.

"Do you even remember anything?"

"Sure. Best fuck I've had in a while."

"Huh. Is that right? What's her name?"

*Fuck.* "Tonya."

Reilly laughed. "No, it wasn't."

He shrugged on his cut and made sure the keys to his '75 Shovelhead were still tucked in the inner pocket. "Yeah? What was it?"

"Not Tonya."

Reilly was known to meddle, but still... "Why would you even ask her?"

"I didn't." She held out her hand. In it was a piece of scrap paper.

"Fuck, that her number?"

Reilly nodded with a grin. "And her name. Should we make a bet on how many times it would take you to get it right?"

"Nope. Let's go. Dutch is gonna be up my ass." Cage ignored the paper when Reilly tossed it on his bed.

"Oh yeah. He's already on a roll, grumping and growling. Everybody's cursing you out for getting him all worked up."

"Great," he muttered under his breath. "Where's Oz?"

"Probably in the kitchen. He said he's making himself a big greasy breakfast this morning to soak up some of last night's booze."

"I could go for one of those, too." *Hint, hint.*

"You're getting a stale donut leftover from Friday, along with a Dutch-sized boot up your ass."

*Fuck.*

Reilly stepped up to him, reached into the opening of his cut and patted his gut. "I'll make you a strong pot of coffee when we get there."

"Then what the fuck we waitin' for?"

She grabbed his cheeks between her fingers and squeezed them together, giving him duck lips. "You're so cute," she teased with a laugh. She released his face and walked out the door.

Cage followed.

"Cage..." she threw over her shoulder as she headed toward the rear exit.

"Yeah?"

"I need to know... Are you a show-er or a grower?"

A snort came from his left. He spotted one of their newer prospects, Tater Tot, standing just inside the prospect's bunkroom.

Cage stopped in his tracks and shot him a searing look. "You supposed to be in here right now? Don't you got somewhere to be?"

The chunky nineteen-year-old's eyes went wide. "Don't gotta be at Pete's 'til one."

"Don't give a fuck where you gotta be at one. Where you gotta be now?"

Tater's mouth dropped open and he stuttered, "I... I..."

"I got a room full of dirty fuckin' laundry. You got 'til you go to Pete's to get it all fuckin' washed, dried and put the fuck away. You get me?"

The kid's Adam's apple jumped. "Yeah."

"I find you missed one thing—a sock under my bed, a pair of boxers in my bathroom, one of Reilly's cum-stained thongs hidden in my sheets—gonna find somethin' even shittier for you to do."

Tater stood frozen in place.

"Go!" Cage roared.

The prospect jerked, then lumbered past him and down the hall to Cage's room.

He sliced his gaze from Tater back to Reilly who was waiting by the back door, appearing amused.

"My cum-stained thong?"

"Was told I couldn't touch you. Never was told I couldn't fantasize." He grinned, stuck out his tongue at her and jerked his hand up and down in the air like he was whacking off.

Reilly arched an eyebrow. "Well, to make your fantasies more accurate, I don't wear thongs."

"No? What d'you wear?"

Reilly shoved the push bar to the back door with both hands, flinging it open. "Nothing!"

Cage stood there for a second, then rushed after her.

Within twenty minutes, they were pulling into the garage lot on his sled with Reilly wrapped around his back.

All four garage bay doors were wide open, which was normal for June.

What wasn't normal was Rev, Whip, Rook and Dutch standing in a half circle around a large cardboard box on the ground.

Either they were inspecting some part that had been delivered or a litter of kittens someone dropped off overnight, which happened way too often. Assholes dumped their cats at their place thinking they'd need them for the storage yard to keep the rodent population down.

Cage was usually the one tasked with taking the abandoned animals to the local humane society. It was either that or taking them over to Tioga Pet Crematorium and...

No, those kittens didn't ask to be born or abandoned.

Just like him and Rook. Unwanted by someone who was supposed to take care of them. Who was supposed to love them.

Cage rolled his sled into the spot next to Rook's and shut it down.

"What's going on?" Reilly asked as she dismounted and pulled off the brain bucket Reese insisted she wear. His attention turned from the men to her as she bent over, giving him a nice view of her perfect, juicy peach of an ass, and shook her long blonde hair out before flipping it back up.

"Don't know. You see what I see," he murmured.

As his gaze fell back on the group, he realized all of them had turned to watch him and Reilly.

Or maybe just Reilly.

A *whoop whoop* made his heart jump into his throat as a Manning Grove PD cruiser rolled into the lot and up to the garage crew.

What the fuck was going on? What the fuck did Rook do now? Did that asshole break parole?

"Someone going to jail?" Reilly whispered.

"Beats the fuck outta me."

She nudged him with her elbow. "She was legal, right?"

"Didn't even know her fuckin' name, Reilly. How the fuck would I know how old she was?" He grimaced. "Hope to fuck she was."

"Better hope so."

Yeah, he more than hoped so. Unlike his brother, he'd only done a couple short bids in the county jail. Mostly for stupid shit when he was underage. Rook tended to like those longer state or federal vacations with bars. And not the drinking type of bars.

On his last *not-so-tropical* getaway, Rook became prison pals with Dodge, who now helped manage Crazy Pete's.

As he strode across the front lot with Reilly on his heels, the black-and-white's driver's door opened and one of the *too-many-badge-wearing* Brysons unfolded from the seat.

Matt Bryson, to be exact. The pig who, along with his

doctor wife, adopted Red's baby, Levi, last November. He stepped up to the half circle.

"What the fuck," Cage heard the cop whisper as he joined the group and stared down into the box. Reilly shoved her way in, too.

Cage glanced down and scowled. "What the fuck is that?" It certainly wasn't a fucking kitten.

"Holy shit," Reilly whispered. "A baby."

"Looks like a newborn," Bryson said, raising his face and his gaze circling all of them. "Is this where you found it?"

"Yeah," Dutch answered. "Came in through the gate and then the back door this mornin', so I didn't spot it."

"Saw the box when I came in the front door earlier," Whip said. "Didn't check it right away thinkin' someone dropped a part off or somethin' overnight."

"Has it cried at all?" Bryson asked as he pulled back the green blanket the baby was wrapped in and ran a finger over its pudgy cheek. Its eyes were open and it made a little noise that sort of sounded like a kitten's mew.

"Nope," Dutch answered, his bushy salt-and-pepper eyebrows pinned together.

"It doesn't look sick. But I'm calling EMS to come get it and take it to the ER."

"You need to find its mother," Reilly said, squatting next to Bryson and also touching the kid.

"Yo, Captain Obvious, maybe you shouldn't touch it," Cage told her.

"It isn't a fucking baby bird!"

He winced. Her shout didn't help his pounding head. "Don't gotta yell."

"Well, don't be an asshole."

Ignoring them, Bryson grabbed his radio mic from his shoulder and called for a "bus." Pig-speak for an ambulance.

"What's gonna happen to it?" Whip asked, his brow furrowed.

Bryson glanced up at him. "We'll have to call Child Protective Services. They can deal with it until the mother's found or someone comes forward to claim it. *If* someone does. But this baby was just born. He's as tiny as Levi was."

Bryson did another quick inspection, then reached into the box full of blankets, picked the kid up and rose to his feet, holding it against his chest. He peeled the blanket back a little more, exposing the fact the baby wore a thick towel around his bottom area instead of a diaper.

Something was pinned to the front of the towel.

"What's that?" Reilly asked. Before she could pluck it off the makeshift diaper, Bryson grabbed it and scanned what looked like a handwritten note.

"Shit," he muttered and his crystal blue eyes hit Cage's.

His dropped from the cop's face to the note as it was shoved into his chest.

Cage's stomach dropped, too, when Bryson said, "Better read that."

# Chapter Two

Better read that.

Cage wasn't so sure he wanted to.

No, he knew he didn't.

He had no fucking choice.

He gripped the note as Bryson's fingers released it. And everything around him went out of focus.

*Better read that.*

His heart was fighting to escape his chest. His mouth became as dry as a desert. An invisible hand squeezed his throat.

"What the fuck does it say, boy?" Dutch bellowed at him. His father had an extreme case of impatience. Today wasn't any different.

Cage pulled the small scrap of paper away from his chest and slowly let his gaze drop from his father to it.

*Christopher,*

*I kept it a secret as long as possible. From you, from everyone.*

*When I couldn't conceal it anymore, my family hid me until the birth.*

*I had no choice but to give our baby up or be shunned.*

*I can't live in your world and you can never live in mine. Nor would you want to.*

*I'm sorry. This is for the best.*

*God forgive me.*

*God forgive you.*

*May God bless this child He made.*

*~ S*


S?

Sarah?

*Fuck. Fuck. Fuck.*

*Fuck!*

He'd only been with her a couple times. At the end of her rumspringa, after she had decided she wouldn't join the church. She stated a few times she no longer wanted to live the Amish life. She planned on leaving her community and living among the "English."

That was what she said.

Before she changed her mind, apparently.

She had shyly flirted with him when she came along with her cousin, Rebecca, and the others to drop off weekly supplies at The Barn.

Then she encouraged him to sneak off a couple times...

To show her what a kiss was like.

And then...

*Fuck.*

She stopped coming. He hadn't thought much about it. He certainly had no reason to go looking for her. It wasn't a thing, it was just a fling. A little forbidden fun on both their parts.

Trip didn't want any of them fucking with the Amish. Especially with what happened between Sig and Rebecca.

His prez would be fucking pissed. Fucking furious if Cage's fuck-up threatened the club's relationship with the plain people.

His eyes slid back to his father, whose mouth was moving, but Cage couldn't hear anything coming out of it. Maybe that was for the best.

His father was friendly with some of the elders...

*Fuck. Shit. Motherfucker.*

He crumpled the note within his fist and walked away, raking fingers through his hair. He kept going until he hit the edge of the concrete sidewalk that ran past the garage. He stopped, planted one hand on his hip and stared sightlessly across the street. Tempted to step out into the roadway when the next big truck sped by.

This was *not* happening.

How the fuck could it happen?

No way. The note was a fucking lie.

It was all a lie.

He'd worn a condom both times. He swore he did.

He had to have. He'd never risk getting saddled with a snot monkey.

He had no desire to be a father. Especially to some Amish baby that probably wasn't even his.

This was all bullshit.

She fucked someone else. An Amish guy or something and wanted to pawn the unwanted kid off on him. Pass it off as his, get the kid out of the community so she didn't look like a slut who gave up her virginity before marriage.

That was it.

It was all a fucking lie. That was what he would tell Bryson. To take the kid and do whatever with it. He wanted nothing to do with someone else's brat.

He spun and strode back toward the group, who all stared at him.

His gaze landed on his brother who looked almost as pissed as Dutch.

His feet stopped moving halfway through the lot. He stood there, helpless, the note still crumpled in his fist.

He closed his eyes and scrubbed a hand down his face.

Out of nowhere, he was standing in a yard of brown, dead grass.

On that day.

The day she left.

The day she deserted him and Rook.

Left them behind without a second thought.

Not giving a flying fuck about what happened to them.

Simply gave up her sons because she was done with the MC life. Done with her ol' man. Done with her own fucking children.

She had abandoned them all.

His eyes popped open when the balled-up note was snatched from his hand. His father unwrinkled it and quickly read it.

Then his dark brown eyes hit his. Cage didn't even bother to duck when Dutch swung. His old man clubbed him alongside the head, rattling his brains for a second. "Stupid motherfucker."

Bryson yelled out a, "Yo! Dutch! You can't do that shit in front of me."

Dutch ignored the pig in uniform. "Taught you boys to wrap your fuckin' shit tight, didn't I? You just made me a goddamn granddaddy before my fuckin' time." He jerked on his long salt-and-pepper beard. He shook the wrinkled note in front of Cage's face. "Makin' me feel old. Goddamn it." He spat tobacco juice on the ground at Cage's feet, splashing his boots.

Dutch took the note with him when he walked back to where Bryson was holding the baby. Rev and Whip were gone, most likely ordered to get back to work by his father. And Rook and Reilly remained with the cop.

Rook's face was now unreadable. Reilly kept glancing back and forth from Dutch to Cage with a worried look.

"You know her? This S?" Matt Bryson asked, gently

bouncing the baby because it was now crying softly. Like a kitten. Which was what should have been in that fucking box in the first place!

"Of fuckin' course he knew her if he stuck his dick in her and got her knocked up," Dutch growled.

"You didn't force her—"

Rook shouted a, "Hey!" cutting the pig off. "My brother don't need to force a fuckin' woman."

Cage looked up from the now red-faced infant in Bryson's arm. "No. Didn't force her. She gave it up willingly."

Bryson stared down at the baby and sighed. "You think it's yours?"

"Dunno," Cage answered honestly. "Wrapped it tight each time... Could be tryin' to pawn her spawn off on me... Not sure."

"What do you want to do?" Bryson asked.

"This isn't like kittens, Cage. You can't take him to the Humane Society," Reilly said behind him, like she was being fucking helpful.

"EMS is already en route. I can call CPS, if you want. Especially if you don't think he's yours."

He?

No fucking way he had a son. And this was all starting to feel a little too real.

He had drank so much last night he'd blacked out. Now he was just sleeping it off and this was just a nightmare.

That was it.

This was all a fucking nightmare to teach him a lesson about drinking too much.

He'd imagined everything that happened this morning. He didn't wake up with some random snatch in his room. Reilly never showed up, riding his ass about being late. And in a little while he'd open his eyes and see his dirty laundry still scattered all over his room.

Yep. He was recovering from the whiskey bender he had last night.

The baby's cry turned into a wail.

"DNA test would be smart," Bryson suggested, as if this wasn't a nightmare. "Then if he's yours, you can put him up for adoption. Maybe Teddy and Adam would be interested."

Right. Hand his son over to a gay couple to raise.

*Fuck*, they'd do a better job than him. What the fuck did he know about babies? Nothing.

He didn't want to learn, either.

"If this is my grandbaby, he ain't goin' nowhere," Dutch groused. "If he's blood, he stays with blood. He ain't goin' to the ER for CPS to take 'im. He ain't bein' put up for adoption. My son's gonna grow a fuckin' set and raise the son he made 'cause he was too stupid not to knock up some Amish girl who he fuckin' *knows* he wasn't supposed to fuck around with." The last came out on a roar. His red-faced father turned toward Bryson. "Now, Matt, gonna kindly ask you to turn around while I clobber some fuckin' sense into my own crotch fruit. Shoulda made his momma swallow that fuckin' load."

Bryson's lips flattened out. "That's not going to happen, Dutch." He held out the crying baby to Cage. "Here. Maybe if you're holding your kid, your father won't want to kick your ass."

Cage doubted that.

He stared down at the bundled infant in Bryson's arms.

Dutch growled, "Take your goddamn kid, Cage."

Reilly reached between Cage and Bryson, intending to take the baby until Dutch snapped at her, "Don't you fuckin' dare." She dropped her arms and stepped back with her palms in the air.

Cage took a deep inhale and took the now screaming baby from Bryson, who said, "I suggest someone head out to get diapers and formula while we wait for the EMTs to check him out."

"I'll go," Reilly volunteered quickly. "I just need to borrow a car."

"Take his Impala. Key's hangin' in the office. His fuckin' baby he loves so damn much and might hafta get rid of now he's got a real one. Hit Walmart for that shit and grab a car seat while you're at it. And whatever else he's gonna need to deal with this little surprise for the next coupla days." Dutch dug into his open coveralls and the back pocket of his jeans, and pulled out his wallet.

Reilly accepted the credit card and disappeared into the garage.

Cage cleared his throat and tried to swallow the lump. "Think he's gonna need changed." The towel and blanket around the baby's lower half were soaked and squishy.

His father's thick eyebrows shot up his forehead. "Yeah, they do that, asshole. They cry, shit, piss and wanna fuckin' tit. That's it. Get used to it."

Cage gritted his teeth as his '65 Chevy Impala SS ripped through the lot with Reilly behind the wheel, the convertible's tires squealing as she shot out onto the road without slowing down. When she smashed on the accelerator, the 409 big-block roared. Then she ground a gear.

Ground a fucking gear.

Cage just might cry seeing and hearing that. No one drove his baby.

No one.

Out of all the piece of shit vehicles on the property, his father had to tell her to take his restored classic.

An ambulance with lights flashing, but no siren, pulled into the lot and parked next to Bryson's cruiser. Two EMTs climbed out and came around to them.

"Got a call for an abandoned infant?" one of them asked Bryson.

Before the cop could answer, Dutch said, "Ain't abandoned. He's where he fuckin' belongs. Just make sure he's fuckin' okay and then give 'im back. My dumbass son will be takin' care of his own fuck-up."

Two sets of surprised eyes went from staring at Cage's pissed off father to Bryson, who nodded.

One of them took the baby from a relieved Cage and went to the back of the ambulance. Bryson followed, a grim look on his face. Maybe he wasn't really sure about leaving Cage alone with Dutch.

He had a good reason to worry.

Uncomfortable silence surrounded him, his father and brother.

Dutch, suddenly looking a lot older than he was, shook his head as he stared at Cage.

"Wore a wrap both times, Dad."

"'Parently you need a lesson on how to wrap it right. Musta failed you on that. 'Cause how else did you knock her the fuck up?"

"Got no fuckin' clue."

"You weren't supposed to fuck with them Amish girls. That's one of the fuckin' club rules."

"It was only twice. And before Sig got caught with Rebecca."

"Don't matter. The rule was in place before then. He fucked up, too. This gotta go to the table."

*Fuck.*

"Broke a fuckin' important rule which is gonna piss off the prez. He set that rule for a goddamn reason. And now I gotta look some of those elders in the fuckin' eye and know you bent over and gave it to one of their innocent girls."

"I doubt they know." She said in the note she'd kept it a secret, then her family hid her away once she couldn't hide the pregnancy anymore.

"If the pigs go lookin' for her, they will."

*Fuck.* His father was right.

"Assumin' you know who S is," Rook grumbled. The first words Cage had heard from his brother.

"Yeah."

"She the only Amish snatch you dipped your dick into?" Dutch asked.

Like he'd tell his father any different if she wasn't. "Yeah."

"You sit on that exec committee, boy, but as road captain you don't get a fuckin' vote. Don't be surprised if your ass is stripped of your colors."

He hadn't even considered that. *Fuck.* "Sig's wasn't."

"You ain't Sig," Dutch reminded him. "You ain't Trip's blood. He don't have great love for your ass, either. You forget that?"

No, he hadn't. It had gotten better over the months between him and Trip. *Hell,* between him and all his club brothers. In the beginning they only tolerated him because Dutch was an Original. His old man had been part of the Blood Fury MC from the club's inception and was there when everything went down.

The Fury's implosion had been the final straw that had his mother packing her shit into trash bags and splitting so quickly Cage's head had spun.

His brother's, "Least she didn't leave it in a trash can somewhere. Or in a field for the coyotes," got his attention.

"What?" he whispered, his stomach churning at the thought of a mother not wanting her kid as much as his mother, Bebe, didn't want him and Rook.

"Yeah, you know, what mothers do when they don't want their baby and get desperate," Rook explained. "We were just too fuckin' old to get thrown in the trash when Mom left."

Dutch grunted loudly, but before he could respond, a

deep voice came from behind Cage. "That's why Safe Haven was enacted in this state."

He turned to see Bryson hoofing it back towards him, holding the kid.

"Newborns can be dropped off at our station, the hospital, or even the firehouse, if the mother is desperate."

Cage frowned. "That happen?"

"Around here?" Bryson shrugged. "Only once, so far, that I know of. The law is the baby has to be less than twenty-eight days old and unharmed, of course, then no questions are asked. They can hand the baby over and they don't get in any kind of trouble. If there are signs of abuse, though, that's a different story." He glanced down at the baby in his arms and took a deep inhale like he was preparing himself for what he was going to say next. "Anyway... got some news..."

"He okay?" Rook asked first before Cage could. *Damn it.*

"Yes. *She* is."

Cage blinked and stared at the quiet bundle Bryson was holding.

*She.*

What?

"They cleaned her up and put on a real diaper. Clamped off the umbilical cord. She's hungry but not starving, so she was fed recently at least. Eyes clear, temp normal. Lungs sound developed. Heartbeat strong. Basically, she appears healthy and no worse for wear by being left outside in a cardboard box. They recommend getting her to a pediatrician right away, anyhow. Also, I still think you should do a DNA test, Cage. If she isn't yours, we need to figure out who her father is, especially if her birth mother doesn't want anything to do with her. Because if neither parent wants the baby, CPS will have no choice but to step in."

"Note says the mother don't want her," Dutch reminded the cop.

"But that doesn't mean she won't change her mind. She might not have been thinking straight at the time."

"Well, she definitely wasn't thinkin' fuckin' straight when she spread her legs for my dumbass son."

"Dad," Rook muttered, shaking his head.

"No, let him get it all outta his fuckin' system now," Cage told his brother. "'Cause there's gonna come a point where I ain't gonna hear anymore and what he did to me over there..." Cage jerked his head toward the location that Dutch cuffed him upside the head. "He ain't ever gonna do to me again." He turned to Dutch. "So, you better get it all out now, old man. Or as soon as Bryson here is gone, we're gonna get things fuckin' straight. The Dietrich way."

If anyone was familiar with the Dietrich way, it was Dutch, since he was the one who taught it to Rook and Cage. Every single time either one of them fucked up and got caught.

Which was a lot.

That pretty much also meant Dutch's way to keep his sons straight wasn't very effective.

Or maybe it was, and both Rook and Cage could have ended up worse off than they were now. Maybe both of them could have ended up in prison for life.

Or dead.

Or just finding out they're the fucking father of a baby born to some Amish chick after poking her twice in a shed.

His nostrils flared.

Even when he didn't try to fuck up, he did.

And that baby in Bryson's arms was one of his biggest. Not because she was born, but because Cage was her father.

The baby might not have a damn chance.

Adopting her out might be the better choice. Like Red did with Levi. She knew what was best for her unplanned pregnancy, what was best for the baby born out of crazy and violent circumstances. She trusted putting Levi in Matt and Carly Bryson's capable hands.

He needed to think about this.

But nothing could be done until he was sure this baby was his. If she wasn't, then...

Then he had nothing to worry about. The baby wouldn't be his problem. She'd be someone else's. Like the state's.

A lump the size of a boulder landed in his gut. Hard and uncomfortable.

"Which one of you want to take her while I talk to Cage privately?" Bryson asked.

"Her pap does," Dutch said, stepping forward. "That other one there don't know shit about babies, either."

"Like you were really involved when we were babies," Rook scoffed. "You knew how to fuckin' make them, not raise them. No wonder Mom split."

"Right now's not a good time to be mouthin' off to the man who put you on this Earth, boy," Dutch warned him.

Rook's jaw got hard and he sucked on his teeth but ate his words. Something Cage knew his brother had a hard time doing.

He had seen Rook and Dutch get into some vicious, bloody brawls when Rook was younger. But Dutch was past the age of getting into scraps. Cage was pretty damn sure his brother could take their father to the ground and Dutch wouldn't be able to get back up so easily afterward. If at all.

As soon as his old man had a secure hold on the sleeping infant, Bryson grabbed Cage's upper arm.

He stiffened and ripped his arm free. "Unless you're arrestin' me, hands off."

Bryson tilted his head and stared at Cage, the pig's narrowed blue eyes spearing him. After a moment, he jerked his chin toward the other side of his cruiser.

Cage reluctantly followed.

When they got there, Bryson pulled a small notebook from his back pocket and flipped it open before sliding a pen from the front pocket of his uniform shirt. "You know who this S woman is?"

"Yeah. She gonna get charged for leavin' her baby?" *His* baby.

*Jesus fuck.* He suddenly felt like puking.

"She left the baby for the father, so... I mean, it wasn't the best circumstances the way she did it... but she meant well for the most part. We *could* go talk to her, if you want. I still will need her name, either way."

Cage shook his head. "Can we hold off on that? For now?"

If the cops showed up to confront Sarah, it would cause more problems with the Amish and, again, possibly screw up the club's relationship with them. The Fury relied on them to farm the fields and give them supplies in return.

And he remembered, only too well, how pissed off Trip had gotten at Sig because of Rebecca. He ordered them all to stay away from the Amish women. Not just once, either.

"How she did it wasn't much different than her droppin' it off anonymously at the fire station, right? In fact, those people would be strangers versus droppin' the kid off with us... with blood."

Bryson ran a hand down his clean-shaven cheek. "If she isn't your baby, Cage..."

"If she ain't, I'll give you the mother's name. Don't wanna cause more shit between the club and the Amish, if this kid turns out to be mine."

Bryson's eyes narrowed on him again. "What do you mean by *more shit?*"

Cage regretted that slip up. What happened between Sig and Rebecca was no one's business but the club's. That shit had settled. He wouldn't be the one to stir it back up.

"Nothin' your brothers in blue need to be involved with. Just a mistake Sig made."

Bryson cocked a dark eyebrow. "A mistake like you made?"

"Sorta." But no kid came out of his. Cage dropped his head and shook it. "Don't make any goddamn sense."

"Just a little reminder, condoms aren't a hundred percent effective. Shit happens."

"Yeah, thanks for the fuckin' Sex Ed lesson." *Asshole*.

"You know, I could still call CPS, if you want. They can take her until the DNA results come back. Then, if she isn't yours, they could put her in a foster home. Unlike older kids, babies are easy to adopt out. Like I said, my cousin and his husband may—"

"No," Cage cut him off.

Bryon's mouth got tight. "Why? Is it because they're gay?"

"'Cause your cuz is a fuckin' pig. No pig's raisin' my kid. Sig didn't have a say with Levi, but if he had..." That was all Cage needed to say. He made his point.

"Well then, good thing Autumn cared more about Levi's well-being than about me wearing a badge."

"Truth? Sig also figured the badge bullshit might help with keepin' Levi safe from the Shirleys."

Bryson didn't have much to say about that. "I'll tell the EMTs they can leave. You want me to stay until your shop girl gets back?"

Shop girl? "Nope. Don't need you. Not sure why you're here in the first fuckin' place."

"Because someone left a newborn in a box in front of the garage, remember? Nobody knew it was yours."

Cage heard the unspoken *dumbass* added onto that. He grimaced.

"Anyway, I'll check back if I don't hear from you in a

couple of days. I need you to let me know as soon as you get those results back. Get the tests done today."

*Right, boss.*

"Do you hear me, Cage? Today. It'll take two or three days to get the results back, if you're lucky. I'm sure you don't want to be changing more shitty diapers than you have to if she doesn't turn out to be yours."

"You mean like how you change Levi's when he ain't really yours?"

A muscle in Bryson's cheek flexed dangerously. The cop leaned in but not close enough to touch Cage. "Levi *is* mine. He's my fucking son. I'll protect him with my last dying breath. He's a Bryson, no matter what you think." The cop straightened. "Oh, that's right, it doesn't matter what you think about it. Now, how about worrying about your own daughter. *If* she's yours."

"She's—" He swallowed the *mine*. Since when was he in a rush to claim a snot monkey?

"Keep me updated," Bryson ordered, then folded himself into his pig mobile.

Cage stood there until he left. Then he turned to see his brother, father and... possible daughter gone.

"Christ," he muttered.

His fucking day went sideways from the moment he opened his eyes this morning.

He had a feeling it wasn't going to get any better.

He just hoped it couldn't get any worse.

But he wouldn't fucking bet on it.

## Chapter Three

"Trip ain't gonna let you keep this kid in your room at the bunkhouse, Cage. You think of that?"

Cage shot a frown at his brother who stood next to the cardboard box on Reilly's desk, staring down at his *could-be* niece. "Did I think of that? Are you fuckin' serious? I haven't had a chance to think about shit. Got no idea what the fuck I'm doin'. My life just fuckin' crashed and burned. Haven't had time yet to think about anything, much less where this kid's sleepin'." He blew out a breath. "Maybe Bryson was right..."

"With what?" his father asked.

"Lettin' CPS take her 'til we know she's mine for sure."

"She ain't gettin' in the state's hands, boy," Dutch growled. "Once they got their claws in her, it's hard to rip them back out. Had CPS sniffin' 'round after your momma left us."

*What?* Cage had no idea.

"No way was I lettin' them have what belonged to me. Fuck that."

"So, you only wanted us because we were your property," Cage concluded.

"No, asshole, wanted you because you were my fuckin' sons. Convinced your useless snatch of a mother to stop swallowin' my loads so I could have you two. *I* wanted you boys, not her. Thought she'd feel differently after you were born. Thought that motherly instinct would kick in. It didn't. Look at you now, you ungrateful shits. Raised you, fed you, put a fuckin' roof over your heads. Gave you fuckin' jobs..." He grunted and stopped his grumping when the baby moved in his arms.

Cage was surprised as fuck when Dutch glanced down and his pissed-off face turned soft.

"She ain't got a dick so can't name her Dutch Jr... Gonna name her Duchess, instead."

*He was gonna do what now?* "No, Dad. You ain't namin' her what you'd name a stray dog. You ain't namin' her Duchess." Cage just about shuddered.

His old man grinned and pressed the tip of his finger to her little button nose. "Yeah, Pap's baby girl, Duchess."

"Her name ain't Duchess," Cage growled.

Dutch shot him a frown. "Then what you gonna name her?"

Good question. "Nothin'. Not 'til I know she's mine. And I recommend you not get attached, Dad. What if she turns out not to be blood?"

"Then I'll name your next fuck-up Duchess."

There wouldn't be another fuck-up. He'd wear two fucking wraps if he had to. Or, *fuck it*, just give up sex.

Yeah, no. The last option wasn't a viable one.

He *could* stick to oral and anal sex. Yeah, that sounded like a better plan.

"Where the fuck is Reilly? Gotta feed Duchess." Dutch hooted. "Can't wait to see you change her for the first time, either." He chuckled as he put the baby carefully back in the box amongst the blankets. "Gonna videotape it."

"On what? Your Betamax video camera?" Rook asked with a snort. "Just use your fuckin' smart phone."

"Phone ain't so fuckin' smart," their father grumbled.

"Smarter than you, old man," Rook said.

"Swear you don't like breathin', do you, boy?"

"You make a lot of threats for someone who can hardly roll outta bed in the mornin'," Rook reminded him.

Dutch grabbed his junk and shook it. "Can't roll outta bed because of my kickstand. Musta got your small dicks from your momma's side."

Rook's mouth flattened out. "We've all seen your dick, Dutch, and—"

Reilly rushed into the office, out of breath, her hands full of plastic shopping bags. "Would've been nice if someone would've come out to help."

"Didn't know you were back," Cage answered.

"You can't hear that thing pulling in?" she asked with wide eyes. "That car is loud."

"It ain't loud. It purrs like it should. Like a woman when I'm eatin' her pussy," Cage told her.

Reilly put a finger to her lips and said smartly, "Bet you don't remember *Tonya* purring like that."

"Who the fuck is Tonya?" Dutch asked.

"Nobody," Cage answered quickly.

"So, anyway, while I was at Walmart, someone hit your convertible with a cart," Reilly announced like it was no big thing.

He spun on her, his mouth hanging open. "What?"

She grinned. "Just kidding." She leaned over the box and brushed her fingers over the baby's sparse downy hair. "But I don't think that car will work for hauling this little one around." She straightened. "You should get a minivan. And sell me that car on payments. It's badass."

No shit it was badass. That was why he restored it. He was the one who stripped it down to the frame and restored it part by part until it was even better than the original. "I ain't sellin' that fuckin' car. It's my baby."

"No," Rook pointed into the box, "that's your fuckin' baby." He added a snort.

"I ain't gettin' rid of my car. It's a fuckin' classic and worth some scratch. And, anyway, we don't even know this is my kid."

"When you gonna get the DNA test?" Rook asked.

Cage looked up from staring at the infant, whose blue-gray eyes were open and staring at him. Her little legs moved whenever he spoke. *Huh.* That was not a good sign.

He pursed his lips as he considered the baby. "Don't know. Today? Got no idea where to go."

"Well, I bought a car seat," Reilly announced. "You'll have to figure out how to latch it into the Chevy. I left it out there with a bunch of other shit I bought for now. Someone needs to go out and bring the rest in. Plus, I'll bet she'll want a bottle soon. I got a bunch of formula. However, I don't know shit about babies. Maybe we need some help from someone who does. And by *we*, I mean you, Cage." She shot him a big grin.

*Great.* "Like who? Red?"

Rook shook his head. "Fuck no. She ain't ready to deal with an infant yet, stupid ass."

"Reilly? You can learn," Cage suggested.

"I'm not taking care of someone else's kid," she huffed. "If I wanted to take care of a baby, I'd have one of my own."

"That's just fuckin' selfish, woman."

"Fuck you. You trying to pawn off your own offspring is selfish. You made it, you take care of it."

"We don't even know she's mine! A note ain't no proof." He groaned.

"Got an idea," Dutch growled.

*Thank fuck.* "Yeah?"

"How 'bout you take care of your own fuckin' kid. Just like I had to take care of you two knuckleheads after your fuckin' useless momma left."

"But I know nothin' about babies."

"Ain't much to know about havin' snot monkeys. When they cry, you shove somethin' in their mouth. When they shit, you change their nappy. When they get older, they break your shit and steal it, too. They eat the last fuckin' piece of fried chicken and put the container back empty in the fuckin' fridge. They cost you a fuckton of scratch. There you go. Now you're up to speed."

"Speaking of a fuckton of scratch, here's your card back, Dutch," Reilly said pulling the credit card out of her back pocket. "I might have hit the limit."

Dutch shook his head. "Gonna take it outta his pay."

"Look, I'll go try to figure out the formula. I'm sure it has instructions on the can. I got everything I can think of to at least get through today. In the meantime, you figure out how to get a DNA test. Then figure out what you're going to do with this sweet little girl during the day while you're working since I'm not going to be a babysitter. Between running the office here and helping out Ozzy in the evening, I have enough to do. Get a house mouse like Cassie and Judge did," Reilly suggested.

That wasn't a bad idea.

*Saylor.* She was an option.

"You still never said where you and your snot monkey are stayin'," Rook reminded him.

*Snot monkey.*

He might have his very own snot monkey now.

He glanced at the baby, whose eyes were drifting closed. "Reilly?"

"Yeah?"

"I'm awake, right?"

"Oh, you're definitely awake." With that and a grin, she left the office.

*Fuck*, he was afraid of that.

―――

THANK FUCK the garage had a spare vehicle. Sometimes they loaned it out to their customers, sometimes used it for a parts run or to grab lunch, or for whatever.

Like strapping a car seat into the back.

While not Cage's preferred method of transportation—that would be his '75 Shovelhead or his '65 Chevy—it had to do. For now. Once he got the results back from the cheek swabs he and the baby just had done—and if the results came back saying he was the father—then he'd reevaluate getting something better to haul the kid around in.

Until then...

"When the results come in, give them to me, I want to do it like Maury Povich does on his talk show." She deepened her voice and shouted, "When it comes to the case of newborn Duchess Dietrich... *Caaaage*... you *are* the father!"

"First of all, I'm done havin' fantasies about you," he muttered. "Second, the fuck if her name is Duchess." Her laughter filled the car, getting on his nerves. "So glad you think this shit's funny."

"I see it as karma for how much you guys are hos. None of you are picky where you stick your dickies. Maybe this will be a lesson to you all."

Cage doubted it.

"At least she didn't do it on purpose to trap you like Ry's mom did to Judge. This was a true accident. Especially if you really did wear a condom." He heard a sharp inhale from the passenger side of the four-door Accord. "Wait, did you even remember wearing a condom with *Tonya*? Or are you going to be surprised with baby number two in nine months."

"Fuckin' Reilly. Shut the fuck up."

She laughed again. It quickly faded when the baby began to cry softly. "Oh, I think Duchess wants another bottle."

"How fuckin' much can a little shit factory like her eat?"

Reilly shrugged, lifted her cell phone, pushed a button and asked, "Google, how often do newborns eat?"

A computerized voice came back through the phone's speaker. "*Most newborns eat every two to three hours, or eight to twelve times every twenty-four hours.*"

"Holy shit," Reilly whispered.

"Fuck," Cage groaned.

Reilly's head spun toward him. "Reese wasn't even eleven yet when I was born. She had to feed me that much?"

Cage shot her a surprised glance. "Your mom didn't feed you at all?"

"I don't know," she answered, still whispering. "I'll have to ask Reese."

"Look, Reese musta did all right and you didn't fuckin' die since you're sittin' in that seat, so let's get back to worryin' about me," he glanced in the rearview mirror at the occupied car seat, "and her. What am I gonna do?"

"You're asking me?" she squeaked.

"I sure as shit ain't askin' the fuckin' baby."

"Well, I guess you're going to feed her as soon as we get back to the garage and then change her diaper when she squirts all that milk back out." Reilly wrinkled her nose. "I'm not doing it again. Your turn. You need to learn."

"Should I even be touching a girl down there?"

"She's your daughter."

His fingers gripped the steering wheel tighter as he shouted, "We don't even fuckin' know that! What the fuck!"

Did she giggle at his suffering?

"Cassie has experience with babies. Maybe she can give you a few lessons."

That was more like it. Some real advice. "Apparently, so does Stella."

"She does?"

"Yeah, nobody talks about it but I heard she had a kid."

Reilly turned wide green eyes to him. "What happened to it?"

"I don't fuckin' know, Reilly. Back to my problems..."

"Okay, then there you go. You call them when we get back and have them stop over to show you some pointers."

He groaned. Just what he needed, the prez and the enforcer's ol' ladies coming over and then spilling the beans to the two people who'll want to knock his fucking block off for breaking the club's Cardinal sin of not dicking with the Amish chicks.

The baby's cry got louder, so he turned up the music.

Reilly turned the music back down. "You can't just drown her out. She's crying for a reason."

He gave her the side-eye. "Okay, expert, what's the reason?"

Reilly hit the side button on her phone again and asked loudly, "Google, why do babies cry?"

Cage gritted his teeth as the computer voice began to list the one million reasons why babies might cry.

On reason one hundred and fifty-three, he turned the Honda into the garage lot and instantly slammed on the brakes. "Oh fuck," he whispered.

"*Oooh.* You're in trouble now."

"Like I wasn't before?" he asked as he stared through the windshield at the lineup of bikes in front of the garage. His asshole actually squeezed the tiniest bit tighter.

As he shifted the car into Reverse, Judge and Trip both

stepped out of one of the open garage bay doors and out into the daylight. They stared straight at him.

"Fuck." He wasn't a pussy. He wouldn't run like a coward. However, today? He'd already dealt with one too many surprises. The day was turning into a nightmare that wouldn't end.

"Are you going to pull up, or am I getting out here?" Reilly asked.

"They all know already," he whispered.

"Well, of course they do. You guys are like a bunch of clucking hens. Gossip didn't travel this fast when I was in high school."

"Reilly..."

"No, I'm serious. You guys are worse than Italian grandmothers."

Cage shook his head and reluctantly put the Honda back into Drive and slowly pulled into an empty spot.

"I'll go in and get a bottle ready. You get Duchess out of the car."

"Stop callin' her that."

"Well then, pick a name! Can't just call her 'baby.'"

"Why not?"

"Because... You just can't. Pick something."

His eyes landed on his Shovelhead parked nearby. "Harley."

She scrunched up her face. "What? No! That's too stereotypical."

"I like it." What biker didn't want to name his kid Harley? *A* kid, not *his*.

"No. Pick something better."

"This ain't your kid."

"And as you told me a few times already—and everyone else, too—she might not be yours, either," she insisted.

Cage closed his eyes and took a huge inhale, beating

back his impatience and a little bit of panic, too. "Just get out."

Reilly rolled her eyes. "Fine." She pushed the passenger door open and climbed out. Before she closed it, she leaned in and peered into the back seat. "You can't sit in the car forever and she's hungry." The door slammed shut.

Cage rubbed at his forehead. His headache was no longer due to his hangover, it was now due to a crying baby and also what—or *who*—was waiting for him.

"*Fuuuuuck.*"

Reilly was right. He couldn't hide in the car to avoid whatever was about to happen.

He got out of the Honda and opened the back door, leaning in and trying to figure out how to unlatch the car seat from the base. Reilly had figured it out at the lab where they went to do the DNA test, but he hadn't paid attention.

He should have.

The kid was crying even more now, her face red, her mouth open, her eyes tearing up.

"It's okay, monkey," he spoke softly, trying to soothe her. "Gonna get you out. Gonna figure it out."

*Squeeze the handle.*

"*Shhh*, little monkey. If anyone should be cryin', it should be me."

*Squeeze the other piece.*

He sighed with relief when the car seat unlatched and he carefully pulled it out, trying not to jostle the baby too much.

Holding the carrier's handle, he glanced down at its contents. "It's okay, monkey. The only one gonna die today may be me."

He quickly made his way toward the garage, noticing Trip and Judge had gone inside. Probably to grill Reilly.

Like she had anything to do with any of this.

He set his jaw and stepped inside.

And saw no one. Where the fuck did everyone go?

"They're all waiting for you out back," came Reilly's voice from the tiny break room behind the office.

"Great," he muttered under his breath.

"Take her with you. I'll bring out the bottle."

"Great," he muttered again.

He carefully maneuvered himself and the car seat through the back door and spotted everyone gathered around the old picnic table where they ate and smoked when the weather was decent. He stopped right outside the door, weighing his options.

Unfortunately, he had none.

The group included, not only his father and brother, but Trip, Judge, Deacon, Rev, Whip and even Sig. Having the prez, VP, and sergeant at arms show up unexpectedly didn't bode well.

He pursed his lips as he stared at the crew as they stared at the occupied car seat. "Before anyone says anything—"

"Nope," Judge cut him off. "Come sit down and put that thing on the table."

*That thing?*

Cage hoped the enforcer meant the car seat and not his kid. *The* kid. He gritted his teeth.

*Do I have to?* was on the tip of his tongue. *Damn it.*

Everyone's eyes remained glued on the crying baby as he approached and set the car seat in the center of the weathered wood table.

"Sit."

Just as he was planting his ass on one of the benches, Reilly burst through the steel back door and rushed over with a bottle and an old towel in her hand. Her gaze circled the group. "Who's going to feed her?" Without waiting for an answer, she turned to Cage. "It isn't hard, just stick the nipple in her mouth. You should know how to do that... very well." She snickered.

Cage pressed his lips together. He wasn't appreciating any of Reilly's ill-timed humor today.

"Her pap will feed her." Dutch came forward, plucking the bottle from Reilly. "It ain't too hot, right?"

"No, I Googled how to check the temperature. It's just right."

The old man nodded, then settled at the table across from Cage, turned the car seat toward him and encouraged the baby to take the bottle.

After a few false starts, she finally accepted it.

And, *thank fuck*, stopped crying.

Finally.

Reilly went to take a place at the table next to Cage and Judge stopped her with a deep, "Get lost, Reilly."

She frowned. "Why?"

"We're talkin' club business."

"So?"

"Get inside, girl," Dutch ordered her. "Someone needs to answer the fuckin' phones and deal with the customers while we're dealin' with this."

"But—"

"Go," Cage said softly.

She stared at him for a second, then nodded and went back inside at a lot slower pace than how she came out. She took one last glance at him before shutting the door behind her.

"How did you—"

Trip cut Cage off. "Don't matter. We were gonna find out one way or another."

True. A baby wasn't something he could hide.

"Issue ain't you havin' a kid, Cage," Judge started. "The problem's who the mother is. And what you're gonna do about it. You can't keep an infant in the bunkhouse."

"First, before you start makin' plans, like a vote, or whatever... Or kick me out of the bunkhouse, can we at least wait to find out if she's really mine?" Cage asked hopefully.

"We can wait," Trip said, which loosened up Cage's chest a cunt hair. "Rook said you went to go get the DNA test done. When do the results come back?"

"They said it could take up to five days. No less than two."

"Fuck," Rook muttered behind him.

Their prez continued, "But no matter if she's yours or not, you broke one of the club rules. That alone needs to go to the table. This *S*... She an Amish girl?"

"Yeah, she... uh..." His eyes sliced to Sig, who stood back a little bit with Rev and Whip, behind the menacing wall Judge, Trip and Deacon made. "Sarah's cousins with Rebecca. Met her when she was deliverin' shit... She chased me." Cage closed his eyes for a second and cursed silently. They weren't going to give a fuck if a skirt chased him, he ultimately made the choice to flip that skirt over her head.

First virgin he ever had. He decided right then and there Sarah would be the last. He would stick to women who knew about birth control. Like the sweet butts. They were all on some sort of birth control even though the brothers all wrapped it tight when they did shit with them. It was double protection.

It also kept his brothers from sharing more than just pussy with each other.

"You wanna strip his colors, then you strip his colors. That'll teach 'im," Dutch grumbled. Just like his father, always so goddamn helpful.

He shot a frown at Dutch. "Sig didn't get—"

Judge lifted one of his big paws. "You're fuckin' right. Sig didn't get shit from us when he got caught with an Amish girl. I get it ain't fair. We can right that wrong at the same fuckin' time."

"He did get shit when her brothers gave him that fuckin'

blanket party." Trip glanced over his shoulder at his brother, Sig. Trip's jaw got tight and a muscle jerked in his cheek. "He got his fuckin' ass kicked. Just not by us."

Their prez struggled with a bad fucking temper. He got it from his father, Buck, the former Blood Fury president. He did his best to keep it under control, but sometimes it got away from him.

Cage was worried this situation was going to be one of those times. Though, if it did, he fucking deserved it. He fucked up. No denying it.

He blew air through his nose, thinking how badly he needed to get stoned right now, and watched his father pick up the baby, put her against his shoulder and bounce her.

Cage frowned. "What're you doin' that for?"

One of Dutch's bushy eyebrows shot up. "Gotta burp the kid after it eats."

Cage was impressed his father knew that much. "You did that with us?"

"Sometimes. Your momma couldn't wait to take you two from her tit and hand you over to me if I was nearby. Like I said, the woman didn't wanna be a mother. But she was good-lookin' and could suck a knob off a door, so I got suckered in. Plus, her pussy was pretty fuckin' tight 'til you two destroyed it. Then I had to move to her ass."

"Christ," Rook muttered behind Cage, who tried not to reflect too deeply on his father's words.

"What're you gonna do 'til you get the results?" Deacon asked, obviously trying to change the subject because no one wanted to picture Dutch having anal.

"He can stay with me," his old man volunteered, "but only 'til then. After that we're figurin' something else out 'cause I'm not raisin' another kid. Spoil? Yeah. Raise? Fuck no. He made Duchess, he deals with her."

"Duchess?" Trip asked with a grimace.

"Yeah, that's her name," Dutch answered.

"The fuck it is," Cage said.

"What's her name?" Deacon asked, leaning over Dutch's shoulder to peer at the baby.

"Ain't got one yet," Cage said. "If she's mine, I'll deal with it then."

Deacon's eyebrows pinned together. "What're you gonna call her in the meantime?"

Cage shrugged. "Does it matter?"

"Suppose not," Trip said, frowning.

"Who's gonna help you take care of her?" Deacon asked.

All these fucking questions he didn't have answers to... But needed to figure out.

"Dunno. Yet." He lifted his eyes to Judge, who scowled.

"No," the big man said immediately. "Cassie ain't helpin' with your kid."

"Not Cassie. Was thinkin' Saylor."

"That's another big fuckin' no." Judge said. "She's only eighteen and got her hands full with Daisy and takin' care of the house. Not dumpin' an infant on her, too."

"Any suggestions?" he asked hopefully.

Cage watched Judge's body expand and contract with the huge breath he took.

*Shit*, the big man was gearing up for something.

Could be good. Could be bad.

Deacon noticed his reaction, too. "Wait. You thinkin' Mom?"

"Fuck no. Lottie's too busy enjoyin' retirement like she should be. Doin' her woman shit. Like cruises with her girlfriends and playin' cards, and whatever other shit she does. Not stickin' her with a baby."

"She might do it."

"She ain't doin' it," Judge told his cousin. "And if the baby's his, we're not talkin' a week. We're talkin' years. Maybe even eighteen."

Eighteen.

*Holy fuck.*

Judge wasn't done. "Anyway, she's gonna be busy bein' a grandma if Cassie and I have one."

"You thinkin' about it?" Deacon asked, surprised.

"Jesus fuck," Trip barked. "Can we get back on fuckin' track? I got shit to do besides talkin' about who's knockin' up who."

"Yeah, so... Know someone who might be able to give asshole a hand temporarily with the kid since she's between jobs."

All eyes turned toward the club's sergeant at arms and Cage held his breath. Judge didn't look too excited about the option he was about to suggest. But Cage was game for anyone who knew what the fuck they were doing.

Or even someone who *kind of* knew what they were doing.

Anyone.

Because he sure didn't.

And he didn't need the DNA test to come back to know the baby now asleep in Dutch's arms was his daughter.

He knew. Deep in his gut.

She wasn't temporary. She was here to stay.

And his father was right. CPS was not getting their claws in his daughter.

No one was.

She was blood.

He'd never abandon his blood. Not like his mother did.

He would just have to grow a set and play with the hand life just dealt him.

But still, he needed to wait for the results to be sure. Because his gut instinct had been wrong before.

Once or twice.

"Aww, shit," came from Deacon who stared at his cousin, Judge.

The big man shook his head, not happy at all.

"You think she'll do it?" Deacon asked. "Basically you're askin' her to be a house mouse. For that reason alone, she might rip you a new one."

"Yeah," Judge grunted. "That's why I'll do it over the phone and not in fuckin' person. I ain't dumb like you."

Deacon grinned. "Just 'cause you say it don't mean it's true."

"Are you talkin' about who I think you're talkin' about?" Trip asked, not hiding his surprise.

"Who the fuck are you all talkin' about?" Cage shouted, getting impatient with this secret talk. "Spit it out."

Judge's nostrils flared. "Jemma."

Cage blinked. Judge's baby sister? Last time he saw her, she was like five. Just a baby herself.

"Ain't she an RN?" Rook asked.

"Yeah," Judge grunted.

A nurse? She might be perfect.

"Then why the fuck would she take a spot as a house mouse?" Dutch groused.

*Fuck*, Cage knew it was too good to be true. His father was right.

"Normally, she wouldn't," Judge answered. "But like I said, she's between jobs and was talkin' to Lottie about comin' home for a bit 'til she finds somethin' else."

"What the fuck happened to her job she had in..." Dutch tilted his head. "Where was it?"

Judge snorted. "The last one? Cleveland."

Dutch made a disgusted face and spat on the ground. "Cleveland. Fuckin' suck-ass Browns. They need a real football team."

"Christ, can we stay on topic?" Trip barked. "Think Jemma will do it? What happened to her job?"

Deacon smirked. "She was workin' with Doctor Handsy and he made the mistake of cornerin' her in a closet."

"Fuck," Rook groaned behind Cage.

"Oh yeah," Deacon said with a grin which quickly turned into a grimace. "Someone got their nads knocked out of alignment."

"Fuck!" Rook groaned louder.

Then everyone took an automatic moment of silence in memory of it happening to them. Not one of them there didn't know what it felt like when their nuts got knocked hard enough to make them crumple to the ground. Maybe even whimper a bit, too. Once they could breathe.

"What the fuck? She got fired for protectin' herself?" Whip asked behind Judge.

"Doctor owned the hospice center."

"Hospice?" Cage asked. "What she know about babies?"

"More than you, asshole," Judge told him.

Cage couldn't argue that. And beggars couldn't be choosy. Or however that saying went. "When she comin' home?"

"Was ridin' out her last month's rent where she was, while puttin' out resumes in Cleveland hopin' somethin' came up in the meantime. She only planned on comin' home if nothin' panned out."

"Can I afford her?"

Judge snorted. "A mechanic payin' for an RN? Fuck no. She's gonna have to do it as a favor while job huntin'."

"A favor to who?" Cage hardly knew her. He'd seen her a few times when she was just a little slip of a kid but that was it. They didn't go to the same school or hang with the same crowd growing up. He couldn't imagine she'd do a favor for him.

"Guess to me. And then you'll owe me a fuckin' favor." Judge lifted one eyebrow. "A big one. That's if we don't skin the fuckin' colors off your back for fuckin' up."

It might be worth owing the big guy a big favor because, right now, Cage was in way over his head. In fact, he was sitting at the bottom of the deep end of a pool holding a cinder block. And the baby had only appeared a few hours ago. He had a feeling things wouldn't get better, but only worse.

"But ain't havin' her come home early 'til you know this kid's yours. 'Cause if she ain't, the state will probably take her."

Nobody said anything for a long moment as they all considered the truth Judge said last. Most of the men standing near the picnic table had shitty childhoods, no one wished that shit on anyone, especially an innocent baby. Not if it could be avoided.

"Just let me know as soon as you do," Judge said.

Cage nodded, his lips pressed together. He had no idea what he was going to do in the meantime.

"Then once we know," Trip began, "gonna call an exec meetin' and deal with the broken rule." He looked at Cage. "You won't be in this one. Judge will let you know the consequences after we vote on it."

"I got any say in it?" he asked Trip.

"If you did, you'd be sittin' at the table with us when we decide."

*Fuck.* "Just wanna keep my colors. Sig's wasn't stripped. I expect the same."

"Not up to you," Judge growled.

"Road captain's the easiest position to fill," Trip reminded him. "Shoulda kept that in mind while you were bustin' a nut in someone you knew was off limits."

"And speakin' of off limits, just a reminder that Reilly and Saylor are off limits, too," Judge said, first looking at Rook over Cage's shoulder, Cage himself, then behind him at Whip and Rev. Though, Saylor was Rev's baby sister, so the younger biker's warning only applied to Reilly. "Picture them in those bonnets and black dresses."

A snort came from Dutch.

"It's a Kapp," Sig corrected him.

Judge's eyebrows shot up his forehead. "Info I don't give a fuck about. And neither should anyone else with a dick in this group."

Trip clapped his hands together once. "All right, got shit to do. Like make some fuckin' money for this club so you all can eat, wipe your ass with more than one-ply toilet paper, and can get fucked up on whiskey and beer every weekend. And so do the rest of you. Let's get to it." He planted his fists on the table and leaned into them to go eye to eye with Cage. He lowered his voice. "Text us the second you hear. Then we'll deal with it."

"Yeah."

Dutch rose from his seat. "All right, you knuckleheads, you've fucked off enough for the day. Those fuckin' vehicles ain't gonna fix themselves."

Whip, Rook and Rev headed into the garage through the back door, while Deacon, Judge and Trip headed around the corner and out the front gate.

Then it was just the two of them left, his father and him. Well, officially, three with the baby.

Dutch stared at him for a long, uncomfortable minute. Cage braced himself for another whack upside the head. He couldn't guarantee he wouldn't strike back this time if his father tried it.

"You ain't workin' today. Your job for the next few days, 'til you figure out what the fuck's goin' on, is to take care of this kid. Ask Cassie for advice if you gotta. But get it from somewhere. I ain't gonna raise this girl for you. I ain't gonna be gettin' up in the middle of the fuckin' night to feed or change her. You are. No one else. You did somethin' really fuckin' stupid and now you might end up payin' for it for a long fuckin' time. Gonna get Rook to grab some of your shit from the bunkhouse and bring it over to the house. You can stay there 'til we find out if it was your swimmer that made this baby. And when we find out it did, 'cause I'm pretty fuckin' sure that'd be your fuckin' luck, then we're gonna deal with findin' you a place of your own. But dockin' you a day's pay for every day you don't work. You also owe me for all the shit Reilly bought. And what she got ain't everythin' you're gonna need. Havin' this kid's gonna cost you. Not just talkin' about money, either. Your life's just been changed forever."

Cage hadn't heard a speech like that from his father in a long time. The speech he gave him and Rook after Bebe left hadn't been that long. In fact, it had only been a couple sentences, if he included the grunts.

Dutch shook his head, took a deep inhale, then turned to go inside. Just as he was reaching for the door, Cage called out, "Dad."

Dutch only turned his head as he waited.

"Thanks."

His father said nothing and just went inside, slamming the door shut behind him.

## Chapter Four

Cage ran down the hallway, something heavy bouncing against his legs trying to trip him up. All he knew was, he had to get back there and quickly. Otherwise, he'd be too late.

He couldn't be late.

He couldn't be left behind.

If he was, he'd be forgotten.

When he got to the bedroom, it was already empty.

She was gone.

"Wait, Mom. I'm going with you!" he screamed as he tore back down the hallway toward the front door, dragging the bag behind him. "Don't leave! Please!"

His full bag became heavier with each step, slowing him down.

"Mom! Don't leave without me!"

The burden was suddenly so heavy, he couldn't pull it anymore. He tried to drop it so he could run and catch her, but he couldn't let it go. His hand was somehow stuck to it.

He tugged and tugged, but the bag would no longer move.

He fell to his knees, unable to control his sobbing. "Mom! Don't you want me anymore?"

With another garbled shout of "Mom!" Cage jackknifed up in bed, his heart racing, his forehead beaded with sweat, his vision unfocused.

He blinked a couple times until it hit him where he was and what woke him.

He was in a bedroom at his father's place.

He took a few deep inhales as he dragged his hands down his face.

"Jesus fuck," he whispered shakily. He snagged his cell phone off the charger next to the bed and hit the side button to light it up.

Two am.

A soft cry came from the corner of the room temporarily turned into a spare bedroom. His head twisted in that direction and he cursed Google for being right. Babies ate a fucking lot.

He groaned and kicked off the bedding.

He'd gotten shit sleep for the past three nights. He was fucking exhausted and he hadn't even gone to work all week.

How could babies be so fucking exhausting? They slept, shit and ate. That was it.

He rolled out of bed with another groan and, without even looking in the thing Cassie called a bassinet, he headed out the door and into his father's small galley kitchen.

He automatically went through the motions of preparing a bottle and making sure the formula wasn't too hot, then he bare-footed it back to the room.

Yep, she was still crying, but now sounded pissed.

"At least I'm not the only one fuckin' annoyed," he told her as he placed the bottle on the little table next to the bed and went over to scoop up the baby.

Who the fuck would want to have a kid on purpose? He felt like a slave to this baby.

He carefully climbed back on the bed with the baby now wrapped in one of the baby blankets Stella had dropped off, along with some other shit.

Both Cassie and Stella had given him pointers, cooed over the baby, then left with smirks on their faces as soon as they could.

They both had also voted no on naming the baby Duchess or Harley. He agreed with them on the first, not on the second.

He settled the infant against his chest and grabbed the bottle. She already started to "root" against his bare skin. They said it was a sign she was hungry.

He had thought the sign was all the crying she did.

He stroked the baby's cheek with his fingertip to let her know the bottle was coming, then tucked the nipple between her little pink bowed lips. Thank fuck she latched on immediately this time. He tilted the bottle up to avoid the air the women warned him about. Once she was sucking strongly, he sighed.

He was tempted to lean his head back and close his eyes. But if he did that, he knew he'd be out instantly, especially with her warm body snuggled against him.

He needed to keep his mind active and awake. He wedged her into the seam of his thighs, bending his knees slightly, and with one hand on the bottle to keep it in place, he snagged his phone with the other. He placed it on his thigh next to her and scrolled through his email until he spotted one he hadn't noticed the last time he fed her.

What the hell? How had he missed that?

Exhaustion, that was fucking how.

His heart lodged in his throat and a ringing filled his ears as he read the subject line. *Paternity Results for Baby Dietrich.*

Baby Dietrich.

*Fuck.*

His gaze bounced from his phone to the nursing baby, who stared up at him as her little lips were busy.

"Christ, monkey, this is it. What I'm about to read decides what happens to you from here."

His finger hovered over the lab's email. He closed his eyes, took a breath, then when he opened them, he tapped the email and it popped up to fill his screen. He skipped all the bullshit at the top, the column with the heading *child*, the column with the heading *alleged father*, and each column consisting of a bunch of numbers called alleles...

Then found the most important part. What he needed to know.

What they all needed to know.

What would determine this baby's future. His, too.

The unbearable pressure in his head began to throb.

Thanks to Reilly, he heard Maury Povich's voice as his brain deciphered what his eyes skimmed over, which was the interpretation at the very bottom in bold:

### Probability of Paternity: 99.9998%

He blinked and read it again, just in case he misread it. Then the little voice in his brain said, "Hey, it's not one hundred percent! There's still a slight chance she's not yours."

Right?

He could ask Google if that was true, but he'd asked the search engine so many damn questions in the last few days that the Google lady was no longer speaking to him.

He pushed the button on the side of the phone, anyway, hoping the Google lady had at least one more answer for him for a very important question. "Google, now what?"

Of course, the only answer he got was silence.

He guessed it was better than hearing, "You're fucked," in an emotionless computer voice.

He dropped his head back against the wall and stared up at the dark ceiling.

His father's words slammed him directly in the chest. *Your life's just been changed forever.*

He could still take the easy route and give her up for adoption. He could.

Red did it with Levi.

And Sarah gave up her daughter.

People gave their kids up every fucking day.

Maybe like Levi, she'd have a better life elsewhere. Not be stuck with a father like him. A man who wasn't ready to be a father.

A father who didn't have a fucking clue.

"Sorry I'm your dad, monkey. I didn't ask for this. Know you didn't, either."

When she stopped suckling, he put the bottle aside on the table and lifted her to his chest to burp her using one of the methods Cassie showed him.

When a tiny burp escaped, he kept her there, against his shoulder, rubbing her back in her little onesie that had the Harley Davidson emblem on the front and *Crawl. Walk. Ride.* on the back.

She was so fucking vulnerable. So fucking innocent. So unaware of the turmoil surrounding her arrival.

Her mother didn't want her. Just like his didn't want him.

He couldn't give her up. He couldn't walk away from her.

He couldn't do that.

She wasn't a mistake he could ignore or erase.

Blood was supposed to be thicker than water. That was how the saying went, right?

And they were blood.

She was his.

No matter what, she was a piece of him.

The weight of his future was pressed against his chest. But he had no fucking clue where to go from here.

*Your life's just been changed forever* echoed through his head.

———

CAGE DROPPED the empty bottle into the sink with the rest of them. Someone needed to wash those bottles so he had some to use.

This kid never stopped eating.

He glanced at the clock on the stove. Six-twenty.

*Christ.* He'd gotten no sleep after reading that email.

Worse, he needed to give Trip and Judge the results. But it was too early yet.

He also needed to tell his dad.

And Rook.

And, *fuck*, everyone.

Then he'd needed to not only figure out where he needed to go from here, but needed to face whatever the exec committee decided would be his punishment for breaking the rule.

If they stripped him of his colors, the support of his brothers would be gone. The help of their ol' ladies, gone. He might end up with just his father and brother, if that.

He threw the dish towel over his shoulder and settled his daughter against him. He moved from the kitchen to the small living room at the front of the house, bouncing her gently as he went.

Then he began to pace. He was too fucking tired to figure out what to do about the situation.

He needed to sleep for days.

He needed gallons of coffee.

He needed a lot of fucking help.

Getting only a couple hours of sleep between feedings

and diaper changings wasn't working. Every fucking cell in his body screamed for rest.

Again, he didn't understand the appeal of having a fucking kid if this was what it was like. Who the fuck *wanted* to do this?

He paced back and forth across the tiny living room, softly patting the baby on her back, waiting to hear the burp.

"I need to pick out a real name for you, monkey." Before his father woke the fuck up and continued to call her a German Shepherd's name. Cage gritted his teeth every time he heard it.

He took a couple of long strides across the short room again and stopped when he spotted photos on the far wall. Pictures he'd seen so many times, he normally looked right through them. His father had framed and hung a picture of himself on every sled he'd ever owned in his lifetime. From his first, a '77 Low Rider to his current.

Cage stepped closer and stared at one in particular.

A framed, but faded, eight by ten of Dutch on his '91 Harley Dyna Low Rider. It had been a special edition called the FXDB Sturgis. A sled he sold years ago when he decided he needed a change.

A sled his father still wished he owned. A sled Cage wished his father had passed down.

He pursed his lips as he studied the Harley, his fingers wrapped around the back of his daughter's neck to support her head while his other hand cupped her tiny diapered butt as he stood in place and bounced her.

Harley Low Rider Dietrich.

He kind of liked the ring of that.

Reilly's comment about the name being stereotypical came rushing back to him. Whatever name he picked would be with her forever.

She wouldn't only live amongst him, his family and his

club—all bikers—she'd go to school. Maybe, unlike Cage, to college. He wouldn't want her to be bullied for her name. Even better, she might become a lawyer like Reese, or an accountant like Red, and get a job in some fancy high-rise office building in some city, like New York or Pittsburgh.

Just as long as it wasn't Philly or Cleveland.

Or Baltimore.

He snorted. Yeah, his baby girl would never dress in anything but Pittsburgh colors. Like her old man. Like his old man.

But he didn't have to worry about that right now. He needed to give her a name. A real name. Not Duchess. Not monkey.

He needed to claim her as his. For real.

He stared at the Harley Low Rider some more.

Harley Lo?

Harlow?

The obvious choice hit him right smack in the middle of his forehead.

Dyna. A nod to a Harley without sounding too obvious.

Dyna Dietrich.

*Fuck yes,* it was goddamn perfect. And badass, too.

The baby lurched in his arms and warm liquid soaked the towel and the back of his T-shirt.

"Fuck!"

He rushed into the kitchen and put the baby in the little bouncer thingy that sat on top of the kitchen table. He grabbed a wet paper towel and wiped her mouth and chin clean.

She blinked up at him with her grayish-blue eyes, not giving a fuck she just puked all over her father.

He froze as she gurgled, then hiccuped. Then followed it with a sneeze.

Was she dying? Did he do something wrong?

What was wrong with her?

She gurgled again as her little fists jerked and so did her legs.

Her skin was a normal color and she wasn't crying. That was a good sign, right?

*Holy fuck*, he had no fucking clue what he was doing. This poor kid was doomed by having to rely on him to keep her alive.

"Sorry, monkey. So fuckin' sorry you're stuck with me." He'd told her that a million times already and probably would tell her that a million more.

He growled his frustration, then scraped his fingers through his hair. When his hair stood up, he realized he'd had spit-up on his fingers.

"Fuck!"

Dyna gurgled again.

"You must think this is funny, huh?"

He turned his head and glanced at the mess on his shirt. He not only needed to change, he needed a damn shower.

His father probably hadn't left for the garage yet. Hopefully, he'd be in a generous mood this morning and could watch the baby while he jumped in the shower quick. He yanked the puke-covered shirt over his head, turning it inside out, and threw it over the back of a chair. He lifted Dyna back out of the bouncer and put her against his shoulder, remembering, once again, to support her neck and head. Both Cassie and Stella had beaten that into him with an invisible club.

He moved down the short hallway of the small two-bedroom unit, which was the bottom half of a two-family house, and opened his father's bedroom door, not bothering to knock. "Hey, Da—"

*Christ.*

Some very pale, naked chick was sprawled on her belly diagonally across Dutch's bed. And worse, his father was just as naked, but his hand was planted on her bare ass cheek.

He quickly covered the baby's eyes, then looked closer to see if he recognized the woman. Girl. Whatever.

She was pretty damn young, whoever she was. But then, most women his father boned were a lot younger than him.

He narrowed his eyes. This woman was definitely not a sweet butt, unless she was a new one Cage didn't know about. However, he'd been out of the loop for the past few days. If she wasn't a sweet butt, Cage had no idea where she came from. He had to assume from Crazy Pete's, since Dutch went there last night for a few beers.

Turned out, he not only came home with a buzz but pussy to boot. His old man still had impressive skills when it came to sweet talking some strange into his bed.

*Go, Dad,* he thought dryly, then grimaced.

He quietly closed the door and uncovered Dyna's eyes. He looked straight into her face. "You're never doin' that at that age." He headed down the hallway. "Fuck that. You ain't doin' that *ever.*"

He needed to get the fuck out of his father's house and soon. But, *for fuck's sake,* he couldn't take Dyna to the bunkhouse.

He needed to seriously figure shit out.

But first, he needed to survive whatever the exec committee decided. In his opinion, being saddled with a surprise baby should be enough punishment. Though, they wouldn't give a fuck about his opinion. Or that he regretted taking Sarah's virginity.

But whatever the punishment was, he'd take it like a goddamn man.

He glanced down at Dyna.

Because he needed the club. He needed his family.

He didn't even kid himself.

There was no fucking way he could do this on his own.

———

CAGE HEARD A GROAN. Then realized it came from him.

He opened his eyes just a slit and saw nothing but sky. A stretch of light blue. A few white puffy clouds. A red-winged blackbird flying overhead.

With his fucked up luck the bird would shit on him while he laid sprawled on the ground. Helpless.

His temples throbbed. A trickle at his lip meant his mouth was bleeding. He might even have a couple of cracked ribs.

He would definitely have more bruises than he'd be able to count.

Everything fucking hurt.

He wasn't even sure a bottle of whiskey and a handful of Percocet would help. Not that it mattered, he could find the first but he didn't have the second and doubted Aleve would be enough.

With another groan, he carefully rolled over to his belly because he couldn't sit up. He wasn't even sure if he could lift his hand enough to wipe away the blood on his mouth. Not yet. He still had to tell his own body to breathe.

Breathe through the fucking pain.

He'd been in plenty of fucking fights before.

He'd been jumped before.

He'd been sucker punched once or twice.

But he never remembered having to simply stand and take a beating until he fell to the ground and then take some more.

All without defending himself.

Not once.

To make things "fair," the exec committee decided that Cage's punishment for breaking the rule—the rule Sig also broke—would be the same price the VP paid.

All those months ago, when Sig had gotten caught with Rebecca, her two brothers had thrown a horse blanket over his head and beat the fuck out of him with a pipe or some kind of club.

So, Cage stood at the edge of the field just beyond The Barn while a heavy blanket had been thrown over him and someone—he assumed Judge—had beat the fuck out of him with something long and hard. Not a baseball bat and not a steel pipe. Maybe a wooden club of some sort.

Cage wasn't sure because he'd been facing the open field away from where all his brothers gathered since he didn't want to anticipate whatever he had coming to him.

Though, it was hard not to.

He pressed his palms into the dirt and lifted his head, making sure he still had feeling in all of his limbs. Making sure he wasn't paralyzed or even had any broken arm or leg bones.

He didn't. *Thank fuck.*

He watched as one drop of blood dripped, then two, making a tiny puddle in the dry dirt below his face. That blood came from his nose.

He turned his neck and shifted his jaw slightly to test it. Sore but functional.

This whole thing could've turned out a lot worse than it did.

He inhaled another painful breath.

Then another before slowly pushing himself to his knees.

He was covered in dirt. He was leaking blood.

But he still had his colors.

He still had his brotherhood.

He still had his family.

He'd heal from the beating. But he might not have recovered from losing everything that was important to him.

He didn't realize how important they all were until Dyna showed up at the garage in a cardboard box.

Discarded and unwanted.

That was when he realized he needed everything he currently had and needed to make sure not to fuck that up.

So, when he was told what his punishment was, he only nodded and accepted it.

He didn't argue.

He didn't walk away.

Instead, he strode to the edge of the field, shrugged out of his cut and held it out until someone came—he didn't see who—and snagged it from his fingers. Then he waited.

When he wobbled on his knees, Rook and Rev rushed up and grabbed him under the arms, helping him to his feet, but not letting go.

"You look like hell, brother," Rook said under his breath.

"Feel like it, too." He tried to smile but his mouth hurt too badly and he could taste the metallic tang of blood along with a little bit of grit.

"No Amish pussy's worth that," Rev muttered.

*A-fucking-men.*

"That was the point of havin' everyone here to watch it," Trip announced loudly.

With the help of Rook and Rev, Cage slowly turned around to face the rest of his brothers. He didn't miss Whip wince when the younger brother saw all the damage.

He also didn't miss the blank expression Dutch wore.

His gaze landed on Judge and he noticed what the enforcer held. Just what he suspected. A wooden billy club. Where the fuck that came from, Cage had no idea, but he could guess it belonged to the Originals because it didn't look new.

No, it looked well used. It had a crack running through it and some of the wood was stained darker. Most likely from blood. The leather loop on the end was still circling Judge's wrist.

The enforcer lifted the club so everyone could see it and a grumble came from deep within his chest. "Gonna hang this fucker in The Barn as a reminder. Ain't gonna tolerate any of you breakin' the fuckin' rules. Trip has them for a reason. You don't like those fuckin' rules, you either pay the penalty or you lose your colors. We all get that?"

A bunch of "fuck yeahs" rose from the group. Not in a shout, but in more of a subdued murmur.

Luckily, only his brothers were there. The women were told to find something else to do and not told why, even when they asked.

They'd find out soon enough.

Trip and Judge didn't want the women stepping in, which might have happened. The ol' ladies could get mad all they wanted after the fact. Once the deed was done.

They had taken Daisy and Dyna into town to get Cassie's *hell-on-wheels* some ice cream. And Ry was sent to Crazy Pete's to help the prospects with the bar so Dodge could be here with the rest of their brothers. Ry's father didn't want him witnessing the shit Judge had been forced to do.

Someone was supposed to record it to show the current prospects and future recruits what the price could be for not following the club rules and by-laws.

Cage knew Judge wasn't happy about having to dole out the punishment. But then, Judge held the position of sergeant at arms, so it was his job to do it. No one else's.

He might not like it, but he did it.

His father, Ox, had done so much fucking worse. Cage doubted that fact made it any easier for the big man.

Cage hadn't always been a fan of Judge, but he respected him. Like Cage, the man hadn't pussed out on what needed done.

"We good now?" Cage asked Trip. The Fury prez had stepped forward from the large half circle of men who stood shoulder-to-shoulder.

The prez's mouth was tight when he nodded. "Yeah,

we're good. Now we can discuss the rest of the shit we need to discuss."

Cage couldn't nod his head without his brains falling out, so he just blinked in agreement.

Yeah, that was what they needed to do next. Figure out where he and Dyna would live. How they would survive.

Decide how they were *all* moving on from there.

This week had been the most goddamn humbling week in his fucking life. He hoped to fuck he never had a week like this again. But at least he could look every one of his brothers directly in the eye because he hadn't pussed out and had taken the beating doled out to him.

He didn't just do it to keep his colors.

He did it for his daughter.

A husky female voice was heard from behind the solid wall of his Fury brothers. "I assume he's the stupid ass who knocked up one of the Amish women?"

A few of his brothers stepped aside to let the woman through, her sunglass-covered eyes landing on Cage. She appeared to assess his condition from head to toe before those dark lenses pointed at Trip for only a second, finally landed on Judge and stuck there.

Her lips became an angry slash as she noticed what Judge still held in his fist. She jerked her chin toward Cage. "You do that damage?"

Judge's nostrils flared enough to be visible and he grunted out a, "Yeah."

"We'll talk about that later," she said matter-of-factly and turned to Deacon. "You let him do that shit?"

Deacon's mouth opened but before he could answer, she shook her head and said, "We'll also talk about that later," to him, too.

If Cage could grin at that moment, he would.

She was fucking tall with legs that wouldn't quit. Her

brown hair was loose and long, a few soft waves framing her face. But her jaw was popping.

Someone wasn't happy to be there.

Not at all.

"Jemma," Rook whispered next to him, just loud enough for him to hear. Cage didn't remember much about her since they both had been so young. Rook probably remembered her better since he was four years older than Cage.

"You're shittin' me," Rev whispered, still standing on his other side, helping hold him up. "That's Judge's baby sister?"

Cage was thinking the same. His gaze slid from Judge to Jemma. How did such a good-looking woman come out of Ox? Did Trixie cheat on her ol' man? He wouldn't be surprised if she did. But her endless legs could only come from the Original, not Trixie, since the woman had been on the smaller side. At least height-wise.

"Move him over to one of the tables under that pavilion there so I can check him to make sure he doesn't have a concussion or anything worse."

He winced when his eyebrows began to rise at her simply walking into the midst of a group of bikers and taking charge.

As Rev and Rook began to assist him toward the pavilion, he heard Trip say, "We're done here. You all go where you need to be. 'Cept for the exec committee. Soon as Jemma's done checkin' Cage out, need to do a sit down and figure out the rest of his shit. Not upstairs. Down in The Barn since I doubt he can climb stairs right now. Plus, someone's gonna need a fuckin' shot or two."

A few fucking someones. Including him.

Cage hissed and bit back a few whimpers as they made the slow, what seemed like endless, trek to one of the picnic tables under the pavilion.

Jemma must have been following because he heard her

next command. "Sit him on top of one of the tables." Once he was settled, she stepped in front of him and said softly, but firmly, "Leave us."

"You good?" Rook asked him.

"Yeah," he muttered. "Go."

"Cut's next to you."

Without turning his head, he reached out and slid his fingertips over the familiar leather and patches, giving him a little bit of solace.

His brothers' boots faded away as they headed toward the barn, but he kept his gaze locked on the woman who stood in front of him watching him with her arms crossed over her tits and her head tilted slightly.

She waited until no one was within hearing distance and whispered raspy words that weren't meant to be sexy in any way, but it still affected him just the same.

"I remember you, Chris."

# Chapter Five

JEMMA PUSHED her sunglasses up to the top of her head, pulling her hair back from her face.

She'd only been five when the original club imploded. Chris had been eight. But, yes, she remembered him. The older Fury kids wouldn't allow Chris or her to hang out with them. They were always pushed away and told to get lost. Even called babies.

To add insult to injury, Chris had wanted nothing to do with her.

But now? He needed her.

How shit had changed...

"You gonna hold a grudge about somethin' that was nothin'?"

Jemma pursed her lips and stared at the beaten man before her. He sat on top of the table with his blood-spattered boots planted apart on the bench. "Nope. My brother just beat the living shit out of you. I'm thinking that's enough karma right there."

"He didn't do it for you."

"No, he didn't." She continued to study him. The boy had grown up to look like a man, but the beating proved he might not act like one. He had done something stupid and paid the price. "I figured you would have turned out a little smarter. Guess I was wrong."

"Yeah," he said in a low, rough voice. "You were wrong. Today proved it."

Her eyebrows lifted slightly. "It's rare to hear a man admit he did something stupid."

"Yeah? Well, got proof of bein' stupid. Someone I can't hide. She cries, shits and eats a lot. Gonna be hard to forget that mistake."

*Mistake.*

The mistake had been made when he broke club rules, fucked one of the Amish and got her pregnant. She figured that was what he was calling a mistake, not the baby which resulted from his bad decision. Because if he was...

She decided to test her theory. "Why don't you just give her up for adoption? You're not obligated to raise her. She could have a better life elsewhere." In fact, Jemma was sure the baby would have a better life somewhere else.

"Who says she'd end up with a better life?"

Maybe he wasn't as dumb as she first thought. "Good point."

"And anyway, she's blood."

Jemma barked out a laugh. "And since when has that meant anything?"

"Means somethin' to me."

His face might be busted up, but she could see the intensity in his eyes. Under the shade of the pavilion, she couldn't tell exactly the color they were. If she remembered correctly, blue.

Even so, she remembered him. And his circumstances. Just like she was sure he remembered hers.

That week so long ago had been the worst for them all. No one—not one of them—survived without scars, visible or not.

"Because your mom left you?" she asked.

He didn't answer. He didn't need to. His silence was answer enough.

She sighed. "Let me take a closer look at you."

"Don't gotta."

"You're right," she murmured, "I don't." She stepped closer to the table. "Take your shirt off."

"Want my pants off, too?"

Typical cocky asshole. *Oh, yes, please, drop your pants, stud. There's nothing I'd like to see more than your fucking tiny dick. Thank you for being so generous. *giggle giggle**

"No. I want to check your ribs. I don't give a shit if your legs are bruised up. I know nothing's broken below the waist because you walked over here."

"Barely."

"Still, you don't have anything major broken because you wouldn't be sitting here calmly. Trust me."

He only hesitated a second before he tried to pull up his shirt. With a loud groan and a curse.

With another sigh, she stepped between his bent knees and did it for him, slowly working the bloodied tee up his torso and over his head, careful not to catch his busted lip or nose.

"Idiot. Why would you let anyone do this to you?" She dropped his shirt onto the table and picked up one hand, inspecting it. She picked up the other and did the same. Not one bruised or split knuckle to be found. Not one. "And not even hit back."

"You wouldn't understand."

"No? Then mansplain it to me. I'm sure you're used to doing that."

"Pretty fuckin' sure your brother explained the whole fuckin' situation."

She knew how the baby came to be, but she hadn't been

expecting to walk into the backlash from that situation today.

"I want to hear it from you."

"Do stupid shit, win stupid prizes. 'Nough said."

"That about covers it." She sighed and decided to assess him from the top and move downward.

She tipped his face up and gently turned it left and right, checking each bruise. He winced and cursed on a hiss when she poked and prodded his injuries. Nothing was broken in his face besides his nose and his lip. Both would heal on their own.

"Your nose has a simple break. Take pain killers and put ice on it for twenty minutes every hour or so to reduce the swelling. You're lucky, it shouldn't heal crooked and mess up your pretty face." Or possibly formerly pretty face. She really had no idea what his face looked like now that he was older and it was a bit fucked up.

"Not worried about my face."

"Maybe you should be."

He almost snorted at that, but muttered a "fuck" at the pain, instead.

"Looks like the bleeding has already stopped. If it starts up again and won't stop, go to the ER."

"Yes, Nurse Ratched."

She ignored his remark and leaned in closer to stare into his eyes. Her heart skipped a beat and her breath stilled as his shuddered from between parted, partially swollen lips.

"What're you doin'?" he whispered.

"Checking your pupils." She straightened. Yep, just as she remembered. His eyes were blue. One just had a nice blood spot in it now. "They look normal. Are you dizzy? Have a headache?"

"Head's poundin'."

"Do you feel like you need to vomit?"

His Adam's apple rolled up and down in slow motion. "Every fuckin' day this week, but not 'cause of the beatin'."

Right, having a baby you knew nothing about just show up one day at your door probably felt like a kick in the gut.

"Can you see clearly? Or is your vision blurry?"

"Can see you just fine, Jem."

*Jem.*

She ignored the goosebumps that swept along her skin at his low grumble. A man's voice had never caused a physical reaction like this. Why was it happening now? With him?

She held her middle finger up in front of his face. "How many fingers am I holding up?"

"I deserve that?"

She arched an eyebrow. "I don't know, do you?"

"Probably."

She grinned. "Sit still."

"Ain't goin' nowhere."

She leaned in again and ran both thumbs over his collarbones from the center of his neck to the outer points, checking for pain or anything out of place.

"Been gone a long time."

Her fingers stilled, as did her heart. Did she imagine those whispered words? "What?"

"Didn't say nothin'."

She must be hearing things. She continued with her exam. "Any sharp pain where I just pressed?"

"No," he breathed.

"Anything hurt besides your ribs?"

"Does the answer 'everything' fuckin' count?"

She ran her fingers lightly down his left rib cage, noticing when he reacted to a couple tender spots. Did it again down his right side. When she got to the area already turning an ugly shade of purple, he hissed when she prodded him there.

After a few more gentle pushes, she straightened again.

"Yep. Cracked. Bruised. But not broken, luckily. They'll heal, like your nose. So will your split lip. You'll have a couple shiners from your broken nose and plenty of bruises." She took another step back and stared at his chest. This time for herself and not for his benefit. He had tattoos down both arms. A few tats on his chest. And she assumed his back bore the Fury's colors.

"So, where is the reason for which you willingly got your ass kicked?"

"If you're talkin' Dyna's mother, not sure."

"Dyna?"

"My daughter."

She didn't think the baby had a name yet. Her brother must have been wrong. "Ah. No. I was asking about the baby. The reason I came home early."

"Not sure of that, either."

"No wonder you need help. You lost your baby already."

"Didn't fuckin' lose her. She's with the club sisters."

"And none of them could help you out?" Or maybe they just didn't want to. She remembered Stella from all those years ago, but didn't know the rest of them.

"Not long term." She wasn't here long term, either. Hopefully, Judd made that fact known.

Not Judd, *Judge*. He'd made that clear in the phone call the other day. She could only call him Judge. She rolled her eyes now just like she had on the phone. At least Deacon hadn't changed his name to something ridiculous.

Like Cage.

She helped him pull his blood-stained shirt back on as she talked. "Anyway, you'll live. You just won't enjoy living for the next few days, maybe even weeks, until you completely heal up."

"Got a kid to take care of."

"Should've thought about that before you agreed to

stand there and allow my brother to beat the shit out of you."

"Had to be done."

"Did it?" She shook her head and decided not to dig deeper right now. "I'm here now. I'll help where and when I can. Where are you living?"

When he hesitated, she narrowed her eyes on him.

"Nowhere, yet."

"Nowhere? Are you being serious right now?"

"Yeah. Livin' temporarily with Dutch. Gotta make other arrangements."

Judge didn't mention the man was homeless. That made raising a baby a little more difficult than normal.

"Well, once you figure it out and get settled in your own place, we can reevaluate my situation and how I'm going to help. But, as I'm sure... *Judge* told you, I'm not here permanently, Chris."

"Cage." He grabbed his cut and tried to shrug it on. He failed and let out a long, low hiss.

Jemma watched him try once more, then took pity on him and helped. "I'm only here until I find another job. I didn't become a registered nurse to raise someone else's baby, Chris."

"Cage."

"Right. *Cage.*" She sighed. "Until you do get your house in order—literally—I'll head home and stay there. I miss Lottie's cooking anyway." She held out her hand and he stared at it. "Give me your phone."

Moving slowly and with another groan, he dug inside his cut for his phone, unlocked it and handed it to her. She snagged it from his long fingers and plugged in her number before handing it back.

"Text me when you have it all figured out."

"Might take me the next eighteen years to figure it all out," he muttered.

"I won't be here for the next eighteen years, Chris. You'll be lucky if you have me for the next eighteen days. It won't take me long to get another job since RNs are in high demand right now. So, get your shit together and soon."

She didn't wait for his response, instead she left him still sitting on the table. Alone. She needed to maintain the hold on her reality and her frustrations with this MC life, not the part of her emotions curious about this wounded biker.

If he needed help to get to The Barn, the Fury's new clubhouse, then that was his problem, not hers.

Her current problem was waiting for her at her Volvo XC40. She sighed as she approached where she'd parked it near the farmhouse. She loved that vehicle. And now she didn't have a damn job to pay for it. Taking care of a biker's surprise baby wasn't going to make that monthly payment.

"What the fuck is this thing?" Judge grumbled. "A fuckin' Volvo, Jem? Really?"

She had bought it in bright white and had the windows tinted dark. With the crossover vehicle's black accents, she thought it looked badass. Apparently, her brother didn't.

Well, he didn't have to drive it.

Or pay for it.

*Damn it.*

"I deserved it."

"Didn't say you don't deserve a sweet ride, sis, but," he shook his head, "a fuckin' Volvo? Even Walt's probably spinnin' in his grave."

"Go take your judgement elsewhere, *Judge*."

His expression went grim.

So did hers. "Brother..." She stopped in front of him, where he leaned against her driver's door, his thick, tattooed arms crossed over his chest. To anyone else his expression and his stance would be intimidating. To her, it wasn't. And she hoped to hell he wasn't scratching her pretty white paint with that damn chained wallet of his, otherwise he was going to hear about it. "You did a fucking number on him."

"Yeah."

"You swore you wouldn't be like Ox. You promised me, Judd."

He took a sharp inhale through his nostrils, even though his expression remained stony. "Yeah."

"Please don't become Ox. Not just for me, but for Lottie." Having to say those words made her chest ache. "Please," came out on a broken whisper.

*Damn it!*

His jaw shifted and his eyes slid to the side to avoid hers. "Nothin' like our old man."

Him avoiding her gaze didn't bode well and after what she saw out at the edge of that field, Jemma wasn't so sure he wasn't turning into their father. When Lottie told her that her brother had taken over as sergeant at arms for the Fury, Jemma couldn't believe it.

Judd hated Ox. He hated Trixie. He was glad when Lottie and Walter took them in and away from that life.

He willingly stepped right back into it.

Jemma was ticked Trip even resurrected the damn club. She figured the Fury had been irrecoverably destroyed. That no one would ever dare piece the club and its shattered past back together.

Somehow Trip had done it.

And the group of bikers who had stood at that field proved just how many men were willing to follow him into the possible abyss.

Even worse, her brother had stepped into their father's boots. The same ones that killed Ox. She didn't want *Judge* ending up with the same fate.

Her brother was a much better man than Ox. He needed to remain that way. For their family. For his own.

Especially now that he was in a serious relationship with Cassie and was helping raise her little girl, Daisy.

And Ry, of all people, had shown up in Manning Grove to get to know his father. To build their relationship.

Jemma didn't want her nephew following the same deadly path as his grandfather. He had a bright future ahead of him with college scholarships. He needed to remain on that path and not let any of what happened on this farm make him take a wrong turn. He did not need to wear the Fury's colors like his grandfather had and now, unfortunately, his father.

"So, where's my nephew? I'd like to meet him."

"Workin'. You can meet him later at dinner. Lottie wants us all sittin' at her table tonight. Got a big dinner planned."

"Okay. I'm heading there next. I just wasn't expecting to walk into what I did here. What have you gotten me into?"

"You can say no, Jem."

Could she? "Don't tempt me." Her brother asked for her help. Even if this favor wasn't for him, she owed him a lot. "Brother, just a warning... Like I said on the phone, I'm not staying long and you know why."

Judge nodded. "Yeah. Just 'til he gets a handle on this shit and finds a long-term house mouse."

"Or another job comes up. A real job," she added. "Can't pay for that beautiful, badass Volvo behind you without one."

Her brother didn't seem to find that funny. But then the whole situation—at least what she knew of it—wasn't funny at all.

That was driven home with what Judge said next. "Jem, that baby didn't ask for any of this shit. Just like we didn't. I'm the sergeant at arms of this club. My job's to protect them all. Even that baby. No matter what."

"I hear you, brother," she said on a sigh.

"I also hear you. Just askin' you to stay 'til somethin'

better comes along for him or you. Jem, he can be a fuckin' asshole, sometimes more than the rest of us, but this kid didn't ask to be born, so she deserves better. You get what I'm sayin'?"

"Yes, I get you. We don't get to choose our parents, but we have to survive them. Good or bad."

"We survived."

"Have we?" With a tilt of her head, she stared up at him. "Look what you're wearing on your back. Look what you did today. Are you proud of that? Are you okay with picking up where Ox left off?"

"Truth?"

Jemma lifted a palm. "You don't have to say it. I already know." She shook her head. "See you at dinner. Think about bringing the asshole and his offspring."

"Not enough room at the table, sis. Besides meetin' my son, you get to finally meet my girls. Saylor, too."

"Saylor?"

He smirked. "Daisy's wrangler."

"Uh oh. She needs a wrangler?"

"Believe me, *uh oh* don't fuckin' cut it when it comes to Crazy Daze."

Jemma couldn't wait to meet Cassie, the woman who put a smile on her brother's face. She wanted to thank her brother's ol' lady. And her spirited daughter.

"Well, I can't wait." She brushed her hands off on her jeans. "I'd like to say I'm glad to be home, but I'm not going to lie. I miss you and Deke and Lottie, but I don't miss the memories that being home brings."

"I hear you, sis."

Jemma stepped up to Judge, and when he pushed off her car, she wrapped her arms around his thick waist. She squeezed harder when he enveloped her tightly in his arms. His lips pressed against the top of her head. She was tall, but he was much taller.

And so fucking solid, he felt good. Calming.

Like home.

She wasn't lying when she said she'd missed him. It was the hardest thing about staying away. An unfamiliar sting in her nose and eyes had her sniffle, then pull back. "Is Ry as tall as you?"

"Almost."

"Gangly and awkward?"

"Fuck no. He's beatin' the women off with a stick. He's fuckin' smart, too. Will miss him when he leaves for college in August. Haven't had enough time with him."

"You'll get it. Just be glad you reconnected. What's he think about his old man doing shit like today?"

"He don't know. Sent him to Crazy Pete's to get him outta here. He don't know much about club life yet. He's only been here a week. Shit's all new to him."

Jemma wished Ry would stay ignorant of an MC's ways. "Is he staying with you?"

"No." He jerked his chin toward the barn structure behind them. "In the bunkhouse."

"With your club brothers?"

"Yeah."

"Well then, he's going to learn real fast, won't he?"

Judge actually chuckled. *Chuckled.* It was music to her ears. Yes, she was going to give Cassie a huge hug. Maybe even buy her a dozen daisies.

"Yeah. Told the sweet butts they can't touch him. But livin' there, he'll see the rest. Just wanted him to avoid today. Don't wanna scare him away before he understands."

"Think he'll understand?"

"Don't know."

"If he doesn't, will you give this all up? For your son? For Cassie? For Daisy?"

Judge's nostrils flared. "Didn't want it in the first place."

"The club or the position?"

"Both."

Jemma locked eyes with her brother's troubled green ones and whispered, "If you really didn't want it, you wouldn't be here." She stepped around him and put a hand on the door handle. "See you tonight."

He moved out of her way, and she climbed into the driver's side and closed the door. She watched her brother's long legs take him quickly back to the barn.

To his club.

To a group of men who had no problem with her brother beating another one of their own.

She rubbed her chest.

Her heart ached a little.

No, that wasn't right.

It ached a lot.

Chapter Six
<hr>

"This is fuckin' insane," Cage muttered as he stood next to Trip staring at the single-wide mobile home.

What sat before him was exactly why he'd tolerated that beating a couple of days ago. Because his club, his brothers, had his back. No matter how much he fucked up.

As long as he didn't screw over the club or his brotherhood.

After Jemma left the other day, he practically crawled back to The Barn but he managed to make it there on his own power. And while they all sat around spit-balling ideas on where Cage could live, even temporarily, he downed about a half of a fifth of Jack.

Simply to dull the pain.

But that also meant he had needed help back to his room in the bunkhouse after their discussion. Or actually in the midst of it, since he missed most of what had been decided.

The next morning he picked up Dyna from Judge and Cassie's house since they kept her overnight due to his inability to do just about anything.

Though, he did manage not to shit the bed.

Luckily.

Now two days later he still hurt like fuck and looked like he kissed a speeding tractor-trailer.

"Crazy, right?" Trip asked. "Stella found a business that specializes in emergency housing. It's fuckin' genius. They set up shit like this when a hurricane or tornado, or even fuckin' Godzilla, takes out your house. Gives a family a place to stay while their home and life are being rebuilt. Or for when your balls are to the wall with a baby on your hip and you need somethin' quick. Like you do. They truck it in and set it up. When you're done with it, they pick it up. Like I said, goddamn genius." He turned and pointed to the shed where they kept their sleds. It was parked right next to it. "It's not the best spot since we had to put it near the large shed to temporarily hook it to utilities. It's a quick fuckin' fix, but it'll do you for now."

Fuck yeah, it would.

Thing looked brand new, too. It wasn't some dumpy damn tin can that had been sitting and rusting in a trailer park for a couple of decades.

"Thinkin' about settin' up a business like this for the club. Gonna talk to Deke about it. Maybe run some numbers by Red. We got the space to park these fuckers. Get some of the guys to get their CDLs and get 'em trained... For what they charge for haulin' and rentin' these fuckers out..." He shook his head. "Once the initial expense is paid off, we might be rollin' in it. Could be a good investment."

Cage didn't have a head for numbers, not like Autumn and Deacon, so he couldn't comment on that part, but he did catch the part about how much it was costing.

He hadn't worked in over a week, his hourly salary at the shop was basically shit, and he already owed Dutch a shit-ton due to all the baby shit he had needed to buy.

Not to mention the fucking cost of formula and diapers.

Having a kid wasn't cheap. And this was only the beginning.

Wraps were cheaper. Unless they were defective.

He stared at the huge expense sitting before him. "Club paid for it?"

Trip turned with his hands on his hips and gave him a strange look. "Dutch."

*What?*

"Yeah, he paid for it. Just asked if we could put it here. I was all for keepin' you guys close. You know how I feel about us bein' spread out. Don't like it. Bad enough Dodge is livin' above the bar, Dutch is in his place in town and Ozzy's livin' in the motel's manager quarters. Beside Dutch, where Oz and Dodge are stayin' is necessary since they're managin' those businesses. And Dutch, well..."

"Enough said."

"Yeah, you know your pop. Set in his ways."

"And from what I've seen since stayin' with him, he'd have a tough time stickin' to the bunkhouse rule of no women stayin' all night."

Trip grinned. "Get the fuck out."

"Not sure where he's findin' them, but he's bangin' chicks left and right. Young ones, old ones. Quiet ones, loud ones. Fuckin' guy. Not sure how he does it, but he does. Gotta be impressed. The old man's got fuckin' stamina."

"They weren't sweet butts?"

"Fuck no. And he's bonin' 'em in every shape and color, too. He's fuckin' his way through a goddamn bag of Skittles."

"Huh," Trip said softly. "If I didn't have Stella, I'd be kinda fuckin' jealous."

"Right? Man's got skills I never realized he had. Not that I really wanted to witness all the shit I've seen lately. He musta found his groove once Rook and I moved out."

"Anyway... Done talkin' about your pop's dick action."

"Yeah," Cage muttered. "Me fuckin', too." He glanced at the mobile home again. "Guess I'm gonna owe him big time for this. Goddamn debt's pilin' up."

"Don't think so. Don't think he's doin' this for you. Think he's doin' it for her." Trip jerked his chin up at the sleeping baby in Cage's arms.

Cage glanced down at Dyna. Her belly was full, her eyes closed and she breathed loudly through her nose. He never realized how loud babies breathed. The Google lady, who was finally talking to him again, told him it was because babies were "obligate nasal breathers." He had to look that up, too. A few times, he'd fallen asleep just listening to Dyna's steady breathing.

He really needed to put her in her car seat because his ribs were aching like hell, but carrying the car seat with her in it seemed to make it even worse. And a stroller wasn't going to work while they inspected his new place, even if he had one.

*Their* new place.

And, if he was lucky, Jemma's temporary digs, too. If she agreed. It would be nice if she was close by instead of at her aunt's house. It would hopefully make things easier and, *for fuck's sake*, a bit less overwhelming.

Jemma got to meet Dyna for the first time the other night at dinner, since Cassie and Judge had taken her along to Lottie's after Cage passed out in his bed at the bunkhouse. Without him asking, Jemma also showed up at Dutch's house the next day to stay with the baby while he tried to recover in bed there, too.

But she had left that night once he dragged himself from his mattress into the living room to check on her and Dyna.

"You still look like the walking dead, but you're upright and breathing, so that's a good sign. That also means you're on duty. Have a great night," were her last words as she scurried out the door and headed who knows where.

Probably back to Lottie's.

Maybe even Crazy Pete's.

All he knew was he was left alone in his state of disrepair to take care of his daughter.

He managed. Barely.

He did what he had to do to take care of his daughter, just like with the beating.

It wasn't for him. It was for her.

"C'mon. Gotta check out the inside. It's two fuckin' bedrooms, too. Perfect if Jemma agrees to stay here. Only problem, there's only one bathroom."

It was more than he ever expected. It was better than living in a tent out in one of the fields.

*Hell*, it was way better than living in the camper Dutch originally suggested. That rust bucket had been sitting in the garage's storage yard so long when he went inside to check it out, his foot went through the floor. Worse, he heard mice scrambling to hide.

So yeah, he could live with only one fucking bathroom. He only hoped Jemma could.

Cage followed his president up the portable wood steps and into the mobile home. The interior even smelled new.

Trip stopped directly inside and pushed a door to the right wider. "Got one bedroom on this end. It's the smaller one. Not quite eight by twelve."

Cage peeked around him. He didn't even think about furniture, but it was already furnished. "It came furnished?"

"It's an additional fee. Dutch is payin' for it. For now."

Cage groaned. He'd never be able to pay his dad back for all of this.

Trip turned and they both checked out the living room. It was a decent size. Bigger than the first bedroom and had an open floor plan into the kitchen/dining area. There wasn't a table in the dining area but there were a couple stools at the counter bar separating the kitchen from the living room. Surprisingly, the trailer seemed to be even roomier than his father's place.

"You can work on gettin' your own shit and then he won't be payin' that monthly fee."

Right. With all the spare scratch he was going to have, he'd go right out and get some new furniture. He wasn't even sure he'd be able to buy used furniture. Maybe he could find some shit at the curb in town when it was large item trash day. He didn't need new shit raising a kid. Dyna would only most likely damage the furniture anyway once she became mobile.

His mother always bitched that she couldn't have nice things because of him and Rook.

Now Cage looked back, he didn't think that was the reason. As an adult, he realized how much his mother lied to her sons. Probably to Dutch, too. However, he never discussed it with his old man.

They stepped into the short hallway off the kitchen. To the left was the full-sized bathroom with a shower stall and to the right was a nice-sized laundry room, which also included another door outside. A back door, he guessed.

"No washer or dryer," he murmured.

"Nope. Dutch said you can use the shit in the bunkhouse. Actually, his exact words were, 'He wants a fuckin' washer and dryer then his ass can buy 'em. Ain't payin' to rent that shit when there's a perfectly good set in the fuckin' bunkhouse. His ass can hoof it over there.'"

Cage grinned. Yeah, that sounded like his old man.

They moved to the last room farthest from the front door. The master bedroom. It was definitely larger in size, had a bigger closet and a bigger bed. He guessed this one was a queen versus the double in the first bedroom.

"You and Jem gotta fight it out who takes the bigger room. If I were you, I'd offer her this one. Sweeten the pot a little bit. Then once you find a house mouse and Jemma leaves, you can switch rooms. Or, hell, by then, we might figure out a better setup for you elsewhere. Keeping this here long term will cost too fuckin' much. Need somethin' more permanent. Your kid ain't temporary, your place shouldn't be, either."

His chest really ached, and it had nothing to do with his cracked ribs or injuries. It had to do with all of the responsibility beginning to close in on him, starting to smother him.

Sometimes even made it hard to breathe.

Like now.

His whole life was upside down, all due to picking the wrong pussy to stick his dick into.

He closed his eyes, willing that heavy weight to lessen.

"You all right?"

He opened his eyes and met Trip's concerned ones. "No. Ain't gonna lie."

Trip's lips thinned. "Yeah. Get it. It's like a direct kick in the nuts, right? One you didn't see comin' and had no time to deflect."

"Yeah," he murmured.

"No one said you had to keep her. Not one of us woulda blamed you if you hadn't, brother. Not one of us. It ain't an easy decision but sometimes it's the right one. It was right for Autumn and Levi. It could be right for you and it also ain't too late to change your mind. Plenty of folks out there would love to have a baby."

Cage slowly inhaled, filling his lungs, the air expanding his chest and shoving that weight off. "Yeah. It's too late."

Trip tilted his head and stared at him for a few uncomfortable, silent moments, then gave him a sharp nod. "Then do whatchya gotta do, brother. And do it right. We got your fuckin' back. That's the whole point of a brotherhood. That's the whole reason I came home and decided to rebuild this club from the ground up. For fuckin' situations like these. You ain't gonna be the only one raisin' this baby.

We all are. It ain't just Dutch and Rook at your back anymore. It's all of us."

Cage stared at a spot on the floor because he couldn't let his president see the tears stinging his eyes. But his voice was thick when he lifted his head and said, "Yeah, brother, you don't know how fuckin' much I appreciate that."

Trip swallowed hard. "Okay, got shit to do. So do you."

Cage stood in the bedroom doorway and watched the Fury prez make his way through the trailer. The whole time Cage kept his eyes glued to the colors on the man's back.

"See, Dyna? You got a whole fuckin' army at your back," he whispered against her soft hair. "Thank fuck for that."

He took a last look at the bedroom and wandered back through his new home.

*Their* new home.

Once he got settled in, he wanted to set up an outdoor space right outside the door. The pavilion wasn't far but it would be nice to sit right outside the trailer to smoke a bowl or drink a beer after a long fucking day.

Or give his baby a bottle.

*Your life's just been changed forever.*

Wasn't that the fucking truth.

# Chapter Seven

Cage had texted her earlier asking her to come out to the farm. He had something to show her. She already knew what it was since Judge had given her the head's up a couple of days ago, but they had wanted to keep it a surprise from Cage.

Being in Dutch's house for the past few days while helping with Dyna, Jemma could see why Cage wouldn't want to raise his daughter there.

She didn't know Dutch well since she had been so young when the club became no more, but she was finding out quickly what a character he was. Being an Original, he was biker through and through. But then, his sons seemed to be the same way. He raised them as any MC member would, even though he hadn't been part of the Fury for over twenty years.

So, it wasn't surprising that Cage and Rook slipped easily into the MC life.

It still surprised Jemma that Judge had. Deacon surprised her even more. Their cousin had never lived the MC life, never grew up like she and Judge had, but appeared to thrive in the environment.

Since she'd been home, she met Reese. The woman surprised the shit out of Jemma. She was an attorney and not one of those sleezy kind. No, she had a lot of confidence, intelligence, and was stubborn as all fuck. She made Jemma smother a laugh one too many times with how skillfully she handled Deacon.

Even so, it was clear to see both her brother and cousin were deeply in love. She never thought she'd see the day. Especially after Judge's first disaster of a marriage.

Cassie was perfect for her brother. Daisy was a damn handful. And again, Reese shouldn't fit in at all, but somehow did. At least with Deacon by her side.

She doubted the MC life was one either women would have chosen if it hadn't already been part of the men they fell in love with. In fact, she was pretty damn sure both women would've preferred their men weren't involved with the club at all.

Jemma understood that inclination better than anyone. Because there was no fucking way she would ever end up with a biker, or even a man like Ox. A man who put himself above his own child, his own family.

A long shed with garage doors sat to the left and parallel to the stone driveway leading to The Barn, what she learned was the official name of the clubhouse. Right past the shed sat a new mobile home about fifty feet long and twelve feet wide. It had no skirting, nor was it sitting on a concrete pad like they normally did, and she could see where the utilities were connected.

It wasn't permanent, but only temporary. Just like Jemma being in Manning Grove.

That reminded her she needed to buckle down and find another job in her field. What she was meant to do. Not raise someone else's child. For free, no less.

She didn't even want to raise her own child. Not yet.

One day she'd be ready, when she found the right man to do it with.

A good father.

A man who would put his children above himself.

A loyal husband.

A man who'd treat her like gold instead of tarnished silver. A man who'd be her best friend.

Basically, a man as far from Ox as she could find.

Another man stood outside the trailer with a baby in his arms. She wasn't sure if he spotted her vehicle yet, so she rolled to a stop about a hundred yards away to study him.

Cage was talking to the baby while he supported both her butt and neck and gently bounced his body up and down. She was pretty sure it hurt for him to do so, but he was putting his daughter's comfort above his own.

She doubted her own sperm donor ever did that with her or Judge. She doubted Ox ever changed a diaper, fed them a bottle or read them a bedtime story.

Cage seemed to be taking the unexpected arrival of his own child pretty damn well. Yes, he was overwhelmed, but he was dealing with it.

The easy way out would've been to give Dyna up for adoption.

Cage didn't take the easy way out, and Jemma respected that. Even though her own opinion was he should've adopted her out instead of planning on raising her within an MC.

But whatever. That wasn't her decision and Dyna wasn't her child.

She was only there to help for a short while. That was all.

Jemma's heart did a little flip when Cage dipped his head and pressed his lips to his daughter's tiny forehead. He held them there for a while. Almost like it wasn't a simple kiss but an actual promise to her. To do right by her. No matter what.

*Holy shit.* Her imagination was running wild.

With a groan, she gave the Volvo gas and pulled up to the biker who stood waiting for her and proudly wearing his colors.

She rolled down the window. "This is it, huh?"

No grin. No smile. Only a solemn, but unneeded, confirmation. "This is it."

She hadn't seen him smile once since she came back to town. Not fucking once. She tried to convince herself that it shouldn't matter to her.

Unfortunately, it did.

She shoved the shifter into Park, opened the door, and climbed out.

What was before her was why she was here. Back in Pennsylvania, in Manning Grove, and involved with a club she never thought in her right mind she would be.

However, here she was. And here they were. The man, the baby and now, the mobile home.

She knew he was about to ask her to move in. Once again, she had been warned ahead of time when Trip and Judge showed up at Lottie's last night to have a serious sit-down with her.

They asked her to consider Cage's request.

They stressed the part where the club was a family and needed to act like one. Unlike the Originals who were all selfish, motherfucking assholes.

Even Dutch. Maybe even Ozzy, but Jemma didn't know him at all. So, she couldn't say for sure.

However, as much as they stressed the whole family bullshit, none of it applied to her. She wasn't part of the club. She wasn't club property. Being born to an Original, or being the sister and cousin to current members, didn't make it so. This wasn't her life.

It never would be.

It stopped being her life when she was five and she wanted to keep it that way.

She approached Cage and kept her eyes on the bundle in his arms. When she stood toe to toe with him, she leaned in and sniffed Dyna's dark downy hair, her own hair brushing against Cage's chest and arm.

There was nothing like the smell of a baby. Unless they shit themselves.

Dyna smelled clean, but Jemma also smelled the combo of tobacco and weed on Cage.

Men with babies. *Fuck.* It shouldn't be a turn-on but sometimes it was unavoidable. It had to be some deep-seated hormonal thing.

"How's my little monkey?" she asked softly and noticed when Dyna turned her head toward her voice and gurgled. Both she and Cage were her source of food, so it made sense the baby would bond with her. Jemma straightened and pulled free a few strands of her hair that had caught in his short beard. "She eat?"

"Yeah."

"She keep it down?"

"Yep."

"Did you remember to wipe her front to back?"

He nodded, but his mouth got tight.

Jemma pressed her lips together to keep from smiling. He was trying his best, she had to give him that much. He wanted to learn and do it right. He didn't always, but he was willing to listen and fix his mistakes.

That was half the battle right there.

She grabbed Dyna's little foot in her cute little onesie and shook it gently. She wasn't sure from whom or where he got all the biker-themed onesies, but today's read: *From the Bottle to the Throttle* with a picture of a motorcycle.

"It'll be a while before she can be your backpack," Jemma murmured.

"Soon as she can, she'll ride in front of me."

"Let's not rush it, biker boy." She patted his tattooed arm and he winced. She made a mental note to check his ribs again. "You know, you don't have to hold her constantly." *Especially when you're suffering,* she added silently.

"She likes it."

She couldn't read his expression because he wore dark sunglasses. He also had a folded up bandana tied around his forehead, probably to keep his longish, messy hair out of his face. It wasn't super long but it wasn't cropped short, either. Just long enough to be annoying.

"You'll spoil her."

The clenching of his jaws was hard to miss. "Then I fuckin' spoil her. Don't got much to give her, but can give her that."

*Damn,* that hurt her heart. "Chris..."

His nostrils flared and every muscle went stiff, so she gave him a moment. She wasn't sure if his reaction was from what he said or from her use of his real name.

"Cage," she finally whispered.

When he stared over her shoulder into the tree line behind the shed and mobile home, she realized it wasn't from her calling him Chris. It was time to change the subject. Right now he seemed to be as vulnerable as the baby in his arms.

"You asked me here for a reason."

"Yeah."

She reached out. "Let me take her. I'm sure your ribs are killing you."

His fingers tightened slightly on Dyna, but a few seconds later they loosened and he handed her over. But it was clear he had a hard time letting her go.

"Did you bring her bouncer?"

"Inside."

"Did you move in yet?"

"Sort of."

She nodded, not expecting more than that, but he continued.

"Got some stuff still in my room in the bunkhouse. Some clothes and shit. Some stuff still at Dutch's. Not much, but then I don't got much 'cause I don't need much."

However, his daughter would. Jemma realized why he'd gotten upset, he was worried he wouldn't be able to give Dyna everything she needed.

"Want to show me the inside? I assume this is where you want me to watch Dyna during the day?"

She wouldn't make it easy for him. She wasn't going to volunteer to stay in this mobile home on the farm. If he wanted that, he needed to be the one to ask. She'd be perfectly fine staying at Lottie's at night and coming over to the farm during the day to watch the baby while she scoured the internet for a new job, emailed her resume and did virtual interviews. And once she found the right job, she could search for a new place to live.

As long as it was anywhere other than Manning Grove.

She didn't wait for his invitation and climbed the portable, three-step wood staircase into the trailer. First thing she noticed when she stepped inside was that it looked and smelled new. She was sure it wouldn't stay like that for long.

She also noticed the furnishings were new. There wasn't a lot since the home was only a single-wide but he had the basics. A couch, a recliner, a TV and a couple side tables in the living room. To the right at the end of the trailer was a small bedroom with also the basics and what looked like a double bed.

She wandered through the kitchen, opening up a couple of cabinets to find some mismatched pots and pans along with some old mugs and dishes. None of the kitchen items were new. They'd either been bought at a yard sale, a second-hand store or donated. Not that it mattered, they would work.

She peeked into the bathroom and the empty room across from it, which seemed to be set up for a washer and dryer. Something needed when raising a baby, but was missing. She frowned.

She heard his footsteps behind her. "You need a washer and dryer."

"In the bunkhouse."

She shook her head. "Fuck that. You need a set in here. Even if it's one of those small stackable sets. Get them."

She didn't bother to look at him when she heard him blow out a loud breath. Instead, she opened the door to the last room on the far side of the trailer. The master bedroom. The sheets were a mess and clothes were scattered on the floor already. She spotted the bassinet that had been at Dutch's house tucked in the corner by the head of the bed.

"That bassinet will work for now, but you'll need a crib. Get a convertible one so she doesn't outgrow it so quickly. You also need a changing table with drawers to keep all her baby biker onesies. If you get a small stackable washer/dryer, then you'll still have space in that laundry room for it. Plus, that room has shelves to keep diapers and supplies organized." Dyna made a little noise in her arms and Jemma ran her fingers over her head. "Hey, monkey, Daddy's going to get you *alllll* set up," she said in a sing-song voice.

During their baby-duty handoffs at Dutch's, she had heard Cage calling Dyna "monkey" a couple times. Jemma smiled whenever he said it, usually before he pressed a soft goodbye kiss to her forehead. It was heart-warming and cute even though she knew it was a shortened version of the nickname the guys called kids, which was not so cute. But Dyna seemed like such a grown-up name for such a tiny human.

Jemma had fallen into the habit of calling the baby Cage's pet name for her. She could see herself calling her own baby that. She had even purchased an adorable, plush monkey for Dyna at Target. She had spotted it right away on the couch when she had entered the trailer.

She turned to Cage, who stood behind her. "Let me check your ribs before I leave. I want to make sure you're healing okay."

"Don't gotta do that."

"We've had this discussion before. I know I don't, but I'm going to do it anyway."

His sunglasses were now folded and tucked into the neckline of his shirt, so she could see his light blue eyes get intense with a touch of confusion. Like he couldn't understand why someone would want to do something for him simply for no reason. Without expecting anything in return.

Though, wasn't that what he was expecting when it came to her helping him out with Dyna? He expected her to do something for him without anything in return.

So, she didn't quite understand his reaction.

Well, he was a man and *sometimes* they were hard to figure out. Most of the time, she didn't even bother to try.

She swallowed a sigh and pushed past him, carrying Dyna back out to the kitchen where the bouncer sat on the counter that separated it from the living area. She jerked her head toward it. "Never put it on a table or counter. She might not be able to move it now, but babies can get some hardcore bouncing action going and it could fall." She placed Dyna into it. "It's okay for now because she can't bounce it off the counter yet and we're going to be standing right next to it, but don't get in that bad habit."

She turned, following his movement as he rounded the end of the counter and came to stand next to her. He stared at his daughter in the bouncer with concern.

"Now," she said, catching his attention. "Take your shirt off."

He had no problems shucking his cut and placing it over the back of one of the stools at the counter, but removing his shirt wasn't as easy. With his back toward her, she watched him struggle for a few seconds before she stopped him and slid it up and over his torso and head for him. Again, careful of his nose, which was still healing.

Unlike the last time she helped him undress, she had a full view of his broad, naked back. A few bruises of different sizes discolored the skin here and there but didn't take away from that view.

He had to work out somewhat. While he wasn't ripped, he also wasn't flabby. He was trim enough not to have even the slightest love handles above his jeans.

His soft, worn Levi's were cinched around his narrow hips by a wide black leather belt but rode low enough where the elastic waistband of his boxer briefs was visible.

His jeans cupped his ass perfectly. So perfectly, she had to drag her attention from it. But before she did, she took note of the black leather wallet tucked into his back pocket with a chain attached to one of his front belt loops. Bikers wore them so they wouldn't lose their wallets on a ride, or in a fight. It also made it more difficult to be stolen when hanging out with questionable company.

Before she checked his ribs, she stepped back and studied the club's colors tattooed onto his back.

Proof this man was *all in*.

He was born to be in this club, he just didn't get the chance until now because of all the fucked up shit the Originals did and were involved in. The Originals had been their own worst enemies. They fucked up what could've been a good thing. They tainted their brotherhood with backstabbing, lies and internal beefs.

She only hoped the new Fury wouldn't follow the same pot-hole riddled road as the old. From what she'd seen so far, she wasn't sure. Especially with what happened with Cage on the edge of that field.

She had to assume both Judge and Deacon bore the same ink in their skin. She hadn't seen it since she had no reason to see her brother or cousin without a shirt or even without their cuts. She also hadn't asked.

Though, she planned on it.

She needed to know how deep into this club they both were. It was bad enough they both held spots on the executive committee. They helped make decisions when it came to what the club did and what the brotherhood became involved in. And Judge, as the sergeant at arms, not only enforced the rules, but was responsible for doling out the actual punishment for breaking those rules.

The very reason she was about to inspect Cage's cracked ribs and bruises. The damage her brother had done to his own so-called "brother."

Brutal.

Disappointing.

Damage that couldn't be undone.

And the man before her wanted to raise his daughter in this life.

Jemma closed her eyes for a moment and simply breathed, pushing away the memories of what it was like to be a little girl being raised in an MC.

When she said, "Turn around," her voice cracked and she quickly cleared her throat and gathered herself before he saw her.

Once he faced her, she handed his shirt back to him,

which he took and gripped tightly within his fist. Without breaking their locked gaze, she noticed his chest expand and retract oh-so slowly.

Something in that movement made her stomach flutter. A sensation that should not be. Not with the man before her. She quickly shoved it away.

Without his sunglasses on, she could see the deep purple under both eyes caused from his broken nose. The bruise surrounding the right eye was worse and crept toward his temple. Judge must have clubbed him upside the head.

If he had not been covered with a heavy blanket, he'd most likely be dead, or at least in a coma. Her brother could've killed him. And that would have made Judge a murderer, just like Ox.

That pissed off Jemma even more at her brother for wearing the club colors. But it wasn't Judge standing before her.

She quickly smothered the flare of her anger, just like she had with the unexpected reaction to Cage, and concentrated on the task at hand. "Any problems with breathing?"

"No." His answer was buttery-soft, so it caught her off-guard and she had to swallow hard to keep her throat from closing. "Jem—"

*Ignore it and keep going.* "You're not sleeping on that side, right?"

She wasn't sure if he answered or not because she was too busy studying the tattoo on his right upper chest. It covered his pec and surrounded his nipple. A helmeted man rode a Harley but his face was only a skull. However, the rider's arms and legs looked normal.

"Is that supposed to be you?"

"Do I look dead?"

He definitely did not look dead. But why was he whispering? Yes, they were standing very close but him keeping his voice soft kept doing something to her it shouldn't.

She shook it off again. "You're lucky you're not. Your little girl could've ended up with no parents instead of only one."

He jerked, which also made Jemma start and lift her gaze to his. She was surprised he hadn't thought of that. He hadn't considered the possibility of dying when Judge beat the fuck out of him. He hadn't realized his daughter could've been left alone on this Earth with only a grandfather and uncle. Because the Amish certainly didn't want her.

The baby was created from sin. To them, she was an embarrassment.

From what Dutch had found out, right after the birth, Dyna's mother was sent to another Amish community in Ohio to marry a widower who already had a bunch of kids. Because of her mistake with Cage, Sarah was now destined to raise another woman's children and most definitely bear more of her own.

More she'd keep this time. Unlike the one she left behind.

"Won't be breakin' that rule again."

"I imagine so." She placed her hands on his right side, his skin warm under her fingertips as she moved them along his rib cage. "How about not breaking any rules?"

She didn't have to look up from her exam to know he was staring at her. She could feel his eyes searing her. Almost as if they were hands. Touching her. Sliding over her skin. She fought a shiver.

What the fuck was going on?

"Can't promise that." Again, a whisper that did things to her it shouldn't.

He needed to stop that. Was he doing it on purpose? Was this a game to him?

Was this how he convinced an Amish woman to hike up her dress and allow him to take her virginity?

She carefully prodded the worst bruise to make sure the

ribs hadn't shifted out of place. Even as gentle as she was, he sucked in a sharp breath.

"Sorry," she mumbled, but hurried to finish.

When she was done, she stepped back, giving herself some space and breathing room.

"They seem to be healing, but you need to be careful. Try to carry Dyna in the car seat rather than in both arms. Just carry the seat with your left arm instead of your right. I'd tell you to avoid lifting anything heavy, but I know you'll ignore it."

When he didn't answer, she looked up from his chest to his face. His eyes held curiosity. And even a little interest.

No, they weren't going there. No chance in hell.

She was here to help with the baby, not scratch some biker's itches. Even if he kind of made her itchy, too.

Even with the busted up face and the broken nose, she could tell he was normally good-looking. However, looks were only skin deep and that tattoo permanently marking his skin, the large one on his back, was enough to not make her search any deeper.

He held out his shirt to her. When she stepped closer again to take it, he murmured, "Jem..."

With her heart racing, she panicked and snapped, "Stop it," before she could bite it back.

His mouth tightened and the interest in his eyes flickered and died.

*Thank fuck.* She was struggling as it was.

She ignored the humming in her veins and helped him tug on his shirt. She watched him carefully shrug his cut back on. That leather vest alone was like an anti-aphrodisiac. It was enough to chill her blood.

The perfect reminder of what she didn't want out of life.

She pulled her attention from Dyna's father back to the baby, now asleep in the bouncer.

She fought the urge to scream at him, "If you love your

daughter, take her far, far away from this fucking club!" Instead, she said, like a civilized, somewhat sane person, "I'm going to head out now. I'll be back Monday morning before you leave for work."

As she turned, he caught her wrist and pulled her back to face him. His blue eyes locked with hers. Once again, she could read the intense, obvious interest in them. She shook off the ribbon of heat threatening to swirl through her.

This wasn't what she was here for.

The only reason to be in this mobile home was for the baby, not the baby's father.

Dyna was proof he didn't make the smartest decisions. His interest in her was another one.

It would never happen. Even casually.

She'd never been a casual sex kind of person. Being intimate with someone was just that. Intimate. Meaningful. A special connection.

She knew plenty of people who could have a one-night-stand, roll out of bed and never say boo to that person again. Deacon previously being one of those people. Judge also. Jemma had never been like that. That was why she never did casual.

"Jem," he began, his warm honey-like voice sliding over her skin. "Got a question for you."

She already knew what he was going to ask. However, after what she just saw and with her disturbing reaction to him, she hoped he wouldn't.

But he had no choice, he would ask it because he was putting his daughter above himself. Once he did, she would need to make a decision. She had previously made it after talking to Judge and Trip last night, but now she was second-guessing that answer.

"More like a favor," he continued.

"Me coming home to help out is already a favor, but not

for you. For my brother." And for an innocent baby who hadn't asked for what life handed her.

"Yeah, get that. It goes along with that."

"If you're asking me for a favor, it doesn't."

"Then this one would be for me, Jem. For Dyna." He grimaced. "But I might not be able to pay this favor back."

She already knew that. Even so, she wasn't going to make this easy for him. Especially now. "Then, is it a true favor?"

He reached up, pulled the bandana off his head, closed his eyes and raked his fingers through his hair.

Doing so messed his hair up even more, but it fit him. That cocky, *don't-give-a fuck* look. He'd look good in ripped jeans, a holey T-shirt and with a damn smear of grease on his face.

Some men could pull it off. Cage would be one of them.

Some women would find it panty-melting. Jemma was determined not to be one of those.

Not here. Not now. Not ever.

That should be her new mantra. A reminder she apparently needed.

However, his next words tugged at her heart, especially when he didn't bother to hide the desperation in them. "If I gotta beg, I will, Jem. I can't do this alone and do it right. *Need* to do it right. Don't wanna fuck this up. Can't fuck her up. I can't."

*Oh God*, it wasn't a tug, he was reaching into her chest, ripping out her heart and squeezing it within his fingers. He wasn't fighting fair.

"You're going to fuck up, Chris. You will. It's inevitable. Perfect parents don't exist." A parent who did their best despite screwing up was as close to perfect as one could be. Parents who recognized they made mistakes, and would make many more, but still provided for, protected, loved and cherished their child.

Being truly loved was more important than the latest gadget or toy.

From what Jemma saw so far, Cage seemed desperate to want to do his best. What his motivation was—either from the loss of his own mother or from something else, Jemma didn't know—but it eased her worries a little bit.

"'Kay, then. Don't wanna fuck it up too badly. Wanna do my best to give her a good life. So, I need to give her a good start."

She stared at him for a minute. Maybe two. *Ugh.* She had this damn deep-rooted need to help people. She had no idea why because she certainly didn't inherit it from Trixie or Ox. But that pull was why she became an RN. It was both a blessing and a curse. Right now, it felt like a curse.

Because just in the little bit of time she'd spent with the man before her, something about him drew her. She couldn't figure out why or what, but it was there.

She was afraid to dig to discover what it was. Staying at Lottie's at night and seeing him only in passing would make ignoring whatever that *weirdness* was between them easier. Living with Cage would not.

In a two-bedroom trailer, not much privacy existed.

"Are you going to ask?" If he got around to asking, she could say no and that would be that.

"Know you're not stickin' in town. I get why. Not only 'cause of the past but the future. You're a nurse, not a babysitter. But," he inhaled deeply, "askin' you... While you're here... 'Til you leave...''

*Jesus*, he was killing her. Should she put him out of his misery?

"You want me to move in here," she said. Last night she hadn't been scared to say yes. But today? It scared the fuck out of her.

"Yeah. I'll give you the bigger bedroom, if you want. If you wanna stay close to Dyna at night. Or... whatever...

whatever you want. I just... I just can't... Don't wanna do this alone. I don't know what the fuck I'm doin' and I'm scared to fuck it up."

He wasn't the only one scared right now.

She reminded him, "You could've stayed at Dutch's if you didn't want to do it alone."

He pressed his lips together. "You saw what went on there. Got strange pussy comin' in and out..."

Yes, Jemma wouldn't like the idea of random strangers being around her baby, either. "When I leave, you'll be on your own again," she warned. Because no matter what this *weirdness* was between them, no matter how attached she got to Dyna, she was leaving.

That wasn't even a question.

"Will look for a house mouse in the meantime."

"A house mouse," she muttered. A young girl without any parenting skills. Most likely someone irresponsible who only would agree to be Cage's house mouse to get closer to the club.

A foot in the door.

Maybe even her ass in his bed.

She remembered what a house mouse was. One had lived with them for a short while to help around the house and to take care of Jemma when she was a baby. Jemma had been too young to remember her well, but Judge told her later that Trixie had knifed her after finding her in their bed with Ox. Not enough to kill her, but enough to scar her face so "no other man would ever want her."

Judge had no idea what happened to her after that. Their parents never talked about it, of course.

"Yeah, like Saylor. She does good with Daisy."

"Daisy isn't an infant." A teenager shouldn't raise a child. They were only children themselves.

"Jem... The way I'm hurtin', it'll kill me right now, but if I gotta, I'll get down on my fuckin' knees and beg."

She ripped her gaze from him and glanced around the trailer. Anything to avoid the desperation in his eyes.

She spotted the stuffed monkey on the couch and squeezed her eyes shut.

"Jem, please..."

She opened them. She would regret this...

"Okay."

# Chapter Eight



JEMMA BLINKED HER EYES OPEN. Like a cold glass of water to the face, it hit her where she was.

The trailer.

She had left Cage and Dyna yesterday and went out for a couple of drinks at Crazy Pete's to clear her mind. While there, she chatted with Dodge, Trip and Stella for a while. Actually, Dodge flirted with her for most of the night and she flirted back to try to scrape Cage out of her head.

That *weirdness*.

Whatever it was.

It had to be because she had a soft spot for men who were good fathers. Since she'd had such a shitty one.

That had to be it. Nothing more.

Cage had been thrown a hard ball and maybe, just maybe, she could help him knock this fatherhood stuff out of the park.

Stella and Trip didn't talk about the Fury's past with her, but instead, the club's future and what they hoped to achieve.

Family and financial security were two main goals.

One thing in their favor was the club's president and his

ol' lady were strong people apart and even more powerful together. If anyone could make the club successful, it would be those two. However, they were trying to sell it to the wrong person, because she wasn't buying it.

While it sounded good on the surface, Jemma had a hard time not looking back at the past. She only hoped they weren't hitching their star on a bunch of false hope.

Ozzy had also stopped in—with some woman hanging all over him—to talk to Trip for a bit. Then he—and the girl stuck to him like glue-paper—left to go drink at The Barn. Jemma didn't feel comfortable doing the same since she wasn't a part of the club.

Ozzy didn't remember her, but then he was barely eighteen when the Fury detonated from the inside out. He mentioned he lied about his age when he became a prospect. And what seventeen-year-old boy remembered a five-year-old girl who had the perfect hiding spot at the warehouse when her mother would drag her there?

Jemma had hated the yelling and fighting, the noise, the smell, everything about being around the club and its members. At the time she didn't know better, but now she knew what went on. The violence, the drinking, the drugs, the shakedowns, the gang bangs, the rapes, and treating women like shit. And that wasn't everything.

All of it, now that she understood what it was, left a bitter taste in her mouth.

When she asked Trixie once why a woman had been forced to her knees, even though she cried and begged to be let go, her mother told her to keep her mouth shut and mind her own business. It didn't concern her.

So, she'd hide in her secret spot with Annie, the dirty doll one of her father's "brothers" had given her, but not until she agreed to pretend he was Santa and sit on his lap. She didn't stay there long because he held her too tightly and his lap wasn't comfortable. He had smelled and breathed funny, too.

She and Annie would have pretend tea parties and sleepovers. Jemma would tell her doll all kinds of stories and sing songs to her just to drown out what went on outside her secret hideaway. Eventually, she'd fall asleep and Judd would come find her and carry her home.

When she asked her brother why some women who visited the warehouse laughed and some cried, Judd wouldn't explain it. He'd simply say, "I don't know."

He knew. Her brother was smart. He just didn't want to tell her. He probably thought she was still a baby and wouldn't understand.

But she was smart, too.

One good thing that happened that day... The day the police stormed the house and Ox grabbed her to use her as a shield from the guns being pointed at him...

She never had to see Trixie or Ox again.

She never had to listen to any women cry in that warehouse again.

She never was forced to sit on anyone's lap again.

She never had to hide in her secret spot again.

Jemma's heart began to thump heavily in her chest.

*Holy fuck*, she hated Manning Grove.

She fucking hated it.

She scrubbed roughly at her eyes and sat up in bed, trying to control her breathing.

Tilting her head, she listened carefully.

Nothing but silence.

She had woken up a few times during the night, once from a nightmare and twice from hearing Dyna cry. She had waited to see if Cage would come ask her for help, but he didn't. He handled whatever his daughter had needed.

She smiled. Yeah, he was going to knock this fatherhood thing out of the park.

She rolled out of bed and tugged down the long T-shirt she wore. An oversized tee she had pilfered from her last boyfriend. She had loved the T-shirt, just not the man. So, she kept the one and got rid of the other.

Wearing the Rolling Stones shirt to bed gave her more satisfaction than he ever did. He wasn't a dick, but he didn't give good dick, either. She could only deal with the bad sex for so long.

He had been a big guy, so the T-shirt was loose and long enough to hit her mid-thigh.

With a sigh, she opened her bedroom door and went still at the sight before her. She didn't know what to expect her first morning living with Cage, but what she saw wasn't it.

Bare-chested and bare-footed, he was sprawled across the couch fast asleep. One arm was folded behind his head like a pillow, the other held Dyna, who only wore a diaper, to his chest. From what Jemma could see, she was sleeping just as soundly as her father.

That view was enough to melt any cold, dead heart.

On the end table next to the couch were two empty bottles—one baby, one beer—a spit-up towel and a cell phone.

She tiptoed past, figuring she'd leave them undisturbed for a few minutes while she emptied her full bladder, brushed her teeth and at least washed her face.

When she finally came back out of the only bathroom, she headed to the couch, where Cage's mouth was now open, and he snored softly.

She shouldn't be standing over him and watching him like she was, but she couldn't resist. While, yes, his face was still fucked up, there was something about it being relaxed in sleep that reminded her of when he was a kid. He looked as vulnerable and innocent as Dyna, even with the busted nose, slightly swollen lip and black eyes.

Her fingers curled to fight the itch to run them through

his messy hair. To brush it away from his face and assure him everything would be okay.

*Holy shit*, she was fucking losing it.

She didn't want to get caught staring, so she concentrated on Dyna instead. The baby shouldn't be sleeping on her belly, so she decided to take her and put her in her bassinet for now.

As she slowly peeled his fingers off her back, trying not to wake either of them, his grip on his daughter automatically tightened.

His blue eyes popped open. "Wha—"

"I was only going to put her down. She shouldn't be sleeping on her stomach."

He glanced down and muttered a soft, "Fuck."

"Let her go," she whispered.

Jemma gently pried Dyna from his hold, moved away from the couch and checked her. Her belly was full and her diaper empty. She should sleep for a little bit.

When she looked up, she saw Cage was now sitting, his bare feet planted apart, his elbows on his knees and his head in both hands.

He looked drained.

"How much sleep did you get?"

He sat upright and shook his head. "Not much."

"You have to be at work in an hour. Do you have time for breakfast?"

"You makin' it?"

"Sure, since I have to eat, too. When's the last time she ate?"

"A half hour ago."

That gave Jemma time to make them something. "Don't let her sleep on her belly. Even when she's on your chest. A little bit of tummy time is okay but not when she's sleeping. Go grab a clean blanket and put it on the floor for now but add a playpen to your shopping list."

She heard his groan and turned her face away to hide her grin. "Ever hear that condoms are cheaper than babies?"

"Used a wrap."

Her head snapped back to him. "You used a condom?"

"Yeah. Both times."

She thought about Judge and how Jen had gotten pregnant with Ry. Jemma doubted the Amish woman came with a condom or would even poke a hole in it to get pregnant on purpose, but that didn't mean someone else hadn't poked holes in Cage's condoms.

And, if that happened, it was an evil thing to do.

"Do you think someone sabotaged your stash?"

"If someone did, I'll fuckin' kill them," he growled. He strode through the trailer and into his bedroom, returning not a minute later with a baby blanket. He spread it out on the floor where both of them would be able to see Dyna. He came over, plucked the baby from her arms and placed her on her back in the center of the blanket that bore the Blood Fury colors.

*Great.* She wondered where that came from. It had to be new, as well as custom-made.

"Did you buy your own condoms?"

"Yeah," he grunted, raking his fingers through his hair in an attempt to tame his messy bedhead.

She caught him grimacing a few times while he did it.

She did her best to stay on topic and not let him distract her. In all the wrong ways. "There are plenty of reasons for condoms to fail. Did you use lube?" Using an oil-based lube on a latex condom could be one of those reasons.

Cage's lips twitched. "Didn't need lube."

"Oh, okay, stud." She rolled her eyes. "Was the condom too big, then?" She turned away to hide her smirk.

He snorted behind her. *Close* behind her. She hadn't heard him move.

"You wanna check the fit for me?" came his low rumble.

She ignored the tingle that shot through her. "I'm a nurse. I've seen more penises in my lifetime than I ever wanted to. It takes a lot to impress me."

"Seein' them and experiencin' them are two different things."

That was for sure.

"How about you concentrate on the most important girl in your life right now instead of trying to get laid, which by the way, got you into this mess in the first place. Not that you should need a reminder. And... if you haven't figured it out yet, she might put a kink in your dating game."

"Don't date," he grumbled.

"Ah, you just prefer strange like your dad, then."

He moved behind her and grabbed the items needed to make coffee from a cabinet. A beat-up coffeemaker was on the short counter next to the fridge. Jemma hoped it worked.

When she didn't get an answer—even though she hoped to hear one—she got back on track. "Anyway, I bet you kept those condoms in your wallet, like most men."

"Yeah," he grunted, opening a can of cheap-ass coffee and scooping some into the filter. She mentally made a note to pick up some better quality coffee.

Caffeine would be very important to survival when it came to sleepless nights and late-night feedings. If she was going to drink a lot of it, she'd prefer it was rich and dark and not watered-down generic swill.

"You know keeping it in your wallet can break down a condom so it's ineffective, right?"

He pushed the start button and spun on her. "Are you fuckin' kiddin' me?"

She shrugged. "Most men don't know that. They tuck one or two in their wallet, but both sitting on it and your body heat breaks it down and could cause it to fail. Never keep it in your wallet."

"Fuck," he muttered.

"Could've been that or could've been a simple leak. Plenty of reasons why one fails. Plus, it's not a hundred percent effective."

"'Specially when you're with someone probably fertile as fuck."

"Those Amish like having loads of kids," Jemma agreed. She sighed. "Well, it doesn't matter how your baby girl came to be, she's here and you've got no choice but to deal with it."

Jemma pushed past him, wishing he'd put on a shirt, and opened the fridge. She peeked inside and grimaced. There wasn't a goddamn thing inside but a six-pack. So much for breakfast. She closed it and turned to him. "What were you planning on eating this morning?"

Cage shrugged. "Hadn't thought about it."

"Well, maybe you should."

"Got food in the bunkhouse kitchen."

"Then I suggest you march your ass over there, go 'shopping' and bring some back. You might not give a shit about eating, but I do. And if I'm going to live here, I need to eat. You don't want to see me when I'm *hangry*."

His lips twitched again. "Can't be worse than Judge when he's got a burr up his fuckin' ass."

"Oh no. I can be way worse. Trust me. We got our pleasant personalities from our father who loved to beat the snot out of someone or simply plug a hole in their noggin when he was pissed. He was worse than an angry Bruce Banner."

"I remember him, Jem," Cage said softly.

"Then you know how he got. You didn't want him turning his anger on you. That's me without good coffee and decent food."

"Like to eat."

"I appreciate a good meal. This is why I'm not a size six." Not even close.

She curled her fingers and dug her nails into her palms to quell her reaction when he raked his eyes over her from head to toe.

"Not seein' the problem."

"I didn't say there was a problem. But I'll never be one of those women who can eat three pieces of leafy greens and a baby carrot and be satisfied."

She wasn't the type of woman who could give up simple pleasures—like sweets—to keep her body in an unrealistic shape. Mostly because she wouldn't be doing it for her, she'd be doing it for the wrong reason, which would be attracting men who like thin, in-shape women, who spent time in a gym. She was none of that and never would be. If she felt like a donut, she would eat a fucking donut and not deprive herself of it. Life was too fucking short.

Plus, she hated to exercise. She tried it once. That was all it took to decide it wasn't for her.

"Takes a lot to satisfy you."

She opened her mouth to deny that in general, but then realized it was actually true. Whether it came to food or sex. "Yes. I'm not easily satisfied."

This was another reason she didn't like casual sex. With every man she'd been with, it took time and guidance for her to teach them what she liked and what made her orgasm. One night with a man wasn't long enough for him to figure it out, and she'd walk away disappointed.

She reminded herself that wasn't what they were talking about, they were supposed to be talking about food.

"Chris," she started.

"Nobody fuckin' calls me Chris. Not since I was old enough to work on cars."

"And how old were you when you started tinkering with cars?"

"When I was old enough to hold a wrench. When Bebe left, Dutch started takin' us to the garage every day. While we were there, he taught us how to work on cages and sleds, and once we knew what the fuck we were doin', he put us to work."

"Huh. Sounds like that might have violated some child labor laws."

The uninjured side of his mouth pulled up. "Think Dutch gave a fuck?"

Jemma smiled. "No."

"Right answer. Gave us a skill and a way to make a livin'. Not to mention, cheap labor for him."

"But not a way to keep you boys out of trouble, apparently."

Cage scratched his chin, considered what she said, then headed into the back bedroom. A second later he came out with a shirt in his hand. "Gonna go grab some grub from the bunkhouse. What do you need?"

"The staples. Milk. Eggs. Bread. For now, stuff to make a quick breakfast. Creamer, if there is some. Sugar, too. I don't drink my coffee black. I might have to make a trip to the grocery store."

He gingerly tugged his shirt over his head but didn't put his arms through the holes. It hung around his neck like a scarf. "Jem."

"Yeah?" She lifted her gaze from his damn chest. *Ugh.* What the hell was wrong with her? Could he see the turmoil brewing inside her?

His expression wasn't of amusement, but of pain, maybe even a touch of embarrassment. "Don't got money for groceries."

*Fuck.*

"Needed to pay my dad back for all the baby shit, still not done doin' that, and you keep addin' to the list of shit I need to buy..."

This was why condoms were cheaper than kids. "Food's important, Cage."

"But the Amish..." He ground his teeth, then sighed. "The fuckin' Amish supply us with a bunch of shit. Gotta make do with whatever they bring for now."

"Which was why Trip was so pissed about you guys fucking with the Amish. You threatened that supply."

"Yeah."

"It saves not only you guys, but the club, a lot of money," she concluded.

"Yeah."

"Then that should've been a good reason not to fuck one of them."

He blew out a breath. She could see the anger rising into his face.

"You didn't fucking think, Cage. You did something stupid that threatened a relationship the club has. All because you were selfish and wanted some tight, virgin pussy." She fed off his anger, letting it bubble in her own gut.

Last night, she had seen how passionate Trip and Stella were about making the club solid and successful. What Sig did, what Cage did, had risked that. Doing stupid shit was what destroyed the original Blood Fury. Both Sig and Cage knew that better than most—since they were both witnesses and victims of the result—and did it anyway.

"Jemma."

"No, you're not getting a pass on what you did. I get why Judge doled out punishment for breaking that rule. I don't agree with how that punishment was delivered, but I get he needs to enforce those rules. They're in place to protect the club."

It also pissed her off that what Cage did forced her brother to beat him with a club and possibly kill him. Which might have potentially thrown Judge in prison like Ox. And if her brother got thrown in prison for murder, she would never, ever forgive Judge or anyone who drove him to it.

Never.

Judge promised he'd never end up like Ox. He needed to keep that promise.

She squeezed her eyes shut.

"Jemma."

"Sorry," she whispered roughly and opened her eyes, not missing the regret in his. "I know you've already taken enough heat. And Dyna will be a reminder for breaking that rule for the rest of your life. But you guys need to stop thinking with the heads between your legs and start thinking with the heads between your shoulders instead."

"Us guys? Or just me?"

"Whoever it applies to."

He glanced around the trailer. "I'm the only one standin' here, Jem. So right now? It only applies to me. And, yeah, I fucked up. I fucked up big time. I don't need you remindin' me when my reminder, just like you said, is lyin' right on that fuckin' blanket." He shook his head. "Gonna go grab some shit from the bunkhouse."

He stormed out of the trailer and, luckily, didn't slam the door.

Jemma pressed a hand to her forehead and blew out a breath, hoping to relieve some of the tension that had tightened every muscle in her body.

She had given him more shit than necessary for no reason other than to distract herself from how she was feeling. But that wasn't the only reason.

She was scared.

She was scared for Judge and what the club might do to her brother. She was also scared for all the children who would be raised within that club.

For the first five years of her life, she had been raised in an outlaw MC. She had seen nothing good, but everything bad. That tiny human asleep on the floor didn't deserve to see or experience the same things she and the rest of the kids belonging to the Originals had.

But pushing Cage's buttons wouldn't change anything. However, anger was easier to deal with than fear.

Anger was also easier to deal with than the *weirdness* between her and Cage. She was sure he didn't feel it, it was only her.

That bothered her more than anything.

She wasn't looking for a quick hookup. She wasn't looking to stay in Manning Grove. She wasn't looking to get sucked into the MC life.

She was a fortunate escapee and wanted to keep it that way.

But it also scared her that Stella had been older, saw the same things Jemma had all those years ago and let Trip suck her back in anyway.

She needed to shower and get dressed but didn't want to do that until Cage got back. Instead, she sank onto the couch near the BFMC blanket and watched Dyna sleep.

*God*, she wished she could sleep just as soundly.

She picked up the stuffed monkey tucked in the corner of the couch and held it tightly to her chest.

She lost track of how long she sat there. She jumped when the trailer door opened and Cage entered, his T-shirt still hanging around his neck, his feet still bare, but now dirty, and a white garbage bag full of stuff in his hand.

He carried it into the kitchen and Jemma popped up off the couch, leaving the monkey behind. She swished his hands away from the bag and began to pull out whatever he had scored.

"Go shower and get ready for work. I'll make breakfast." Plus, it was hard to stand next to him and not touch him. Not like a nurse, but like a woman.

She really wanted to shake some sense into him. That was what it was.

Without a word, he went into his bedroom, left the door open and shucked off his jeans, then went into the bathroom wearing just a pair of boxer briefs. Not that she was looking...

She sighed.

She dug fresh cream—in an actual glass bottle—and a bag of generic sugar out of the unorthodox grocery bag and made herself a large mug of coffee, sucking down the caffeine in hopes that it would help her think more clearly.

Her reaction to Cage made no sense.

She searched the lower cabinets and found an old fry pan. In the garbage bag, she also found a half loaf of homemade bread and a container of churned butter. She discovered a dozen farm fresh brown eggs and a butcher-paper wrapped package of thickly sliced bacon. There were only a few pieces left, but it would be enough for this morning.

These guys had access to the best food. It truly would've been a loss if the Amish had broken ties with them. She might have to take Dyna over to the bunkhouse later and check out what else these guys had and what she could use. From what she saw so far, the selection was way better than any grocery store.

She made up two plates of scrambled eggs, bacon and toast and placed them both in front of the stools.

She was sitting on one of those stools, sipping her second mug of coffee when he came out of his bedroom, once again shirtless and only wearing a pair of old jeans. She fucking *knew* he'd look good in holey jeans.

*Damn it.*

These weren't as clean as the previous pair he had on, so she figured he only wore certain pairs to work since they probably got ruined by working on cars.

His damp hair was only toweled dry, so it was still a mess. She wondered if he owned a damn brush.

He paused at the coffeemaker, poured some coffee into an old, chipped mug and then, without a word, came around the long counter to settle gingerly on the stool next to her. She shifted when his denim-clad knee brushed her bare thigh. She should've put on some damn pants.

"Shit looks good, Jem." He forked a small mountain of eggs into his mouth.

"Are you done being angry?"

He lifted his blue eyes to hers. "Are you?"

"I think you know where I'm coming from, Chris. We share a similar past of which I don't want to repeat."

"Not lookin' to relive the past, Jem."

"Good."

"Ownin' up to my fuck up. Now we need to move on."

She would like to move on, but... "It's hard to move on when I was asked to come home."

"You've been home before." His almost perfectly straight, white teeth sank into the buttered toast.

*What the fuck?* Why was she imagining those teeth sinking into her inner thigh?

*Good lord*, coming home was making her lose her sanity.

She cleared her throat. "Only to appease Lottie. That's it."

"And now for me."

She picked up her fork and gripped it tightly in her hand like a switchblade. "For Judd," she corrected him. She needed to eat before her meal got cold, but her stomach was fluttering strangely like it was full of butterflies.

Or murderous moths.

She needed to kill those fuckers with bug spray.

"Judge ain't in this trailer right now, Jem. I am. Dyna is. Judge wouldn't have blamed you if you had said no."

"I have time on my hands until I find a new job."

"Still could've said no."

She should've. Her nightmare last night was the same that she had whenever she was back in town.

"If I said no, where would you be right now?"

"Here in this trailer, strugglin' on my own. I'd be lucky to be eatin' a leftover stale donut at work, not a breakfast like this. That's even *if* I went to work. Mighta been stuck here without anyone to take care of Dyna."

"I'm sure one of the women would've stepped in temporarily."

"Yeah, Jemma, one of the women did. You." He took another crunchy bite of his crispy toast, then turned on his stool until his knee pressed against her outer thigh again. "You don't know how much I fuckin' appreciate it, Jem. Know you hate comin' home. Judge told me how much. But you did it... For me. Even though you keep sayin' you did it for him. Ultimately it was for us, Dyna and me. Can't fuckin' thank you enough."

"Chris..."

He dropped his head for a minute and Jemma put her fork down, since she hadn't even touched a bite of her food yet, and stared at him. She swallowed, trying to loosen her closed throat.

She tentatively reached out and brushed her fingers over the top of his damp hair. "Chris," she whispered.

Stella had warned her last night about what a cocky asshole Cage could be. But Jemma hadn't seen much of that. Not yet.

For the most part, she'd seen him act nothing but humbled.

But then, she guessed getting kicked squarely in the balls might take a man down a peg or two. And having a surprise baby dropped off at your work one morning was equivalent to a direct knee to the nuts.

Her lungs locked up when he slid long, warm fingers

around her bare knee. She was still only wearing panties and that long tee, which had worked its way up to her upper thighs when she sat on the stool.

She'd had plenty of time to put on pants. Why hadn't she?

When he lifted his head, he locked eyes with her and her nipples instantly reacted. And when he leaned in, her breath hitched and her blood began to hum.

With the one hand on her knee, he curled his other hand around the back of her head and pulled her toward him as he leaned in even farther.

*Holy shit.*

*Holy fucking shit.*

She tried to get his name out, to stop him, to tell him this was not a good idea and she didn't want this, but nothing came out.

Nothing.

She closed her eyes and waited for the press of his lips.

Her eyes popped open when she felt them, but not where she expected them. They brushed over her forehead instead. He pulled back just slightly and whispered, "Thanks."

He released her head, gave her knee a quick squeeze, straightened and turned back to his breakfast.

Jemma had to tell herself to breathe because in that instant she forgot how.

He bit into a slice of bacon and chewed, staring straight ahead.

*What the fuck just happened?*

She couldn't remember getting this worked up over any man. In fact, the last time she had gotten this flustered was when she was fifteen and sixteen-year-old Bobby Miller had French kissed her, shoved his hand up her shirt and honked her boob behind the shed at the house.

Judd had found out—Jemma had no idea how—tracked

Bobby down, punched him so hard the kid ended up knocked out cold. He also threatened Bobby that if he ever touched his sister again, Judd would slice his throat. Bobby had told Jemma that Judd actually pulled a real knife when he made that threat and did a slicing motion across his throat. Then Bobby told her never to speak to him again because she wasn't worth dying for.

Well, the news of that incident ran rampant through her school and fucked up Jemma's chances of dating all throughout high school. It wasn't until she got a car and could drive herself to parties in surrounding towns, where no one knew Judd Scott was her brother, that she not only could get kissed, but finally lose her virginity.

Admittedly, it had sucked.

So had the second time.

And the third.

But eventually she found someone who knew kind of what he was doing so it wasn't as bad. Out of desperation, Jemma bought her first vibrator at eighteen and discovered what an orgasm was. But that kind of backfired. Once she experienced a real orgasm, she was more disappointed in most of the guys she slept with since they had no clue how to help her achieve one.

But less than a minute prior, Cage's touch, and then the anticipation of a possible kiss, had not only those butterflies pounding their monster-sized wings inside her belly, but had her pussy pulsing.

She pulled her gaze from his profile, since she was probably staring at him like a lunatic and dropped it to her plate.

Right now, she had no desire to eat the meal she'd prepared, but instead, she felt like grabbing a handful of his hair, dragging him to the floor, stripping him of those soft, worn jeans and riding his cock until those butterflies stopped beating up her insides and her pussy got what it was throbbing for.

Unfortunately, there were several problems with doing any of that.

One, she didn't do casual.

Two, she didn't do bikers.

And three, that would really fucking complicate things since they were temporarily living together in a small space.

Oh, and four—and it was a big one—Judge would club Cage again. Though, this time probably skipping the protection of the heavy blanket, that meant he would die and Dyna would become an orphan.

Cage might not be the perfect parent for her, but he was better than nothing.

"Gonna eat your bacon?"

That question brought her tumbling back to the here and now, and the reality of their situation.

She slid her plate next to his. He grabbed a slice of her bacon and shoved it into his mouth. While he chewed, he grumbled, "Got home late last night."

*Home.*

That word alone was enough to rip the wings off those fucking butterflies.

## Chapter Nine

CAGE DID his best to bring them both back to Earth. Because, *Jesus Christ*, the way her breathing had changed and how she had stared at him—like she was a cannibal and he was her next meal—just about made him drag her to the floor, yank up that damn T-shirt, pull off her panties and go balls deep inside her.

And if he did that, he might actually die the next time he saw Judge. He was pretty damn sure it would be a slow death, too.

The club's sergeant at arms had convinced his sister to come home to help him. Sticking his dick in her was included in the *you-better-treat-Jemma-with-respect-or-else* threat Judge had given him before she'd showed up.

"I needed a drink."

*Huh? Oh yeah.* Why she came home late last night. He was kind of pissed she did.

Not that he could say anything. She wasn't chained to the trailer, to his daughter or even to him.

"Booze in The Barn." She could walk the hundred yards to church and grab a beer or a shot without having to go to a bar, even if it was a club-owned one.

"I don't belong to the club."

She did. Whether she liked it or not.

She was born to an Original. She was the sister to the Fury's enforcer, cousin to the treasurer. Fury blood ran thick through her veins. If anyone belonged to the club, she did.

He opened his mouth to argue that point, but knew he'd only be beating his head against a wall and he already had enough bruises to last a while. Instead, he asked, "You head to Crazy Pete's?"

"Yes." She plucked a piece of toast from her plate and took a bite.

"Were you lookin' for somethin' in particular?"

"A drink."

"Nothin' else?"

Her eyes burned a hole into the side of his face as he concentrated on the mug in his hand.

"Like what?"

He almost shrugged but caught himself in time. "What's normally at a bar?"

"Booze?"

"And company."

"Wasn't looking for company but found some anyway."

He twisted on the stool and put his mug down. "Yeah? Anyone I know?"

"Trip, Stella and Dodge. Ozzy also did a drive-by. I'm not sure who the woman was who was glued to his side."

"Maybe Lizzy."

"Don't know and don't care. That's his business. Just like where I went last night was mine."

"Just worried."

Her eyebrows shot to her hairline. "You worried?"

"Yeah."

"Why? Were you worried I'd hook up with some random dick and if he killed me and chopped me up into little pieces, you wouldn't have anyone to help you?"

A muscle in his jaw popped. He tried to conceal his rising irritation with sarcasm. "Yeah, Jemma. That's why I was fuckin' worried."

"No reason to worry about me. I've been on my own a long time. And I don't do random one-night-stands."

"Good. 'Cause it was bad enough at Dutch's. Don't want strange comin' in and out of this trailer."

"Oh, suddenly *Mr. Let-me-knock-up-an-Amish-girl* has morals?"

"Ain't about me, it's about Dyna." That was both the truth and a lie.

"Of course it is." She shot him a big smile he didn't like. "Don't worry, if I decide to slide down some strange dick, I'll do it elsewhere."

"Just said you don't do randoms."

"They're only considered random the first night. The second night they're not so random."

He curled his fingers around his mug and took a much needed, calming breath. "Jem—"

"How about if you don't worry about my sex life and I don't worry about yours?"

"That'd be best." Not really, but it would have to be for now.

"Okay, then," she huffed.

"'Kay, then." He popped her last piece of bacon into his mouth and carefully slipped off the stool. "Gotta get ready for work or I'm gonna be late."

Without looking back, he went in his bedroom, carefully put on his socks and boots, slipped a belt through the jeans' loops and snagged a shirt out of his stash of old T-shirts he wore to work. Once they got a hole or became threadbare, they moved to that category.

Once again, he had a hard time putting his arms through the sleeves without excruciating pain, so he left it hanging around his neck and headed back out to the kitchen.

Not only was his baby helpless to get dressed, so was he.

But, *hey*, at least Jemma was a lot better looking and smelled a lot better, too, than his previous help. Before moving into the trailer, he'd had to get whoever was available in the bunkhouse or The Barn to help him. And that had been a little weird. Just being that close to another man alone proved he'd never do a threesome or a train with any of his brothers.

No fucking way.

But now Jem was here and could help him with his shirts and his boot laces, if he needed it.

Which he did.

Even better, it was a great excuse to get close to her again. Especially with her only wearing that damn T-shirt. It barely covered her long-assed legs and when she had sat on the stool, it had inched up even higher. He'd actually gotten a couple glimpses of the pink panties she wore.

He'd never wanted to lift a pair of panties to his nose and inhale a woman's scent so badly before. It was so fucking weird. He didn't have any kinks, so he was never into sniffing women's panties or clothes, or even hair.

But there was something about Jemma that made him want to do that. Like if he inhaled her, she would be inside him and a part of him.

It was the strangest goddamn thing.

One, she was off limits. Judge had been crystal motherfucking clear about that.

Two, he didn't want to do anything stupid and lose her help with Dyna.

And three, it could get really fucking awkward since they had to live together—even temporarily—in the trailer.

The best thing for both of them would be if he stuck to

his side of the mobile home and she stuck to hers. They could just meet in the middle when dealing with Dyna.

He stopped in front of her, where she was scraping the plates into the now empty garbage bag he'd used to carry the food over from the bunkhouse.

She looked up and without a word, placed the dishes in the sink and turned toward him. He only hissed twice with pain as she helped him get his arms into the sleeves. Once she did, he pulled it the rest of the way down his torso.

"Can you get my laces?"

She arched one dark eyebrow at him, but with only a twist to her lips, squatted at his feet and snugly laced up his boots.

The sight of her almost on her knees before him made him grin but he quickly hid it as she rose back to a stand.

"Anything else I can help you with?"

He bit back a snort because he actually had a nice little list of things she could help him with, but he doubted that was what she meant. "Nope."

She took a step back. "Where are her onesies, diapers and the rest?"

"On the shelves in the laundry room like you suggested."

She nodded, a pleased look on her face. Probably because he'd taken her suggestion. But it had been a good one and he would've been stupid not to consider it.

Now he just needed to get some sort of changing table in there. As well as a crib for Dyna to sleep in.

*Fuck.*

He needed to figure out how to get those things for free or at least as cheaply as possible.

Or he could sell his perfectly restored Impala convertible, buy a practical car and the shit he needed for his kid.

He grimaced. Even if he did that, it would take a while to find the right buyer for the right money, and he needed shit before then.

But still…

No, he couldn't get rid of his baby. Giving up his classic Chevy would almost be as bad as if he had given up Dyna for adoption. It was his. And he'd restored it from the frame up himself.

He didn't have much but he had his daughter, his car and his sled.

And right now, a roof over their heads.

The rest he'd figure out. He'd get whatever she needed, even if it meant selling sperm or plasma.

Both their heads turned toward the blanket in the living room when the baby made a squeak.

"Someone's awake."

Cage watched Jemma move into the living room and held his breath as she bent over to pick up Dyna. Not only did he get a good look at her long bare legs, but he had an unobstructed view of her ass covered in pink cotton.

He groaned softly. Her ass was sweet perfection. *Fuck him.*

She turned with Dyna in her arms and holding the baby pressed the soft cotton of that tee to her unrestrained tits underneath it.

Dyna began rooting against those luscious tits with her face. He almost groaned again. *Yeah, kid, I'd like to suck on those, too.* If he tried, he might get a fist to the face and his nose still had a way to go to heal.

He needed to get the hell out of this trailer before his hard-on got any bigger and became obvious. "Gotta go or I'm never gonna pay off my debt to Dutch."

She carried Dyna into the kitchen and grabbed the container of formula that was sitting out on the counter. That shit was expensive as fuck, too. No wonder women breastfed. It had to save them a fortune.

"You'd think him being her grandfather, he'd be in no rush to be paid back."

"Then you don't know Dutch." He filled one of the empty baby bottles with the right amount of bottled spring water, took the scoop of formula from her fingers, dumped it in, and handed the scoop back to her. She sealed the can back up as he tightened the nipple onto the bottle and shook it enough to mix it. He ran it under the hot tap for a few seconds to warm the formula up just to the right temp, then handed it to Jemma.

He could now make formula in his sleep. In fact, he might have actually done it while sleeping a couple times. Not only were babies expensive, they were fucking exhausting.

But now he was just as much an expert at mixing baby formula as he was rebuilding a Holley two-barrel carburetor.

"He's payin' for this place," he reminded Jemma as he stepped even closer.

Her green eyes lifted to his and he stared down at her for a couple of heartbeats.

A flush rushed up her throat when he reached toward her. He was tempted to touch her lips, which were parted slightly, but instead he did what he originally intended. He brushed his fingers over Dyna's sparse soft dark hair.

Jemma's breath ruffled his own hair as he leaned closer to give his daughter a kiss. "Bye, monkey," he whispered, only a couple inches from the baby's face. Dyna's eyes were glued to him and she was no longer fussing for her bottle.

It wasn't just Dyna watching him.

Jemma had gone completely still. Like she was afraid to move. Cage noticed goosebumps had broken out over Jemma's skin and her nipples pebbled under the thin cotton.

He didn't pull away, but hesitated there, near her neck, and he took a slow, deep inhale. When he exhaled just as slowly, he let it sweep over her skin.

Cage heard her breath slip in almost a sigh from

between her lips. He straightened and stared down again into her face. The flush had crept from her throat into her cheeks, her eyes seemed a little wider than normal and her grip on Dyna had tightened.

"Gotta go," he whispered.

He turned and exited the trailer before he decided to skip work altogether.

When he walked down the steps, he wore a grin.

---

DYNA FINALLY HAD A STROLLER. Jemma had no idea who dropped it off, but a brand-new one, still in the box, sat outside the door when Cage had come home. He dragged the huge box into the trailer and unpacked it to find a stroller and a matching carrier that could be used as part of the stroller or as a car seat. It was perfect since Cage only had one car seat and kept it in the old, beat-up Honda he'd been driving around, not just to haul Dyna but because riding his sled was still too painful for his ribs.

She could put the second car seat in her Volvo, or use it as a carrier when she couldn't use the stroller.

Whoever bought it had spent a nice chunk of change. But the gift that showed up mysteriously on their doorstep was proof this brotherhood had each other's back. They weren't going to let Cage and his daughter go without. If he couldn't afford the shit he needed, someone else who could wouldn't hesitate to help.

However, by not putting their name on the gift, Cage wouldn't feel pressured to pay that person back. The selfless-ness both impressed Jemma and warmed her heart.

She decided to give the new Cadillac of strollers a spin this morning and take Dyna on a little journey over to The Barn. Jemma hadn't had much of a chance to explore since coming to the farm a couple of days ago. Even though she wasn't officially a part of the Fury, she was curious about the club's church and how the guys were living, including her nephew who had a room in the rear bunkhouse portion.

While eating leftovers Lottie had dropped off when she'd popped in for a quick visit—her aunt's excuse for a chance to cuddle with Dyna—Cage had mentioned that their meeting room was on the upper level of The Barn and two apartments took up the second floor of the bunkhouse.

Sig and Autumn lived in one. Deacon and Justice lived in the other, but Reese crashed there with him on the weekends. During the week, her cousin took the twenty minute or so drive to Mansfield to shack up with his ol' lady in her big house on a mountain.

The idea of that made Jemma smile. Deacon was more like a brother to her than a cousin, so she was happy to see him happy. He'd always been a dog, so she had been shocked when he told her over the phone a few weeks ago he found "the one."

*The one.* She shook her head.

While visiting yesterday, Lottie seemed to be thrilled with both of *her boys'* choices in women to settle down with. Not that either was exactly "settled." They were just in a serious relationship.

What her aunt wasn't happy with was *her boys* wearing Fury colors. They were forbidden to wear their cuts in her house. She had cut ties with Jemma's father, Ox, when he got involved with the original Fury and the MC began to cause problems in town. And elsewhere.

Like Jemma, Lottie didn't want to see Judge follow in his father's footsteps, meaning in prison and then six-feet under. Her aunt also tried to talk Ry into staying with her for the summer instead of on the farm, but both Ry and Judge put their foot down about that. The whole reason he was in the bunkhouse was to take the summer to get to know the father he was stolen from. At least by staying on the property, he was close. If Saylor hadn't already been a part of the Judge/Cassie household, he probably would've ended up staying with them.

Jemma pushed the stroller over the uneven ground past the pavilion and to the back of the building that housed both the club's church and quarters. She rolled Dyna through the rear steel door.

What she had noticed as she walked along the outside of the building was the lower level had no windows. Neither in the barn or the bunkhouse portion. She found that interesting and wondered if that had been done for a reason.

At the very front of The Barn were large windows on the second floor and two large windows at the back where the apartments overlooked a field. Plus, a couple along each side. One for the apartment in the back and one, she assumed, where the meeting room was.

She wondered if that was done for safety reasons. She'd have to ask Cage.

The bunkhouse was as quiet as expected since it was the middle of the day and even though the occupants were bikers, they had to do their part by working.

Trip had said the other night at Crazy Pete's that everyone had to pull their weight. He didn't want any "lazy motherfuckers" as part of the club. He also quoted a saying about idle hands being the devil's workshop. Jemma took that as Trip doing his best to keep his brothers out of trouble and out of prison by keeping them focused.

The fucking man was smart. And driven. He also wasn't going to take any shit from anyone inside or outside the MC, or let his brothers get caught up in shit which would take themselves or the club down.

He had his work cut out for him since Jemma learned most of the guys had done more than their share of time behind bars. They weren't strangers to making or getting into trouble.

But something the club president said the other night stuck with her. A club didn't exist without members. And if those members spent more time in jail than out, it could weaken the club and effectively destroy it.

He certainly learned from the Originals' mistakes. Jemma also wondered if Trip had been part of a more solid and grounded club in the past and got his cues from it.

It didn't matter because the club wasn't Jemma's reason for coming home. The tiny human in the stroller was. And Cage's daughter would never wear a Fury cut.

*Thank fuck.*

Jemma took her time wandering through the bunkhouse, peeking into rooms as she went. The large shared bathroom, the room with bunkbeds, the single rooms with private bathrooms, then another bathroom right outside the door leading into church.

That one was smaller than the one just inside the back door and it didn't have a shower. It was probably used when there were parties or pig roasts. Or by guests.

She imagined any guests to the farm had to be invited. As much as Trip kept a tight grip on the club, she couldn't see parties being a wild free-for-all.

Many parties at the old warehouse had been total clusterfucks. There were many times Jemma didn't recognize most of the people inside and outside the building. She knew now that some of the females had to be underage. Some of the guys, too. It wasn't like the Originals cared that a sixteen-year-old would be doing drugs or drinking with them. Or that a sixteen-year-old girl brought along her four-teen-year-old friend.

They probably thought bikers were cool or badass and would be fun to party with.

Sure they were.

Those girls probably didn't leave with the same attitude about bikers that they showed up with.

Hearing Trip, and knowing Judge and Deacon, she knew that kind of shit wouldn't be tolerated here. Teenaged girls weren't going to wake up the next morning bloodied and bruised and full of cum from a few different men.

Jemma stopped dead when her pulse began to race. She squeezed her eyes shut until she could get her heart back into her chest. When she did, she glanced down at Dyna. She would grow up in a club and she didn't want Cage's daughter to think that shit was normal.

Or okay.

It was far from it.

At the end of the hall across from the smaller bathroom was a grey swinging door on the left. This had to be where Cage pilfered all the farm fresh food. She swung the stroller around and backed through the door. Once she had Dyna safely through it, she parked the sleeping baby to the side and out of the way so she could take a good look around.

Impressive couldn't even begin to describe what the kitchen was like. She'd never worked in a restaurant but she figured this kitchen—with all the commercial appliances and stainless steel—had to rival one. It had a walk-in cooler and also what looked like a huge freezer. Loads of storage shelves and cabinets full of all kinds of food lined a couple walls

Was it sparkling clean?

Hell no.

Take a whole bunch of bachelor bikers, let them eat, drink and cook and it was going to be a mess. The double sinks at the far end of the kitchen were overflowing with dishes, mugs, cups, pots and pans. So was the counter next to it. Of course, not one of those plates had been scraped clean.

She wondered whose responsibility it was to keep the kitchen clean. Whoever it was hadn't done their job. But even so, it wasn't worse than what a restaurant kitchen would look like at the end of a busy night.

Since Cage didn't have money for groceries, she planned on doing some "shopping" and grab stuff she could make for the next few days for both breakfast and dinner. Plus, grab some mid-day snacks.

Not surprising, plenty of fruit and vegetables were available to choose from, but when it came to the junk, like snack food and sodas, most of it was slim pickings. She'd have to shake a box or a bag first to see if it was even worth taking. Anything she found completely empty or with just crumbs at the very bottom of the package, she tossed in an already almost full metal trash can.

She probably spent a good ten minutes perusing their supplies and picking out stuff she could use, but making sure she left enough behind for the rest of the guys. Just in case one of them decided to make a fruit tart or a spinach quiche.

She snorted.

In truth, more than enough food was available. And most of it high quality like what Cage had brought back for breakfast two mornings ago.

The deal they had with the Amish more than paid off. It was genius.

And, again, the main reason Trip was so pissed at Cage for getting involved with one of the Amish girls. *Women.* Hopefully, Dyna's birth mother had been old enough to be considered a woman and not underage. Jemma never asked.

The whoosh of the swinging door made Jemma jump and almost drop one of the bags of bounty she pilfered.

She turned and froze at who walked in.

Her mouth opened and her breath hissed out as they blinked at each other.

She had long dark hair that looked like she'd freshly rolled out of bed, wide blue eyes with slightly smeared mascara, a little bit of lipstick clung to her upper lip, and pale skin.

The reason Jemma knew she was pale was because the woman—or girl, she didn't look very old—was completely naked. Oh, wait. That was wrong. She was wearing cute striped socks or stockings—whatever they were—that came up mid-thigh.

Jemma also couldn't help notice the girl had small perky breasts, a completely shaved pussy, a belly ring and was willowy thin.

"Hi!" Jemma squealed like she was a high school cheerleader, and quickly plastered on a big smile.

Why did she feel guilty about being caught with her fingers in the cookie jar?

She shouldn't. Both Trip and Judge had told her she had free rein to anything in the kitchen or the bar in The Barn. The club paid or traded for all of the food, drinks, beer and booze. Cage and Dyna were part of the club.

"Hey," came the answer on a sort-of giggle.

The dark-haired girl inspected Jemma from head to toe. Jemma was dressed way more conservatively, like with actual clothes.

"Are you new here?" the naked woman-child asked.

"Oh, yeah. Just getting the lay of the land," Jemma answered, trying to keep her eyes above the girl's shoulders.

"Are you making breakfast for one of the guys?"

She pursed her lips. Was that normal around here? Naked breakfast served in bed? That sounded like a service a five-star hotel might provide. For a big, fat extra fee. "Do you normally make breakfast for them?"

"No... It depends. If they tell me to."

Jemma hoped to fuck she was at least eighteen. "Do you normally do whatever they tell you to do...?" She let the last hang.

"Angel," she answered and frowned. "Of course. Didn't anyone tell you that?"

"Tell me what?"

"You do whatever you're told," Angel answered in an exaggerated way that made it seem she thought Jemma was a dimwit.

That slightly amused Jemma, so she decided to play along. "Oh. I... I just thought they meant sexually."

"Oh no. I sometimes do laundry and dishes. And clean their bathroom. Whatever they need."

"Do all the... Do all of you do that?"

"Pretty much."

Jemma was no longer amused and decided she didn't like this game. "And then if they want to fuck you, they just point at you and crook their finger?"

"Crook their finger?" Angel somehow made a confused expression look cute. Jemma wondered if she practiced it.

"You know. Like this." Jemma demonstrated by crooking her finger at her.

"Well, yeah. But that's the whole point of being a club girl. Except for the prospects. They can't order us around or fuck us." She plugged a hand on her bare hip, which, unfortunately, drew Jemma's gaze downward, something she was trying to avoid. "Who brought you in?"

Brought her in? "Cage."

Angel's voice had gone from high-pitched to husky when she groaned, "*Oh God, yessss. Mmm.*" She closed her eyes and bit her bottom lip. She even did a cute little shudder.

Jemma might have imagined it, but did Angel's perky boobs get even perkier? Maybe she had a mini-orgasm or something.

"That good, huh?"

"Most of them are *really* good."

Most. She assumed with Angel's reaction, Cage was

included in that "most." That meant Cage had crooked his finger at Angel. Presumably more than once.

That shouldn't annoy her, but, *damn it*, it did. "That right?"

"You're definitely new here if you don't know yet." Her blue raccoon eyes went wide. "Wait! Are you his new house mouse? I heard he got stuck with that Amish bitch's brat."

Jemma opened her mouth to say no, but snapped it shut. *Holy shit*, in reality, she *was* a house mouse. She was taking care of Cage's baby, his trailer, cleaning up, and stealing food to feed his ass. All without a dime in compensation.

She wasn't even getting any of his apparently "good" dick. Good, at least by Angel's standards.

"I'm just helping out temporarily," she said weakly.

"Well, lucky you. I offered to help but he turned me down. You know... since he doesn't have an ol' lady yet..."

Jemma didn't know.

"It would be like a trial run," the "club girl," aka sweet butt, clarified.

Oh, sure it would.

Angel scrunched up her face. "But really, I don't think I want to become someone's ol' lady who already has a kid from another bitch. There are plenty of other guys around here who don't have an ol' lady yet and don't have that extra baggage." She wrapped her arms around her waist and did a dramatic shiver. "You know diapers and puke and all of that when the kid didn't even come out of my own pussy."

*Uh.* "Well, I gotta go before Dyna wakes up."

"Who's Dyna?"

Jemma moved to where she had pushed the stroller out of the way. Apparently, Angel couldn't see it from where she stood. As she pointed it toward her escape, Angel squealed out a high-pitched, "O... M... G!" She practically shoved Jemma out of the way, squatted—yes, squatted in all her naked glory—in front of the stroller and *booped* Dyna's nose with her finger.

If Angel woke up the baby, Jemma was going to *boop* her. She grabbed the woman by the shoulder—she barely resisted grabbing a fistful of her hair—and yanked her away from the stroller. "She's sleeping," she hissed.

"So?"

"So, if you wake her, you're going to be the one to get her back to sleep."

"It can't be that hard," Angel huffed.

Tell that to her father at three in the morning.

"Can you get the door for me?" Jemma asked with saccharine sweetness, trying to sound more civil because she didn't need to make enemies right off the bat.

Angel swung the door outward and held it open as Jemma pushed a—luckily—still-sleeping Dyna past her.

She hooked a left.

"Hey, if Cage ever needs me to babysit..." Angel called out from the open doorway.

"I'll let him know." No, she wouldn't, and she also doubted Cage would leave Dyna in Angel's hands.

If he did, Jemma would never forgive him, even though Dyna wasn't her daughter and she had no right to judge.

But, too bad, in this matter she was going to judge.

Jemma hesitated at the closed door to The Barn. "Hey, Angel?" She glanced over her shoulder to make sure the sweet butt was still there.

"Yeah?"

"Just curious. Who are you making breakfast for?" It was actually past breakfast and heading into lunch. Maybe Angel was planning on a brunch spread, other than what was between her legs.

Jemma lifted a palm to stop the sweet butt's answer and shook her head. "It doesn't matter for who. All that matters is, it's a nice gesture."

As long as it wasn't for her eighteen-year-old nephew.

# Chapter Ten

JEMMA PUSHED THE STROLLER—NOW filled with a sleeping baby and a bunch of groceries, both hanging off the handles and stuffed underneath the seat—through church.

She couldn't believe what she was seeing. It was nothing like the old warehouse.

Not even close.

At first glance, one wouldn't even guess it was the clubhouse to an MC. No, it looked like a lodge—or something similar—with the center, see-through stone fireplace, the handcrafted wood bar and more.

Old green bus benches lined the walls and a couple sat in front of the fireplace. Two pool tables sat on the opposite side of the building from the bar. A couple dart boards hung on the walls. Bike parts and Harley memorabilia also decorated the space. Not garbage, but really cool shit.

However, one thing hanging on the wall near the bar caught her attention. She rolled the stroller a little closer, parked it where she could see it, and approached. On display, and lit by a small spotlight, was a Fury cut spread open so both the front and back could be seen.

The colors belonged to Crazy Pete. Stella's father.

She reached up and brushed her fingertips over the old patches, tracing the sewn edges and the embroidered letters. Doing so felt like reaching into the past. She yanked her hand back as if that past seared her fingers.

If she remembered correctly, a cut was supposed to be buried with the member. Obviously, Pete's hadn't been. Though, neither had Ox's because Judge wore their father's, which was disturbing in itself. Judge had replaced the name patch but the rest was all original. The cut was the one Ox wore when he murdered his own brothers. And who knew who else.

A chill spiraled down Jemma's spine.

*Christ*, she hated that Judge chose this path. Deacon, too.

If anything, during her time home, maybe she could convince them to rethink their choices. They had good women, a loving family and neither needed to be a part of a brotherhood that could potentially destroy their futures with those women and family.

Judge finally had Ry back and was discussing adopting Daisy. So, if he went to prison for something like their father had done, he'd desert his own children. Like Ox and Trixie had.

In truth, their parents weren't a loss. Their parenting skills had been lacking, or, for the most part, non-existent. She and her brother lucked out by being taken in by Lottie and Walter, who acted like real parents should.

The problem was, while Jemma had benefitted from their solid parenting, Judge had been sixteen and by that time, bad habits were already instilled in him. Walter did his best to straighten Judge out. Jemma knew her brother had loved and respected their uncle, so he tried to follow their uncle's advice and guidance. To an extent.

Fortunately, Judge wasn't Ox, at least not yet, and he'd be a great father to both his son and future adopted daughter. Even so, he needed to be there for them no matter what.

Especially since he missed the first eighteen years of raising his son.

Jemma's chest became tight as she stared at Crazy Pete's cut and blew out a frustrated breath to try to loosen it. She loved her brother and cousin to pieces, and she didn't want anything bad happening to either. Plus, Walter's loss affected all of them deeply. Lottie had remained strong throughout Walter's cancer and death, but Jemma was sure she'd be devastated if anything happened to her son or nephew and might not recover so quickly from another life-altering loss.

She turned and let her gaze slide through church again. It didn't create a knot in her gut like the warehouse always did. Just the atmosphere alone had a totally different vibe. The warehouse had been dingy, dirty and dark. The upkeep done on it was minimal. While The Barn didn't have windows, it wasn't nearly as dark or depressing.

It also was free of bad memories.

Except for Pete's cut, of course.

She moved behind the bar and grabbed an unopened bottle of Jack Daniels to go along with the six-pack of cola she had snagged from the pantry in the kitchen. If Cage wanted beer, he could get it himself. The stroller was already overloaded with goodies.

Anyway, coming over to the bunkhouse to grab food and drinks gave her an excuse to get Dyna out of the trailer and give Jemma a change of scenery. Even if that scenery was a naked sweet butt.

She tucked the bottle securely under the stroller seat and took one last spin around the interior to take in the details and, as she did so, one of the double doors on the side opened just a crack and someone slipped inside.

Not just anyone.

Ry.

Her nephew was sneaking into church. That made no sense since he lived here. He didn't need to sneak anywhere.

"Hey!" she called out, causing him to visibly startle and spin toward her with wide eyes.

He quickly schooled his *oh-shit* face. "Uh... Hey, Aunt Jemma!" He sounded a little too enthusiastic to see an aunt he'd only met recently.

She smiled and rolled Dyna closer. She'd head out through the same door Ry just entered. "Just Jemma. You don't need to add the 'aunt.'"

He nodded and scrubbed his fingers nervously over his short hair. He was so clean-cut compared to the rest of the men on this property. Not one tattoo, short, neat hair, and he looked comfortable wearing a turquoise polo shirt with khaki shorts.

Both fit him well. He wasn't as gangly as Judge had been at that age. He was very handsome and solid. She could see girls chasing him.

Or boys. Whatever he was into.

Well, at least she knew now Angel wasn't bringing Ry a smorgasbord of food and pussy to his bed. She would have a little discussion with Judge to make sure the sweet butts were told to stay hands-off with his son.

"So... Where are you coming from?" *And why do you look so guilty?*

He glanced nervously over his shoulder at the now closed door. "Uh... nowhere."

"Nowhere, huh?" She raised both eyebrows and watched him closely.

"I... I was just checking to see if my dad was home."

"He's probably working."

Her nephew's Adam's apple shot up his throat and then dropped like a rock.

She pursed her lips and studied him. "Was Cassie home?"

"N-no. She went to work."

"Ah, yes. Most people are at work right now. So, was anyone home?"

"Only... uh..." Color tinged Ry's cheeks.

While Jemma had to smother her smile at his reaction at being busted, she also became a tad concerned. "Only..." she prodded.

"Only... Saylor. She told me Dad wasn't home."

"You didn't know that before going over?"

"I texted him to ask, but he didn't answer."

Or Judge did answer to tell Ry he wasn't home, giving Ry the head's up that the coast was clear.

Jemma had met Rev's younger sister, Saylor, at dinner the other night. Her brother's house mouse was very pretty but way more experienced in life than Ry. Not only with the topics she talked about, but how she dressed and did her makeup. Her nephew reminded her of a boy, while Saylor looked like she had a penchant for trouble. It was one reason Judge and Cassie took her on and into their home. Saylor needed to learn responsibility and Daisy, along with the housekeeping duties, was enough to keep her busy and keep her out of that trouble.

For the most part.

While all the Fury members were warned not to touch Saylor, not just by Judge but by Rev, Jemma wondered if Judge had told his son the same. Because it wasn't hard to miss that Ry only had eyes for Saylor all during the dinner at Lottie's. Jemma wasn't the only one who noticed. Judge did, too.

While both kids were eighteen, they seemed years apart in life experience. Jen must have sheltered Ry. While Saylor had spent time in juvie.

Not the best start for a teenaged girl.

Living with Cassie and Judge would help give her a good foundation to move on from her troubled past. But really,

Saylor was legally an adult. She could do whatever she wanted.

Jemma wondered if Saylor wanted to do Ry. Because no doubt remained that Ry wanted to do Saylor.

She hated to be the one to tattletale to Judge about Ry sneaking over to his house when he and Cassie weren't home, but she also didn't want Ry stuck with a surprise baby, like Dyna.

He needed to get his degree first, get settled into a good career before he got saddled with a family, which could possibly derail his plans if it happened before it was time.

Jemma was the first in the Scott family to get a college education. She wanted Ry to be the second. The kid had a lot of potential.

Ry seemed poised to sprint toward the bunkhouse to escape his aunt's questions. She didn't blame him since she remembered what it was like to be a horny teenager. She had been eighteen herself only nine years prior.

"Ry—" The start of her *please-be-careful* lecture was interrupted by a crying Dyna. Someone was awake and most likely hungry.

She pulled Dyna from the carrier hooked into the stroller base and straightened out the baby's onesie, which today read: *Warning! Protected by a Biker Grandpa,* with a picture of a motorcycle, of course.

It was easy to figure out who bought that one. Especially since Dutch had taken a black Sharpie and drawn a top rocker on the back of it, filling it in with the name "Duchess."

She was sure Cage just loved that fact, since he grimaced every time Dutch called her that. But then, so did Jemma.

As Dyna continued to cry softly, Jemma knew it would become an angry wail soon if she didn't get her fed. But instead of rushing back to the trailer, she stepped up to Ry and forced him to take her.

"Make sure you support her head and neck." She moved his hands to where they needed to be, then stepped back, watching his expression turn panicked.

Dyna would be a great reminder of what could happen if he wasn't careful. She had no idea if Ry knew the truth of his own conception. Most likely, he didn't.

Judge was still pissed about Jen trapping him by poking holes in his condoms, but Jemma doubted he'd ever tell his son what a real piece of shit his mother had been.

Ry probably learned some of it when he found out his "dead" father was very much alive and his mother had lied about it for eighteen years. He'd also found all the text messages and listened to all the voicemails Judge had left for his son over the years, hoping Ry would contact him.

So, yeah, after Ry's mother died, he discovered some of the truth. But not all of it and maybe not about the whole condom sabotage. There was no point in bringing that up at this point in Ry's life. Unless it could be used as a lesson.

Both Dyna and Ry's existence were hard lessons on how condoms could fail. Either on purpose or by accident.

Ry looked like a deer in headlights ready to get plastered by an eighteen-wheeler. He'd probably prefer that to holding a still crying Dyna.

Good.

"Bounce her gently to try to soothe her. Rub her back, too." Jemma knew that probably wouldn't help since Dyna was ready to eat and wasn't just being fussy. "Now, hum or sing to her a little bit... She's a good lesson of what not to do, Ry. You have college and your whole future ahead of you. Don't screw that up."

His Adam's apple bobbed again. "I... I wasn't..."

"Right." She gave him a smile. "I'm in the trailer by the shed. You can always stop by to talk if you need to. I'm not only your aunt but I'm also a nurse. If you have a question,

I'll do my best to answer it. I know losing your mom like that had to be hard."

His expression went blank. "Yes, it was difficult." His answer was robotic as if he was used to saying it automatically. "I miss her."

"I'm sure you do," she murmured, finding it weird his words lacked any sadness. His mother didn't die long ago, so it still should be very fresh.

If Jemma let it, she could still cry while thinking about Walter. Especially with how he suffered toward the end. It had been heartbreaking.

She was sure Jen's death had been difficult for a teenager, too. From what Ry told Judge, Jen had died from lung cancer. She was a heavy smoker her whole adult life and that habit got her in the end. It also left a barely-baked boy without a mother.

Not that Jen was a perfect one. But Ry was a good, clean-cut kid, so his mother had to do something right.

"I miss Walt. He was like a father to me. I wish he could've gotten to know you. He'd be super proud of you heading to college and I know Lottie is, too. And it's also important to your dad. Even though you didn't know he was alive all these years, he knew you were and loved you the second you were born. He wanted nothing more than to be your father."

*And your fucking bitch of a mother robbed him of that chance.*

The same could've happened to Cage. If Dyna's maternal family had given the baby away to someone in their community, Cage would've never known he had a daughter and Dyna would've never known her father.

But at least in that case, Cage wouldn't be pining away for a child he knew nothing about. Not like Judge, who knew, and everything he did to try to be in his son's life failed.

Cage would've been blissfully unaware.

Ry still looked absolutely miserable holding Dyna, so Jemma took pity on him and took her back. The baby immediately began to root at her boob and get frustrated.

It was time to go.

Jemma settled Dyna back in the stroller and before she wheeled the baby back to the trailer, she paused and reached up to cup her nephew's cheek, because even at eighteen he was much taller than her. If he wasn't already as tall as Judge, he would be soon.

"Thank you for giving your father a chance, Ry. You don't know how much that means to him. And me. I'm here for you if you ever need anything. Please, please, please don't hesitate to come to me, or even Deacon. You're blood. Don't forget that."

Ry pinned his lips together and nodded.

"And don't worry, I won't snitch to Judge that you visited Saylor today. Just promise me you won't do anything stupid."

A look of relief crossed his face and a small smile curled his lips. "I promise."

Jemma dropped her hand from his face and grabbed the stroller handles.

"I'm going to hold you to that. Now, get the door for me, please."

As soon as he did, Jemma took a now wailing Dyna back to the trailer to get her belly full.

# Chapter Eleven

CAGE PARKED his sled in the shed, pulled what he brought home from his saddlebag and headed out of the open garage door toward his trailer.

*Their* trailer.

He needed to start looking for something more permanent. He just wished he had more money to do so. They'd only been in the trailer for two weeks and Dutch wasn't bugging him about finding something else. At least, not yet. But Cage knew it would be coming.

He was still borrowing the Honda, the shop's loaner, too.

Dutch may not be bitching about the trailer rent, but he'd been bitching about the Honda. Everyone at the shop used it during the day to run for lunch or parts, or whatever, but Dutch didn't have a loaner to offer his long-time customers when Cage needed it.

Since Cage didn't have the money to buy a car, he and Rook had scoured the yard to find something in half-decent shape they could fix up after hours.

Rook suggested he sell the Impala. Doing so would make Cage flush for a while. But his brother also said he should leave that option as a last resort, since he knew Cage would never be able to recover close to the amount he'd invested in just parts alone.

But, with his ribs not bothering him as much, he was back to riding his sled and only needed the Honda when he had to take Dyna somewhere. With Jemma around, she hauled his daughter in the Volvo to places like the pediatrician while Cage worked.

However, he knew, like the trailer, Jemma was only temporary.

He needed to get his shit together and at least make a plan, not only for a permanent home but for when Jemma left. She'd been sending out resumes and having phone, as well as virtual, interviews. He couldn't imagine her being unemployed long.

That scared the shit out of him.

Knowing Dyna was in her capable hands during the day helped him concentrate at work. But he didn't want to take advantage of Jemma by getting a second job, even if it was bartending at Pete's part-time. He couldn't stick her with Dyna for longer hours when she wasn't even earning any scratch to do it as it was.

He was just relieved she took the day shift and most times she'd help him with the nightshift. Even though he never asked. If she helped him during the evening or night, it was because she wanted to or maybe because she felt sorry for him being so in over his head.

Too many times he'd sit on the couch with a crying Dyna, not knowing what she needed, and was close to crying along with her. When he'd almost be at his breaking point, Jemma would swoop in and save his sanity.

She seemed to have the golden touch with his daughter.

Since the evening wasn't too humid, she sat outside the trailer with Dyna on a blanket in front of her. His daughter was getting stronger every day. He wasn't sure if he'd be excited or scared once she was mobile. At least now, she couldn't get into trouble on her own.

Jemma looked relaxed in one of the plastic Adirondack chairs Deacon and Judge had brought over. They had also dropped off an old grill and a couple small plastic tables and helped Jemma set up a little outdoor area to hang out at. While the pavilion wasn't far, it was nice to be close to the trailer in case of a necessary feeding or diaper change.

All the outdoor area needed now was a pop-up tent or an awning to protect them from the rain and sun when they sat outside. He spent time out there to smoke, have a beer or toke on a joint when his nerves were shot.

How anyone survived raising a kid and kept all their hair, he had no fucking clue. But a few hits on a bowl, or joint, and a beer helped. He just kept it to a minimum while he was on Dyna-duty, and did his best to not partake at all if Jemma wasn't around.

So, most of the time he and the rest of the guys at the shop, including Dutch, shared a bowl or bong out back at lunchtime. Doing so grounded him and kept him from hopping in his Impala, spinning the tires out of the garage lot and never coming back. Because every time he thought he was getting a handle on taking care of his baby, life punched him in the nuts and fucking cackled like an evil witch.

As soon as he got home, Jemma usually bailed on them, so she was gone a lot.

Most nights she'd make a plate for him before she left, or leave a meal in the borrowed crockpot, then head some-where else for dinner. Sometimes Lottie's, other times she'd walk over to Judge and Cassie's. She had gone to Mansfield to have dinner with Deacon and Reese twice already.

She and Reilly even went to Dino's Diner the other night. They were close in age and, at the shop the next day, Reilly told him she'd had a blast hanging out with Judge's sister. She wore a huge smile as she told Cage how Jemma was a lot of fun. She confessed they hit Crazy Pete's afterward to sing Karaoke, shoot some pool and drink some beer. Afterward, Jemma took Reilly home to The Grove Inn since she didn't have her own set of wheels yet.

Cage had no idea why Jemma didn't stick around to eat with him, but after spending all day taking care of a baby who wasn't hers, he couldn't blame her for taking a break.

Did he like it? No.

Could he bitch about it? Fuck no.

He wasn't going to say or do anything that would push Jemma away. He needed her too badly.

*For fuck's sake*, more like desperately.

So, he was smart and kept his fucking trap shut.

As he approached, she said, "You're late. Your shift started a while ago. I'm now on OT."

"Good thing I'm not payin' you, then." Sure, he was late but he had a good reason.

"Oh yeah, good thing." Her words dripped with sarcasm. Her gaze dropped to what he carried. "What's that?"

He grabbed the eyehook he'd welded to the top and let the rest of the mobile fall free.

Jemma's gasp and her slapping a hand over her mouth made him ask, "What?"

Did he fuck up?

"A mobile," she whispered, getting to her feet. She took the last couple steps to bring her close and her eyes were suspiciously shiny.

*What the fuck?*

"I've never seen one like that," she breathed.

Of course not, it was custom made. "Reilly said Dyna needs a mobile for above the crib to keep her from bein' dumb like me." She had been fucking with him, but knew he'd do anything to help Dyna's development. "She's been lookin' online at all kinda baby shit and tryin' to spend scratch I don't fuckin' have. Figured I'd stay a little late today and make one. Rev helped 'cause he's also good with weldin' and cuttin' metal."

His blood began to rush as Jemma reached out and touched the aluminum mobile. He'd used the light, shiny metal to make the pendants that would hang above the crib and would catch Dyna's eye and help her focus. He'd cut out decorative snowflakes, clouds, stars, and crescent moons.

Jemma spun it and the pieces clinked together lightly making a tinkling noise.

It wasn't one of those battery-operated ones Reilly wanted him to get where the dangly things were made of cloth and it spun on its own, but it would have to do for now. Something was better than nothing. And maybe one day his daughter could use it for her daughter.

He struggled to swallow at that thought.

Sarah was someone's daughter, too. What if the same thing happened to Dyna? She innocently flirted with a man, then got caught up in the moment, like he and Sarah had done, and she came home knocked up?

His nostrils flared and his jaws clenched.

He'd fucking kill the bastard.

He squeezed his eyes shut. The bastard was him.

"Hey," Jemma whispered, her fingers sliding over his forearm, the one not holding the mobile.

He opened his eyes, took a deep breath and shook it off.

He could see some conflict in her expression and eyes, so he drew a blank mask over his own face.

After studying him for a few seconds, she asked, "How did you get so much detail?"

Thank fuck she hadn't asked what he'd been thinking. She seemed to be getting pretty good at reading his moods, just like she was good with figuring out what bothered Dyna. She had a fucking gift.

He used her question to lighten the mood. "Good with my hands."

She arched a dark eyebrow. "You're a mechanic. I should hope so."

"Wasn't what I meant."

"I know. But I'm choosing to ignore your inuendo."

"You're not ignorin' it if you're commentin' on it."

"Let's pretend I didn't."

His grin drew one from her, too.

"Will you also build her a crib?"

He had thought about it but he wasn't good with wood—of the tree type—and he was pretty damn sure a crib welded from scrap metal wouldn't be safe. The yard behind the garage was full of metal, so that was all he had to work with. He sand-blasted off any paint on the stainless steel and cleaned it thoroughly before he made the mobile. He also made sure to smooth any sharp edges by sand-blasting the pieces after he cut them with the jigsaw. To test it, he drew every edge across his own skin to make sure it wouldn't cut him.

He would also make sure to hang it high enough so Dyna couldn't reach it and before she could, he'd take it down.

"No, but I'm gonna build her a changin' table out of an old dresser from The Grove Inn. Ozzy brought it over to the shop, stripped and repainted it already. I'll work on finishin' it tomorrow after work. So..."

"So, you'll be late again."

"Yeah."

"I guess it's better you're late because you're making the shit your baby girl needs instead of going out and drinking and whoring it up, trying to avoid coming home."

She still stood close and smelled so goddamn good. He dropped his head and stared down into her face. "Ain't avoidin' shit."

"I know you aren't. I..."

He waited, but after a few heartbeats, she still hadn't finished. "You what?"

"It's really not for me to say, but... I'm proud of you."

*Fuck.*

He hadn't expected that. Maybe he was doing something right. But he probably couldn't have done as well without her.

"Jem," he said softly, not sure what to say. But, *fuck it*, he needed to say something. He didn't feel he could express his appreciation for her and what she was sacrificing for him well enough with only words.

She turned away, breaking their locked gaze, and quickly changed the subject. "She was a little fussy today, but seems to be better now, which is good news for you." She gathered her cell phone and the tablet she read on, as well as her oversized bag or purse, or whatever the fuck it was.

She was leaving.

*Fuck.*

He didn't want her to leave. Not because of Dyna, but because of him.

She secured her bag over her shoulder, tucked her cell phone and tablet in the bag and went to move past him toward her Volvo.

He reached out and snagged her wrist, stopping her. With a gentle tug, he pulled her back to him. "Don't go."

His fucking pulse was trying to thump right out of his neck.

She looked up at him, quickly narrowing her wide green eyes. "I'm starving. I made you a plate."

He never asked her to do that, she got into that habit on her own, but he was tired of eating alone. He was tired of her rushing out of the trailer as soon as he got home. "There enough for both of us?"

She hesitated. Her chest rose and fell slowly. She was thinking too hard for an easy answer.

He answered for her. "Don't wanna spend time with me."

"It's not that I don't want to spend time with you..." She bit her bottom lip and not in a sexy way but one that showed her inner struggle.

"Then why the fuck do you bolt every day as soon as I get home? You didn't at first, and for the past week and a half, you have. What the fuck changed?"

He was trying to tamp down his anger and frustration, but he was at the point he couldn't hide it anymore.

Her eyes slid from him to her Volvo just beyond where they stood and back to him. She was looking at her escape. She didn't want to answer.

"Jem..."

"Chris... You..."

"I what? Piss you off? You hate me 'cause of what I did to Sarah? What? You hate that Dyna's stuck with me and I didn't give her up like some people thought I should? That she'd be better off with someone else?"

"I don't hate you."

"Then you hate Dyna's stuck with a father who's a biker, like me. You think her future's fucked. 'Cause bein' a girl raised in a club fuckin' sucked for you."

"I don't know what her future holds, but that's not it."

"Then what the fuck is it?"

"She's done with her tummy time."

*Goddamn it.* "Gonna grab her in a sec. Once you answer me. You just think I'm a motherfuckin' asshole then, that it?"

Jemma shook her head. "You haven't been an asshole once. Everyone says you are. Jokes about what a dick you can be. Truthfully, I haven't seen it."

"Maybe you don't see it 'cause you're used to bein'

around assholes. It ain't like your brother ain't one. And your father sure was the ultimate asshole."

"Judge isn't an asshole." She sighed. "Neither are you. Just because you don't fart rainbows and glitter all the time doesn't make you an asshole. It makes you human."

"So, what is it?" he asked in a rough whisper.

She hadn't tried to pull free of his grip, so he slowly brushed the calloused pad of his thumb back and forth over the delicate skin of her inner wrist.

A shiver shot through her, once again causing visible goosebumps along the skin he could see. Which was a lot. She wore a dark pink V-neck, short-sleeved top that framed her generous cleavage and was also too thin to hide the way her nipples had responded to his touch. He was tempted to slide his tongue along her neck and taste her there.

Fuck the shiver, he wanted to make her shudder.

He also wanted to hear his name on her lips for something other than discussing his daughter. The thought of her moaning his name while tasting her soft skin shot blood south and woke up his dick.

This wasn't the first time he'd gotten a chubby around her. Most of the time he could hide it from her. This time he didn't bother. If he went full-blown hard, he wanted her to see how touching her affected him. He wanted her to know she wasn't the only one feeling whatever it was between them.

He fought the urge to press the hand he held to his dick, but figured she might take offense to that contact and neuter him right on the spot. He liked his dick, as well as his balls, and would like to keep them attached to his body.

"Jem, why d'you keep runnin' away?" At first he thought she simply needed a well-earned break, but now it was smacking him upside the head it was something else.

Something deeper.

"I'm not running away... I'm just..."

"Just?"

She blew out a breath and the warm air swept over his throat, making his dick twitch and grow even harder. He would soon have full wood.

"I'm just trying to be smart."

"Smart about what?" He was going to get a goddamn straight answer from her before he'd let her escape this time.

He needed to know why the fuck he was sitting alone eating a fucking dinner she made but didn't enjoy. Wanting to spend time with anyone and everyone other than him seemed to be the answer, but he needed to hear it from her.

"You tempt me."

He tempted her? "What d'you mean?"

Was it the same way she tempted him? Was it the same way that caused him to wait until Dyna was sound asleep so he could whack the fuck off every night? And sometimes in the morning, too? All because he wanted to head to the other side of the trailer, kick open her door and fuck her brains out.

Since he couldn't, he did the next best thing. He'd close his eyes and imagine his fist was her tight pussy, or her hot mouth, until he shot his hot, what seemed like endless, load all over his own stomach. She washed some of his laundry a couple of days ago, did she wonder why a couple of his dirty T-shirts were stiff?

"You know what I mean. I need to minimize my time around you as much as possible."

"Why do I tempt you?"

She frowned and drew her free hand across her forehead, like she was wiping away invisible sweat. "I don't know, but I hate that you do."

*Christ.* She *hated* that she wanted him. "Why d'you hate it?"

"Because I didn't come here for dick, Cage." She was on the verge of shouting.

"Don't mean you can't get some dick."

"We need to live together right now for Dyna's sake. Like I said, it's not smart."

"We all got needs." He needed to stop jerking off and experience the real thing. Because nothing beat a warm, wet, tight pussy. His own rough, calloused fingers weren't even close.

He considered getting a Fleshlight or latex pocket pussy, like Judge and probably some of his other brothers had, but right now he couldn't afford one. He wasn't paying for a goddamn fake pussy to blow his load into when his daughter needed shit.

His pleasure would have to wait.

Unless there was a warm, soft and wet woman willing to help him out with his dilemma...

"I can get my needs filled elsewhere. Not with someone I need to see every fucking day. Not with the father of the baby girl I'm helping with. It's just a sticky situation because I'm not staying and you have your hands full. And the idea of just fucking to fuck seems way too problematic."

Why was there anything wrong with just fucking to fuck? Humans have done it for thousands of years. Cavemen probably fucked just to fuck. She probably didn't want to hear that, though. "Don't have to be problematic."

"Really? Tell that to yourself. Look what a couple quick fucks in a shed did to your life. Sex can get complicated, even when it's not supposed to be. And, anyway, I don't do casual."

She didn't *do casual*. "Just said you could get your needs filled elsewhere. That means you'd be doin' some strange. So, which is it? You don't do randoms, or you do? You're confusin' the fuck outta me."

If she only did relationships, why wasn't she in one now? Or why hadn't any of her past relationships been successful enough that she was married, or at least still with the guy?

"You're not the only one confused. To me, casual and randoms are two different things. One is someone you casually have sex with whenever you're in the mood. It's the same person but no commitment. Randoms are just that. One-night-stands. It's a hi, fuck, bye situation. Deacon's an expert at those. Or was, until Reese."

"So, wait. You're sayin' you won't do casual but you'll do a random fuck?" His fingers tightened on her wrist. His blood was beginning to simmer and not in a good way.

"I normally don't do either. But..." She shook her head. "I'm not getting into this with you. Just know this, I have no desire to get mixed up with a biker, even if I *was* into casual sex."

"Why?"

"Because I don't ever want to be with a man like my father."

"I ain't your father."

"So you say."

"I know the shit your father did. I know what he did to you, Jem. I'd never do that to Dyna."

"Again, so you say. You can't say that for sure."

He set his jaw. "I'd never put my daughter in fuckin' danger." The simmer was turning into a boil.

"You don't know what you'd do if you had a shitload of guns pointed in your direction and a convenient shield nearby who you knew the cops wouldn't fire at."

"Fuck, Jem. You're pissin' me the fuck off."

"Good. Then let me go," her eyes flicked down for a second to where he held her, "so I can go get dinner."

"If you're so fuckin' hungry, you got dinner here. You just don't wanna eat it with me because I fuckin' *tempt* you."

"Do you really want to risk fucking this up?"

He knew what she meant. If he fucked her and things went sideways, she'd be out the door in a fucking flash, leaving him alone with Dyna and no help.

No, he couldn't fucking risk that.

He also didn't want to risk Judge's wrath if he ever found out Cage had boned his sister. The big guy made it clear not to fuck with her, and Cage took that warning seriously.

He wasn't really fond of attending blanket parties, unless he was the one throwing the fucking party. His ribs were still healing from the last one and he'd only just begun to breathe more freely through his broken nose.

More importantly, remaining upright and above ground was necessary to raise his daughter.

That same daughter took that opportunity to start crying.

His head twisted toward Dyna automatically and he released Jemma's wrist. Unfortunately, that connection had been the only thing keeping her from leaving. Of course, she immediately took advantage of her freedom.

She mumbled, "I gotta go," as he moved to get his daughter.

As much as he wanted Jemma, Dyna came first.

He reached down for the baby and noticed her head turned toward him as he said her name. Whether that was coincidence or not, he had no fucking clue, but he hoped it was because she knew he was her dad.

He scooped her up, along with the pacifier which was lying on the blanket, and cuddled her to his chest.

His anger quickly dissipated when his heart just about fucking melted as he read today's onesie: *Daddy's New Riding Buddy*, with a child-like stick drawing of a motorcycle.

*Jesus fucking Christ.*

He'd be disappointed when she outgrew all the cute onesies.

He offered her the binky hoping it would curtail her crying so he could continue the conversation with Jemma. She took it and stared up at him with her gray-blue eyes.

*Jesus fuck.*

This was his blood. He created her.

How could Ox use his fucking daughter as a shield? The thought of putting Dyna in danger, especially for selfish reasons, just about cut him off at the knees.

Once Dyna was sucking strongly and had quieted down, he turned to see, and hear, the Volvo's door slam shut.

"Jem!"

Their conversation wasn't finished. Not even close.

But not even a minute later, all Cage saw was her taillights as she drove faster than she should down the rough lane past the farmhouse.

"Fuck."

With one arm holding Dyna against him, he curled the fingers of his other hand around his hip and dropped his head. With his eyes closed, he took a couple deep inhales. When he opened his eyes, he stared down at his future.

It wasn't a woman.

It was his daughter.

Jemma was right. Fucking her wouldn't be smart.

It still didn't mean he didn't want to.

## Chapter Twelve

The Volvo's headlight beams sliced across the dark figure sprawled in one of the Adirondack chairs.

*Fuck.*

Jemma had hoped she'd return after he'd already gone to bed. Or at least be passed out on the couch in front of the TV. Her goal had been to come home late enough to avoid continuing their earlier conversation.

She feared, if he pushed hard and long enough, she might cave.

To what she wanted. To what he wanted.

Which was the same thing. The exchanging of orgasms and body fluids in a horizontal, vertical or even diagonal fashion.

But when she thought about it with a clear head, which was what she did every time she wasn't around Cage, she confirmed it was stupid.

So, so fucking stupid.

She could easily walk away and rid herself of the temptation. Nothing held her in Manning Grove. She was only there to help him.

So, really, if he wanted to screw that up, that would be on him, right?

Or would she feel guilty for abandoning him?

No, not him.

She'd feel guilty abandoning her. Dyna. She was here for the baby, not Cage. Dyna was the most important thing for both of them right now. Sex was not.

Simply put, she could find anyone for sex.

*Hell*, after drinking with two Fury members all night, she could probably return to Crazy Pete's and ask Dodge to take her upstairs and, as long as she promised Judge wouldn't find out, he'd most likely drag her up those steps with a sexy grin and a hard-on.

Or she could head over to The Grove Inn and pound on Ozzy's door and, as long as he was alone, he'd probably invite her into his apartment and his bed to pound her into his mattress and give her brush-burn with his beard in several key areas.

Or, *shit*, she could walk the few hundred feet or so to the bunkhouse and find a willing volunteer there, too. A couple shots of whiskey and a condom later, she could be naked and drumming up a decent orgasm or two.

Guaranteed, none of those guys would say shit about it to anyone because of Judge and Deacon. Her secret would be safe.

But she didn't want that.

She didn't want to crawl into and then back out of some biker's bed. She really didn't want to do that in *any* man's bed.

In her first five years of life, she had seen way too much casual sex all around her. It meant nothing to any of the participants except for power or a quick release. It wasn't until many years later she realized none of what she saw had any meaning. None of it meant anything to the people involved.

The Originals who forced women didn't do it for the sex, especially since they had their choice of volunteers who would fuck them without being forced.

No, they did it because they could.

Because they liked the fight.

Or the fear.

Or the sense of power it gave them.

Or because they thought they were teaching a female a "lesson" on which gender was stronger.

Or smarter.

Or whatever their fucked up reasoning was.

But to most of them, the sex meant nothing. It was a quick bang and a release of their load until they picked their next target.

For the women... Well, Jemma didn't want to judge. They had their reasons and so did the men. If a woman took multiple dicks voluntarily, that was on her. If she was forced to take them, that was on the men.

Jemma never remembered any of the Originals showing any mercy to a woman who was crying or begging to be released. Or not conscious, whether by the excessive use of drugs or alcohol, or even being beaten.

Not once.

They figured if a female showed up at the warehouse, they only showed up for one thing. To be used and abused.

That's what they got.

The only women who received some level of respect were the ol' ladies. But all the ol' ladies had to get their foot in the door one way or another.

Which made her think of Angel and her false hope of becoming an ol' lady.

Jemma always wondered how many bikers Trixie had to do, what abuse she had to put up with, until she finally got to wear her "Property of Ox" cut. Once she wore that, she was protected. But Jemma was sure it took a hell of a lot to earn it.

Once a woman was claimed by a brother, it was her choice who she did and when. *If* her ol' man allowed it.

They usually didn't. And if they got caught cheating, there was hell to pay.

Unlike all the cheating their ol' men did. That was a given. That was expected. They could stick their dick into any woman they wanted and their ol' ladies couldn't say shit. If they did, it usually went badly for them. So, they accepted it. For the most part.

Jemma shoved her XC40 into Park, hit the ignition button to shut off the engine and sat in the dark interior, her eyes on the still figure sitting outside the temporary mobile home.

He had waited up for her.

He'd never done that before. Even when she came back at an earlier hour.

He also never waited outside. He'd be crashed on the couch or actually passed out in bed, if Dyna was asleep.

But he sat there looking way too relaxed in one of those chairs. When she looked closer, she could see the glow of one of the hand-rolled cigarettes he smoked as he lifted it to his lips. She saw the lit end flare brightly as he took a deep inhale.

Those movements were the only ones he made. He reminded her of a lion lying in wait to pounce.

She considered her options. Get out and hope he didn't stop her from heading directly to bed? Or drive away and try again even later?

Neither was going to happen. She wasn't a coward, but she was also too tired to continue discussing something she didn't want to admit to.

Which was just how much he got her blood pumping and her pussy throbbing.

If he kept trying to convince her they could do casual without any fallout, she might break and agree. But fallout always occurred with casual. One reason why she didn't do it.

Not that she'd had any luck with anything more serious, either.

Her groan filled the interior of the car.

She'd been hanging onto the excuse she "didn't do casual" by her fingernails, hoping it would help her resist him. But, in truth, no man had stuck in her life. Not because she wanted them to, but because she didn't.

She wasn't in a rush to settle down, but she also liked steady. She *needed* steady in her life. She wasn't going to get that by letting men in and out of her life or bed, like a revolving door.

However, her answer was not sprawled in that fucking plastic chair.

No, what was sprawled in that chair was her problem.

A big problem she would have a difficult time ignoring.

She sighed, then mumbled a "fuck." She could start her car and go. And never come back.

The problem in that trailer wasn't hers. The problem in that chair shouldn't be hers, either. If she got out of her Volvo, she was making them hers.

She could do her best to stick to her guns and leave when she got the right job offer. She knew it wouldn't be too long before the right one came along.

Sticking around until then was what she promised Judge. It was what Cage expected.

She needed to stop being a coward for Dyna's sake.

"Motherfucker," she whispered as she shoved open her driver's door and grabbed her big slouchy purse. She slammed the door shut, threw her key fob and phone inside her bag and slowly made her way closer to the trailer entrance. Like a dead man walking. Her heart thumped in rhythm with each step she took.

When she got closer, she realized he was wearing a baseball cap pulled low. Even if he wasn't, she wouldn't be able to read his eyes or expression since the night was so damn dark. The promise of rain was now in the air, so the moon was in hiding.

Once her eyes adjusted to the inky-darkness, she saw he'd shed his cut, his belt and his boots, and sat in only jeans and a dark, most likely black, sleeveless undershirt, what was commonly called a wife-beater.

Weird how a tank would make his shoulders seem broader than when he wore his cut or even when he went shirtless. Which was a lot.

Another reason she needed to keep her distance as much as possible. It was like he had a sixth sense that, when she was close to him, she could barely resist touching his skin. Which meant he rarely wore a shirt while home like he was purposely trying to break her will.

If skin to skin contact wasn't so good for Dyna, she'd ask him to put one on. But he loved to recline on his bed or the couch with the baby on his bare chest. It helped father and daughter bond and was a medically-proven good practice for infants.

That meant she kept her mouth shut and tried to remain strong.

Too many times she caught herself reaching out to brush her fingers over his chest, or the breadth of his back, when he was near. She'd pull back just in time before contact was made and she'd move away to give herself space and keep her sanity.

The only time she allowed herself to touch him was during the unavoidable contact when handing him the baby or taking her from him, or when checking his healing ribs.

He sat in the seat next to the wood steps. As she went to

take the first one, his hand came out in a blur and snagged her forearm. His warm long fingers circled her arm and slid slowly down to her wrist.

She didn't pull away because he gripped her loosely. He wasn't forcing her to do anything, but his hold was more of an ask. A "don't go inside yet" without words.

She stared at the door for a couple heartbeats, then cleared the thick in her throat to ask, "She asleep?"

Without a word, he lifted the used baby monitor from his lap. The one Jemma was lucky enough to score at the consignment shop in town. While there, she'd left her name and number in case a convertible crib came in.

He gently tugged her arm, and she went with it, moving from the steps and around him. When she sighed, he released her and she settled into the plastic chair next to him.

She stared up into the sky. She couldn't see any stars because of the cloud cover. The night had become humid and overly warm.

Not only could she smell rain in the air, she could smell him. The scent of the soap he used combined with his shampoo, a faint mix of tobacco and pot, along with exhaust, oil and grease.

The only thing that was missing tonight was the scent of warm leather. It was too hot to wear his cut and he was nowhere where he needed to represent his brotherhood.

She took his cue of looking relaxed and kicked off her sandals so she could curl her legs underneath her.

He lifted the hand-rolled to his lips again. With these guys all smoking hand-rolleds, it was hard to know if it was tobacco or weed unless you asked or inhaled.

She preferred not to inhale any pot since she was job hunting and could be drug tested. Marijuana wasn't legal for recreational use in most states yet and she had no idea where she'd land a job. Plus, legal or not, most employers frowned on a hot piss test for medical professional applicants.

On the flipside, pot was recommended for cancer patients, and others, to help relieve their pain and suffering.

"Is that pot?"

He shook his head. "Tobacco. From the Amish. Saves us a lot of fuckin' scratch. Got a joint in my wallet, though, if you want a hit."

Jemma shook her head. "I don't want it to screw up my employment chances."

He blew the stream of smoke up and away from her.

She hated cigarettes but she had no right to bitch about his smoking. He was good about not smoking around Dyna, so she couldn't use her as an excuse.

"Did you know Ry's mom died of lung cancer? She was a heavy smoker."

"Cancer sucks," was his only response as he took another drag. "Walt have lung cancer, too?"

"No. He had smoked when he was in his twenties but quit and never started again. It's probably one reason Deacon and Judge never picked up the habit."

"They smoke weed."

She sighed. "Yeah, well. Quality pot isn't going to kill you like the poisoned shit from the big tobacco companies."

"The shit from the Amish is pure. No additives."

"I know, but it's still not good for you."

"So, you're sayin' I should only get stoned instead of smokin' tobacco."

"I'm not saying that. Do what you want. Just keep Dyna away from it all."

He got quiet, finished his cigarette and then flicked it out into the dark after pinching out the end.

He reached down, picked up a bottle she hadn't noticed and tipped it to his lips.

"She give you any trouble tonight?"

She was staring straight ahead but out of the corner of her eye could see him turn his head to look at her.

"Only one female gave me trouble tonight," he said way too softly.

"Yeah, did you have a visitor?"

"Ain't you fuckin' funny," he grumbled. "She was good. Went down easy. Fed her again just a while ago."

"You're doing good, Chris," she said quietly. It was true and he should know.

"Yeah," he said on a sigh. "Who'da thunk a dumb fuck like me could be a good dad?" When she didn't respond, he asked, "Where'd ya go?"

Here came the conversation she wanted to avoid. "Pete's."

He didn't say anything for a few moments, but she could feel his searching gaze.

"Don't ask."

"Jem..."

"Not your business, Chris."

"Could be."

*For fuck's sake*, now she was really regretting not hooking up with Ozzy or Dodge, or anyone at the bar. It would have delayed her coming back here and getting into this conversation again. "It's not on the table. And I'm done talking about it."

"Could be on the table. The bed, the floor, wherever. I ain't your father, Jem." He said the last part so softly, her heart skipped a beat.

It was true, he was proving that he was nothing like her father. He actually cared about his daughter and wanted to do right by her.

However, it wasn't enough. "Doesn't matter."

"Yeah, the fuck it does. What the fuck does it matter if the random you choose is a fuckin' biker? It's a fuck, not a forever."

Why the hell did he have to keep pushing this?

"It matters when I wake up on the other side of the same trailer. As I see him every morning so I can feed his daughter and make him breakfast."

"Don't need to make me fuckin' breakfast. Never asked you for that."

*No, but I want to.*

*Your life's going to be hard enough being a single parent. So, for the time I'm here, I want to do that for you. Make you breakfast before you head to work. Have a meal ready for when you return. It isn't much, but it's something.*

She didn't admit to any of that, instead she said, "No, you only need to snap your fingers and Angel will do it for you."

"Angel?"

She squeezed her eyes shut for a second. *Holy shit,* was that a flicker of jealousy? "Never mind."

Angel could sleep with any of the guys and not have a problem with "casual." She'd had Cage without strings. But the sweet butt also didn't have to live in close quarters with him.

At least Ozzy and Dodge lived elsewhere.

*Christ!* Why was she even thinking of those two? The one who got her heart thumping and her pussy pulsing was sitting right next to her.

"I've fucked other women since Sarah, Jem."

"Well, yeah. I didn't think you were a choir boy, but that was before you knew you had a daughter."

"Hold up. I shouldn't wanna fuck now that I have a kid? I'm supposed to just lose my fuckin' desire for women 'cause I'm now a dad? How do couples make more kids if that's true?"

She twisted her head to stare at him. "You want more kids?"

"Can't afford more. Can't afford this one."

"If you could…"

"Already strugglin' with this one. She's enough."

"Keep that in mind the next time you find a willing part-ner." It just wasn't her. It was bad enough in the couple of weeks since she'd been back to Manning Grove, she was losing her heart to his daughter.

She didn't need to lose it to the baby's father, too.

Because she wasn't staying. She never wanted to stay in Manning Grove. She'd escaped as soon as she was able. She even kept her visits home short.

There were too many bad memories. Ones she'll never be able to scrub from her mind. She wished she could.

She really didn't want to rip herself open and expose her fears but when he reached over and brushed his fingers over hers and, *fuck*, even though she liked it and it sent warmth through her like drinking a shot of whiskey, she still pulled her hand away and curled her fingers tightly into her palm.

Maybe if he had a better understanding, he'd back off.

"I drove past the house on my way home tonight."

He remained quiet but his hand remained on the arm of her chair. As if he was keeping it close in case she needed it.

She waited for him to ask what house. When he didn't, she realized he knew which one. What happened was common knowledge among the current Fury members, especially the ones who grew up in the club, like Cage had.

"When I do, it all rushes back."

His voice was deep, but quiet, when he said, "Then don't do it."

*Don't do it.* She wished it was that easy.

"I can't. I'm not sure why, but I can't. I know I shouldn't. I pull up anyway, sit out front and relive everything I heard and saw in that house from the moment I could remember. Then it brings the nightmares back."

At least a half dozen officers pointing guns in her direction wasn't even the worst one. She tried to swallow but her throat had tightened.

"Every time I come home, I have nightmares of the father who didn't deserve me. And nightmares about the father who did."

"Walt."

"Yes, it's one reason I don't come home often or, when I do, don't stay long. This has been the longest I've been home since I moved away."

"Doin' it for me."

"For Dyna," she reminded him. "Let me explain why I agreed to come here for Dyna and to help you. You chose to keep her instead of giving her up. Was that selfish? Maybe. Was it selfless? Possibly. I don't know. Time will tell. But I came because Judge asked me to help you since you had no clue what you were doing but you wanted to try. And I didn't want a child to suffer. I hope my time here makes a difference, even if only a little, for you *and* Dyna."

"Jem..."

She shook her head. She needed to get this out and over. "At five, I thought my father loved me. His actions proved otherwise. Did it hurt? Yes. Will I ever forget it? No."

She knew his story, too. It was similar. His mother up and leaving both of her sons because she'd had enough with the club. She didn't take her boys with her. She never came back. She never called or visited. She scraped her family clean.

A mother who loved her children didn't do that. Dutch, at least, fought to keep his sons. He might not have been the perfect father, but he loved them. He cared for them the best way he could.

The same way his own son was doing with his grand-daughter.

The best he could.

Maybe it wouldn't be perfect, but as long as Dyna felt loved and cared for... then she'd be okay.

She didn't need to mention any of this to the man who had experienced his mother abandoning him. He'd lived it.

He felt the pain and betrayal firsthand.

Just like Jemma had when she couldn't ignore the truth.

The truth being, she'd been held in her father's arms, not because he loved her and wanted a hug, but because she was a tool for him to ensure his own safety.

Ox was a selfish bastard.

So was Bebe, Cage and Rook's mother.

Her story wasn't over yet. "Walter was more of a father to me than Ox ever was. Then I helplessly watched the father who loved me and never disappointed me suffer away to nothing. I stayed by his side until he took his last rattled breath. I held his hand until it went cold. I closed the lids on his sightless eyes. I kissed his hollowed, paled cheek. I whispered goodbye to someone who could no longer hear me.

"I lost two fathers in ways a daughter should never lose them. But I relive how Walt died. How he suffered at the end. How I felt helpless and could do nothing but watch him wither to a shell of the man I loved deeply and finally die. All I could do was comfort him in the end. That's all any of us could do. Be with him, let him know we loved him. Ensure he knew our lives would never be the same when he was gone."

She closed her eyes and waited for the sharp sting to pass.

"It's why you became a nurse," came softly from beside her.

"It's why I became a hospice nurse. If it wasn't for Walt's, he would've suffered even worse. His hospice nurse became my heroine. I was amazed at how she could remain so strong while witnessing so much death and sorrow. Do you know Lottie is still friends with her?"

Of course he didn't. How would he know?

She didn't wait for his answer. "I would sit for hours next to Maggie and talk to her about her job. She had so many stories. Happy. Sad. She touched so many lives. She witnessed so many deaths. Like I said, she was so strong, and I wanted to be just like her."

"You are, Jem."

"I guess." Not strong enough, apparently, to resist Cage.

"Was that story for you or me?"

It was supposed to be for him, but, honestly, she wasn't sure now. Sitting out in front of Ox and Trixie's house had caused a huge knot in her stomach, then heading back to the trailer had turned that knot into a huge ball of anxiety.

She didn't want complications. She wanted to help, find a job and head out without regret.

"Maybe I hoped letting it out would cleanse my soul."

A fat drop of rain plopped on her arm. Then another. Neither of them moved.

She closed her eyes and lifted her face to the sky. The drops felt like warm tears on her cheeks.

She heard him rise and, when she opened her eyes, she saw him standing in front of her, offering his hand.

She shook her head. "The rain feels good. I'm going to sit outside for a little bit and let it wash away the memories." He turned to go in. "Can you take my bag and sandals inside? I don't want my stuff getting wet."

Without a word, he grabbed her things and she waited until she heard the door shut before turning her face up again and letting the summer shower wash her "clean."

It went from slow, fat drops to a steadier rainfall.

She had just stuck out her tongue to catch some drops, like she had with snowflakes as a child, when the door opened again.

He was going to tell her to come inside.

But he didn't.

He came back out, only wearing his boxer briefs and surprised her by sitting back in his chair. "Could use a little bita soul cleansin', too."

What he said wasn't even remotely sexual, but the gentle rumble of his voice made her toes curl and her lips part.

The rain was beginning to soak her shorts and top, but it wasn't cold, and it felt soothing on her skin. Almost like a hug from Mother Nature.

Since it was dark and no one would see except Cage, and since he was already in his briefs, she decided to join him. She stood up and pulled her shirt over her head dropping it with a wet plop onto the chair she'd abandoned. She peeled her shorts down her damp legs and tossed them on top.

Then, in just her panties and bra, she took a few steps away from the chairs and stretched out her arms with her palms up, dropped her head back, closed her eyes and stuck out her tongue again.

The rain clung to her eyelashes, weighed down her hair, washed down her body and collected in her palms. She breathed slowly in and out of her nose and cleared her mind.

It felt freeing.

Wonderful.

Cleansing.

Healing.

# Chapter Thirteen

His HEAT and presence touched her even before he did. At first she thought it was his lips lightly brushing over hers. She realized it was the tips of his fingers.

She lifted her head and opened her eyes to stare up at him in the dark. In the now pouring rain.

His eyes were hooded, his own lips parted, and he stood toe to toe with her, his body slick with rain. His chest rose and fell as if he'd run a mile.

She was sure, if she allowed herself to check, he'd be hard.

A violent shiver raced through her and it wasn't from the downpour. It was from the electric charge between the two of them.

He had to feel the shock of it, too. Two lightning bolts, not coming from the sky, but from each other's center. Sparking and cracking as they connected.

With a quickness she wasn't expecting, he grabbed the back of her neck with one hand and her jaw with the other, crashing the two of them together. The shock of their mouths meeting made her gasp, and he took that opportunity to take control of the kiss and invade her mouth.

She pressed her palms to his chest to shove him away. To break this unexplainable pull, but when her hands made contact with his damp skin, she didn't push, the touch grounded her instead.

His pounding heart beat against her palm, like her hand was the only thing keeping it from breaking free of his chest.

After a few moments, he pressed his wet forehead to hers, breaking the kiss, and both of them simply breathed.

Before she could say something... anything... he claimed her mouth again, not soft and gentle this time. Hard. Rough. Powerful.

The hand holding her jaw slid down her arm and around to her back, dropping to grip her ass and yank her against him, close enough so his erection was sandwiched tightly between them. Only two layers of soaked cotton separated them.

Her panties were not only soaked from the rain but from his kiss. From his commanding touch.

From the deep groan that vibrated through his chest under her fingers.

From the hard press of his erection against her lower belly.

With excruciating slowness he rocked his hips, his cock sliding against her, making her pussy throb even harder, making her nipples want to punch right through the fabric of her bra.

It wasn't rainwater dampening the crux of her thighs. It was her aching need to have him inside her.

To have him on top of her.

Beneath her...

She needed to stop this.

Before it was too late.

Before it went beyond a kiss.

She twisted her head, ending it, and he panted against her wet cheek. His groan filled her ear, "Jemma."

"Chris…"

"Lemme show you how good it could be…"

No, she didn't need proof.

He grabbed her upper arm, spun her around and pulled her against him, his cock now pressed into the crease of her ass. The fingers that had been curled around the back of her neck, now gripped her throat firmly.

His heaving, bare chest pressed into her back as the sky continued to open up upon them, not even slowing a little. His right hand cupped her breast over her drenched bra, and her breath caught as he slipped inside to roll the hard, aching tip between his thumb and forefinger. Her back arched and her head slammed back against his shoulder. The fingers around her throat tightened even more, holding her hostage against him.

"Chris…" His name spilled from her lips on a ragged whisper.

She needed to stop this. To collect her wits and go inside. To free herself from his hold. Not the physical one, that was easy. From the sexual and emotional one, which was more difficult.

When she reached to pull his hand away from her throat, she kept hers there instead.

When he pulled the other from inside her bra and planted it on her belly, she covered it with her own. She pushed it, not away, but lower.

Not discouraging him. But encouraging.

Not telling him this was wrong. But right.

He splayed his fingers along her lower belly, the tips brushing along the elastic waistband of her panties. Playing with the very edge.

Teasing her.

His name got caught in her throat and she was glad it did. Because she wasn't going to tell him to stop, but to keep going.

He didn't need the words, he took his cues from her. From the encouraging way she slid the crease of her ass along his steel-hard cock. From the beat of her breath against his cheek, from her endless groan as he slipped his hand into her panties and drew a finger between her slick folds.

"Fuck," he breathed into her ear. "Fuck, Jem..."

One finger, then a second glided easily inside her. She was open and ready for him.

She bit the inside of her cheek so she wouldn't beg him for more.

With a slow, steady rhythm, he pumped his fingers in and out of her. As deep as he could go. His thumb twirled and pressed her sensitive clit, sending shockwaves all the way to her fingers and toes.

She began rocking against him at the same pace as his thrusting, but it wasn't enough. With each tip of her hips, she encouraged him to go faster.

"Need to be inside you," he growled.

*Oh fuck*, she did, too...

No. She was losing her mind.

No. What she needed to do was slam her foot on the brakes and stop this.

No. This was not a good idea.

It was a horrible idea.

Everything about this was wrong.

Wasn't it?

His hot breath beat against her wet skin in rapid pants. His erection thickened and pulsed between her ass cheeks.

A growl rose from the back of his throat and caused a shudder to shoot through her. Her breasts felt swollen, her puckered nipples painfully hard. Her mouth had gone dry.

"Wanna fist your hair while I fuck your mouth," went into her ear and landed directly in her core, making her even wetter.

Right now, she was so far gone, she'd give him whatever he wanted to send her over that steep edge.

Right now, nothing existed but him.

"Ride my fingers, baby. That's it. Stay with me." His voice, an octave lower than normal, had a rough edge to it as if he had to force the words from the bottom of his gut.

He whispered, "Keep soakin' my fingers just like that. So fuckin' wet, Jemma. So goddamn slick and hot. You're squeezin' me, pullin' me deeper just like you would my cock," and sank his teeth into her earlobe.

Her breathing became strained and shallow. Every time he plunged his fingers deep, his voice swirled through her mind, making her lose it.

"Wanna bury my face in your tits. Suck your nipples. Slide my dick between them. I dream of that, Jem. Fuckin' your mouth, your tits. Your pussy. Your tight ass."

*Oh God,* he needed to shut up before she screamed at him to bend her over and fuck her hard and fast in the downpour.

"Gonna take you everywhere. 'Til there's no place I haven't touched, tasted, marked with my cum. Wanna eat your pussy 'til you scream for me to stop. 'Til you can't take anymore."

*Yes,* she wanted all of that. And more.

She bowed against him as far as she could, tilting her hips sharply and riding his erection with her ass as he relentlessly fucked her with his fingers. As he worked on coaxing an orgasm from her with his thumb.

His words, his touch, the grip on her throat.

Powerful. Demanding. Titillating.

Her thighs quivered, her knees wobbled. Her breathing caught in her restrained throat.

She rode his fingers and cock harder and faster, in a complete frenzy, and a whimper finally escaped.

"Jem, you're gonna make me blow in my fuckin' underwear."

She didn't care but she'd forgotten how to form the words to tell him that.

She just didn't want him to stop.

Not yet.

Not until she came. Not until the ball of tension at her center burst into a million little pieces.

"*Fuuuck*, baby, I fuckin' feel you."

What started in her toes, shot up her legs and, when it hit her center, it exploded. Through her, around him.

His deep grunt was muffled by her cry.

He held her pinned against him because the orgasm stripped every bone from her body and her legs shook like Jell-O.

She didn't pull away, but let him hold her as she tried to gather her strength, control her breathing.

His fingers were still gliding in and out of her, but now it was slow and gentle.

His rough "Fuck," another deep grunt, his muscles tightening and one more hard thrust against her ass had her eyes popping open and the air rushing from her lungs, but she let him ride out his own orgasm.

It was only fair.

And with his long fingers still inside her, it sent her spiraling into another surprise orgasm of her own. Not as intense as the first, but just as satisfying.

She released a sigh when he stilled both his hips and his hand and simply held her close, his rough, whiskered cheek pinned to hers.

She slowly became aware of her surroundings once more. The rain had slowed to a light drizzle. The quiet only broken by their strained breathing and her heartbeat thumping in her ears.

As reality closed in, she realized what they did and how

it would complicate things. Technically, they didn't fuck, but they might as well have.

She had let him inside her and he had made her vibrate with want and need and then gave her the best damn orgasm she'd had in a long time. He knew what to do, how to do it and proceeded to shock the shit out of her.

The white-noise of the falling rain was broken by a deep rumble and this time it wasn't from Cage.

This time it was from something else.

A single headlight and the loud exhaust of a sled was headed in their direction.

A Fury member returning home.

Cage went completely still behind her, every muscle tense, as he slipped his fingers from her and his hand from her panties.

She surged away from him and he released her neck just as whoever was on the back of that sled pulled it into the shed next to them.

Jemma spun on him, just as he drew the fingers he'd used to make her come from between his lips.

"Fuck, Jem. So goddamn delicious."

She pressed shaky fingers to her mouth. Not because they'd been caught but because what they did suddenly became too real. A reminder that their world wasn't centered on only two of them and what they just did.

No, their world was an intricate web of family and "brothers." With a baby girl at the center.

All connected.

*Holy shit.*

"Don't ever do that again," she hissed right before whoever had been on that sled got within hearing range.

She took a step away from Cage, her legs still a bit weak, her mind spinning with the possible fallout of being caught. She wanted to escape into the trailer, but as Shade approached, she found herself frozen in place.

The man wasn't going to ignore the two of them standing out in the rain in just their soaked underwear. She was glad the dark night hid the heat in her cheeks for them being caught with their pants down. Or off.

His narrowed eyes sliced from Cage to Jemma and back. "Everythin' good here?"

That seemed to snap Cage back to the situation. "Yeah. Where you comin' from?"

"Nowhere." Shade turned toward her. "You good, Jemma?"

While she was shaken by what just happened, she needed to sound calm so Shade didn't misconstrue the situation and run to Judge or Deacon with what he saw. Which was probably Cage grabbing her throat and pinning her against him. To anyone else it might look like he was forcing her to submit.

And, *for fuck's sake*, if her brother got wind of that, Dyna might end up fatherless.

She licked her lips and swallowed her worry to give him a slight smile. "Yes, I'm good. We were just out here enjoying the warm rain. When we were kids, we used to strip down to our underwear and play in the rain, jumping in the puddles and... stuff." Her added laugh sounded dry and forced.

She hoped to fuck he didn't go to any of the rest of the Fury kids, like Trip or Stella, and ask them to confirm that lie.

Shade, with his hair pulled back tightly against his head, most likely due to the rain and the ride, focused on her for way too long. Even in the dark, the intensity of his stare sent a shiver sliding through her, and not the same kind Cage had caused. "That's what it was?"

She opened her mouth, but Cage answered first. "Yeah, just a little reminiscin'."

A soft cry came from the baby monitor on the chair.

That was her cue to escape. She snagged it and bolted inside.

Cage could handle Shade. It would be in his best interest to make sure Shade believed her. That it was nothing other than them goofing off.

She ran into her room, quickly stripped out of her soaked panties and bra and pulled the T-shirt she slept in over her head. She yanked a pair of dry underwear out of the dresser, yanked it up her legs and hurried out of her room, across the trailer and into his, where Dyna was crying.

She lifted the baby from the bassinet and cooed to her, trying to figure out what she needed. She realized it was a diaper change. She should make Cage do it since it was his "shift," but simply holding Dyna settled her nerves a bit.

She had fallen in love with Cage's daughter. And she'd be the reason Jemma would be heartbroken when she accepted one of the job offers coming in. It would be hard to say goodbye and not watch her grow up. To be with her through every stage of her childhood.

Simple things like crawling, getting her first tooth, standing and then walking.

*Oh God*, and hearing her say "Da-Da" for the first time.

She also wanted to see Cage's face when Dyna finally said it. Simply imagining that moment made her eyes leak at the corners a little bit.

"Do you need your diaper changed, monkey?" With one hand, she cleared a spot on Cage's messy bed and laid a waterproof pad down on the mattress. She settled the baby in the center of the pad and kept one eye on her while she located a small stack of clean diapers on the floor under the bassinet.

She cooed and made silly baby talk as she cleaned her up and put on a fresh diaper, wiggling the baby's feet and hands, and blowing raspberries on her bare belly. She wrangled her back into the onesie, and, as she picked her back up for some cuddles and kisses, she heard the front door to the trailer slam shut.

*Shit.*

She was hoping Shade would've kept him occupied long enough for her to make her escape back into her bedroom. But maybe Shade didn't consider standing out in the rain a cleansing of his soul.

"Jem," came from the doorway. Deep. Rough. Even a bit tortured.

Her heart began to pound again, just like it had done outside while he touched her, kissed her, made her shatter from the inside out.

She couldn't look at him. Not yet. Not when her emotions were still simmering along the surface.

She needed time and space to bury them deep again.

To remind herself of the reality of the situation.

She pressed a kiss to Dyna's forehead and carefully placed the baby back in the bassinet. She stared down at her, her hand covering the baby's chest and belly, making a connection through touch.

A warmth hit her back, even through the cotton of her oversized T-shirt. He now smelled like damp heat and a touch of sex, not from her, but his own release caught in his boxer briefs.

She avoided direct eye contact as she turned and began to push past him.

"Jem, wait." He went for her arm and she pulled it out of reach before he could stop her.

She noticed his blue eyes appeared troubled and his wet hair was slicked back from raking his fingers through it.

Clenching her jaw, she steeled herself against the pull between them she could no longer deny.

The *weirdness* was no longer weird. Tonight it became something else.

She realized for the first time in her life that a person could fall in love with someone without sex bonding the two. She had mistakenly thought intimacy was needed to make a true connection. The problem was when there was a connection established and intimacy was added, it only made the bond stronger.

So, she needed to avoid that. She couldn't risk falling any harder for Cage than she already was. And if they added sex to the mix, it might tear her heart out when she left.

Leaving a baby she loved would almost destroy her.

Leaving a man she loved would finish the job.

"Don't ever do that again. Not if you want me to stay." She left his room and kept walking until she was in her own and the door was locked behind her.

She scrubbed at her lips to try to erase the feel of his on hers. The kiss that led to more.

The kiss that made her want him more than ever.

She promised Judge she'd stay until she found the right job, but staying might become unbearable, since resisting Cage might become impossible.

## Chapter Fourteen

Cage groaned. He couldn't stop thinking about Jemma.

He couldn't touch her without chasing her away. He also wasn't in the mood for another motherfucking blanket party. Even so, he'd been struggling to keep his hands to himself. He barely managed it by making his hand his willing partner, instead.

He didn't even get to fuck her and that night in the rain was the hottest fucking sex he'd ever had.

How she felt against him, how slick she got from his touch, her gasps and whimpers and cries, how her delicate throat felt vulnerable under the press of his fingers. Holding her like that had made him so hard he thought his dick would split open like an overcooked hot dog.

He not only whacked off every morning and every night, every time he was in the shower, it took him back to those moments in the rain and he'd get hard as a fucking rock. His shower would get longer and the water would get cooler. Then, instead of him shooting his load in his boxer briefs like he had, it would swirl down the drain.

His current shower was no exception.

All he had to do was turn on the water, shut his eyes, and he'd quickly go back to that night.

When they sealed their mouths together and touched tongues.

When he pinned her against him with the hand on her throat.

When he twisted her nipple and she shuddered against him.

When her hand guided him lower, when she actually encouraged him to take it further instead of pushing him away.

When his finger first slid through her swollen, slick lips. He wasn't sure if he'd ever been with a woman who'd gotten so wet so fast.

When her hot sheath surrounded his fingers as he pumped in and out of it, and he wished it was his dick instead.

When the nub of her clit hardened beneath the press of his thumb.

When her cunt squeezed and rippled around him.

When the intensity of her orgasm soaked his fingers even more.

The way his hard dick fit perfectly between her soft, round ass cheeks and the harder he pushed, the more she rocked and grinded against him.

He had to clench his teeth to keep from ripping her panties down and plunging into her ass right then and there. Outside the trailer for anyone to see.

He groaned again and tightened his grip around his hard-on, pumping into his fist as the lukewarm water rushed over his head, chest and everything else.

He'd been using her shampoo to jack off because it made his palm feel as silky as her pussy had been. How slick he wanted to make it again.

If she'd let him.

Which she wouldn't.

Because she was stubborn as fuck, determined to not let them have more of what they had the other night.

Because she didn't do "casual," she only wanted steady. She couldn't have steady if she had one foot out the fucking door.

But, *for fuck's sake*, she'd do randoms. However, he didn't count as a random because he lived in the same trailer with her.

He was damned either way he looked at it.

So, he had his fist, and the shampoo that smelled like her, and however long it took him in the shower to do himself what he wished he was doing with her.

With a hand splayed along the shower wall, he leaned into it and tipped his head down so the water wouldn't sting his eyes or run into his gaping mouth.

His chest heaved, his heart raced and his breath chugged like a locomotive. His fingers flexed. Squeezed. Pumped. To the tip. To the root.

Over and over as he thrust inside her tight, hot pussy. The pressure in his groin increased as his orgasm built. Squeezing his eyes shut harder, he pictured Jemma in his mind's eye. Naked and writhing under him as he fucked her hard enough her heavy tits rocked back and forth with each thrust. He stared at her face, her mouth parted, her eyelids heavy, her green eyes focused on him.

And only him.

She plucked, pulled and twisted her own nipples, teasing him. Tempting him to take one into his mouth. He thrust harder until he was buried to the root. Balls deep.

His thrusting ground to an abrupt halt as the bathroom door burst open.

*What the fuck?*

"I need to pee badly and you're taking too long," he

heard yelled over the spray of the shower. "I couldn't wait any longer. Just stay in the shower until I'm done."

That wasn't a problem. He wasn't going anywhere.

Unless she invited him to her bed. Or to bend her over the sink.

His fingers remained frozen mid-stroke on his dick. "Jem..."

"I'll only be a second."

He lifted his head and noticed the curtain wasn't pulled completely shut. A small gap existed between the plastic and the shower wall.

A gap that clearly showed part of the toilet.

Where Jem was settling her naked ass, her shorts down around her knees.

He only hoped she didn't have the same view as he did.

That hope was quickly destroyed as she turned her head and looked right at him.

*Fuck.*

He was literally caught with his dick in his hand.

Her wide green eyes went from his face, when she realized he could see her pissing, down his chest, to what he was holding.

*Fuck.*

Her gaping mouth slammed shut and her eyes narrowed as she stared at his dick and said, "I'm assuming I won't have any hot water to shower now that you've used it all up. You do realize the water tank in this thing only holds enough hot water for a ten-minute shower at most. You've been in here almost twenty. It can't take that long to whack off. If it does, you need better jerk-off material."

*If she only fucking knew...* "Can you get the fuck out so I can at least finish? You bitchin' is ruinin' my fantasy."

His fantasy didn't include Jemma being a bitch. No, in his memory she was pliable and willing, and begging him for his dick.

She took her time reaching between her legs to wipe. Then somehow she wiggled up her shorts so he wasn't lucky enough to get the same view she was getting. As if in slow motion, she turned, put her hand on the toilet's lever and twisted her head toward him.

"Don't," he growled.

She grinned and slammed the lever down.

When the water temperature changed, he howled.

"How about not wasting water and doing it in your room with lotion and a sock like every other man in this zip code?"

"Jemma, get the hell out!"

She disappeared from view. "Or what?"

"Or get in the fuckin' shower with me and help me finish, so I can stop wastin' water."

He waited for her answer and heard nothing but the shower running.

Did she leave?

The door slammed shut.

Her hesitation had only meant one thing...

She had considered his suggestion. He grinned.

He closed his eyes again and a few minutes later his load circled the drain.

———

A HARD SLAP on his ass made him jump, shoot straight up and bean his head on the hood of the cage he was working on.

*What the fuck!*

"You got company, brother," Rook told him with a grin.

He rubbed the top of his head. He didn't need any more goddamn injuries. He grabbed the rag he had nearby and wiped his hands. "Who?"

"My niece and your house mouse."

"Jesus fuck, don't call her that if you value your nuts remainin' attached to your fuckin' body."

Rook's grin widened. "Ain't that what she is? She makes your meals, cleans your pad, takes care of your snot monkey... Sounds like a fuckin' house mouse to me. Only thing missin' is her droppin' to her knees when you tell her to. She probably ain't interested in your inverted micro cock. Only pops out when you're hard."

Cage clenched his teeth and growled, "Shut the fuck up before she hears you and I have to knock you the fuck out."

Rook chuckled. "Yeah, right. *You* knock me out. Name the last time that's happened?"

Cage pulled his shoulders back and locked eyes with his brother. "Will put it on my fuckin' calendar for when my ribs are fully fuckin' healed."

Rook sucked sharply at his teeth. "Lookin' forward to it. Maybe we'll make a fuckin' bet to see who knocks out who first."

Both of their heads cracked together without warning and they spun on their father. "Knock it the fuck off, you assholes. Told you, no fightin' here. You do it again and you're fired. Then you can go cryin' to the mommy who left your asses about how you no longer have a job. Though, doubt she's gonna care 'cause she don't give a shit about either of you."

"Trip don't want us fightin' amongst ourselves," Whip reminded them from the next bay over, standing under a Chevy up on the lift and watching the whole thing.

"Shut the fuck up," Rook and Cage shouted at the same time.

They turned, glanced at each other and smiled.

"Asshole," Rook grumbled, still grinning.

"You probably had yours stretched in prison," Cage said. "Bet you can fit a whole fist up there with just a little bit of spit."

"Don't knock it 'til you try it."

"Will take your word for it. I prefer hot, tight pussy that doesn't have hairy balls and a deep voice attached to it."

"A dark room and some lube and you won't be able to tell the fuckin' difference."

Cage faked a gag.

"How the fuck did you two come from my damn nuts?" Dutch grumbled, shaking his head. "Swear your momma took a couple loads in her snatch from someone else when I wasn't lookin'." He wandered out of the open bay door.

Cage followed his father as his old man headed toward Jemma's Volvo parked next to his sled. She had the back hatch open and was removing the stroller and the rest of the baby paraphernalia.

Dutch practically pushed her out of the way, unfolded the stroller and set it up for her like he did it every day. Cage was impressed that his father was that good with that contraption. It had taken him a couple times and a few curses to figure it out.

"Where's my grandbaby?"

"In the car seat, Dutch," Jemma answered, her tone pretty much insinuating his father was a stupid ass.

Cage chuckled and opened the rear passenger door to the Volvo to see Dyna asleep in her seat. "There's my little monkey girl," he whispered.

It was fucking crazy. It had only been about four hours since he last saw her and he couldn't believe how much he missed her. How much his heart swelled in his damn chest when he looked at his own daughter.

He wondered if Dutch had felt the same when he looked at him and Rook when they were babies.

He glanced at his grumpy old man. *Nah.*

He probably sat them out in the dirt with no diaper and gave them a stick and a rock to play with. To turn them into "real" men.

He unhooked the car seat from the base, carefully finagled it from the car, and carried it over to the stroller. He latched it in securely, all without waking the baby.

"She's fuckin' out," he murmured.

"Yes, she'd been crying. As soon as I began driving, she was out. Keep that in mind for the future if she won't settle."

*The future.*

For when Jemma was gone.

His swollen heart deflated.

"That's my Duchess," his father boasted after reading today's onesie.

*Some Grandpas play Bingo*
*My Grandpa rides Motorcycles*

A cartoon drawing of an old man with a long beard riding a sled divided the two sentences.

If that didn't gain brownie points with his old man, nothing would. Might be a good time to ask for a fucking raise. For his grandbaby's sake.

As Dutch reached to unbuckle Dyna from the car seat, Jemma stopped him. "Wash your hands first, Pap-Pap."

The old man grumbled, "A little dirt ain't gonna hurt my Duchess. Build up her immune system."

"And what medical journal did you read that in?" she asked with a dark eyebrow arched.

Cage didn't bother to hide his grin.

"Bah!" The old man flapped a dirty hand at her and stalked back inside, grumbling the whole way.

Cage stepped closer, leaned over and brushed a kiss over Dyna's forehead. When he straightened, he tipped his head down and stared into Jemma's face.

Neither said a word for a few long seconds. Probably

because they were both reliving what happened in the bathroom this morning.

The thought of how that could've ended differently woke up his dick. He also didn't miss her pupils dilate and her lips part the slightest bit.

*Fuck yeah*, she might be thinking the same thing.

He was surprised she came to the shop. He figured she'd want to avoid him like she'd been doing most of the time since the night it rained.

But here she stood, with her long brown hair sweeping around her bare shoulders, looking hot as fuck in black shorts that rode high on the soft thighs he wanted to feel gripping his hips. Sandals that showed off red-painted toes he wanted to suck. A sleeveless, blood red button-down blouse that emphasized her generous cleavage and showed way too fucking much of that soft flesh. She wore a little bit of makeup, but his eyes were drawn to her lips that matched her shirt. She was wearing fucking bright red lipstick. In the middle of the fucking day like she was ready to go to a bar or something.

*What. The. Fuck.*

"You trollin' for random?"

She rolled her eyes at him. "Yeah, here at the garage. Maybe you can watch your kid while Rook pins me down over the hood of a car and fucks me silly."

He sucked in a deep breath to keep the grenade in his belly from exploding. She was fucking with him, but it didn't matter. The thought of his asshole brother nailing Jemma made his blood pressure soar.

He unclenched his jaw. "That what you want? He ain't so random."

"I don't have to live with him."

She was trying to burst a vein in his head. Just trying to take him down and out for the count. "Jesus fuck, Jem."

"Don't ask a stupid question if you don't want a stupid answer."

"Ain't the first time my brother woulda taken what was mine."

Her green eyes narrowed. "What was *yours*?"

"You know what I mean." *Fuck.*

"I'm not yours, Chris." She pointed to Dyna. "She's yours."

Like he needed that fucking reminder. He stopped grinding his teeth to ask, "Why you here?"

"Do I need a reason to bring your daughter to see her family?"

That wasn't why she was here. "Nope. Why you here?"

She sighed and glanced toward the garage. "Reilly texted me and asked if I wanted to go to lunch."

She smiled over his shoulder and Cage glanced that way. Reilly and Rook were coming out of the garage together, beelining toward them.

If his brother started sniffing around Jemma, they would both end up fired. He was not going to sit back and watch Rook fuck another woman Cage had his sights on. Or one he already fucked, like he had in the past.

Rook thought it was fucking funny when he could steal one of Cage's women. Cage never found it so funny. Especially when Rook would use the excuse that he was doing Cage a favor by showing him what a "cheating bitch" she was.

Unfortunately, Rook wasn't the only one using that excuse. It seemed to be the family motto.

Once when he was seventeen and had managed to nail a woman four years older, he came out of his room to check why it was taking her so long in the bathroom only to find her on her knees in the kitchen sucking off his father.

That time was the last time he brought any women home.

Dutch said—after the bitch swallowed his load, of fucking course—he hadn't realized she'd come from Cage's room. Like women just magically popped up in their kitchen to help him with his morning wood. As if Dutch was the Pied Piper of horny women just out there searching for stray hard-ons.

They'd almost come to blows.

But there'd been plenty of times when Cage and Rook had gotten into brawls over pussy. Until they remembered women weren't worth fighting over. Then they'd wipe off the blood, put a bag of ice against a swollen eye or jaw, and go share a beer and a bowl.

It was one thing to share a sweet butt, it was another to share a woman who wasn't.

If Rook had known about Sarah, he probably would've tried to do her, too.

*Fucking motherfucker.*

While he loved his brother, he fucking hated him sometimes, too.

He swung his attention back to the woman his brother better not dare touch. Not if Rook wanted to continue breathing. "You bring me lunch?"

"No," was her answer as Rook and Reilly joined them.

"Hey, baby," Rook said softly, leaning in to kiss her cheek.

Jemma turned her head and rolled her eyes again. "Really, Rook?"

Rook stepped back and let his gaze slowly slide down her from top to toe. "Fuck yeah. Lookin' smokin' hot today, Jem." He shook his hand like it had been burnt. "Hard to believe you're that big ugly fucker's blood." He said to Reilly, "This is how you should dress for work, woman. Shorts could be a little shorter, though."

If Jemma's shorts were any shorter, her snatch would be feeling a breeze.

"I'll make a note of it," Reilly said dryly.

"Is he always an asshole like this?" Jemma asked her.

Reilly grinned. "Yep. One hundred percent asshole, one hundred percent of the time."

"I don't know how you put up with it," Jemma continued like Rook wasn't standing right next to her.

"It's easy. You do things to get him all worked up, then tell him to his face he won't ever get a piece of this." Reilly swept a hand down her body. She snagged her bottom lip between her teeth and gave Rook a sexy, slow wink and blew him a kiss.

"Saved your fuckin' ass from that psycho motherfucker who wanted to bat your head right out of the park with a home run. Don't forget that, woman."

"It doesn't give you the right to be a dick."

"Ain't a dick. Can't help but appreciate a hot as fuck woman. If you ladies wanna make a Rook sandwich for lunch, I'm available."

Both women looked at each other, then burst into laughter so loud it woke up Dyna.

Rook grinned and shrugged. "Just puttin' it out there."

Cage ignored his asshole brother, pulled Dyna out of the stroller and held her against his shoulder, murmuring nonsense to settle her.

Reilly pressed herself against his side and just about squealed. "She's so adorable. Oh my God! How did you make such a cute baby, Cage?"

"Probably ain't his, that's how," Rook teased, even though his brother knew the DNA test proved Dyna was.

"Doubt he'd put up with sleepless nights if she wasn't," Jemma murmured.

"Can think of way better reasons for sleepless nights than dealin' with a baby. I got a list of them if you wanna help me check some off, Jem."

"Give it up, asshole," Cage growled, rubbing Dyna's

back. "Doubt you want Judge fisting your fuckin' asshole, even as stretched as it is. If you hadn't noticed, he's got big fuckin' hands."

Reilly snorted. "Let me hold her."

"Your hands clean?" he asked.

"Yes, I don't diddle myself all day like you guys do. Never saw a group of guys who had to touch their dicks so much. Like you all have to keep checking that they haven't fallen off." Reilly pulled Dyna from his arms and began to do the obligated baby talk to his daughter while patting her diapered butt.

"Cage's fell off the second he realized he had a kid. Now he's just a big pussy."

"I heard Cage was an asshole, *Randy*," Jemma said, "but I'm beginning to believe it's you."

"It's in the blood," Rook said with a crooked smile. He hooked a thumb over his shoulder at their old man heading back in their direction. "Learned from the master."

"Well, you seemed to have turned out to be a real charmer, *Randy*. I bet you can't get any pussy besides the ones that have been shared by all your brothers and who aren't allowed to say no when you drag them like the Neanderthal you are back to your room."

Cage dropped his head and snorted.

"Most of the time, don't even bother draggin' them anywhere. Do them right on the spot," Rook corrected her.

If his brother wasn't careful, he would soon get a knee to the nuts.

"Like I said, a real charmer."

"I can be charmin' when I need to be," Rook assured her, giving her a wink.

Forget Jemma teaching Rook a lesson, Cage was about to pop him in the face. "She don't want your crooked-assed, deformed dick. Give it up."

"That crooked dick hits all the right spots."

Cage turned back to Jemma, trying to relax his fists and change the subject before things got ugly.

Whip was right, if they started fighting, not only would Dutch have a fit, but so would Trip and Judge.

He took another good look at Jemma since her attention was turned toward Reilly and Dyna. He couldn't blame Rook for wanting a piece of her. But if anyone was going to get it, it was going to be him.

Fuck his brother. Rook wasn't snagging this one from under his nose. "Where you goin'?"

The slight curl on her lips while watching Reilly and Dyna flattened when she turned back to him.

*Damn.*

"Probably just to Dino's. We can walk from here since it's nice out. I could use the change of scenery."

"Gonna bring me somethin' back?" Thinking about their loaded fries made his stomach growl a little.

She thrust out her hand, palm up. "Do you have money?"

He grimaced. She knew he didn't. Every fucking dime he made went to pay Dutch back to get him off his ass and to buy shit Dyna needed.

Rook pulled out his wallet, dug out a twenty and slapped it into her open palm. "Two burgers and two loaded fries. I'll buy this broke-ass bitch lunch today. He'll owe me a quick hand job later."

Reilly scrunched up her face. "Gross! You might have to move up that mountain with those inbred Shirleys. Dutch said they do family circle jerks."

Rook laughed. "Yeah, everyone stands in a circle and grabs the dick to their right. Don't matter if it's their brother, cousin, uncle or father."

"Sounds like you've taken part in it," Jemma said. She frowned at Cage. "Who are the Shirleys?"

*Fuck.* "Judge or Deke didn't tell you about them?"

She shook her head.

"Will tell you all about them," he purposely added, "at dinner."

She ignored the last part. "How do you boys want your burgers?"

"Pink, warm and juicy in the center, just how I like my pussy," Rook said.

"I'll make sure to tell them to pound your meat extra hard before they form the patty."

Rook smirked. "You can pound my m—"

"*Brother*," Cage growled. "Medium rare. For both of us. Thanks, Jem."

"You ready?" Jemma asked Reilly.

"Yep! I need a break from Stud Muffin here." She handed Dyna back to Jemma, who strapped the baby into the stroller. "Let's hit it."

"I'd like to hit—"

Cage shoved Rook toward the garage, cutting off his remark.

"Later," Cage called over his shoulder as the women headed toward the sidewalk.

He turned before going into the darker interior of the bay and stopped to watch the two women make their way toward the center of town.

Jemma looked natural pushing a stroller with his daughter. He couldn't pull his eyes away until she was out of sight. Even when Rook elbowed him and said, "You know I'm fuckin' with you, right? Can see you got a hard-on over her even though she's not stickin'."

"Fuck you, asshole."

Rook laughed all the way into the garage where it echoed back at him.

## Chapter Fifteen

SIX BLOCKS SEPARATED Dino's Diner from the garage. Both businesses were on Main Street with the diner closer to the center of town and Dutch's Garage at the west end. While taking the long stroll back, Jemma took her time checking out the businesses along the way. Usually when she came home for a visit, Lottie wanted to make her homecooked meals and Deke and Judge would join them, so Jemma rarely went into town. She wasn't aware how much things had changed over the years.

All for the better, from what she could remember.

The town was still quaint, and for the most part quiet, but Jemma noticed more tourists were coming to Main Street to shop the locally-owned businesses. Most came to the area to enjoy the nearby Pennsylvania Grand Canyon whether by hiking, biking, horseback riding or whatever.

Jemma didn't have to wait for dinner for Cage to tell her about the mountain clan, Reilly spilled the info she knew. Reese's younger sister admitted she didn't know everything but knew some key things.

Like the basics of what happened to Autumn. How Sig saved her. About Levi. About one of the local cops and his wife, an OB/GYN, adopting the baby Sig's ol' lady had by the former leader of the Shirley clan.

She learned the Shirleys considered themselves a "sovereign nation," a group who didn't follow any laws but their own.

All of it sounded kind of worrisome.

Reilly said something big went down on the mountain after the clan abducted an already pregnant Autumn, but none of the guys would tell the twenty-four-year-old exactly what.

If the current club was anything like the Originals, the retribution probably involved mass death and destruction.

She'd have to ask Judge, who, as the club's enforcer, would know the details. Whether he'd share them or not was another story. Jemma wasn't a member and also being a woman, he'd probably tell her that club business wasn't her business.

However, Dyna was her business, and the baby was club property.

Hearing about these "inbred hillbillies" who cooked meth, made moonshine and had a stash of guns made Jemma worry even more about her brother stepping into their father's boots as sergeant at arms. Her brother was responsible for the safety of everyone under the Fury's protection. That also meant if any violence went down he'd be front and center.

Deacon probably would be, too.

Lottie fretted over and despised the fact they were both wearing Fury colors. Jemma could see why. This wasn't a weekend riding club, this was a motorcycle club. This wasn't a social club, this was a lifestyle.

One they'd protect any way they'd need to.

Jemma only hoped Judge did it with a cooler head and more smarts than Ox. Trip was nothing like his father Buck who ruled the original Blood Fury with an abusive fist. She'd heard a few comments here and there about Trip having the same temper as the former Fury president. So did Sig. But both were doing their best to keep it under control.

Trip, for the club and Stella. Sig, for his "Red."

Their women seemed important to them, unlike the way the Originals treated theirs. That made Jemma optimistic, but it didn't settle her fears.

She had no idea if the Shirley clan existed when Buck and Ox ruled the Fury. If they had, she didn't remember hearing about them, not even as a kid growing up with Lottie and Walter. Possibly, they'd kept to themselves or had been, at the time, a much smaller group.

Hearing everything Reilly told her over lunch turned Dino's famous loaded fries in Jemma's gut to a slab of concrete.

Jemma might have waited until later for Cage to explain if Reilly hadn't seen a sketchy vehicle slowly traveling down Main Street toward the end of town where all the chain stores, like Walmart and Target, were located. Justice Bail Bonds was also at that end of town.

"Did you notice that rust bucket had no plate?" Reilly had whispered after the primered, four-door sedan with the missing exhaust passed them.

"I wasn't paying attention." She was too busy checking out the new stores in town and window shopping.

"I wonder if a couple of Shirleys were in that car. I've been keeping an eye out ever since I was warned about them. The boys said their cars are never inspected or registered. They don't have driver's licenses or insurance, either. They never bring their vehicles to Dutch's to get repaired, they do it themselves."

Jemma had looked for the car but by then it was too far in the distance with a cloud of smoke billowing from behind it. "Why do you need to keep an eye out?"

"Because they hate the club," the blonde answered.

"Because of Autumn?"

"Yes. And whatever the club did to them to get her back after they stole her."

*Stole* was an interesting word Reilly used. Jemma gripped the stroller handles more tightly as ice settled in her veins. "So, they went up there to get club property back and did whatever they needed to do to achieve that goal."

"Yes," Reilly practically whispered. "But they won't tell me what. They always give the answer that," she dropped her voice as deep as she could to mimic one of the guys, "*club business ain't your fuckin' business.*"

Jemma grimaced. She hated that shit.

Reilly might not be official club property, like the ol' ladies, but working at Dutch's, as well as being Reese's sister, she was under the club's protection.

Just like Jemma was.

Now they were almost back to the garage, with Jemma pushing the stroller with an awake, but quiet, Dyna, and Reilly carrying the wax-paper sack of take-out from Dino's for the two Dietrich brothers.

She was sure their food would no longer be hot, but she doubted either would care if they were anything like her brother and cousin. They'd hoover food hot or at room temperature. And cold pizza was like cocaine.

A half block away from Dutch's, Reilly suddenly put on the brakes, grabbing Jemma's arm to haul her to a stop.

"What the hell?" she whispered and nudged Jemma with an elbow to the ribs. "There's that fucking car again. It's such a piece of shit, it has to be them."

Jemma turned her gaze toward the sedan Reilly was staring at. It was now parked at the curb along the same side of the street they were walking. They would have to pass right by it.

From where they stood, she could see what looked like

two male figures in the driver and passenger's seats, but only the back of their heads were visible.

Her heart leapt into her throat. "I don't think it's much worse than that Honda Cage sometimes drives." Jemma wasn't sure why she mentioned it or even if that mattered. It didn't. But maybe she was trying to soothe her own fear. If the Shirley clan was dangerous and, if the club had done a bunch of shit to their family, then they might want revenge.

The parked vehicle was close enough to observe any activity at the garage.

"What do you want to do?" Reilly whispered, her blonde head close to hers so they wouldn't hear her, since all four windows on the sedan were open.

What did she want to do? "What do you mean?"

"Should we cross the street?"

"For a half block?" Jemma asked, apparently a little too loudly since Reilly shushed her.

"They're giving me the creeps."

"They're not doing anything but sitting there."

"They don't give you the creeps?" Reilly asked with surprise.

Fuck yes, they did, now that Reilly had told her about their existence. "We don't even know who they are."

"Who else drives around town without a plate?"

"Someone who lost it and doesn't realize it?"

Reilly snorted.

Jemma pressed her lips together and pushed the stroller. "We're being ridiculous."

"I hope so. But what if they try to grab us?"

Her heart began to thunder as they got closer. What if Reilly was right? She was spooking the hell out of Jemma. "They have no way of knowing we're a part of the club."

Right? Was she assuring Reilly or herself?

"Maybe. Maybe not. They grabbed Autumn right out of

Sig's apartment. They had to have been watching The Barn to know where she was."

Jemma's steps faltered, but she didn't want to stop so close to that car, so she pushed on. "What?"

Reilly lowered her voice to the point Jemma almost couldn't hear her. "Yes, they were watching the farm. Maybe they still are." She sucked in a sharp breath. "Maybe they've been watching all the businesses!"

"Reilly, you're freaking me the fuck out," Jemma hissed, the hairs on her arms and the back of her neck now standing. Why hadn't anyone thought to warn her about them before this? Especially with Dyna!

She and Cage were going to have words tonight. That was after she had words with her brother and cousin.

She'd been living on the farm for a few weeks now, why hadn't anyone thought to tell her she or Dyna could get snatched or attacked by some toothless, *Deliverance* wanna-bes?

Now she wasn't scared. Hell no, now she was angry.

Men were so stupid sometimes!

With a little growl, she walked faster. Both of them moved closer to the edge of the sidewalk farthest from the street. That, at least, would give them time to fight or scream if those men in the car tried anything.

*Holy shit*, it was bad enough being home in Manning Grove brought bad memories to the surface, now this. She couldn't get out of this town fast enough. She was going to flood every employment website with her resume when she got back to the trailer.

Reilly grabbed her forearm and dug her nails into Jemma's skin as they quickly walked past the car.

Jemma tried to act as if everything was normal, and, without being too obvious, let her eyes slide toward the car as they passed. She couldn't see too much but from what she did, she'd describe them as typical mountain men or rednecks. Their hair and beards were unkempt, and their heads followed both Jemma and Reilly as they passed.

She shivered, like a ghost had run its fingers down her spine, once the car was behind them. She didn't like that vulnerable feeling and kept her ears peeled for any opening car doors or footsteps behind them. Her paranoia was at a level one hundred on a scale from one to ten.

They heard nothing except the start of the exhaustless engine and the transmission clunking into gear, but by then their feet were hitting the edge of the garage's lot. They'd be within hearing and vision range for the guys in the shop.

Even though Jemma's heart was still pounding in her throat, she breathed a little easier.

Reilly finally extracted her nails from Jemma's forearm and practically sprinted into one of the open garage bays, leaving Jemma and Dyna behind.

She could hear Reilly yelling about something. She assumed it was the car when all the guys rushed outside, rags in hand and heads on swivels. Even Dutch.

Cage jogged across the lot to her. "You okay?"

Her fear swirled and mixed with her anger until that was the only thing left. "Yes, but you have a lot of explaining to do."

"Told you I'd give you the lowdown tonight over dinner."

"You should have told me on day one!" she yelled. "Or my brother should have." She released the stroller handles and covered her face with trembling hands and just breathed to try to regain control.

"We warned them not to fuck with us again," Cage said in a low voice. "We fuckin' warned them. You sure it was them?"

She dropped her hands and stared at him with incredulity. "You *warned* them?" *Damn it*, now her voice was shaking, too. "You fucking *warned* them?"

"Yeah. We told them we'd burn their mountain to the ground if they ever touched, talked or looked at what's ours again."

She shook her head. "You have a three-week-old baby, Cage." A reminder he certainly shouldn't need.

"Yeah, and they haven't fucked with us since that night last fall when we went and took back Red."

Jemma groaned. "Do you think they're smart enough to heed that warning?" If the clan was created from incest, then they might have very few IQ points and the ones they had they might be sharing.

"If they want their women and children to keep breathin', yeah."

"Jemma!" Reilly yelled and waved her over. She stood right outside one of the bays and was surrounded by the men who'd rushed outside.

With a sigh, she pushed the stroller to join them. Cage followed on her heels, sticking close.

"I really think they were casing the joint," Reilly was animatedly telling them. "Don't you think, Jemma?"

Rook made a face. "Casin' the fuckin' joint? Who says that shit?"

"Whatever, Rook! You know what I mean. Like they did with Autumn. They watched until the timing was right and had an opportunity to snatch her."

"Who fuckin' told you that?" Rook barked and eyed the two younger men in the circle.

Jemma had run into the younger one before at the farm when she was scouting for food in the kitchen one day. The oval embroidered name patch on his navy coveralls said Whip.

That was right. She remembered him. He had been kind of sweet. He looked to be around Jemma's age.

"You two runnin' your fuckin' mouth about club business?" Rook asked, exuding all kinds of unhappy.

"Wasn't me," Whip said with a shrug.

"Not me," the other mechanic said. "Probably the women runnin' their mouths. Stella was there with us and Red lived it, remember? They know exactly what happened."

Rook scrubbed a hand down his beard in agitation. "Fuckin' women. Gotta run their fuckin' mouths."

Jemma wanted to address Rook's assholery but got distracted by the blond with the most stunning blue eyes. His hair was cut short and spiked on top, both ears had several piercings and he had a hoop in one nostril, like Deacon did. He looked to be about in his mid-to-late twenties and was absolutely gorgeous. He wore navy coveralls that weren't buttoned from his waist up, just like Whip's. She could read the name patch on his, too. Rev.

Like rev an engine? Or Reverend? She wondered what it was short for. "Is Rev your real name?"

The blond tilted his head and let those beautiful blue eyes slide down her body. He wasn't even subtle about it. The air shifted sharply behind Jemma.

"Nope. Nickname. Real name's Mickey. Surprised I haven't run into you yet at the farm."

"You hang out at the farm?"

One side of his mouth pulled up. And it was sexy as hell. *Damn.* "I live at the farm."

"Oh. You're a member of the Fury, too." *Jeez*, everyone at the shop was. She had no idea.

The other side of his mouth pulled up into a blinding smile. "Yeah."

Jemma heard a loud grunt right behind her and she rolled her eyes at the caveman claim.

"*Anyway*," Reilly shouted to get everyone's attention back on her. "A rusty piece of shit was sitting a half block down. After we passed it, it pulled away. It would've driven right by the garage."

"Those motherfuckers occasionally come into town to hit a store. They ain't supposed to even talk or look at our women," Rev said, moving closer to Reilly until they were almost touching. Almost as if he was her personal protector.

Just like Cage was doing with Jemma. Hovering so closely behind her, she could practically feel his heat and his breath.

"How would they know we're *your women*?" They weren't ol' ladies, they weren't wearing "property of" cuts. Nothing Reilly or Jemma wore would tie them to the club.

"They would know now since we were seen leaving and returning to the garage," Reilly surmised.

Jemma was momentarily distracted when Rev's hand curled around Reilly's hip, almost as if to reassure her. She wasn't the only one who noticed. Rook's head snapped up and he scowled at that hand until Rev removed it.

Whip, unaware of the unspoken exchange between his brothers, said, "But they could just be customers leavin' their car here and, instead of waitin', headin' to Dino's to get grub. Happens all the time."

"Could be." Dutch grumbled, tugging on his long salt-and-pepper beard. "Ain't likin' the fact they were parked nearby. If they come to town they need to get where their goin' and get the fuck back up that mountain. We ain't gonna tolerate them loiterin' or stalkin' our women."

"We're not your women," Jemma reminded him.

"The fuck you ain't," the old man grumbled with a scowl almost identical to Rook's.

"Maybe it wasn't us they were watching," Jemma suggested.

"Right. That's what I'm fucking saying! It could be your garage, Dutch," Reilly exclaimed, sounding exasperated.

"Gonna give Trip and Judge the head's up," Cage said behind her. "If they're watchin', we need to know. Need to prepare. Wish we had more prospects besides Tweedle-

Dumbass and Twattle-Dumbfuck to shadow the women 'til we know what the fuck's goin' on or can confirm it was them sittin' and watchin'."

"Most of the time they're covered," Rev said. "Reilly's with us during the day and with Ozzy at night at the inn. Stella's with Dodge and the prospects at Pete's. Cassie's with Shade and Easy during the day at the pet crematorium. Reese..."

"Yeah. Reese. Saylor's alone at the house durin' the day with Daisy. And," Rook glanced over Jemma's shoulder, she assumed at Cage behind her. "Jem's at the trailer durin' the day with Dyna. Got two prospects, three women not covered."

"Those prospects are needed at the bar," Cage reminded his brother. "Stel will have a fit if we leave her shorthanded."

"Yeah," Dutch mumbled, tugging on his beard some more like it helped him think. "Let Trip, Sig and Judge figure it the fuck out. They ain't gonna want us makin' those decisions without 'em."

"Sig's gonna fuckin' flip," Whip said.

"He ain't the only one," Rev added.

"We don't even know if it was them and what the fuck they were doin'," Dutch reminded them all. "Coulda been nothin' and the girls are just imaginin' shit. Always gotta cause drama."

Jemma took a huge inhale to address Dutch's bullshit when a warm hand splayed along the small of her back, causing all the air to rush out of her. Cage started stroking her back the same way they did when Dyna was upset.

*Son of a bitch*, it fucking worked, too.

But his touch also caused what felt like an electrical current along her skin even with the blouse between them.

*For fuck's sake*, this was why she'd been trying to avoid him as much as possible while living in close quarters.

She took a step to the side and broke the contact so she could breathe and think.

Reilly was staring, her mouth agape, her wide green eyes sliding back and forth between Cage and Jemma.

*Fuck.*

Jemma gave her a look that told her to keep her mouth shut and only hoped the woman got the message. The other woman's surprise turned into a sly smile as she glanced around the rest of the circle to see if anyone else picked up on what she saw.

Jemma decided it was best to ignore it all. If she ignored it, it didn't exist, right?

She wished.

What they couldn't ignore was the flashy vehicle that pulled up next to the group and parked in front of one of the empty bays. A newer, bright yellow Mustang convertible with the top down.

A male with short dark hair twisted his head toward them, did a finger wiggle and yelled out, "Yoo hoo!"

Several groans rounded the circle.

The driver's door was flung open and a tall, slender, very well-dressed man quickly joined the group and slid his dark sunglasses down his nose enough to peer over them at all the men. Jemma swore he licked his lips like he was thirsty. Parched, even.

"Look at this circle of handsome hunks. Mmm. Lord have mercy. I need to set myself right in the center. All you hard-working boys can certainly make a man's toes curl."

In those few seconds, Jemma was one hundred percent certain whoever he was, he was not straight. Not with the way he was eyeing up the men, even Dutch, like they were lollipops and he wanted to figure out how many licks it took to get to the center.

"Aren't you married now, Teddy?" Cage asked dryly.

Had he stepped behind Jemma even more, like she was a shield?

She was no one's shield. She side-stepped again to let Cage fight his own battle.

"Why yes!" this Teddy exclaimed with an extraordinary amount of enthusiasm. "My Bryson Buck finally bit the bullet and put a ring on it. Haven't you seen my ring?"

A couple of the guys groaned again as he flapped his hand with its long, well-manicured fingers toward the center of the circle. A wedding band on his left ring finger sparkled in the sunlight, just like the man wearing it. Not a *Twilight's* Edward Cullen type of sparkle but more of a sun creating a colorful rainbow type.

Jemma was amazed at how the arrival of Teddy instantly derailed the dark and serious mood of the group.

"What do you need, Theodore?" Dutch grumbled.

Teddy leaned into Cage's father and grabbed Dutch's bushy beard at the top and slid his hand down the length and all the way to the older man's belly, where it settled. "To sit on Santa's lap and tell him how good I've been so far this year." His fingers walked their way back up to Dutch's barreled chest. "And you know it makes me feel like a naughty boy when you call me by my full name. I promise Santa, I've been good." He did an exaggerated wink.

Dutch grinned at the man's flirting, leaving Jemma speechless. The grumpy old grouch turned into someone she didn't recognize.

She turned and bugged her eyes out at Cage. He simply closed his for a moment and shook his head. Jemma slapped a hand over her mouth to contain her laughter at the change in Dutch.

She also had no idea why this man was calling Dutch Santa, but him doing so rattled a forgotten memory. Of her sitting on Santa's lap. But not the same "Santa" that had a super hard lap and stinky breath.

She closed her eyes and pushed back any and all of those memories. She didn't care if any were good. Drawing out the good ones also drew out the bad. They seemed to intertwine with each other no matter how hard she tried to separate them.

Cage touched her back again and her eyes popped open. *Christ*, why did he have this effect on her?

"Don't need your hubbie harrassin' my ass," Dutch was saying. "So, gotta keep it to business. What d'you need?"

"*Wellllll*," Teddy announced loudly with a sharp single clap and a frown. He flapped a hand toward his Mustang. "I got screwed and not in a good way. Now I need plugged." He grinned and wiggled his very on-point dark eyebrows.

"A screw or a nail?" Rev asked, not aware he was stepping right into the trap.

Teddy sidled up to him and batted his eyelashes at Rev. "Yes, please." He waved his hand around between them. "Is there a difference? Is one rougher than the other? Tell me." The last was whispered.

Rook sighed. "You know, Teddy, we don't need Adam down here poundin' on his uniformed chest like—"

"Like a jealous gorilla?"

"And causin' problems 'cause you're a damn flirt," Rook finished.

Sounded like Teddy's husband might be one of the local cops, which, of course, with his past, Rook wouldn't want to tangle with anyone wearing a badge. Cage mentioned he only got out of jail about a year and a half ago and managed to remain free of cuffs and bars since then. Which was a record for his brother, apparently.

But then being a part of the Fury now, if Rook got busted for something stupid, he'd have to deal with more than the law. He'd have to answer to the club's executive committee.

Trip told Jemma he was determined to keep everyone

out of jail or prison when they talked that night at Crazy Pete's. He probably told her that to ease her fears about Judge and Deacon being a part of the club.

The club president could say that all he wanted, it didn't mean he could have complete control over the situation. But him feeling so strongly about everyone staying out of trouble could mean the guys worked a little harder at not doing stupid shit that might land their asses behind bars.

Still, it was no guarantee.

"Oh, handsome. He knows good and well I'm a flirt. I can flirt, I can look, I just can't touch."

"Is he allowed to do the same?" Reilly asked, her worry about the Shirleys long gone as she smiled at the newcomer.

"Wait." Teddy's eyes narrowed on Reilly. "*Whoooo* are you?" They landed on Jemma next, like he only noticed them. "And you? How did you two ladies slip by me?"

Were women invisible in his world? Or was he just temporarily blinded by the five handsome bikers? Glancing around the circle, she looked at them all in a new light. She could see that happening. All five of them, including Dutch, who was just a little more seasoned than the rest, were hot as fuck.

Teddy's gaze dropped from Jemma to the baby in the stroller. He bent down toward Dyna and whispered, "Oh, who's this little muffin?" He wiggled Dyna's foot.

"That's Cage's snot monkey," Rook said with a grin.

Dutch wacked his oldest son in the gut so hard, Rook grunted and almost bent in half. "That's my grandbaby Duchess," said the proud pap-pap.

"Duchess?" Teddy glanced up from the baby to Cage, then he looked at Rook. "Didn't know either of you two were taken." He straightened and cocked an eyebrow at Jemma. "But I could see why. You're not only beautiful but have a great head of hair." He looked at Reilly. "You, too.

And I'm not sure why your tushes haven't been in my chair at Manes on Main yet." He pouted.

"You have a salon?" Jemma asked.

"Oh yes, girlfriend. I'm not sure why any of these leather-loving gorillas haven't told you. Right down on Main Street. Past the square, next to the butcher shop. You can't miss it. Big lettering on the window." He raised his hands together in the air and then spread them apart, like he was revealing a marquis or a banner. "Manes on Main. New customers get their first wash and trim for free."

That was good to know, especially since she'd need a cut soon and wanted to look good for any interviews coming up.

Teddy leaned closer to Jemma and winked. "I'm the best in town. Ask Dutch. I'm the only one he'll let touch Santa's beard."

"I'm in," Reilly said. "I haven't had a cut and lowlights since leaving Philly."

Teddy spun on her and clapped his hands. "Can't wait! But, girlfriend, you need to stop tugging on your hair like that. It'll give you a bald spot." He stepped up to the blonde and tipped her face up, turning it back and forth as if he was inspecting it. "I see you're trying to cover that scar. That ain't but a thing, girl. I can style your hair to minimize it and then show you how to cover the rest with makeup if it bothers you. But honestly, it doesn't change how gorgeous you are. So," he plugged one hand on his hip while jutting it out, "who are you?"

"Reilly," she answered with a smile. "I work here at the garage."

Teddy clapped his hands again and bounced on his toes. "Oh goodie! That means you'll be a regular. You let me know when you want to sit your cute tush in my chair and I'll clear my schedule."

He moved to stand in front of Jemma next and fluffed the sides of her hair. "Just as gorgeous. The color of your hair is how I like my coffee and men. With lots of cream. And who are you?"

As she opened her mouth to answer, Cage's hand settled on her lower back again. "This is Judge's sister Jemma."

"Judge... Judge..." Teddy stared up at the sky, tapping one finger against his pursed lips. His eyes went wide. "Oh! The big beast of a man with roadkill on his face." He scrunched up his nose. "I offered to *snip snip snip* it," he mimed cutting scissors with his fingers, "to let his handsome face show, but he got a little..."

"Grumpy?" Jemma asked with a muffled snort.

"Growly. Let your brother know the offer is still available. I expect to see you in my chair soon." Teddy spun on Dutch. "You're looking a little ragged there, too, Santa. Time for you to come visit."

"Why does he call Dutch Santa?" Jemma asked Cage in a whisper.

"He dresses up as Santa for the Christmas parade every year."

"Oh, well... that's... sweet." Jemma never remembered Dutch playing Santa as an Original, but then he'd been a lot younger back then. Maybe Dutch was her good Santa memory. She also never went to the Manning Grove Christmas parade. She never even knew there was one. She wondered if it started more recently.

"Cage drives his Impala in it, too," Whip said next to her. "Let's the chief of police ride in the back."

That surprised the shit out of her. But then, the club had only been reborn within the last two years. Maybe the current Fury members didn't have an issue with the current batch of cops.

"Yes, he does," came Teddy's voice so close, Jemma jumped. Was she still rattled from seeing that car and learning about the Shirleys? "Max looks so handsome in his dress uniform with his just as hot chauffer. Christopher, I know you can pull off the disheveled look." He glanced at Jemma for affirmation. "Right? But don't let it get out of control so you look like one of the bums down at the tracks."

"There are bums at the railroad tracks?" Reilly asked, sounding in awe.

"Fuck no," Dutch answered. "All right, assholes. We've stood around long enough. Get the fuck back to work before I dock your pay. Rev, pull Theodore's 'Stang into the garage and plug his tire."

Rev headed toward the Mustang and everyone but Cage wandered inside.

It was just the two of them and Dyna. He tilted his head and stared at her.

She tried not to shuffle her feet at his intense gaze. "Your food's probably cold."

"Got a microwave in the kitchenette."

"Not the same as when it's fresh." She needed to get Dyna loaded and go back to the farm. "Are we going to be safe out in the trailer?"

"Would you feel better spending the day with Saylor and Daisy?"

She sighed. "No. But you should have told me, Chris. Reilly told me more than you did and she doesn't know everything."

"Honestly, ain't worried about the Shirleys. We taught them a lesson and haven't seen or heard from them since. They'd be stupid as fuck to fuck with us."

"Doesn't mean they won't."

"You're right. Don't mean they won't. Just keep an eye open, that's all. Takin' Reilly's word that the car belonged to the Shirleys. We don't know that for sure. If it was, they mighta had a reason to be in town."

"So, you're not worried."

"Not yet. Gotta work to pay for shit. Can't be home with you all day."

"I didn't ask you for that." Nor would she. She was struggling to keep her hands to herself as it was.

"Wanna gun? I'll get you one."

"A legal one?"

He gave her a look and that was all she needed as an answer.

"Then no." Plus, she never shot a gun in her life. Unless she had training, she'd be worried about handling one. As a nurse, she'd seen what damage a gunshot could do.

"If you get spooked, call me. Me or one of the guys can be there in ten, if needed."

Ten minutes could be forever in a violent situation. She wasn't liking any of this.

"Just keep the door locked when you two are inside. Wait 'til someone's at The Barn or bunkhouse to head over there. Or wait 'til I'm home."

"That means we'll be prisoners in the trailer while everyone is gone during the day."

He blew out a breath and scraped his fingers through his hair. "Jem, doin' the fuckin' best I can here. Gotta work with me. Gonna talk to Trip and Judge."

"I'm going to talk to my brother, too." She chewed on her bottom lip.

He went toe to toe with her and pulled her lip from between her teeth. He brushed his thumb over the lower one. "It'll be okay. Can't tell you the details of what happened on that mountain that night, but can tell you we made a strong statement. Know they ain't the smartest, but they can't be that fuckin' stupid, either."

Or they could be stupid enough to try. "What are you going to do with Dyna when I'm gone? I can't stick around much longer, I need a paying job to pay my bills. I need to settle somewhere other than here. This isn't my life, Chris.

Dyna isn't my child. You need to seriously get your shit in order before I leave."

His blue eyes darkened and he dropped his head slightly. "Truth?" he whispered.

"Nothing but," she whispered back, trying not to focus on how close his lips were to hers.

"Got no fuckin' clue, Jem. That's the hard truth. It comes down to it, I'll sell my Impala to pay for daycare. Don't know what else to fuckin' do. Can't shit out money I don't got."

"Your daughter is more important than a car," she reminded him needlessly.

"Ain't just a car and I'll take a loss by sellin' it quick."

"And you won't be able to haul the chief's ass around in the parade."

Cage snorted softly. "Yeah, well. Dyna's more important than that. But besides my sled and my Impala, the only thing that's truly mine is her."

"Then you need to make a plan. And soon. I'm heading home."

*Home.*

She didn't miss the slight raise of his eyebrow when she said the word. But right now, that was what it was. Even if it was only temporary.

"Jem..."

"Help me load up the stroller, will you?" She went to push it toward her Volvo, but he stopped her with a hand on her arm.

"Jem."

She glanced up at him. "What?"

"You don't gotta leave."

"I can't stay. I can't afford to." In more ways than one.

She broke free of his grip and he followed her when she went to where her car was parked.

"Think about it," was the last thing he said as she finished buckling in the carrier portion of the car seat.

"Nothing to think about, Chris. You knew what the deal was. It hasn't changed."

His jaw got tight as she closed the back passenger door. He remained where he stood as she moved around the car and climbed in the driver's seat.

And he remained standing there as she backed out of the spot and drove out of the lot. She couldn't help but glance into the rearview mirror a few times before the garage disappeared from sight.

*You don't gotta leave.*

Yes, she did. And she needed to do it sooner than later.

Because there had been nothing she wanted more than for him to kiss her when they were standing face to face out in the lot.

She almost thought he was going to do it. And was surprisingly disappointed when he didn't.

Disappointed or not, it was for the best.

# Chapter Sixteen

JEMMA CLICKED through her email inbox, deleting spam and newsletters left and right.

Despite warning Cage that he needed to prepare for her to leave, he hadn't shared any type of plan with her.

She'd stopped by Justice Bail Bonds after leaving the garage that day and Judge assured her that they'd keep an eye out for the Shirleys. Not only at the trailer, but the whole farm and at all the club's businesses. While he took the possible threat seriously, he'd kept his cool about it.

And, of course, he wouldn't share with her what exactly, if anything, he'd do about the "inbred fuckin' hillbillies" if the threat was real.

Her brother was far from happy when she reamed him up one side and down the other about not warning her before asking for her to return home to help Cage out. She actually heard a chuckle from Deacon as she stomped back out of their office after flipping them both off.

From there, she went back to the trailer and did what she planned, which was flood the job market with her resume again.

While jobs were plentiful, they weren't for her niche.

And the hospice care facilities with job openings were as slow as molasses when filling positions.

She glanced through new emails stating they'd received her resume and, if she was the right candidate, they would contact her soon for an interview.

The *right* candidate.

If they reached out to her last employer, she might not get contacted at all. She had kneed the head doctor and part owner of the private hospice center in Cleveland right in the nuts. But it had been an effective and quick way to get his unsolicited hands off her ass and breasts.

Most of the nurses and admin staff called the asshole Dr. Grabby. For the most part, the female staff knew how to avoid the "accidental" brushes against their chests or rears. They also did their best to not be alone with him if—more like *when*—he had his sight focused on them.

However, that fateful day the doctor followed Jemma into the supply closet and crossed the line to the point he couldn't brush it off as "accidental." In turn, she "accidentally" knocked his nuts up into his body cavity with her knee. Hard enough he dropped instantly to the floor and actually blubbered. With real tears, too.

She then calmly walked out of the closet, went down the hall saying goodbye to her patients and went home. It wasn't long before the HR person called her about her termination.

No surprise.

*She* had inappropriately touched *him*. Imagine that. She was also *lucky* he wasn't pressing charges. Jemma laughed and hung up.

The result was her previous employer was a smudge on her resume that might be difficult to overlook by some prospective employers.

While she'd received three job offers already, either the pay or the location, or both, were shitty. She might have to take one in the meantime, anyway, just to get her through financially until something better came along. She'd barely made her last car payment and was scraping the bottom of her bank account.

No matter what, she needed to keep paying for her car and her storage unit in Ohio. Even if she had to borrow money, which she really didn't want to do. She'd leave that as a last resort.

She needed to make a serious decision. She'd been caring for Dyna a little over six weeks now and as much as she loved her, taking care of the baby wasn't a paying job nor what she wanted to do as a career, even if she was paid.

Her calling was to be a hospice nurse. To ease a person's journey into the next stage of their life or afterlife, whatever that destination was for her patient. Heaven, Valhalla, worm food or a return to being stardust.

She was not a nanny.

She was not a house mouse.

She had a career she loved, even when it was heartbreaking. Though, it always seemed to be heartbreaking. Even so, at the end, she was truly appreciated by the patient and their loved ones.

She tried to be a little bit of light during a very dark time. Just like Maggie had been a shining light during Walt's.

Her cursor landed on an email from a private hospice organization that specialized in home hospice care. Their closest office was in Williamsport, which was only about an hour away.

She opened the email to see the offer for an interview. Since it was in driving distance, it would be in person, unlike some of the virtual interviews she'd done recently.

Her heart began to beat faster when she realized they wanted to do it in only three days. She needed to prepare and put her best foot forward. She'd take Teddy up on his offer of a wash and trim and head over to Lottie's to iron her dress slacks and a blouse.

She had crossed her fingers and toes for this job when she'd emailed her resume. It was close enough to Manning Grove to do a day visit with Lottie and the rest of her family, but not close enough to constantly stir up bad memories.

She pressed her fingers to her lips because she wanted to squeal with excitement but Dyna was napping in her bouncer on the floor next to where Jemma sat at the kitchen counter with her laptop.

She glanced down at the baby.

*Fuck.*

She'd be gone for hours and Cage would need to find someone to watch his daughter, or he'd have to take off from work to stay with her himself.

She needed to let him know right away. She also needed to make an appointment with Teddy as soon as possible. She'd call the hairdresser first thing in the morning, since she was sure his salon would be closed at this late hour.

Cage had already come home from work, but wasn't in the trailer. He asked if she'd mind watching Dyna while he went to the shed to work out for a half hour or so, since he hadn't been able to do so for the last six-plus weeks.

She agreed only if he allowed her to check his ribs before he did. She had held her breath as she ran her fingers over his bare skin, testing for any soreness or pain.

He claimed he had none.

"Just don't do anything stupid. Take it easy," she ordered as he walked out of the trailer wearing only long, loose nylon shorts and an actual pair of sneakers. She had wondered if any of the brothers owned anything other than biker boots. Now she knew.

She closed her laptop and slid her feet into her flip flops, gently scooped up Dyna and groaned softly at how heavy she had become. She had to have put on at least four pounds since Jemma had come back to Manning Grove, but then, she ate like crazy and pooped as much, too. They were flying through the diapers.

She did a quick diaper check before heading out of the trailer and across the grass. She hoped to get to the shed and back before Dyna woke and demanded her next meal.

The shed that had been converted into a mini-gym wasn't far. It actually was closer to the trailer than The Barn. She had explored it one day with Dyna when she was bored. It wasn't anything fancy. It didn't have any cardio equipment, like treadmills and stair-steppers, but had free weights, some weight benches, a speed bag and some heavy bags. Just the basics.

What the guys would consider "manly" gym equipment.

As she got closer, she heard *Enter Sandman* by Metallica blasting and wondered if Cage was alone.

She glanced down at Dyna in her arms. Somebody would be awake soon from the loud music if she continued.

Good. Then it would be on Cage to take over her care for the evening if Metallica woke her up and she began to fuss.

She hesitated outside the propped open door to the shed, took a bolstering deep inhale and walked inside.

Dyna immediately awoke in her arms, but she didn't start crying... yet. She'd eaten not long ago, so her belly was full. Luckily, for the most part, she was an easy baby. *Thank fuck.*

Jemma's eyes skimmed the shed, which was much smaller than the one the guys parked their sleds in. She was searching for the radio to turn it down, but her gaze locked on Cage first.

His bare, tattooed back was turned toward her and his skin glistened with sweat. A rolled bandana around his forehead held his hair back from his face, but, from what she could see, beads of sweat still slid down his temples. His loose, light gray shorts were soaked at the small of his back and the silky fabric clung to his ass cheeks like a second skin.

He stood in front of the heavy bag in the corner, a loud grunt escaping him with each punch. His hands were protected by black gloves that were thicker over the knuckles but open at the ends, leaving the ends of his fingers visible. A flap of Velcro secured the gloves tightly.

Cupping Dyna's head, Jemma rocked back and forth to keep the baby quiet as her feet remained frozen in place. She watched his muscles ripple and flex with each powerful strike.

That couldn't be good for his just-healed ribs. She told him not to do anything stupid.

But, in reality, stupid was standing and watching him when he had no clue she was there. She couldn't pull her eyes from him and her thoughts tumbled like clothing in a dryer.

She imagined his back and ass flexing as he pumped into her over and over. Not with his fingers, like that night in the rain, but instead, with his cock. Thick and long, sliding in and out of her.

A trickle landed in her panties. *Christ,* this was what he did to her.

She'd resisted for weeks. *Weeks.* Convincing herself that doing anything more than what they'd already done would be stupid and reckless.

She didn't do casual.

She didn't do casual.

*Fuck.*

She did *not* do casual.

Touching him like she wanted to would only complicate their situation. It would only make things messier when she left.

She knew that.

Unfortunately, her brain didn't want to hear common sense.

No, her mouth wanted to taste the salt on his hot skin. Her fingers wanted to slide through the sheen of sweat on his back and chest.

She wanted to grip his ass tightly as he plunged deep inside her, to encourage him to go even faster. To make her come as intensely as he had that night weeks ago.

All she had to do was ask.

All she had to do was offer.

All she had to do was say yes.

Because he'd been waiting. Patiently. Like he knew there would come a point when she wouldn't be able to resist anymore. She did, too, but she'd hoped to be gone before then.

However, here she stood. Watching the man she wanted but couldn't—shouldn't—have. Holding his child in her arms.

That child, and the reason she came to be, should be enough motive to resist.

But it wasn't.

It wasn't.

Everyone made mistakes.

If anything, Cage had done nothing but owned his mistake and did his best. Day after day. Night after night.

His actions impressed Jemma.

Dyna made a little noise like she was trying to call out to her father. She was staring at him just like Jemma was. She actually smiled and then cooed, her legs kicking and her arms flapping. She wanted her Daddy.

She wasn't the only one.

Jemma finally located the radio and went to turn down the volume so Cage could hear her. As soon as she did, he spun toward her with his fists still up in the ready position.

He quickly masked his surprise and dropped his hands to his side, his slick chest pumping.

"What you doin' in here?" he asked, out of breath. He swiped his damp forearm over the beads of sweat collecting on his forehead. After grabbing a towel hanging on one of the nearby weight benches, he scrubbed it down his face and ran it haphazardly over his chest.

Jemma followed the motion, then tried to swallow.

She couldn't.

He walked over to a banged-up minifridge in the corner, opened it and grabbed a bottle of water. Cracking open the top, he tilted the water to his lips and Jemma watched his throat undulate as he guzzled it down, a little bit of water escaping the corners of his mouth and disappearing into his short beard.

*Holy hell. Stay on point, Jemma.*

"You weren't supposed to push it, Chris. You don't want a set-back."

"I'm fine," he said after sucking down half the water and wiping his mouth with the towel now tossed over his shoulder. "Got goddamn weak these past few weeks not bein' able to work out."

"Getting clubbed for being stupid will do that to you."

He grimaced, finished the rest of the bottle and chucked it into a nearby bucket. He ran the corner of the towel over his face again. "Why you here, Jem?"

"I needed to talk to you."

He lifted one brow. "Couldn't wait?"

*Probably.* "No."

"What is it?" He frowned as his gaze landed on his daughter, who was now moving actively in her arms. "Dyna okay?"

"Yeah. She's... good." When she moved closer, Dyna grunted and made a face.

"She gotta fart?"

"No, she's smiling."

Both eyebrows hit the edge of the soaked bandana. "Get the fuck out."

Jemma smiled, too. "No, she's smiling at you. She loves her Daddy." Her heart squeezed and flip-flopped at her own words.

"Too sweaty to hold her."

"I didn't bring her out here for you to hold her."

"Then, why you here, Jem?" he asked again.

"First, let me check your ribs again." She looked around and found a couple of what looked like clean towels piled on a weight bench. She grabbed them, spread them out on the floor and set a happy Dyna down on her back. She gave the baby a couple coos and feet wiggles before straightening and when she did, Cage was right behind her, his scorching body heat rolling off him in almost visible waves.

She tried to swallow again, but her throat was too tight.

His scent was all Cage but with an added metallic tinge because of his sweat. She stared at his tattooed chest, which seemed to be pumped up more than normal. She caught herself before she licked her dry lips. Her order of "turn around" came out breathless.

*Fuck.* That wasn't too obvious. Nor were her pebbled nipples. She wore a snug camisole and she didn't even need to look to know they were standing at attention. Begging for *his* attention.

Cage studied her face for a couple seconds before dropping his gaze right to the evidence. His lips moved slightly, not quite into a smile but close, as he took his time turning around. It was easier for her to check him when he wasn't staring down at her when she did so.

"Do they hurt at all now?" *Damn it,* why was she whispering? And why were her fingers trembling?

He shook his head and she became mesmerized by a heavy bead of sweat dripping off his hair and rolling down his spine until it landed in the small of his back and was absorbed by the damp elastic waistband hanging low on his hips.

When she placed her fingers along his ribs where they'd been cracked, the shock of the current between them made her want to rip her hand away in self-preservation. She sucked in a breath and pushed forward.

"Jem..."

*God*, every freaking time he said her name like that...

It was unfair. She didn't have a chance. She needed to be stronger. She'd held out this long...

She could do it.

She could make it.

Not much longer.

She cleared her throat in an attempt to get herself together and not fall down the deep and dangerous rabbit hole. "Not even a little?"

He slowly turned and as he did so, her fingers dragged along his hot, damp skin from his ribs to his gut, just like she was working wet clay on a pottery wheel.

His blue eyes were dark, his lips parted. "No."

She needed to resist.

*Resist.*

"Good," slipped from her. So, *so* good.

When he reached up to cup her face, she knocked his hand away and shoved both palms against his chest. He stumbled backward and landed hard against the wall with a grunt. His eyes went wide as she stalked toward him.

They quickly narrowed. "Not sure if I should be fuckin' scared or excited."

"Both," she answered. Because that was what she was feeling, too.

Excited for the moment, fear for the future.

This could fuck everything up.

This could derail her plans.

This was a bad, *bad* idea. But right now, she gave up the fight. Threw in the white towel.

She couldn't resist what was between them anymore.

Whatever it was.

Whether it was simply physical attraction, sexual tension, or more, she didn't want to know, she just wanted to feel.

She'd deal with whatever it brought afterward. After she got what she wanted. What he wanted.

Finally.

She grabbed his face and pulled him down, taking his lips, shoving her tongue inside to kiss him deeply. To claim his mouth.

Their groans merged as their tongues sparred.

He should stop her. One of them needed to keep their head on straight. One needed to recognize this wasn't a good idea.

It was no longer her.

So, it had to be him.

But he didn't stop her when her fingers slid into his hair, gripping firmly enough to keep his mouth where she wanted it, pulling sharply enough it knocked the bandana off his head and to the floor.

*Jesus*, he tasted too good. His mouth was like cool water in a searing hot desert. She craved it. She couldn't drink him down fast enough.

Her thirst wasn't quenched with just a kiss. She wanted more.

She wanted everything.

She just needed to hang onto her plan with her fingernails. No matter what happened, that couldn't change.

He tugged at her cami, yanking it from her shorts, but it was snug and now damp from his sweat, so she'd have to be peeled out of it.

He managed to do so, yanking it over her head, freeing

her breasts while breaking the kiss for only a moment, and dropping it to the floor. He took her mouth this time and his fingers found the button and zipper on her shorts. He undid them, his hands steady, unlike hers as she hung onto him tightly.

She wiggled her hips to help him shove her shorts and panties down as far as he could without separating their mouths. They were both panting now, like she had been his sparring partner. Even though they both struggled for breath, neither could stop tasting, licking, nibbling, searching.

Her nipples ached, her pussy twinged, especially when he drew his finger through her now slick folds. His soft growl filled her mouth and her breath stuttered.

"Need to fuckin' see you," he panted as soon as he twisted his head to break the connection of their lips.

His erection was hot and thick in his silky shorts, pressing against her lower belly. It flexed, begging to be released. "Need to fuck you," filled her ear.

Yes. She needed that, too.

His finger slid back and forth, teasing her, and she buried her face into his chest, sucking his salty skin with her lips and licking it with her tongue.

"Fuck, Jem," he whispered roughly. "Need this. Need you."

She sank her teeth into one tattooed pec and a deep groan bubbled up from his gut. She hooked her fingers into the waistband of his shorts, desperately wanting him naked, too. Being soaked with sweat, the light fabric clung to his skin and didn't cooperate as easily as she hoped.

She whimpered when his finger disappeared from her pussy and his hand from her hair to strip himself of his shorts. As soon as he did, she circled her fingers around his hard cock and stroked the delicate, velvety skin. She drew her thumb over the slick crown, then her fingers back down to the root.

"Fuck," he breathed.

He grabbed her wrist to halt her motion but didn't break her contact. He lifted her face to his with one thumb under her chin.

Her eyes slid to the side. To avoid the reality of what was about to happen.

"Look at me," Cage ordered softly. "Tell me you want this." He tilted his hips, so his cock fucked her fist once.

At this moment, there was nothing she wanted more. Tomorrow morning might be a different story.

Reason and need warred with each other. "Chris..."

He lowered his lips to hers and whispered, "Tell me."

*Good lord*, his husky voice alone could cause her to orgasm.

He lightly brushed his lips over hers and hers parted, encouraging him to take the kiss deeper.

"Wanna be inside you. You want me? Wanna feel me deep inside you?"

*Holy fuck*, yes.

Everything about him was intoxicating. Blurring her common sense.

"I need you inside me," she whispered.

"Fuck yeah, baby," he said on a sigh.

She swallowed those words, his breath, as she crushed her mouth against his again, driving him back against the wall again. Holding him there.

She couldn't get enough of him.

She needed more. She needed him now.

He gripped her ass and pulled her up. She went with him, practically climbing his solid body. His head tilted and he drove his tongue into her mouth while she clung to his shoulders and neck as he hauled her higher until her wet pussy pressed into his belly. Each pounding beat of her heart matched the throb in her pussy.

Nothing separated them now.

Not a damn thing.

Gripping the back of her thighs, he spun and pinned her to the wall. She wrapped her legs around his waist as he shifted her up slightly, until the crown of his cock pressed against her entrance, which had thrown out the welcome mat.

She should be thinking about the baby, not her father, but she couldn't pull her focus from him. He was right there.

Right there. The head of his cock nudging until it found the right spot.

"Jem," he grunted as he thrust upward and she sank a little lower to meet him.

He filled her, thick and hard, his breath harsh in her ear as he remained still for a moment, just letting them both breathe. Letting them both feel their connection.

Because it was undeniable.

She couldn't deny this felt right. Even though it shouldn't.

And they hadn't even moved yet.

"You fit me perfectly."

Did he say that or did she imagine it?

Even so, it was true.

With this, they fit. Outside of this, they didn't. They couldn't.

He lived a life she didn't want. A life she didn't want to remember.

She couldn't forget that.

She couldn't.

But when he began to move, she did.

Nothing in her world existed but him. Sex had never been like this with anyone. This instant, crazy connection she couldn't explain.

Like they were meant to be and that couldn't be right.

It was just the oxytocin flowing through her veins. Making her feel things more strongly than they should. A hormone released during intimacy. A hormone that created bonds.

Even when it shouldn't.

His fingers dug into her ass and thighs as he thrust upward with brute force and pulled her downward, slamming them together. The top of her back was pinned against the wall, helping hold her in place so he could fuck her as hard as he wanted to, as hard as she needed.

His eyes locked with hers. His dark and hooded. Each plunge accompanied by a primal-like grunt which made her gasp.

The movement, the sound.

He was right. So damn right. They fit like a lock and key. He used that key to unlock something from deep inside her. Something she didn't want escaping.

Like her own groan when he raked his teeth down her throat. When he sucked at the hollow of her neck. When his fingers separated her ass cheeks and the tip of his finger pressed a place she'd never given anyone.

Over and over, he pounded her into the wall.

"So fuckin' hot. So wet. You were fuckin' made for me, Jem."

No, no, she wasn't made for him. That was impossible.

Her arms tightened around his neck and she took his mouth again to shut him up. He instantly took control, shoving her tongue from his mouth and using his to plunder hers.

She let him.

Melting against him, she closed her eyes and let him do whatever he wanted. It was crazy, she'd never remembered giving any man this much control. She always had a finger on what and how it was happening. Always.

But he knew what he was doing and she simply let go. She let him sweep all thoughts away and, with her eyes closed, she concentrated on his movements, concentrated on the sounds coming deep from within his chest.

All of that took her there.

To that very edge. Faster than expected, especially in the position they were in, one she had never orgasmed from. But he was doing something with his hips to hit all the right spots, inside and out.

He ended the kiss once again and pressed his damp cheek to hers. "That's it, baby. Fuckin' feel you squeezin' my dick. So much better than I ever fuckin' imagined. Your pussy's a hot, slick fist, pullin' me in, demandin' more, not gettin' enough. Can feel how close you are. Just gotta let go. Just gotta give me you. Give it to me, Jem. Want it all."

For a second, she wanted to give him it all. All of her. Even more than that.

His hoarse words made a white, searing fire swirl through her and land in her core.

She was about to come.

No, not just come. Explode into so many pieces, she'd have trouble finding them again. Have trouble gluing herself back together afterward.

"Chris," she breathed. She moved one hand from the back of his neck into his hair and gripped a handful tightly. "Kiss me when I come."

Without hesitation, his mouth found hers again and he accepted her cry as she detonated around him like a Fourth of July fireworks grand finale. Sparks and heat flickered in her center as he continued to fuck her through the intense contractions.

How could he do this? How could he make it feel like this? Make *her* feel this way?

No matter how, he did it. Her head slammed back into the wall, her eyes opened and so did her mouth as a low wail rolled from her. He again buried his face in her neck and powered his cock up and into her, continuing to drive hard and deep.

Her thoughts were gone. Her vision unfocused. She was only aware of his body moving against hers, getting ready to rip another orgasm from her when the first one was hardly a memory.

And he did it. He achieved it when he thrust one more time, as if he was attempting to climb inside her, to become one with her. He shuddered and stilled, a low moan vibrating against the skin of her throat as he spilled inside her. The pulsations of his cock getting lost amongst her own as she came a second time.

She closed her eyes again and simply breathed as the aftershocks rocked them both. Reminded them of what just happened.

What the two of them created.

Sex had always been simple for her.

What just happened was far from that.

It was complex and complicated.

And troublesome.

He didn't let her go, even after he slipped from her when he no longer had a choice. He kept holding her, his face hidden in her neck, his warm breath beating a rapid pattern against her skin. Hers doing the same.

"Fuck!"

The sharp jerk of his body and the unexpected outburst startled her from her euphoria.

Well, that ruined the moment and brought her back to reality. "Are you worried about Judge finding out? I won't tell him. Don't worry."

"Jem..." He pulled his face back so he could look directly into hers as he let her slide down both his body and the wall until she stood on her own feet.

She blinked and frowned when a trickle of cum slid

from her and dampened her inner thigh at the same time he said, "No goddamn wrap."

She blinked again and let the words swirl in her muddled brain until she understood what he just said.

*Holy shit.*

She wasn't worried about pregnancy, but all the rest...

She had no idea how many women he'd slept with since Sarah. Or even in the last year.

She could count her own number on one hand.

She bet he'd lost count.

*Holy fucking shit.*

They had both lost themselves in the moment and became careless.

He pulled away from her and grabbed his shorts, jerking them up his legs, clearly agitated.

"Fuck," he bit out again, raking his fingers through his damp and already disheveled hair.

She grabbed a discarded T-shirt hanging over a weight bar. She had no idea whose and didn't care. She only knew it would cover her quickly and enough to get back to the trailer without streaking out in the open. She plucked her clothes from the floor and balled them to her tight chest, struggling to breathe.

Without looking at him, she pushed past him and rushed out the open door.

They'd had sex with the door open.

They'd had unprotected sex.

They'd had sex.

What she'd been trying to avoid for weeks.

She fucked up.

He fucked up.

They both fucked up royally.

"Jem!" she heard him shout from inside the shed.

She ignored him and ran the short distance to the trailer.

When she burst through the front door, she realized, in her panic, she left Dyna behind.

It was okay.

It was okay.

Her father was with her.

Cage was with her.

She needed to get into the shower to scrub off what just happened.

Not Cage. Not his sweat. Not his scent. Not even his cum. No.

But she needed to purge everything else that had bubbled up.

The desire. The need. The want.

All of it.

Because it was all dangerous. It threatened her escape.

And she needed to stick to her plan. No matter what.

He wasn't a random.

He wasn't a casual partner.

He wasn't someone steady.

She had no idea what would come from this.

Nothing could come from this, she reminded herself. She couldn't get lost in what just happened. She couldn't lose her way.

She couldn't forget what this place, what this club reminded her of.

She also couldn't forget herself. Her dreams. Her goals. Her career.

None of those things were in this shed, on this farm, in this town.

Or in his bed.

None.

## Chapter Seventeen

Cage carried his daughter into the quiet trailer. His lips flattened into a hard line when he noticed Jemma's bedroom door closed. A dampness, as well as the scent of her soap, hung in the air as he moved into the kitchen and put Dyna in her bouncer while he made her a bottle.

So, Jemma had run inside and showered, washing away everything from him on and in her. His touch, his sweat, his cum.

Now she was avoiding him.

Even though he needed a smoke badly—maybe even a few puffs off a joint—he fed Dyna, changed her diaper and put her down in the used crib he finally could afford last week. It took up a whole corner of his bedroom.

He needed to get serious about finding a permanent residence where he could set up her own room and have an extra room for a house mouse. Because after tonight, he was sure Jemma would find a quick way out the front door.

"'Night, monkey," he whispered as he kissed his daughter's forehead, fingers and toes. He stood staring down at Dyna until her eyelids became heavy. She fought falling asleep but, with a full belly, sleep won out.

*Thank fuck.*

He shucked his shorts and boxer briefs, threw them into a basket in the laundry room and headed into the bathroom, not caring he was completely naked.

He scrubbed off the sweat dried onto his skin, and regretfully washed away the result of Jemma's orgasm from his dick and balls, toweled his hair dry as best he could and yanked on a clean pair of boxer briefs.

Fuck the jeans or shorts. She'd seen him naked anyhow.

He went back out to the kitchen, pulled a beer from the fridge and downed half the bottle while staring at her closed bedroom door.

Debating what he should do.

She might not realize it but this wasn't over.

None of this was over.

Not even close.

He'd tolerated her dancing around him after what happened between them in the rain. He'd done his best to be patient.

But his patience was gone. He was done.

He wasn't going to let her shut him out. Not after what just happened in the shed.

No fucking way.

He hadn't been with another woman in over six fucking weeks. Not because he didn't want to, but because the minute he laid eyes on Jemma he knew what—or who— he wanted.

So, he waited.

He closed his eyes as he replayed what just happened in his head.

It was so worth the goddamn wait.

Even though he screwed up, lost his head and fucked her without a wrap.

He didn't need another fucking kid right now. Dyna was more than he could handle on his own. And, unlike his mother, he was determined to do it right. Adding another unplanned baby would make things more difficult.

Even if it was Jemma's.

And he was pretty sure, he wouldn't live to see that baby born, anyway. Judge would make sure of that. The enforcer wouldn't shake Cage's hand and congratulate him for knocking up the man's sister.

Fuck no.

That previous blanket party would be like a toddler's birthday celebration in comparison to what Judge, and maybe Deacon, would do to him.

If Jemma wanted to be with him, he'd need to approach those two first. It was only courtesy. Especially since she was club property.

She wasn't some woman not connected to the club. She wasn't a sweet butt. *Hell*, she wasn't even an Amish chick.

She was the daughter of an Original. She was Judge's goddamn blood.

While brotherhood was important in an MC, blood was, too.

Fucking the sergeant at arms' sister and getting her pregnant could be looked upon as disrespecting both his brotherhood and her family.

If she wanted it, he'd be willing to run out and get her a morning-after pill, just to be safe. He doubted she wanted to be tied to him permanently and having his kid would do that. But to figure out what their next step should be, she needed to be willing to talk to him.

And, anyway, she had come out to the shed for a reason. That reason got derailed when she slammed him against the wall.

"Fuck," he muttered, combing his damp hair back from his face with his fingers. He tipped the bottle to his lips and downed the remainder, letting the cool beer slide down his throat into his churning gut.

He waited a few more minutes to let the alcohol seep into his bloodstream, to help keep him calm because he anticipated a battle.

He tossed the bottle into the trashcan, took a breath, focused on her door and strode the eleven feet to her bedroom.

He listened.

Nothing.

"Jem..." He softly rapped on the door with a knuckle.

He waited. No answer.

"Jem. You had somethin' to tell me. Guessin' it was important." It had to be for her to search him out. He only hoped whatever it was would get her to open the door and talk to him.

"Jem, come out and talk to me or I'm kickin' in the fuckin' door." He grimaced at his demand. Jemma wasn't a woman who'd put up with any kind of bullshit and forcing her to do something was the kind of bullshit she wouldn't tolerate.

He heard soft footsteps, then the door cracked open. "You can't afford to fix it."

Right.

She knew how to stab him right in the fucking chest.

He expected a battle and she was willing to give him one.

He could only see a few inches of her in the gap. She was wearing the oversized T-shirt she slept in. Her long legs were bare. Her brown hair was pulled up in some sort of sloppy knot. Probably from her shower.

When she rid herself of him.

"Can I come in?"

She blinked at him through the three-inch space between the door and the frame. "It's not a good idea."

"Had somethin' to tell me, Jem. Wanna hear it."

"I—"

"Not from a fuckin' gap in the door. You don't want me in, come out and talk to me."

The door opened wider and he let his eyes roam from her loose hair tucked into a hairband at the top of her head, down her pale face and over that damn T-shirt. One that probably had belonged to another man.

He wanted to fucking burn it.

If she wanted to sleep in a man's tee, it should be his.

He ground his teeth so he wouldn't spout that out like an asshole. It wouldn't help the situation if he acted possessive.

Though, he wanted to. *Fuck*, he wanted to.

He wanted to throw her over his shoulder and march her right into his bedroom and make her sleep naked next to him. Where he could touch her, smell her, make her his.

It was where she belonged.

She just didn't realize it yet.

But he was tired of being patient. Especially now that he'd had her. All that did was cement the idea that they belonged together.

She fit him.

And not just during sex.

She waited until he took a couple steps back before stepping out and closing the bedroom door behind her.

Why? He had no idea. He normally stayed out of her room. He let her have her own space, even as small as it was.

She moved to the center of the living room and turned to face him. The living room and kitchen were always a neutral space for them.

The worn cotton of that fucking T-shirt pinched at her hips when she planted her hands there and also emphasized she wore no bra.

No surprise, her guard was up.

Which raised his.

"Got somethin' to say but you had somethin' to tell me when you came out to the shed. Wanna hear that first."

"Dyna okay?"

"She's sleepin'."

Jemma nodded. "It's about her."

His brow dropped low. "What about her?" Did he miss something? Did he suck at being a dad so much that he'd missed something wrong with his baby girl?

"I was offered an interview and I accepted it. I'll need you to find someone to watch Dyna on Thursday. Or you need to stay home. I'm not sure how long I'll be, but I do know I'll be gone for hours."

"Hours," he echoed, plugging a hand on his own hip, letting his mind flip through his mental Rolodex of people who might be able to watch Dyna.

"Yes. It's in Williamsport. It's a good job and I don't want to miss this opportunity."

"Saylor can probably watch her for a few hours. Talk to Judge."

She shook her head. "*You* talk to Judge. She's *your* daughter and *your* responsibility and I told you to prepare for when I leave, Chris." Her voice rose higher as she talked. "I haven't seen you doing that. You act like I'm going to stay. I'm not. I told you I wasn't and that hasn't changed."

"Jesus fuck, Jemma," he muttered, his blood pressure surging.

"Yeah. *Jesus fuck*, Chris. You knew this was only temporary until I got a decent job offer. I've been clear about that from the beginning. If I get this offer, I'm taking it. If another good offer comes in beforehand, I'm taking that. The sooner, the better. I need to work, pay my bills and get out of this town."

*Get away from you*, he heard in his head.

She flapped a hand in the direction of the shed. "What happened out there hasn't changed anything and won't."

"Jem, about that..."

"I don't want to talk about it."

*Fucking goddamn it.* "Don't gotta except for that one thing. Don't need to fuck up again, Jem. Can't afford it."

Her face became unreadable. "While we fucked up, we didn't *fuck up*."

His eyebrows fused together. "What does that fuckin' mean?"

She sucked in a breath through her nostrils, raised her chin and her eyes held his. "I've been on birth control since I was a teen, Chris. Unlike an Amish woman, I've been sexually active for a long time now."

He grimaced and swiped a hand down his bearded cheek.

"Pregnancy isn't my worry."

Maybe it wasn't hers, but it was his main one. If she worried about catching something from him... "Always wear a wrap."

"Yeah, well, you see how that worked out for you."

He ground his teeth. "Jem, haven't had sex with anyone since..."

"Since?"

Did she hold her breath after asking that? Would it bother her if he had sex with someone else since Jemma had come into his life? That gave him a sliver of hope. "Dyna showed up."

"No one?" Her mask slipped in her surprise.

*Fuck yeah.*

Her response fueled his fire to get her to admit the connection they had. He needed to prove to her he only had one woman in his sights, one woman he wanted, and it was her. And it had nothing to do with Dyna. "No one, Jem. Just you, just now. That's it."

"Still doesn't mean..."

"Yeah. Got that. Never had an STD."

"Me neither and I'd like to keep it that way."

"Jem…"

She lifted a hand. "It was my fault, not yours. I take full responsibility. I lost my head—"

He grinned which abruptly halted her spiel. Unfortunately, he couldn't help it. She admitted he'd made her lose her head.

Just like she made him do.

She needed to stop fighting what was between them and see they fit. More than just with sex. She knew the lifestyle, even though she hated it. But she only needed to open her eyes, and her mind, and see the current Blood Fury was nothing like the Originals.

Trip, and everyone else, was working hard to keep it that way.

If she let him, Cage would do what he could to help her get past what happened to her when she was a young child. He understood it because he lived it, too.

Any offspring from the Originals had to get over their rough beginnings and see the current Blood Fury for what it was.

Their future and their family.

She needed to see it was a good thing Trip had rebuilt. He had learned from Buck's mistakes and was doing everything he could to not repeat them. The prez wanted a solid brotherhood and not one with so many fucking holes punched through it, it looked like Swiss cheese.

But time would show her that, not his words. Right now he needed to concentrate on convincing her to accept him first. Then he could work on her accepting the Fury. Because the fuck if he was giving up his brotherhood. Not unless he was forced to by being stripped of his colors and he would do everything in his power not to have that happen.

He took two steps toward her, close enough to detect the

scent of her shampoo but not enough to cause her to step back. Though, her spine straightened just slightly.

Right now he needed to lay shit out and be crystal fucking clear about what he wanted.

Which was her.

"You do shit to me, Jem, no other woman has ever done before. And it's got nothin' to do with sex. Tonight proved it. I fuckin' waited. Six fuckin' weeks I've been with no one but you. I knew you wanted me as much as I wanted you. Could see it. But I waited anyway. Wasn't gonna push it. Didn't wanna be blamed for pushin' you. You took the first step tonight. It was hot as fuck. Being inside you was like nothin' else I've ever experienced. Waited for you to be ready. Never been so fuckin' patient in my whole goddamn life."

"What happened doesn't change things, Chris."

The fuck it didn't. As he had been speaking, a flush ran from the neckline of her T-shirt up into her cheeks. If she needed more patience from him, he'd give it to her, but that didn't mean backing off.

He didn't have a lot of time before she ran out the door and left him and Dyna behind.

"Don't gotta change shit. We live under the same roof, share the same space, what's the difference if we share the same bed?"

"That's a huge difference, Chris. One is a roommate, the other..." Her words ended in a soft hiss.

"Nobody gotta know you're in my bed. Ain't gonna say shit to anyone. But I want you there, Jemma. You wanna deny what's between us, but deep down you can't. You think I wanna chase someone who's got one foot out the fuckin' door? You think I wanna beg the one person who my daughter thinks of as her momma?"

She squeezed her eyes shut and whispered, "This isn't about Dyna."

"No, it ain't about Dyna, Jem. It's about me and you. What you do to me. What I do to you. Simple as that."

"It isn't simple."

"Could be. You're refusin' to see it."

"I can't get invested here, Chris. I can't. Not in Manning Grove, not with this club, not with you. I told you what coming home does to me. It'll be hard enough when I leave Dyna behind."

"Love my girl."

Her green eyes locked with his and the agony he saw in them shocked him to the core.

"Yes."

"Baby, love that you love my girl as your own. Love that you love her despite that she came from me."

If he was ripping himself open, he wasn't doing it half-assed. Just like he didn't want to raise his baby half-assed.

Both his girls deserved better than that.

"There's nothing wrong with you, Chris," she whispered. "I barely knew you when we were Fury kids, but I know you now. I didn't know you in the time between. What you did, how you acted. But I also know what shaped you. I know what shaped me. So I'm sure, however you were, whatever you did, our childhood had something to do with it. The Originals affected us all. Some more than others."

"You can move past it, Jem. We all gotta move past it. Every fuckin' one of us. Trip, Sig, Judge, Rook, Stella, me... You."

"I wish I could, but it's not that easy. Anyway, it's more than that."

"Right. Can't offer you much. Don't got a home, no money, don't got shit besides this brotherhood, my job and my baby girl. But I want you. Even if it's just 'til you leave. Just give me that, Jem. However long that is. And I'll give you what I got to give. Which is me. That's it. That's what I can give you for as long as you want me. When you leave, ain't gonna stop you. I know you want better for your life than what I can offer you. Know it. Feel it. Want whatever's best for you. Just like I want whatever's best for Dyna. You saved my ass, Jem. Wish I had a way to repay you for that."

Never in his goddamn life had he ever thought he'd want a woman so much it fucking hurt. But in the last six fucking weeks, he'd watched Jemma. How she sacrificed to help him and Dyna by suffering with nightmares simply spurred from coming home, how she could've left at any time, but stayed anyway.

How she loved his baby girl like her own.

He was unlucky she would leave as soon as she could, but he was lucky that they had her for the time she'd given them.

She'd helped him become a better father when he was floundering. Calmed him when he was panicked. Patiently taught him when he had no clue what the fuck he was doing.

When he was afraid he'd hurt Dyna, she assured him his daughter wasn't breakable. When he did something wrong, Jemma showed him how to do it right. When he was overwhelmed, she stepped in.

He could now do it without her.

But he didn't want to.

In those six weeks, the three of them had become a little family. She wanted to rip that family apart.

He would do his best to keep that from happening. "Jem..."

She hadn't said a word and that worried him.

He dropped his head, stared at his bare feet and pinned his clenched fists to his side. Her hand crossed his line of vision and planted on his chest. Solid and warm.

"Even if you could repay me, I'd never accept it."

He covered her hand with his own and lifted his head.

"I came home for Judge. I fell in love with Dyna. And now..."

He waited, his heart thundering like a bass drum beneath her palm.

Her chest rose and fell slowly under her baggy T-shirt. "And now... I need to move on."

Yeah, she knew how to wield that fucking knife. "Feel nothin' for me, Jem?"

Her mouth opened and a rush of air escaped. "Sure. I have no doubt you'll be a great dad. You *are* a great dad already, Chris. You'll be fine without me."

"Not what I meant."

"I know what you meant. But that's my answer."

"Won't admit that your heart's beatin' so hard right now I can see it poundin' in your throat. Wanna feel that with my mouth, my tongue, Jem. Want to spread you wide on my bed and bury my face between your thighs. Wanna taste you. Kiss you. Make you come like you did that night in the rain, against the wall in the shed. Wanna give you new memories to chase out the old."

"You think you can do that," she breathed.

He shifted even closer, keeping her hand trapped against his chest. "Know I can. But you gotta give me that chance. You need to remember the good times. With your real family, not Ox and Trixie. In your aunt and uncle's home, not at the warehouse. The time you had with Walt. With Lottie. With your brother and cousin. And now here with me. With Dyna. Here you're surrounded by family who will love and protect you better than Ox and Trixie or any of the Originals ever fuckin' did."

"I don't do casual."

She kept looking for a goddamn excuse to push him away. To protect herself.

"Nobody said shit about casual."

"It can't be anything more."

"The fuck it can't. You just won't let it."

"Not won't, Chris. Can't."

"Bull-fuckin-shit. Jem, you're strong as fuck. You ain't scared of shit."

"I'm scared of this."

"Yeah, well... you ain't the only one. But I wanna try. Just need you to try, too."

"I'm not sure what you're asking of me."

She fucking knew. But he'd give her that. For now. "Just give me a chance 'til you get a job offer. That's all I'm askin'."

"Judge..."

*Fuck Judge.* He managed to bite that back. "Ain't gonna tell him shit. What we do's our fuckin' business. This way when," *if,* "you go, there won't be any shit from them. We go on livin' our life like it never happened." *Lies.* "No harm. No foul." *More lies.* He squeezed her hand. "Now, I'm done askin', now you gotta answer."

Silence stretched between them. And he waited. He wouldn't say anything else. It had to be her decision on where they took it from here.

Though, *for fuck's sake,* the wait was killing him.

She didn't avoid his gaze, she kept her eyes locked on his. And he heard a clock ticking loudly in his head.

*Tick... tick... tick...*

Five seconds. Ten seconds. Thirty seconds.

If she turned him away, he was done. He never begged a woman for shit. He never would again. He wanted Jemma but he also wanted to keep his fucking pride. If she said no, she would damage it, but he'd live.

He had a baby girl to take care of, to provide for, he'd concentrate on that. Dyna would become the center of his fucking world.

His sole purpose for moving forward.

For being better. For doing better.

For staying out of jail. For getting the fuck up and going to work every day. For keeping patch whores out of his bed. For staying out of fights.

For no longer taking advantage of an innocent virgin. Especially one who didn't know any better. Who got caught up in a moment that created a lifetime obligation.

He'd promise his daughter he could be better for her. But if it was up to him, if she let it, he'd do it for Jemma, too.

They both belonged to him. His to protect, his to care for.

*His.*

A pressure built in his chest and caused an ache only Jemma could cure.

*Tick... tick... tick...*

One minute...

He couldn't take much more.

She deflated before his eyes. The air releasing from a balloon. All the tension held within her shoulders disappeared.

She continued to stare at him but said nothing.

"Say somethin', Jem." *Fuckin' anythin', just put me out of my fuckin' misery.*

"I..."

He hung on that one single fucking letter.

"I..."

*Jesus fuck.*

"I'll give it to you until I leave."

He blinked. *What?* He wanted it so badly, he imagined it, right? "What?"

"Until I leave. You have until then."

In truth, he wasn't expecting her to agree. He expected her to fight it until the very end. She was Ox's daughter, she had his stubborn blood running through her veins.

But she was giving him a chance, which to him meant he got his chance to convince her to stay. That's what he wanted. He just wanted her to give him that opportunity.

Now he had it, he couldn't fuck it up.

289

# Chapter Eighteen

THE BELL above the door jingled when Teddy held it open for her. Jemma maneuvered the stroller out onto the sidewalk in front of Manes on Main. The hairdresser with a flair for the dramatic followed her out.

"Goodbye, girlfriend." He leaned in with a smile to air kiss both of her cheeks. He then did the same to Dyna, causing the baby to release a happy gurgle. "Bye, munchkin. So damn cute. She's making my ovaries explode."

Jemma laughed. Teddy was a trip and she'd had a blast the whole time she sat in his salon chair for her cut and blow out. He even gave her a few makeup pointers for her interview tomorrow.

The man was a town treasure, that was for sure.

She promised him that if she got the job in Williamsport, she'd become a permanent client. That got him wiggling his tush, doing a twirl and pretending to throw glitter up in the air.

He'd been great with Dyna, too. Very patient and understanding when Jemma had to take a quick break to give the baby a bottle.

And burp her.

And change her diaper.

But now with a fresh cut and style, Jemma was ready to slay her interview.

She pointed the stroller toward the municipal lot which was located across Main Street and two blocks down. She took her time walking back to the Volvo, enjoying the July sun on her face and the warmth in her bones. The light summer breeze helped keep it from being a sweltering day.

She smiled down at Dyna in her *Future Biker Babe* short-sleeved onesie.

Jemma had not only fallen for the baby girl in the stroller, but for the baby's father.

The last couple of mornings, waking up with Cage wrapped around her, proved it. The uncontrollable heat between them the last couple of nights proved it, too.

Sex had never been like that with any of her previous partners or boyfriends. Even though she'd had some spectacular sex before, with Cage, it was on another level.

It could only be chalked up to the crazy, unexplainable connection they shared.

The *weirdness* she didn't understand.

After fucking against the wall in the shed, she had run into the trailer to escape what they did, escape him, escape how that sex made her feel.

Which was scared.

Scared it would make her fall even deeper for Cage and she wouldn't be able to leave.

But he flayed himself open, made himself vulnerable, something she never expected a man, and a biker, like Cage to do. That speared her right in the heart. And the feelings for the man she'd been shoving down came bubbling back up.

As scared as she was to say yes, she found she couldn't say no.

Alfred Lord Tennyson once said, "'Tis better to have

loved and lost than never to have loved at all." Jemma looked at their situation as the poet did.

Cage knew she was leaving, he accepted it, so what could it hurt to give them both what they wanted? For whatever time left she had in Manning Grove, she'd allow herself to have Cage and for him to have her.

And, *damn*, did he know how to take what he wanted…

As soon as she'd agreed, he grabbed the baby monitor off the counter bar and tossed it at her without warning. As she instinctively caught it, he rushed over and knocked the wind out of her when he threw her over his shoulder. She muffled her squeal as he barreled into her room only a few steps away.

He fell to the bed with her and, on his hands and knees, caged her beneath him. His longish hair fell free and curtained his face.

"Your ribs!" she scolded.

"They're fine." He gave her a panty-melting, crooked grin. "We're fuckin' in here, then sleepin' in my bed after."

His growled demands caused fire to flicker all the way to her very core. "I can sleep in my own bed."

Did she want to sleep in his bed next to him? Yes.

But did she still need to protect herself? Also yes.

"Fuck that. Takin' the time you're givin' me and makin' the most of it."

He smothered her response with a long, deep, toe-curling kiss. By the time he was done, she'd forgotten what they'd been talking about.

Now on the sidewalk, she gasped softly as the memory overtook her. Her breathing shallowed, her pussy clenched, her fingers tightly clutched the stroller's handles in an attempt to keep herself grounded in the here and now.

It became impossible.

Lost in that night, she came to a complete stop in the

middle of the sidewalk and let that memory sweep her away.

The way he claimed her lips. How he controlled her breathing, her heartbeat, with every single touch, with every kiss, with every stroke of his tongue.

He yanked her old T-shirt over her head and tossed it behind him. After peeling her panties down her legs, he stood and removed his own briefs.

She rose onto her elbows to watch him, his cock long and hard, flexing within his own fingers as he stared at her naked on the bed, and fisted himself slowly.

His blue eyes had darkened but remained readable.

Very, very readable.

She knew exactly what he wanted. She didn't bother to hide exactly what she wanted, either.

If they were only going to share a short time together, no games could be played. He was right. They needed to make the most of it.

"Show me," was all he had to say to cause her flesh to goosebump.

Their eyes held for a long moment as he stood naked at the end of her bed. She tucked two pillows under her shoulders so she could watch him. The same way he watched her.

She slowly dragged the soles of her feet along the bedspread until her knees were bent.

He held her eyes until she separated her legs. Then he honed in on her center, where her arousal began to build. She didn't need to touch herself to find how slick she'd become, but she did it anyway.

She drew a finger through her folds, from the bottom to the top, only brushing lightly over her hard, swollen clit.

Her breath stuttered as she remembered how intense the orgasm was when they were in the shed and wondered if this time it would be the same. Or would it be even better since they were in an actual bed with more freedom to move?

"Again," came from him. Thick, coarse.

His chest pumped at the same pace as his fist. The overhead light caught the gleam of the bead of precum clinging to the very tip and she waited for it to fall like a spider from its web.

His cum was already deep inside her, what she couldn't wash away. That thought shouldn't turn her on, but it did. That thought should worry her, but it didn't.

Even on birth control, the only time she'd had sex without a condom was if the relationship lasted longer than six months.

Their time together had only been six weeks. And most of that time, they simply existed in the same space for the same reason.

His daughter.

But the idea of him spilling inside her again, filling her with his cum, had her touching herself more frantically and with purpose. No longer as a tease, but a means to an end.

The small of her back bowed off the bed as she slipped two fingers inside, coating them with her own natural lubricant as she worked them in and out. When a noise caught at the back of his throat, her eyes flicked up from where he pumped his fist.

His eyelids were heavy, his lips parted, his nostrils flared just slightly. "Wanna watch you come, then I'm gonna taste it before I make you come again."

She forced her eyes to remain open and on his, even though her head rolled back as she worked her fingers all the way in, all the way out.

She slipped her other hand over her chest, her breasts, her peaked nipples and down her belly until she reached her target.

Her clit.

With two fingers pumping inside her, she used two more to stimulate her sensitive hard nub. When his tongue swept over his lower lip, she imagined the fingers circling and pressing were his tongue instead.

She only hoped he'd be able to hold out, so she could feel it for real.

"Jem." Her name came out like a lion's deep huff. Maybe a warning he was at his limits. "Come for me."

With him watching her touch herself, with him touching himself, too, it wouldn't take much longer.

She tried to swallow, but her throat seized. The pressure in her lower belly increased. And then it overwhelmed her.

Starting at her toes, the climax worked its way up her legs to land in her center and rock her as she came. Her cry filled the space between them.

Then he filled that space with him.

Before the aftershocks of her orgasm were even over, he slowly climbed back on the bed, trailing his fingers from her toes, up her calves, over her knees, and inside her thighs. He paused before touching her center and she caught herself panting in anticipation as she moved her hands away.

Giving herself over to him.

He dipped his head, his warm breath sweeping over her swollen, sensitized flesh.

"Please..."

She was surprised to find that came from her. She rarely begged anyone for anything, especially when it came to sex. But she was dying for his touch. To feel his mouth on her.

Many nights she imagined what that would feel like and now she would know.

If he'd hurry up.

"Chris..."

She glanced down her body and his head was low enough between her thighs she could only see the upper part of his nose and his eyes. He watched her, waiting.

"You want me to beg." Again, a surprise.

"What do you want, Jem? Tell me." The raspiness of his voice was like the brush of sandpaper along her heated skin.

"Make me come." She made it more of a demand than an ask. She was stubborn like that.

"You just did."

"*You* make me come."

"With my mouth or my dick?"

"Both," she breathed. *Oh God yes, both.*

The tip of his tongue flicked out and touched her clit so softly, it was like butterfly wings flapping gently against her.

She groaned. He was such a tease.

That was okay. She'd get him back. Maybe not tonight, but in the near future.

Before she left.

They still had days, if not a couple of weeks or so to explore each other's every inch, every desire, every sexual need.

Her thoughts floated away when he was no longer gentle.

He ravaged her pussy with his mouth. Licking, sucking, fucking. With his lips, his fingers, his tongue.

Every time her eyelids would drift close so she could simply concentrate on what he was doing, she forced them back open to see him watching her.

Studying her reactions.

Reading her body.

Learning.

He was very fucking observant.

That was good.

And it could be bad.

Great for sex.

Not so great for protecting herself. To prevent the fall that could wound her. Break her heart.

He sucked each labia into his mouth and when he was

done tasting those, he stroked the tip of his tongue up the slit and drove his fingers inside. Planting his lips on her clit, he sucked hard and stayed with her when her hips bucked wildly.

Then he stopped.

Simply stopped before she reached the precipice.

He shifted slightly, releasing her clit, slipping his two long fingers from inside her. He dipped his pinky, instead.

What was he doing? Why was he doing that?

A pinky wasn't enough for her to orgasm.

Was he trying to torture her?

Seconds later the pinky was gone from her pussy and pressed to a place she wasn't expecting.

No...

No one had done this to her before. No one ever asked or dared.

He wasn't asking.

He was daring.

His order to "relax" came muffled. Because his mouth was full. Of her.

Her hips jerked when his two fingers resumed their place inside her and his skilled mouth clamped onto her clit once more.

He worked her up again, slowly drawing those fingers in and out while his mouth did its magic. Driving her toward her destination on a one-way ticket.

Every plunge was a step closer to the abyss, where she went willingly, wanting to take that leap, to completely free fall.

He worked his pinky, pressing, circling, urging her to let him in.

"Chris," she groaned.

He pressed harder. Biding his time. Waiting for her to unlock that door.

To invite him inside.

Whatever he was doing...

She couldn't take anymore.

She wanted him.

Everywhere.

She forced herself to relax and hissed out a, "Yes."

He took his time, almost too slowly, breaking the plane with the tip of his pinky. Working it, stimulating all the nerves found in that area.

*Oh God*, it felt different, but good. She wanted more.

"Please..."

He sank his pinky in to the middle joint and she gasped. It was nothing like what his cock would feel like in the same area. She knew to accept him there like that would take time. And effort.

But, *holy hell*...

Finally, he was completely inside her. Two fingers deep in her pussy and the other in her ass.

He worked her with skill and patience. His groan against her pussy drove her hips up. She wanted more.

She wanted it faster.

She wanted to come.

She wanted him filling her up with his cock, driving her beyond sanity to the point where she'd lose her mind.

She gave in to the movements of his mouth and fingers. Along with the sounds that came from him. Like he hadn't tasted anything that good in his life.

Her breath caught and her hips shot up... "I'm coming."

He said nothing, nor did he slow his pace. He continued until the orgasm hit her so intensely, she dislodged him herself.

Seconds later when she hadn't even landed from her free fall, he moved quickly, flipping her over onto her belly, covering her body with his, pinning her hands to the bed with their fingers interlaced.

Was he going to try...?

No.

Air escaped her lungs as he slid easily inside her. His hips beat a hard rhythm against her ass as he pounded her, driving as deep as he could.

"Gonna fill you up, Jem," he growled in her ear. "With me. Gonna still be inside you tomorrow mornin'. When I think of me inside you, gonna get hard all over again. Will wanna come home and fill you up some more."

*Jesus.*

She'd be thinking about that all day tomorrow. Until he came home and did what he said.

She had no idea how she'd survive the day. How she'd survive the wait.

He kneed her thighs open even wider, adjusted his angle, and rasped, "Tip your ass."

She did and his hand snaked between her and the mattress, finding her clit, finding their connection, as he powered forward. Sending her to the edge of madness before reining her in sharply by sinking his teeth into the tender spot where her shoulder and neck met. The bite. The deep grunts. The relentless plunge of his cock. It all continued until his body hiccuped, he ground deep and spilled inside her with a guttural grunt.

Wrenching another orgasm from her, the intense pulses of her pussy and his cock blended together. She didn't know where one ended and the other began.

His teeth and hands held her in place as they both rode out their orgasms. Until every throb, every twitch, faded away.

*Fuck yes* whispered through her as she imagined him coating her inside. Marking her. Claiming her.

Even though that didn't—*couldn't*—really happen, it drew something from deep within her.

What she was desperately trying to avoid.

She knew sleeping with him would be dangerous. So, it

shouldn't be a surprise what having sex with him would invoke.

But she couldn't explore it. She needed to stay focused. She couldn't allow her future to become derailed simply due to a man.

No matter who he was.

She needed to remember, above all else, what he was. What he was a part of. Something he stepped back into willingly. Unlike her.

He unclamped his teeth from her flesh, licked the spot slowly, sensually, then whispered, "Want you to be my dessert after dinner every fuckin' night."

Yes, she wanted that, too.

For however long she had left here.

For the time they had left together, she reminded herself once more.

Only until then.

"Don't wanna move," he said softly, still draped heavily over her back.

She didn't want him to move, either. Not yet.

However, it was inevitable and she could only take his crushing weight for so long. Plus, physiology had proven their physical connection would be broken soon anyway.

"Fuck," he muttered when that happened, separating the two of them. He sighed and shifted his weight off her and rolled from the bed to his feet.

Unmoving, she only turned her head on the pillow to watch him, his hair disheveled more than normal, his cock slick from their combined cum and a flush from exertion flaring up his tattooed chest.

"Gonna clean up and bring you somethin', too. Don't move. Be back in a few."

He wasn't asking, he was telling. Normally that would bother her, but satisfaction caused a deep-seated laziness within her bones. She was in no rush to go anywhere.

A few minutes later he was back. Beads of water still clinging to the short, dark wiry hairs from which his now soft, but still impressive, cock was showcased.

In one hand he held a wet washcloth, in the other one of his T-shirts. "Roll over."

With a soft sigh, she did.

"Prefer you naked. But if you gotta wear somethin'..."

He tossed the cotton tee onto her belly. At first, she actually thought he'd toss the wet cloth on her belly, too, expecting her to clean herself up and was surprised when he did it himself by gently parting her thighs and wiping her clean.

She would head to the bathroom soon, anyway. Otherwise, Cage would be leaking from her all night. A reminder that, once again, they were relying on her birth control pill to not get her pregnant. She hoped to hell she wasn't playing Russian Roulette with any other possibilities.

He could say he wrapped it tight with every female he'd ever been with, but Dyna was proof of prophylactic failure.

Well, there went her afterglow from being sexually satisfied.

He didn't join her in bed, but instead, once again, told her they were sleeping in his.

She doubted the night would only be filled with sleep. It was early yet. And she had a feeling he wasn't done with her for the night.

Dyna would most likely wake a few times, too. Another good reason for her to sleep in her own bed.

When she told him that, he wasn't having any of it. She could force the issue, but decided it wasn't worth it. And, *for fuck's sake*, she wanted to curl up next to him and sleep. To feel his presence within arm's reach.

To maybe even spoon.

Again, she reminded herself, for only as long as she stayed in Manning Grove.

She tugged his shirt over her head and let the worn cotton fall around her. His cum was planted deep, his scent encompassed her.

He was claiming ownership inside and out.

*It's only temporary. Let him have this.*

*Let yourself have this. It isn't forever.*

On their way out of her bedroom, he snagged the old Rolling Stones T-shirt she'd been wearing previously and balled it within his fist.

"What are you doing with that? It's my favorite."

"Burnin' the fuckin' thing. You pick any of my shirts to wear. Whatever it is will be your new favorite."

She glanced down at the one he'd picked for her. She wondered how much thought he'd put into it, if any at all. The shirt she wore only covered her to the top of her thighs, but on the front it read *Life Behind Bars* with a skeleton torso behind the handlebars of a motorcycle.

Yeah, she wasn't sure if he thought that one through. Ox would've spent life behind bars if he hadn't been killed in prison. Another reminder of why she had no desire to be a part of this, or any, club. Why she worried for Judge and Deacon.

Now, even Ry.

Her only hope for her nephew was that he'd continue on his current path, just like Jemma planned to continue on with hers.

If Cage insisted on her wearing one of his shirts to bed, she'd pick out a different one in the morning. Tonight she'd ignore that play on words.

Tonight...

Jemma started as she was pulled from her memory and returned to the present. To her current reality.

Brush burn on her inner thighs from his beard. Soreness in places that hadn't been sore in a long time. And not because she hadn't had a sexual partner in a while, but because she hadn't had one like Cage, who was trying to cram it all in in a short amount of time.

She somehow made it back to the municipal lot with both her and Dyna in one piece. How? She had no idea. But her panties were now soaked from reliving the other night.

Maybe she could talk Cage into coming home at lunchtime for a quickie. If not, she might have to take Dyna home, settle her down for a nap and do a little self-service to tide her over until he walked through the trailer door.

Dinner might be delayed.

Dessert before dinner sounded like a plan she could get onboard with. She doubted Cage would complain.

At the back corner of the municipal lot, she'd parked the Volvo under the shade of a tree. While it was the farthest spot from Main Street, she didn't mind walking the extra steps. In Pennsylvania, summer days could be unbearable with the heat and humidity, but today was bearable. Pleasant, actually.

Things were looking up. Her hair, her interview...

All the orgasmic sex she was having with Cage...

She parked the stroller, unlocked the doors, leaned in and started the engine to blast the A/C to chase out the heat. She steered the stroller to the rear door on the passenger side, buckled in Dyna and the car seat, and left the door open since the interior was still too stifling to close her in.

She moved to the rear hatch, powered it open, collapsed the stroller and loaded it into the back storage area. Before she could close the back, a crunch of stones on blacktop came from behind her. That wasn't the last thing she heard.

Hell no.

That was, "You took what was ours. Now gonna take what's yours."

The bright July sky suddenly went dark. And everything in her world around her disappeared.

# Chapter Nineteen

JEMMA BREATHED.

Breathed again.

Her head throbbed so painfully, she was having a diffi-cult time catching her breath.

Beneath her, the hot blacktop burned her skin, even under her clothes.

She needed to move. To get up. To figure out what the hell just happened.

She had heard a voice and then nothing. Everything went black.

Did she get hit by a car? Was she mugged?

She had no idea.

With a groan, she forced open her eyes, and a trickle at the back of her scalp had her pressing her fingers there. Warm liquid. Tenderness. Sharp pain. A possible gash.

Holding her fingers in front of her face, she saw what she suspected.

Blood.

She had been struck from behind.

She heard the crunch of stones on the pavement again.

*Fuck!*

This time it wasn't from feet, it was from tires.

A door opened.

More crunching but now under heavy footsteps.

*Shit.*

The gash on the back of her head began to throb as fast as her racing heartbeat.

A squawk and a voice came over a radio nearby.

*Fuck.*

Cops.

She forced herself to her hands and knees, the tiny stones digging into her palms. Her head pounded and began to spin, her knees wobbled weakly, but, by grabbing the rear bumper of the Volvo she managed to pull herself to her feet. Blood trickled faster under her hair.

She wondered how bad the gash was and if it would need stitches.

Stitches or not, she had a situation to deal with first. One she was fuzzy about the details since someone had scrambled her brains with something a lot harder than a wire whisk.

Her first instinct was to ask the approaching cop for help. But that instinct was quickly squashed by an older memory. By a strict rule the Originals had lived by. A rule taught since birth.

Men in uniform weren't there to help.

The pigs were there to hurt. To harm. To steal children away.

To split up families by throwing them behind bars.

To point guns at innocent people.

"What happened? Were you attacked? Did someone hit you?" The voice was deep, calming.

Her vision was a bit blurry yet, and spots came and went. She blinked to try to clear them away. Unsuccessfully.

She took a couple of full breaths before answering

because she was trying not to panic. Trying to look natural. Like she had been a klutz or something.

She glanced at the dark-haired cop who wore a concerned expression. His steel blue eyes assessed her as she tried to focus on his name badge.

*A. BRYSON*

Didn't Teddy chatter on and on about his husband who was a local cop? Her brain was too muddled to remember his name. She swore his first name started with an A.

It didn't matter. She wasn't there to make friends. She needed to leave and take care of her wound. "No, I... I accidentally cracked my head on the corner of the hatch. It was dumb of me... Rushing and being careless..."

He stared at the folded-up stroller in the back, then his gaze slid through the interior of the Volvo. "Did you have a baby with you?"

Jemma blinked. Ringing began in her ears and not from the hit. She moved as quickly as she could, without face-planting in front of the cop, to the side of the car, where the door still hung wide open.

That was how she left it, wasn't it?

But that didn't matter.

Not fucking at all.

Because she realized what she was staring at.

Her heart was ripped right from her chest.

The car seat was empty. Dyna was gone.

Cage's daughter was fucking gone.

She bit back her scream, barely containing it.

She should ask him for help.

She should ask him for help.

She should...

*Fuck.*

Dyna belonged to Cage.

Cage was BFMC.

Dyna was Fury property.

"No. I..." *Fuck!* "She's with her father. I have to go. I'm fine... officer. I just clunked my head by accident. I'm clumsy like that." She pretended to rub her head above the gash, trying not to wince and forced out a stilted laugh. "I'll be fine. Thank you for checking on me."

He stared at her a little longer. The concern turning to suspicion.

Her blood was rushing, which made her scalp bleed faster under her hair. It would soon soak her shirt if she didn't get the hell out of there. If he saw how much she was bleeding, he'd call for an ambulance. And things would go to shit.

She didn't need cops or an ambulance. Every minute she was delayed was one more minute Dyna was missing.

She tried not to scream in panic. She needed to appear as cool as possible on the outside even though she was completely unraveling on the inside. "I... I have to go, officer, I'm going to be late."

He stared at her a few seconds longer, his eyes narrowed, and finally nodded. "Get your head checked if you feel any worse."

*Oh, thank fuck.* "Will do."

He closed the hatch for her and stood there as she climbed in the driver's seat. She glanced into the rearview mirror at the empty car seat, then at the cop still standing behind the Volvo.

She needed to call Cage. She needed to call Judge. She needed to call *someone*.

She was about to lose her shit any second now, but she couldn't do it in front of the cop. If she did, they'd get involved.

One thing instilled in her at an early age was club business remained club business. No outsiders.

As her shaky finger stabbed the Start button, Ox's deep

voice bellowed through her head, "Fuck the pigs. We handle our own shit."

The Fury needed to handle this.

*For fuck's sake*, they needed to handle this right now.

———

FIRE ANTS MARCHED like soldiers under his skin. He couldn't stand still. One hand gripped the back of his neck, twisting it back and forth to keep himself from exploding. The other was balled into a fist as he paced the lower level of The Barn.

A clear path had been left for him to do so. Though, Sig stood nearby. Just in case.

In case of what, Cage didn't know. He didn't care.

He only cared about one thing right now.

His fucking daughter.

His fucking daughter.

His. Fucking. Daughter!

He stopped, raised his face and tried to release the tension in his chest with a loud roar.

The crowd around him froze.

But he didn't care. He ignored them.

He needed to find Dyna.

He needed to get his baby girl back.

Alive. In one piece.

Without one fucking scratch.

They had no time to waste.

All those months ago, they had gone up that mountain to get Red and while there, they had taken out a bunch of Shirleys.

Now the Shirleys who they left breathing took Dyna.

They took her.

They had her.

They had warned those motherfuckers not to touch anything belonging to the Fury.

And that clan dared to do just that.

They stole his flesh and blood.

*"You took what was ours. Now gonna take what's yours."*

Those were the words they uttered.

Those were the words Jemma barely remembered. Before they struck her from behind.

Before they injured his goddamn woman and stole his fucking baby.

They could've killed Jemma.

They could still kill Dyna, if they haven't already.

His brothers needed to move.

But they weren't. Not yet.

They "needed a plan first." Just like the plan they made to recover Red.

They "needed to be smart." To "use their heads."

But he lost his.

He lost his the moment Jemma sped into the garage lot, the Volvo's tires squealing. She had barely put it in Park before exploding out of the driver's side, almost stumbling to her knees, her shirt drenched with blood.

She was screaming, crying.

How she was reacting, how she looked, the panic in her eyes, made his heart seize.

Everyone in the garage rushed outside to her and she talked so quickly no one knew what the fuck she was saying.

They pieced it together and figured it out.

His blood had turned to ice. Invisible hands crushed his heart and squeezed his throat.

His thoughts spun with the horrors that could be happening to his baby girl at the hands of those motherfucking inbred hillbilly goat fuckers.

Sig had wanted to burn down that mountain. They didn't.

They should have.

A mistake they would regret.

Dutch got on the phone, Rook on his cell. Everybody but him began to make calls and close up the garage.

Cage had packed Jemma back into the Volvo with Reilly in the driver's seat. He ordered Reese's sister to take her to the nearest urgent care center to get her examined, to stitch up the gash. To check for a concussion.

Before they left, Dutch ordered Reilly to take her to the farmhouse as soon as they were done. All the women, including Daisy, needed to gather in one spot, to be protected. Cage's father repeated the order which came directly from the sergeant at arms.

Crazy Pete's was shut down. The prospects took up posts at the farmhouse with the women.

His brothers gathered in The Barn.

All of them.

Every single one.

They were making a plan and Cage had no idea what it was.

His focus was on one thing.

Get his daughter back.

That was it.

What else happened he didn't give a fuck.

Sig could burn that fucking mountain to the ground.

Shade could make a blood river by slicing all their throats.

He didn't give a fuck.

Men. Women. Their spawn. All of them.

Every last goddamn Shirley needed to be wiped from the Earth.

And once the clan on that mountain was gone, he'd go with Sig to Ohio and wipe out the rest.

The Shirleys and their kind needed to become extinct.

A distant memory.

But that wasn't going to happen.

Fuck no.

They'd make a plan.

That was what Trip said.

That was what he was doing.

Standing on top of the bar so everyone could see and hear him. Judge stood on the floor in front of their president, his thick, tattooed arms crossed over his chest. Formidable. His face an angry mask.

The bearded giant watched Cage closely, carefully.

Probably making sure Cage didn't slip out undetected. Making sure Cage didn't head up that mountain on his own.

"Those motherfuckers kicked us right in the fuckin' nuts again," Ozzy yelled out and a chorus of agreement rose from everyone surrounding Cage.

Trip raised a palm and his voice to catch everyone's attention. "We need to decide, not if, but how we handle this. 'Cause we gonna fuckin' handle this. Not just get our property back, but—"

"Dyna," Cage muttered, cutting the prez off.

Trip's eyes fell to him. "What?"

"Dyna. My fuckin' daughter. Not property." Cage jammed the heels of his palms into his eye sockets and snarled.

She was a living, breathing part of him. Not an inanimate object.

His baby could feel pain and discomfort, unlike the fucking wood bar Trip stood on.

Judge's gruff voice rolled over their brotherhood. "Brother, yeah, she's your daughter, but she belongs to all of us. She's Fury property and under our protection. Those hillbilly ass wipes need to learn to stay away from what's ours."

Trip took over from there. "Yeah, so... This ain't just about gettin' Dyna back but finishin' this once and for all."

"We warned them last time," Sig growled, the cords on his neck tight and his own hands formed into fists. "Fuckin' warned them. Should've burned that goddamn mountain to the ground. Took them all out."

"We gotta do this smart," Trip reminded his half-brother.

"We gotta do this now," Cage screamed.

"Brother, Trip's right," Rook said quietly next to him. "Gotta do this smart. What's the point of us cleanin' house up there if we all end up back behind bars? What will be left of this club? Who will be here to protect our women and children then? Who will raise Dyna? Think."

"They're not gonna hurt her. They wouldn't fuckin' dare," Dutch growled. "They took her to replace Levi."

"You don't know that!" Cage yelled, his head feeling like it was about to spin off his neck like a top. "You can't say that, 'cause you don't fuckin' know. None of us do. They're out for revenge. We killed some of their brother-cousins. Took out their leader. You don't think they're pissed enough to hurt Dyna? Maybe even fuckin' kill her? To make a fuckin' statement?"

He sucked in a breath and continued before anyone could interrupt him.

"Why didn't they take Jemma? Why only Dyna? During daylight, in the open, in the middle of town where anyone coulda spotted them?"

A quiet voice rose out of the crowd as the man moved forward. "Easier to snatch a baby than both a baby and her mother. Only takes one person to do it. Coulda been one of their women who did it. Someone unassumin'."

Cage opened his mouth to correct Shade about Jemma being Dyna's mother.

The man knew Jemma wasn't his baby's mother. Everyone knew who Jemma was to Dyna. So, why did he say that?

Then it hit him that Shade was right. He was so fucking right.

Jemma was as close to a mother Dyna could get.

"They all gotta go. Every last fuckin' one of them," Ozzy stated.

Dodge spoke up. "What about the kids? The babies? What happens to them if we wipe out all the adults? They didn't ask to be born on Hillbilly Hill, born to these backwoods back-assed rednecks. We might not like it, but innocents live up there. We're no better than them if we take out the innocent, as well as the guilty."

"Those kids will grow up to be just as depraved as their fuckin' father-uncles and mother-aunts," Sig said and spat on the floor.

"We don't know that," Dodge stated.

"They'll know no different. They're born up there and die up there. They never fuckin' leave. They'll never know there's a broad world out there. Somethin' other than what you call Hillbilly Hill. They'll only live a narrowly focused life," Cage shouted.

"But who the fuck are we to decide?" Dodge asked softly.

"The Fury," Judge bellowed. "That's who the fuck we are. They fuck us, we're fuckin' them back even harder."

A roar rose from all of them, giving Cage a little bit of hope. But still...

Time was ticking.

Every hour, minute, second that passed was another hour, minute, second that clan had Dyna and was doing who knew what to her. That had his fucking blood boiling to the point it was about to explode like a grenade in his gut.

"Listen up," Judge shouted. "Didn't share this shit 'cause it was on a need-to-know basis. Shade's been doin' some recon on that mountain. He approached me, I approved it, as did our prez. He's been watchin', makin' a map of their compound, learnin' their fuckin' inbred ways."

"Also makin' sure they didn't kidnap any more women for breedin' purposes," Trip added.

The floor went back to Judge. "He's been watchin' who stepped into Vernon Shirley's shoes. Also, who's now second in command. Who's comin' and goin'. Their numbers. Inventoryin' their buildings. Their stockpiles of weapons. Where their moonshine stills are hidden. Where they're makin' meth. All of it."

*Fuck.*

Shade had gone up on that mountain by himself, putting himself at risk. For the club. For the brotherhood. He had no woman or children to protect but he was doing it for all of them. Just like it should be. Like the old Fury motto:

*For one! For all!*

*For our brothers, we live and die!*

A motto the Originals shouted but, in the end, never followed. If they had, they wouldn't have turned on each other.

The man named Shade, the brother with the long, curly brown hair, stepped up next to Judge. He didn't like the spotlight, but preferred to remain in the background. Unseen, unheard. A quiet cornerstone of the Fury.

He'd shown his loyalty the last time they went up the mountain. Enough so, he was patched in early.

After that night everyone saw him with new eyes. Judge originally distrusted him, but apparently that changed if he sent Shade up to spy on their enemy.

The group settled down and became really quiet to hear the man speak.

His voice was low but confident. His words were well-chosen before he spoke them. Like he had to pick each word carefully before saying it. Cage knew stutterers sometimes did that, but he'd never heard Shade stutter even slightly. "Got twenty-six women up there. Eighteen men. About forty kids under eighteen."

"Forty," someone repeated near Cage and whistled softly.

"Why more women than men?" Whip asked.

Judge answered. "We took out some of their men the last time."

"Vernon Shirley also had three sister-wives," Shade reminded them. "The male that took his spot—can't figure out how he's related—took those three wives. The youngest one," he found Sig out in the crowd and spoke directly to the VP, "the one you forced to watch what you did with Vernon... She's now knocked up by her new man. They live in the main house. Shit continued without a hitch, like Vernon Shirley never existed."

"After Sig chopped off the head of the snake, the fuckin' thing grew back," Cage grumbled.

"Figured it would," Sig muttered next to him. "They weren't goin' away quietly. They're too fuckin' stupid to do that."

"Now that fuckin' snake's wrapped around my baby girl's throat. Time to chop that motherfucker up and burn the pieces."

"Need to break up into teams," Judge announced. "Leavin' Ry, Tater and Possum here with the women and Daisy. Got them tricked out with what they'd need to handle a threat. Only one not in that house right now is Reese." He shot his cousin a look that spoke volumes.

Deacon shrugged. "Just got a text. She'll be here in twenty. But she's fuckin' pissed to be pulled away. She might take any threat out with her bare hands."

"She can be pissed all she fuckin' wants," Judge said, clearly not giving a fuck.

"That's what I told her. Didn't like that answer. Sure I'm gonna hear about it later."

"*Any-fuckin-way*," Judge said. "There's twelve of us without Dutch—"

"Fuck that!" Cage's father bellowed. "They got my Duchess. My ass is goin' up there to get her back!"

"All right…" Judge continued, "There's thirteen of us. Some are gonna head up and take care of business. Some are gonna sit down at the bottom of the lane, watch for pigs, watch for anyone comin' and goin'. Prevent anyone from comin' up our rear flank. Some are gonna spread out in the woods, make sure no one sneaks off with Dyna."

If his daughter was still alive.

*For fuck's sake*, she better be alive.

A single downy hair better not be out of place on her head.

If there was…

Well, those backwoods motherfuckers would get what was coming to them whether there was or there wasn't.

But still… there had better not be.

Because Hell hath no fury like the Blood Fury.

Every last one of that clan would be begging for Cage to end it for them.

Begging.

His club needed to move.

And now.

They've jawed long enough.

Judge quickly laid out in more detail what each group would do, using Shade's intel. And when they were done, the stomping of boots against the wood plank floor and the hollers of warriors heading into battle rose to the rafters.

"Got somethin' to say first," Cage called out, catching everyone's attention before they filed out.

No better time than now to resurrect the Original's motto. It was the only one they had, it would have to do.

"For one! For all!" Cage yelled. "For our brothers..."

"We live and die!" came the answering roar.

"Let's fuckin' ride!" shouted Judge and led them all out of The Barn.

# Chapter Twenty

THEIR PHONES WERE ON SILENT. Most of them carried the weight of at least one gun under their cuts. A few had knives strapped in various locations on their person.

And everyone was on high alert.

The sun had lowered behind the trees, giving them patches of shade to move between and remain undetected. The biggest worry as they traveled on foot was the possibility of booby traps.

They went up assuming the rumor was true, that the mountain was littered with them. However, nobody knew where and what kind.

It made for a slow go. And the darkness was creeping in like a homicidal stalker.

Whip and Easy were posted at the bottom near the road. The rest were scattered in various locations, moving closer to the clan's compound in the shape of a tightening noose.

All kept an eye open on their surroundings and also their footing. Looking for trip wires. Disturbed undergrowth. Anything suspicious hidden among the trees.

They searched for markings on tree trunks. Those

fuckers had to mark the location of their own booby traps somehow.

Cage was with Shade and Rook. They were the "team" tasked to locate and get Dyna out.

No matter what.

The rest were circling the clearing of the main compound, where the livestock barn, the large main house and a few outbuildings of various sizes were situated.

It also included the shed where the Shirleys had imprisoned Autumn and they'd...

Cage sucked dank forest air deeply into his lungs.

The thought they could have snagged Jemma and what they could've done to her...

They didn't.

But they did have their daughter. Jemma was relying on him to bring Dyna home safely.

Dressed in camo from head to toe, Shade stopped behind a tree. All of them had shed their cuts before leaving and dressed in dark clothing. Black jeans, if they had them, and dark or black shirts. No one wore anything with designs or colors. Nothing that could catch someone's eye.

They needed to do this smartly. Not become targets themselves.

The Shirleys had shot up Trip's wrecker when he tried to repo one of their piece of shit vehicles a while back. If they did that for a rust bucket, they'd do worse to keep his baby.

Shade pointed ahead and lifted both hands with his fingers spread. Ten.

The edge of the clearing was ten yards ahead.

The crack of a twig had Cage's head twisting toward his brother, who had frozen in place and grimaced at his mistake.

All three heads swiveled back toward the compound.

Besides their own footsteps, their collective breathing

and his heart beating in his ears, the mountain was eerily quiet.

Cage took his cues from Shade who had learned the lay of the land—or, in this case, mountain. His club brother jerked his chin and moved forward.

Rook and Cage followed him, stepping carefully and moving as quietly as they could.

They were no Army Rangers, no Navy SEALS, no Green Berets. Neither had time in the service, but they both had done time.

They had no special skills other than being mechanics and good with their hands. But they both knew how to survive prison and they had a purpose. An important one.

They could do this.

Shade stopped again another few yards ahead, pinning his back to a tree and silently indicating for Cage and Rook to move closer.

As they did, Cage noticed no movement in the clearing. No one was around. All the buildings in view were dark. They could see the main house on a ridge just beyond the barn and some sheds. Not one light was lit in any of the windows.

It was goddamn spooky and set the fine hairs on the back of his neck on end.

This scenario was unlike when they had recovered Autumn.

"Somethin' ain't right," Shade said under his breath.

That observation twisted Cage's gut.

"It's way too fuckin' quiet. Not one damn light on in any of the buildings. Nothin' rustlin' but the livestock. Nothin'."

*Fuck.* "They're expectin' us," Cage assumed, his gaze slicing through the compound again, searching for any signs of life.

"Yeah. They didn't snag Dyna to keep her. Those

fuckers snagged her as bait," Rook whispered, sidling up to them.

"Fuckin' motherfuckers," Cage muttered under his breath.

"If they don't wanna keep her, then they might not think twice about hurtin' her." His brother said out loud what Cage was unfortunately thinking.

"Goddamn ambush. That's what this is," Shade said. "They're waitin' for us. Not sure where. Never seen it this dead up here."

"Don't say dead," Cage growled.

"Know what I mean," Shade mumbled, keeping his eyes focused at the center of the clearing. "With the number of kids up here, quiet ain't a thing. They took 'em somewhere. Maybe one of the cabins higher up the mountain. One harder to get to."

"Ambush or not, we gotta find Dyna," Cage said. "Ain't leavin' this mountain without her."

"Agreed," Rook said beside him.

"Can't afford a gun fight without knowin' where she is, either," Cage added. He didn't need his baby caught in crossfire. He glanced at his brother. "Text the rest. Warn them it's an ambush and we need to regroup."

"Tell 'em not to leave their locations. We'll use text to figure out a new plan. We got this far, ain't goin' back," Shade told Rook. "You two stay here for now. Gonna check some shit and will be back."

Within a blink of an eye, Shade was gone, following the shadows, tracking silently among the trees and brush.

"That fucker can be scary. He's gotta have some special ops trainin' or somethin'," Rook said as his fingers moved quickly over his phone, typing out a group text.

"Or somethin'," Cage muttered, looking for signs of where Shade went.

The man had become completely invisible.

"Just glad he's on our side," Rook continued. He lifted his head. "'Kay, message sent."

"Don't know who's on those inbred motherfuckers' side, though. Don't know their skills. They're survivalists at worst. They live off this fuckin' mountain. They're resourceful."

Rook squeezed Cage's shoulder. "They're dumbfucks, brother. Too stupid to live."

"Yeah? Then how are they breathin'?"

"Won't be for long," his brother assured him.

"Wanna wipe them the fuck out, but can't, not all at once. But we're not lettin' this slide. No more goddamn warnings."

"If we gotta quietly take them out one by one, we will. 'Cause it was bad enough when they stole Red from Sig, now they stole my fuckin' niece. They're done. All of 'em. Don't care what Trip or Judge says. They all gotta go in one way or another. Women and kids, too. Can't let 'em keep breedin' a new redneck army."

The thought of killing children, even if they were inbred Shirleys, made his stomach churn. There had to be another way. Whatever that solution was wouldn't come into play tonight. Dyna's safety was priority number one. But if a few adult Shirleys were taken out in the process? So be it.

In fact, that was preferred. Whoever touched his daughter needed to die. Male, female, he didn't give a fuck.

Then they'd remove the rest from this Earth, from this mountain, like a surgeon's knife. Steadily and carefully one at a time. Even if it was slow and methodical.

But the clan's actions today guaranteed their demise.

Their extinction.

One way or another.

———

CAGE HUNKERED down behind a thick shrub just beyond the cabin. Rook and Shade remained in his line of vision.

Shade had a huge fucking knife in his hand. A Rambo-sized fucking knife. Who the fuck carried shit like that?

That crazy motherfucker apparently.

Their new plan was to move in groups of two and check every fucking building at every cleared level up the mountain.

The only problem was, the compound was pretty fucking vast. Off the main clearing, where the leader's house was located, were narrow, rutted dirt roads that reminded Cage of the spokes on a wheel. One directly north, one northeast and one northwest. Then off those lanes more rough roads spidering out into the thick woods.

Shade said he'd explored each one. He memorized the layout of the area. After every recon trip, he'd add to the crude map he drew of lines, squares, squiggles and symbols. Before they got on foot earlier, Cage had glanced at it. It wasn't detailed but basic and he found it strange that Shade hadn't made any notes on it. Just marked it with some letters, numbers and symbols.

The numbers were for how many occupied a cabin he'd discovered. O for occupied living quarters, X for unoccupied shed or lean-to. L for buildings that housed livestock, like the pigs, goats or chickens the Shirleys raised. M for locations where the Shirleys cooked Meth. S for the moonshine stills.

A for their armory stashes. At least the ones he could find. He suspected they also had some sort of root cellars and bunkers, some kind of underground storage. But he hadn't been able to find any but two.

One was full of canned goods. The other a stash of old rifles and some old moldy boxes of ammo.

Cage now knew more about the clan's compound than

he wanted to. All he really wanted to know was Dyna's location.

Where his baby girl was being kept.

And who was keeping her.

But they had a new plan they were carrying out. The only way they would abandon their plan was if someone found Dyna before Cage's small group did.

He hoped that happened but knew it wouldn't be that easy.

No, if they were using Dyna as bait for an ambush, they'd want to draw Cage's brothers as deep and as high into their compound as possible. Somewhere where the Shirleys would have the upper hand and the MC members wouldn't find it easy to escape.

While Shade, Rook and Cage took the lane going directly north, the others took the other two narrow lanes.

This was after the three of them had cleared the main house.

While it had been empty, handmade toys were scattered on the floors and dirty dishes covered the tables and counters. Like someone had told the occupants to drop everything and leave.

He thought the Shirleys had planned the whole abduction, but maybe they had jumped on a good opportunity, instead. Which was Jemma going to town to get her hair done. Because who would plan that kind of kidnapping in the light of day in the middle of a municipal parking lot?

No one with any kind of sense.

No matter what, what they did had worked. Planned or not.

The three moved quickly along the lane but stayed just off the path, using the edge of the woods as cover from being seen or shot at. It would be stupid for them to march up the dirt lane like they owned the place.

Though, that was exactly what Cage wanted to do.

*Gotta be fuckin' smart. Your baby's life depends on it.*

They checked a few small wood sheds along the way. Most were falling apart. All of them full of junk but empty of anything breathing.

Junk vehicles also littered the woods here and there. Some just rusty shells slowly becoming one with the earth beneath them. They checked every single one of those, too. Just in case they'd hidden Dyna in one.

"There's a smaller cabin on the right ahead. Then just beyond that, a short lane to the left with another cabin," Shade whispered to him and Rook.

Both he and his brother nodded.

"How many buildings are up here?" Rook asked Shade.

"Don't know. Didn't count 'em all. Not sure I found them all, either. Was hopin' to get a better handle on what's up here before somethin' like this happened."

*Before somethin' like this happened.*

Whether Judge was simply wanting to be prepared, just in case, or expecting something to happen, Cage wasn't sure. But the man had thought ahead to put Shade on it.

Shade had delivered, too. The intel they had was much better than going in completely blind.

"If they're using Dyna as bait to lure us in, wouldn't they want us to know where she is?" Rook threw out there.

"You'd think," Cage answered.

"They ain't gonna put her somewhere too obvious," Shade said. "They'd probably want us to have to break up into smaller groups to pick us off easier."

"Which is what we fuckin' did," Cage's brother muttered.

"But we figured out it's an ambush before steppin' right into it. So, maybe they weren't expectin' us to be smarter than them," Shade concluded.

"Ain't a hard thing to be." That was for fucking sure.

"Just gotta be cautious," Shade reminded them.

"They're expectin' us. But now we're on notice and they don't know that. That's to our advantage."

"What branch did you serve in?" Rook asked Shade.

"None," came the quiet answer. And then they were done talking.

Not because they needed to be quiet, but because shots began to ring out, echoing through the woods.

All three ducked, hunkering down, making their bodies the smallest target they could.

They had no idea who was shooting, who was being shot at or even what direction the shooting was coming from.

But Cage's heart leapt into his throat. He didn't want his daughter in the middle of a firefight. It was too fucking risky.

They remained eating dirt as they waited for the cracks of gunfire to stop. They also waited to see if trees exploded over their heads from stray or intended bullets.

Cage's cell phone vibrated in his back pocket and he slid it out with minimal movement, pressing the button and blocking the lit screen so he could read the message. The text was from Judge. He assumed everybody got it since Rook and Shade were pulling out their phones, too.

*Found Dyna.*

Was she safe? Cage's heart thumped heavily.

Before he could shoot off a response another text came in. And kept coming.

*Can't get to her.*

*Can hear her crying. Good sign.*

*In a shed w/ heavily armed motherfuckers.*

*AR-15s. Shotguns.*

*Not sure what else.*

*Around shed heavily booby-trapped w/ trip wires.*

*Need a way in. Not thru woods.*

*Need to use lane. Only safe approach.*

Safe except that made them an easy target. Since his

brothers were out-armed, they needed to outsmart the clan, instead.

"Now what?" Rook asked after reading the same texts.

"Need to find the key for the lock," Shade murmured.

"What?" Cage wasn't quite picking up what the man was trying to put down.

"Need a negotiation tool. That's the key. Need to find the right key to open that fuckin' lock," Shade explained.

"Eye for an eye," Cage whispered, finally getting it. Sort of. "That's what this was. We need to look at it in the same way. They got what's mine. We need to take what's theirs. Do a hand-off."

"Yeah," Shade agreed softly.

"Got any idea where they'd take their kids? Their women?" Rook asked.

"Bunker, if they got one," Shade answered. "Couldn't find it, though."

"Sure they have one?" his brother asked. "They're on a fuckin' mountain, hard to dig deep before hittin' rock. Could see them hidin' their weapons underground, but not diggin' a hidey-hole big enough for a bunch of people."

"They knew we'd hit the main house first. There's another good-sized house, not a cabin, up a few more hundred yards. Could see them all huddlin' there, with armed guards to protect them," Shade informed them.

"You said eighteen men remain," Cage said, "If we had a count for the number with Dyna, we'd know how many were left. How many might be either guardin' the women or hidin', just waitin' for us to fuck up."

"We got the advantage. We know how many they have. They don't know how many we have."

"We got less than them. Ain't armed like they are, either," Cage reminded Shade. AR-15s were no fucking joke.

Rook looked up from his phone. "Got six with Dyna

from what Trip could see. Could be more, though. They couldn't get any closer." Rook read another text that came in. "They inspected one booby-trap... Handmade nail bomb. Old grenade with a trip wire under a container of nails and screws, glass, metal, shit like that."

"Jesus fuck," Cage whispered, scraping a hand through his hair, then down his beard.

"We need one of their kids for an exchange," Rook said.

"No the fuck we don't," Shade started.

Rook and Cage waited for him to finish.

"Need three of their fuckin' kids. One for each of us. Gonna use them as shields and then as bargainin' chips."

*Fuck.*

*Fuck.*

*Fuck.*

"Jemma..." Cage breathed.

"Ain't gonna ever know," Rook finished, giving him a look. "We're gonna save your kid and gonna do it any way we can."

Cage thought about what Ox did when Jemma was only five. How that incident haunted her her whole life. But then, Ox was someone who was supposed to love and protect her.

Like Cage was supposed to do for Dyna.

They didn't owe the Shirley kids shit. And, while Dyna was too young to remember today, the Shirleys hadn't cared about fucking up Autumn for the rest of her life.

So, fuck them all.

They were going to do just that. Take three of their kids and use them to get his daughter back.

"'Kay, we need a plan to get three of their brats," Rook agreed.

"Need to find them first," Cage reminded his brothers.

"Oh, we're gonna find them," Shade assured him in a low voice. "We're gonna fuckin' find them. Just a matter of time." He pressed the screen on his phone and talked into it.

Even though he spoke slowly, using talk-to-text was probably faster than typing it out. Their phones vibrated a few seconds later.

Cage read the text.

*Hold your positions. Keep them in shed. Keep eye on baby. Gonna get bargaining chips.*

Bargaining chips.

Just like Dyna was.

## Chapter Twenty-One

"STICK WITH THE FUCKIN' plan," Shade said beside him with their backs plastered to the mismatched clapboard siding of the house deep within the woods.

Dutch, Judge, Trip, Sig, Deacon and Rev kept their positions around the shed where Dyna was being held.

Once Shade, Rook and Cage found where the Shirley women and children were being holed up—exactly where Shade predicted—they hunkered down and waited for Dodge and Ozzy to join them. All of them, except Shade, palmed their handguns. Shade still had a firm grip on that crazy-ass knife.

"We go in and split up. Gonna use the element of surprise and anyone with a gun or hair on their balls dies. No exceptions. It's the only way we all walk off this mountain breathin'. And with Cage's girl. Need three kids minimum as insurance to get his girl back. No matter fuckin' what, we're gettin' her back. Even if my plan goes sideways."

Shade spoke more today than in all the time since he'd joined the MC. He didn't speak fast, but carefully. Again,

Cage wondered what that was about. He'd probably never know and was A-fucking-okay with it because Shade knew his shit.

How? Cage would probably never know that answer, either.

"Dodge," Shade held out a rock to the bar manager, "break a window at that end of the house. Wait thirty seconds, break another one. Want their attention focused at that end. Women and kids will move away from the noise, men will move toward it. Keep your head down. They might just start blindly shootin'. If they do, that'll cover the noise of the rest of us goin' in. Oz and Rook, find and gather the women. Assumin' all twenty-six are inside. Lock them up in a room. Don't worry about the kids but watch any old enough to be a threat. Me and Cage are gonna take out the men."

Shade and Cage made eye contact and he jerked up his chin in agreement with the plan. This had to work. His daughter's life depended on it.

Dodge stayed low and moved around to the opposite side of the house.

The rest of them waited to hear the first window break.

Once they did, along with men's voices yelling inside, they moved fast and low to the back of the house where they found a rear entrance. Ozzy pulled something out of his back pocket.

A lockpick.

Within seconds the door was unlocked and Shade slowly opened it before slipping inside. Another second later he opened it halfway, indicating they should enter.

They did.

More glass broke. More men yelled.

Twelve uncle-daddies could be in that house. They needed to move fast and efficiently.

The back door had taken them directly into a rustic

kitchen where Shade grabbed a six-pack of Mountain Dew in plastic bottles off a long roughly-made table. He freed a bottle from the plastic rings and handed it to Cage.

"Silencer," he mouthed.

*Christ.*

Cage nodded his understanding.

Shade pointed at Ozzy and Rook and signaled the order to go. The two disappeared up the back steps with the assumption the women and children were hiding on the second floor. Cage and Shade headed toward the sound of the men and a third window breaking.

Trying not to make too much noise, Cage twisted off the bottle's cap and dumped the soda as they moved through the rooms, sticking close to the walls, doing their best to be invisible. Because once they were seen, they'd be in a fight for control, maybe even their lives. They needed to pick off as many clan members as possible before that happened.

Shade came to an abrupt stop at the end of the hall and the beginning of what might be the front room, where Dodge had just broken a fourth window. He peeked his head around the corner, then snapped it back and lifted up his hand with all five fingers in the air.

Cage read that hand signal as "five soon-to-be dead motherfuckers." The palm holding his gun itched and his fingers flexed in anticipation.

Shade then counted down from three using those same fingers. *Three. Two.*

*One.*

Cage and Shade rushed forward. He lifted his gun, held the empty bottle over the muzzle and shot three right in a row, taking them down.

*Pop. Pop. Pop.*

They crumpled to the floor, their long guns spilling from their hands, but still within reach.

Shade grabbed a fourth Shirley at the same time Cage

was shooting and sliced the man's throat with crazy efficiency.

As the fifth guy was pulling the business end of his shotgun in from the broken window, Shade sank the large blade deep into the man's back, where the man's heart would be. The fucker remained on his feet and tried to turn. As he did, and as Shade jerked the knife back out, Dodge appeared in the window with his gun drawn and pointed at the clan member's forehead.

"No!" Shade shouted.

The Shirley somehow still stood, but barely, as blood poured from the fatal stab wound. Shade used a handful of the man's hair to yank his head down while kneeing him in the face at the same time. Once he collapsed all the way to the floor, Shade pressed a knee to the man's chest and unceremoniously sliced his throat.

The man gurgled one last time and blood seeped from the newest wound.

"Was gonna take that fucker out," Dodge complained, appearing disappointed he didn't get to take out one of the goat fuckers.

But their mission wasn't over yet.

"Don't want the rest of them hearin' shots if we can avoid it. Don't wanna give them a head's up to hurt Dyna before we got our bargainin' chips," Cage explained. "Get in here and let's clear the rest of the house. And find Ozzy and Rook."

Dodge disappeared from the window.

Shade and Cage moved toward the stairway to meet him at the rear of the house. Then the three moved up the steps, which creaked under them.

Cage doubted any of the buildings in their compound were built to code, so he wondered if the staircase could manage the weight of all three of them at once. Since

Shade led the way, Cage slowed down and held out a hand to Dodge to get him to stop. As soon as Shade hit the upper landing, Cage followed and waved for Dodge to proceed.

Ozzy stood guard at the opening of one door, while Rook stood at another. Both had their guns in their hands and pointed into the rooms. What Cage could assume were bedrooms.

"Got half the women in here. He's got the other half," Ozzy said gruffly. "Those assholes taken care of?"

"Yeah. The ones in this house. Still too many breathin'," Shade answered.

Cage peered over Dodge's shoulder to see about a dozen women of various ages. Some sat on a bed, the rest sat on the floor around it. Only a few were crying and looked scared. The rest? If it was possible, they'd shoot poisoned daggers from their eyes.

Well, fuck them.

All were wearing the same style of homemade dresses and their hair was worn similar.

A goddamn cult. That was what it was.

Brainwashed motherfucking cult.

"Only twelve women in here. And some teens. My count had twenty-six total," Shade said. "Brother, you got the rest in there?"

"Fuck no," Rook answered. "Another twelve. And some kids."

"Fuck. Two women unaccounted for," Cage stated the obvious.

"Maybe they're down with Dyna," Rook suggested.

"No one mentioned any women with Dyna," Ozzy grumbled.

"Or they're hidin' out somewhere in this house," Shade said with his head tilted like he was listening for any movement of the two missing women.

"Could be. Keep your eyes and ears open," Cage ordered. "This ain't lookin' like forty kids, either."

"Nope. Not close to forty here," Dodge said after checking the room Rook was guarding. "Not even fuckin' close. Must got them elsewhere. Maybe with the two other women."

"Can't worry about that shit now," Shade said. "Need to pick kids young enough not to fight, big enough for effective shields."

*Fuck*, Cage hated that word.

Rook jerked his chin to a room with a closed door. "Youngest are in that room. We kept the older ones with the women to keep an eye on them. Ain't trustin' anyone with Shirley blood, no matter how fuckin' young they are."

Shade went to another bedroom with a closed door and Cage followed him.

"This one. This one. And that one." Shade pointed out three kids with his huge knife like he was picking out prime cuts of beef at a fucking butcher. "Got a knife?" he asked no one in particular.

"Yeah," Cage answered. He was taking one of those kids.

"Got one, too." Dodge moved into the room with Shade, his own knife now in hand.

*Jesus Christ*, this was happening.

"Want us to stay here and keep watchin' these brainwashed bitches?" Ozzy asked.

"Fuck no," Cage answered. "Soon as we got Dyna, we're splittin'."

"What about burnin' this fuckin' house down first?" Rook asked. "Another warnin' since they didn't take the last one seriously."

"Gonna take too long," Cage said. He didn't want to discuss any future plans that had to do with the Shirleys in front of the women. Or even the kids. He didn't want them knowing that they weren't finished with them. He wanted that to come as a complete fucking surprise.

They *could* burn down the house but it was summer and dry. It might light up the surrounding forest, catching the PD's attention and bringing them and firefighters up the mountain.

Last thing they needed was the pigs getting involved and doing an investigation. The Shirleys would never go to the pigs on their own. Even to report murders. Like the Fury, they didn't want law enforcement or any government agencies involved in their business. Even if it had to do with threats to their safety or their compound. They distrusted any and all government.

That was good for his club since it would make it easier to thin out the Shirley herd. On their own schedule. To do it smart and efficiently.

The three kids Shade had picked out to use for their safety, and Dyna's exchange, were boys all around the age of three or four. Not strong enough to fight, but large enough to use as a damn shield and light enough to carry.

Three Shirley spawn to exchange for his one and only baby girl.

They needed to move. Darkness was creeping in by the minute.

Shade gave the women a warning to stay upstairs until their menfolk came and retrieved them. He also warned them to not try anything stupid or the boys would die. Cage wasn't sure if Shade meant that last part and he didn't want to find out.

However, if the Shirleys harmed Dyna in any way, the three boys would be sacrificed. Because, no one... Not one fucking person would get away with that. He would do what he needed to do to avenge his daughter. His blood. His little monkey.

"We gotta go." Cage hauled a crying toddler up into his

arms. "You be quiet and stay still, you hear?" he warned the kid, not sure if the boy would understand. "You be good and you'll be back with your momma soon."

*That* the kid understood and he nodded as he hiccupped-sobbed, tears streaming down his face and snot bubbling from his nostrils.

*Jesus fuck,* he wondered how much Dyna had cried since they took her. If she was hungry. If her diaper was dirty. If she was scared.

As the five of them turned to head down the steps, they heard a banshee-like scream from the end of the hallway. One of the women had a shotgun in her hands and was raising it to her shoulder as she screamed, "Let 'em go!"

Cage was standing at the top of the steps. Shade was right behind him with Dodge on his heels.

Shade shouted, "Duck!"

Dodge did and just in time.

The man's hand became a blur and so did the knife until it stuck dead center in the woman's forehead. Cage was surprised it didn't twang from the impact. The woman's eyes went wide and her mouth opened as she collapsed in slow motion, the shotgun dropping from her fingers.

"Damn! Gotta show me how to throw knives like that," Dodge shouted, running over to pick up the shotgun. Shade, with a crying toddler of his own tucked under one arm, followed him. He planted his boot on the dead woman's face and unwedged the knife from her skull.

As a final parting gift, he leaned over and wiped off the bloody blade on her homemade dress.

In front of Cage, Rook asked, "Where the fuck she get that shotgun?"

"Probably got 'em stashed everywhere," Shade answered calmly.

Well, that was fucking reassuring. "Eyes and ears open,"

Cage reminded the rest of them. "Let's go. Want my fuckin' daughter back."

It took almost ten minutes to get to the location where everyone else was spread out, waiting. Everyone except for Whip and Easy, who remained at the base of the mountain still on lookout.

When they got to where some of the Shirley inbred motherfuckers were holding Dyna, the rest of his brothers faded into the background. They kept the shed in their view, their ears open for any other Shirleys approaching, and their guns ready in case of a shootout.

Thank fuck Jemma wasn't seeing this. Using kids as shields. As pawns.

But then, the Shirleys were doing the same with Dyna. Using her as a game piece in their fucked up game.

"We got three of your boys. Three of your blood. You got one of ours," Cage yelled out toward the quiet shed. Too quiet for Cage's liking. He'd rather hear Dyna crying because then he'd be assured she was still alive. "Thinkin' it's more than a fair trade. Three for one."

Shade stood next to him with one boy held to his chest, Rook held another. His brother insisted on standing next to Cage, risking everything for his own niece. Cage was pretty fucking sure Dutch would have swapped out with Shade, too, if Shade would've allowed it.

He didn't.

He said he had no family, no woman, no kids, he didn't have a goddamn thing to lose. Unlike some of the rest of them. Like Cage.

But there was no way Cage was letting anyone else do the talking. Judge didn't like it, but fuck Judge. He didn't have to like it. He only had to respect Cage's decision.

The club enforcer did, even though reluctantly.

"One of you motherfuckers come out with my girl."

"Fuck you," came a male voice from inside the windowless shed. The door was partially open and the interior was pitch dark.

"Which of these boys d'you want dead first?" Cage asked. "Pick one. Which one means the least to you? This one?" He lifted the toddler he held higher. "He disposable to you all?"

"Send 'em all into the shed an' will let your baby go," the faceless voice shouted.

How the fuck was Dyna going to get outside to them? Crawl? She was barely seven weeks old.

Dumb motherfuckers.

"Send out whoever's got her and will swap with the one boy I got."

"Want 'em all."

"You'll get them all once I got my girl back and we're safely off this hillbilly hill."

"Don't want you fuckin' with us after this," came a warning from inside the shed.

*No deal.* "Just want my girl back. That's it. You fucked with us first by takin' her. By injurin' my woman."

Judge shuffled behind Cage. He ignored the big man's reaction to his claim to Jemma.

"Send someone out with her and I'll hand over this boy. He's been cryin' for his momma. We'll take the other two to the bottom, then let them go. Deal?"

"Let 'em all go now."

"Nope. Once we reach the road. Not before. Ain't negotiable. You can send someone down to get them then. When we're gone."

"Ain't likin' this deal," another one of the Shirley men called out.

"Daddy!" the boy in his arms cried out and tried to wiggle free. Cage tightened his grip.

*Shit.*

Shade, Rook and Cage all exchanged looks. The smile Shade now wore had nothing to do with being happy.

Cage lowered his voice. "That your Daddy?"

The boy nodded. "*Daaaaaddy!*" he cried.

"Got your boy," Cage called out. "You got my girl. Let's trade. Father to father."

Silence answered him. It stretched out for a full fucking, heart-pounding minute.

The wood door creaked open wider and a man stepped into the doorway with Dyna in his arms.

Cage's pounding heart seized.

He couldn't see his baby girl's face. He couldn't see shit. Dyna—if it was her—was wrapped in a stained blanket.

"Better not be pullin' any shit," came from Judge behind him. "Better be her in that fuckin' blanket or all three boys die right here. Right in front of your fuckin' faces."

"Show me!" Cage yelled. Ten yards separated him from his baby.

Ten fucking yards.

He wanted to sprint those thirty feet and snatch Dyna from that Shirley's filthy motherfucking hands.

He didn't. Instead, he kept a firm grip on the man's son and held his ground.

"Halfway," the inbred, toothless motherfucker demanded.

Cage gritted his teeth and gave him a nod.

"Got your back," Judge said softly behind him.

Cage adjusted the knife he held close to the toddler's throat so he didn't slice it by accident. He moved slowly and carefully, his eyes focused on his daughter. When he got closer, he stopped. "Lemme see her face."

Dirty fingers peeled back the blanket enough to see the wrapped bundle was indeed Dyna and she was awake but quiet.

His kid was the goddamn best.

"Halfway," Cage reminded the goat-fucking hillbilly.

One side of the bearded man's lips pulled up in a sneer, but he moved closer.

Cage continued until they met amongst dead leaves and mud. His brothers were behind him, the Shirleys in front of him.

His brothers all had his back.

Finally, they only stood a couple feet apart. Two fathers. Two children.

And a whole bunch of hatred filling that empty space between them.

"Let 'im go," the boy's father demanded.

Cage put the toddler on his feet, but kept one hand clamped on the kid's shoulder as he held out his other arm. "Hand her over. Carefully. You hurt her, we got two more behind me."

The man's mouth tightened and he gave a sharp nod. He held out Dyna with both hands. Like a fucking sacrifice.

Cage's heart stopped beating, his lungs failed to take in air, as he released the boy and grabbed Dyna at the same time.

Then, *fuck him*, he had her. His baby in his arms.

He didn't take the time to check her, instead he backed away quickly as the boy wrapped himself around his father's leg.

"Once we're safely off this mountain, the other two will be waitin' at the bottom," Cage reminded the clan member, who said nothing and didn't even hug his damn kid.

When he got back to the line of Fury members, Judge muttered, "Let's get the fuck outta here now. Gotta get your girl home."

That sounded like a plan.

"They're all gonna die, right?" Cage asked his sergeant at arms.

"Fuck yeah," Judge whispered back. "They're all gonna die."

Cage gave the man a nod, turned and headed toward the lane. They'd all take that back down the mountain, using the two remaining boys as insurance for their safety. They wouldn't have to worry about tripping any booby traps by taking the main dirt road.

Cage stayed in front, cuddling Dyna against his chest, occasionally peeking down at her to make sure she was whole and uninjured. But he had to concentrate on his footing. He didn't want to trip with her in his arms since the mountain road was rough with water-filled potholes and deep ruts. Traveling in the limited light made it even more treacherous.

Everyone else stayed behind him, keeping watch, with guns drawn and heads on swivels as they moved as a group toward Copperhead Road.

It was a long fucking hike back down and Cage was getting anxious to get Dyna home. At first, he thought someone stumbled behind him. Until he heard his brothers shouting and scrambling.

"Take cover!" Rook yelled at him, yanking on his shoulder and almost knocking Dyna from his arms. "Fuckin' motherfuckers!"

Cage caught her before she tumbled and he jumped off the road and into the brush, picking the biggest tree he could find as a shield.

More shots rang out, landing in the dirt and surrounding trees, causing tiny explosions.

"Fucking motherfuckers," Rook muttered again under his breath, gun in hand, and a tight grip on the kid who had been his shield. "They're stupid as fuck."

"Guess they don't give a shit about the other two boys. They'll just make more," Cage said.

"Goddamn worse than the Amish when it comes to poppin' out snot monkeys."

"Ain't a conversation to be havin' right now," Cage reminded him.

Rook pressed his lips together and shook his head. "Should put a bullet in this kid's fuckin' head right now."

"But you won't," Cage said firmly.

Rook's nostrils flared and his lips flattened out. "Goddamn it."

More shots rang out, some even whizzing way too closely.

"Everybody still upright and breathin'?" Trip asked, ducked behind a tree.

Everyone verbally checked in.

"See any of them?" Judge asked from a few trees away. Somehow the man found a tree big enough to hide his giant ass.

"No," "Fuck no," and "Nope" came from a few of them.

"Move tree to tree, then. Stay behind cover. Move carefully. Take extra care where you step," Trip called out from ahead of them. "Stay low if possible. Don't let those fuckin' kids go. The second we do, we're gonna be in a fuckin' shootout. They got long guns with scopes. We don't. We'll lose."

*Christ.* More good news.

In a group, they slowly moved through the trees and brush along the edge of the dirt lane, taking the two boys with them. But the hairs on the back of Cage's neck were like the quills on a fucking trapped porcupine. Especially when he heard footsteps in the dead leaves and undergrowth that didn't belong to any of his brothers.

The Shirleys were tracking them and getting closer.

"Maybe we can take more out," Cage said, "as our parting gift."

"Yeah. Game for that. But hangin' onto this kid will fuck up my aim." Rook whistled softly to catch Rev's attention. "Take this fuckin' inbred snot monkey."

Rev carefully worked his way over to them, grabbed the crying kid by the arm and kept moving until he found cover again.

"Trip's a great shot," Rook whispered, sweeping the area by looking down the barrel of his 9mm Beretta.

Trip had been a Marine. He'd better be a good fucking shot. "But will he pick some of them off?"

The prez wanted to keep the club as clean as possible. Cage wasn't sure if Trip would just start killing people, even in self-defense. Trip stated quite a few times he wasn't going back to prison no matter what.

"Most of us are felons already, brother. None of us should have weapons. But, you know what? You got your baby in your arms right now. That's all that fuckin' matters to any of us. I see any movement that ain't one of us, I'm shootin'. We start shootin', you take Dyna and get the fuck down this hell hole."

"Dad can take Dyna. I can stay."

"Fuck that. She needs her fuckin' father. You take her. Hear me?"

"Yeah, brother, I hear you." Sometimes he hated Rook, but at this very fucking moment he might actually love him.

Now wasn't the time to get sappy. Now was the time to get his ass moving and get his daughter home safely.

"Be careful," was the last thing Cage said to his brother as he moved from tree to tree down that fucking mountain. A mountain that needed to be reduced to a canyon from a whole bunch of dynamite.

He kept moving even though more shots rang out behind him and he wasn't sure from which side.

Since he was walking so slowly and being extra careful, it wasn't long before the rest of them caught up. Ozzy had both arms draped over Deacon and Sig's shoulders and a huge splinter—more like a chunk of wood—sticking out of his thigh.

"Fuck!" Ozzy bellowed, his fingers wrapped around the wood fragment.

Cage grimaced. "Holy fuck. What happened?"

"Shrapnel," Ozzy groaned. "Sounded like a fifty-caliber round struck the goddamn tree next to me. It exploded, and the next thing I know, I'm speared like a fuckin' beef kabob."

"Don't pull it out. Don't know what it hit. Don't need you bleedin' out on this mountain," Trip yelled with one hand on Dodge, who was walking under his own power, but also injured.

"Hurts like a fuckin' bitch," Ozzy griped, his face twisted in pain.

"Hurt's better than dead," Trip reminded the motel manager.

"Got that fuckin' right," Dodge agreed, blood soaking the sleeve of his T-shirt and dripping down his arm.

"You get shot?" Cage asked him, holding Dyna closer to the center of his chest in case bullets began to fly again. One would need to go through him first to get to her.

"Let's fuckin' go," Judge bellowed at them. "They can pick us off easier than we can them. Stop jawin' and start movin', we're almost there. I ain't carryin' anyone's ass. I'll drag you by your fuckin' foot 'til we hit pavement. Then I might drag you some more."

Deacon snorted, but everyone listened to that order. Gunshots were still heard higher up the mountain. They felt like a herd of deer being driven into a trap made up of waiting hunters.

He hoped to fuck that wasn't true.

"Anyone check with Easy and Whip?"

"Yeah," Rev answered him, still hauling around one of the crying toddlers. "They're good. They're waitin' on us."

*Thank fuck.*

When they got to Copperhead Road, Easy was waiting, looking anxious.

"Thank fuck!" the young brother yelled, turned and waved his arm in a signal.

Within seconds, Whip pulled up with the plain black van used for the Tioga Pet Crematorium business.

Judge took the hands of both Shirley boys, guided them a few feet back up the mountain road and pointed upward. He gave them both a gentle, but firm, nudge and watched for a second while the two boys joined hands and began to walk.

Cage figured the two Shirley boys were related to each other. Probably brother-cousins.

Judge jogged like Sasquatch over to the van and climbed into the passenger side.

Even though it was a tight fit, the rest of them piled into the back, sitting on the floor since the van had no back seats.

Before Easy could even drive away, Trip was on his phone. "Stel, we got Dyna. On our way back. Got two injured. Grab Granddaddy's first aid kit from the upstairs' closet. Tell Jemma we'll need her nursin' skills. Will be there ASAP."

Now that he could breathe a little easier, he took the time to unwrap the filthy fucking blanket and check Dyna from head to toe. Surprisingly, she had a semi-clean cloth diaper pinned on her. Other than needing a bath to wash off the Shirley filth and a bottle to fill her tummy, his baby girl was perfect.

*Thank fuck.*

His eyes burned as he stared into Dyna's gray-blue ones. He tried to blink the sting away as she smiled up at him and let out a surprising squeak, her arms and legs jerking. Then her face scrunched up, turned red and she began to cry.

Best. Fucking. Sound. Ever.

He closed his eyes and simply listened for a moment.

She was alive, she was well and back in his arms.

"Boy."

He glanced up at his father, who didn't hide the look of relief on his weathered face as he stared at his granddaughter in Cage's arms.

"Good fuckin' job."

*Damn.*

Cage leaned back against the side of the van and propped Dyna in the crease of his thighs before glancing across at Trip. "We're not done."

He needed to hear that reassurance. He had gotten it from Judge, but he needed to hear it from their president, too.

Trip's expression was grim. "Yeah, we're not done. This was the beginnin' of their end."

He could no longer hear Dyna crying when the inside of the van became deafening with all the hollers and stomping of his brothers' boots.

*Fuck yeah. For our brothers we live and die!*

———

As soon as the van pulled up to the back of the farmhouse, the women were running out the back door and down the porch steps.

"Get them inside," Trip ordered their brothers in regards to Ozzy and Dodge. "You grab the kit?" he yelled out to his ol' lady.

"Yes, in the kitchen." Stella held the screen door open to let the guys inside.

Cage had waited for the two injured men to get out of

the van first before climbing out of the sliding side door with an upset Dyna in his arms.

When Jemma rushed over, their eyes met for only a split second before she took Dyna from him, giving her a quick onceover, then pressing her lips all over the crying baby's face.

"She's okay." Jemma tried to soothe Dyna, but his daughter was having none of it.

"Yeah, she's okay. Hungry. Gotta get her a bottle."

Without taking her eyes off the baby, she asked, "Who's hurt? Just Ozzy and Dodge?"

"Yeah. They were shootin' at us."

"Oh my God," she muttered. "What the fuck, Chris?" She spun on her heels and headed back up the porch steps and into the kitchen.

Cage followed.

Trip was inside giving orders to anyone uninjured. "Clear the table. Get Jemma whatever she needs to get these two fixed up."

Their prez wasn't the only one shouting demands, so was Judge. "Saylor, get Daisy out of here. Ry, walk them back to the house and stay with them 'til we get back. Hear?"

"Yes," Judge's son said. Looking shell-shocked, he was taking in everything around him. The men, the blood, the injuries and a wailing Dyna in Jemma's arms.

*Welcome to the Fury, kid.*

"Sis, gonna have to give up the baby. Need your help," Judge told Jemma.

"Get Ozzy up on the table. Someone cut off his jeans. Dodge, sit down in that chair," Jemma ordered, pointing. "Take off your shirt."

She could still get bossy while holding tightly onto a wailing Dyna. Cage had felt the same way once his daughter was in his arms. He didn't want to let go. So, he understood it.

"One of you ladies clean up Dodge's arm so I can see how extensive the damage is."

With a last kiss to Dyna's head, she glanced up at Cage. Her face was stony, unreadable. "Take her back to the trailer, give her a bath and put her in a fresh diaper. Give her a bottle. She'll need a nap after all this shit. As soon as I'm done here, I'll be home."

He took Dyna from her arms. Though, he could tell she was reluctant to let go. "Jem..."

"Do it, Cage," she barked, brushing him off to concentrate on the injured.

*Cage.*

*What. The. Fuck.*

Everyone who was left in that kitchen froze at her tone and most of them knew she never called him by his road name.

He would give her this. This once. He figured she'd been freaking out the whole time they were gone, on top of dealing with her own head injury.

He wouldn't doubt this whole thing stirred up bad memories, too.

So, yeah, he'd give her this.

For now.

But she wasn't the only one reeling after what happened. With how close they came to losing Dyna. With how close they came to losing some of his fellow brothers.

Shit could've really went sideways. They were lucky they walked away with only a couple minor injuries.

But this wasn't over yet.

Not even close.

However, this was not the time for that discussion.

Now was the time for Jemma to do her thing and help

the club out. While he needed to go take care of his daughter.

Priorities.

Then the club would deal with the remaining Shirleys.

Then Cage would deal with Jemma.

Because he knew it was coming.

She hated the MC life.

What happened today probably just cemented it.

However, he couldn't do anything about it but deal with the fallout.

With one last look at her shouting orders and dealing like a pro with Ozzy and Dodge, he held his baby girl tightly to his chest and headed out of the farmhouse back to the trailer.

## Chapter Twenty-Two

JEMMA FIDGETED in her seat and an unexpected shiver shot through her.

Whether it was from the A/C making the office an ice box, or her memory of last night, she didn't know.

After she had finished removing the shard of wood from Ozzy's leg, cleaned and bandaged his injury, she had moved onto Dodge, cleaning the wound where a bullet grazed his bicep.

He'd have a scar, but he thought that was cool. A war wound, he called it.

Right.

Jemma didn't think it was so cool.

Some of them could've died up on that mountain. They were lucky only two had somewhat minor injuries.

Dyna could've been badly hurt or even killed. Luckily, she wasn't.

But what happened on that mountain weren't the only injuries.

Her scalp had stitches at the back. Jemma hoped her hair covered them enough to make them unnoticeable. She hoped the makeup she'd applied over the half-moons of worry under her eyes covered them enough, too. She didn't want to discuss her injury or exhaustion with a prospective employer. If asked, she'd have to lie.

She thought about cancelling today's interview. Then, after a sleepless night, decided she would go no matter what. She needed this job. She needed to get the hell away from the MC.

This job might be her quickest way out.

It would also be the perfect excuse for her to walk away. To get free once more.

From a life she knew could be disastrous. Even heartbreaking.

Like yesterday when she was jumped and Dyna was stolen from her.

Yesterday was a reminder of how dangerous the MC life could be.

Dyna had been lucky. Cage had been lucky. Dodge and Ozzy were lucky they'd heal up without any issues. The whole club was lucky there weren't more casualties.

Jemma was damn lucky she had this interview.

As she sat in front of the director's desk of the hospice organization, she chewed on a fingernail and her knee bounced uncontrollably.

It wasn't the interview that worried her.

It was Dyna growing up in an MC.

When she finally headed back to the trailer last night, she had been ready to collapse. The day had been long and exhausting, and her adrenaline was finally crashing. Her head throbbed and all she wanted to do was soak in a hot bath.

The problem was, the trailer didn't have a bathtub. She settled for a quick shower, pulled on one of Cage's T-shirts, and after eating a plate of lukewarm leftovers and checking on Cage and Dyna in his bedroom, she crawled into her bed.

It wasn't long before her door opened, Cage came in smelling like he had just smoked a bowl and, without a word, carried her to his bed.

She should've resisted. But didn't.

She wanted to be close to Dyna. And, if she admitted it, Cage, too.

He laid Dyna next to Jemma in the center of the mattress and settled in on the other side, sandwiching the baby between them.

They laid there quietly.

She was pretty sure they were both reflecting on everything that happened.

In the dark, Dyna's loud breathing filled the silence as she slept. In the end neither Cage nor Jemma got much sleep. Each kept a hand on Dyna, making sure she was still there.

Between them.

She drifted off eventually because when she awoke, Cage and Dyna were already up. He was in the kitchen feeding his daughter.

The only conversation they had was with the baby, not with each other.

Everything seemed still too raw and the possibilities of how badly the previous day could've gone still weighed heavily on them both.

He ended up staying home from work and she eventually left, hoping to nail this interview.

Hope was pretty much all she had at this point. What she clung to.

The door opened and a woman strode in, wearing heels and a very light scent which filled the office space. Not cloying but fresh.

Jemma stood and they shook hands. Georgette Anthony introduced herself as the regional director of the hospice organization, then moved around to the other side of the desk and they both took a seat.

The brunette appeared super-polished with her makeup, her nails, her posture. She was well-spoken. Flawlessly dressed. Completely professional.

In contrast, Jemma felt like leftovers a raccoon dragged out of the trash.

After a little bit of small-talk the director got right to the crux of things. Jemma, too tired for unnecessary conversation, was relieved.

"Let's get right to it. First off, your resume is impeccable. Honestly, this interview was unneeded, but required by the board." She leaned forward, like she was about to tell Jemma a secret. "Truth is, I'm extremely short-handed. I have patients who desperately need our help and I don't have time to nitpick about what we women are forced to do to protect ourselves from over-eager hands."

Jemma opened her mouth to defend her actions.

Georgette lifted a well-manicured hand to stop her. "No need to explain. Been there, done that. I have the pink-slip to prove it. We have a zero-tolerance policy when it comes to that kind of behavior. I don't care who it comes from."

Georgette dismissing the false accusation that Jemma sexually assaulted the doctor made her sit back and relax a tad. She figured what happened to her out in Cleveland would be her biggest hurdle.

Thank fuck it wasn't.

"You haven't burned out yet?"

Jemma hadn't expected that question and Georgette studied her face, waiting for her answer. Burnout was common with hospice nurses due to the nature of the work.

"No, I... I need to do this. I watched my uncle die from cancer, but I also watched his hospice nurse help ease his way into his next life. That's what made me want to take this path. I do it for him and others like him."

The director nodded, looking pleased at Jemma's answer. "While the work can be gratifying, it can also be hard on your psyche. Unlike working elsewhere where you can help a patient get better, see them heal and walk out of the hospital, in hospice work, you are helping a patient to the end. There's no getting better. No miracle. No happy ever after. You're only twenty-seven, Jemma, you haven't been doing this as long as I have. But just know, within our organization, we have opportunities to move up once you've proven yourself, to get out of the trenches when it becomes too much."

"I love dealing directly with the patients and their families. Of helping a patient spend their last days at home, surrounded by familiar things and their loved ones. But, if needed, having other options would be wonderful." None of that was a lie.

"And you're willing to travel to wherever we need you?"

"Yes, I have no..." *Family.* Jemma's heart raced and the pressure on her chest became almost unbearable. She pinned her hands to her lap so she wouldn't rub at it. "I have no problem with that."

Georgette smiled. "Well then... How soon can you start?"

Jemma returned the smile, though hers wasn't as big or as bright as Georgette's, who stood. Jemma rose to her feet, too.

Was the interview over already?

Georgette held out her hand and Jemma shook it. "Expect a contract in your email later this afternoon. Look it over. If it's acceptable, you can start Monday. You'll spend your first day with HR to get your paperwork in order, get your ID and some of the staff will go over our policies and procedures. Then, on Tuesday, we'll place you with another nurse and once you get to know that patient, you'll be on your own."

*What?*

Monday? Today was Thursday.

That meant she had three days to get organized and find a place to live in Williamsport. She might have to find a motel temporarily. Where she settled also depended on where the majority of her patients would be located. So much to think about. So much to plan.

She took a deep breath. She also needed to break the news to Cage.

*Fuck.*

She had warned him to prepare. He didn't. He had arrogantly assumed she'd stay no matter how many times she told him differently.

But still...

Dyna.

After a few last words with Georgette, she walked out of the office building and back to her car. She climbed in and sat in the driver's seat.

Her heart was already breaking and she hadn't said goodbye yet.

Yes, she wouldn't be far. Yes, she could stop back to visit when she had time. But she would take as much overtime as her new employer offered to get her finances back on track.

She'd need first and last month's rent, a security deposit, to make her next car payment, to buy groceries. Not to mention, get her things from storage and have them shipped from Ohio.

Even so, it was a new beginning. A fresh start. Which was what she'd been looking for.

Then why wasn't she feeling more excited about it?

*Damn it.*

———

CAGE SLOUCHED in one of the Adirondack chairs with his boots planted wide and his knees cocked. He stared at nothing in particular. He was lost inside his head more than anything.

He finished a hand-rolled, ground out the butt on the wide plastic arm of the chair and grabbed the beer by his foot, downing what remained in the bottle.

One bottle wasn't going to be enough.

A six-pack wasn't going to be enough.

A goddamn case *might* be enough to dull the unbearable tightness in his chest.

Jemma came home from her interview hours later than he expected and when he asked how it went, she shook her head and told him they'd discuss it after dinner, once Dyna was down for the night.

During that time she kept Dyna close, constantly picking her up and hugging her, getting down on the floor during the baby's tummy time and entertaining his daughter every moment she was awake.

While Cage watched his two girls, his chest was cracking open and dread was rushing in to drown him.

From the other arm of the chair, he picked up the glass pipe with an already packed bowl and, lifting it to his lips, lit it. He pulled the hit deep within his lungs and held it as the trailer door opened.

He blew the smoke upward as he waited for it to close.

*For fuck's sake,* Jemma was about to shut the door all right.

On being Dyna's mother.

On being with him.

She was going to leave them both.

He closed his eyes and tried to push away the sour memory of the day Bebe left. Watching his mother pack, then running outside to see she was gone without even saying goodbye.

Jemma would say goodbye.

But what good was a fucking goodbye for him or Dyna? It wouldn't ease the loss. Or the disappointment.

He turned his head to watch her slowly take the three steps down to the trampled-to-death grass, two beers in hand. She offered him one in passing and settled with a sigh next to him in the other plastic chair.

He stared at her as she picked at the corner of the bottle's label with her fingernail, her bottom lip caught between her teeth.

He reached over and cracked the top off for her, then opened his own, letting the brew slide down his throat to cool the burn in his gut. He took another long swig and put it down before taking another hit of the pot in his pursuit to become numb.

Totally pain free.

When he was done, he held the pipe out to her.

She shook her head and took a sip of beer instead. "I might get drug tested on Monday. I can't risk it."

*Don't fuckin' ask.*

He did anyway. "What's Monday?" He knew. He fucking knew.

He wanted to rage at her, to scream that it wasn't fair. She couldn't leave them. Not now.

Not ever.

Instead, his hand shook as he lifted the bowl again and took another long hit, waiting for her answer.

The answer he didn't want to hear.

"The interview went extremely well. I start my new job on Monday. They're short-handed, so they want me to start right away."

"In Williamsport," he forced out.

"That's where the regional offices are located. But I'll be working in patient's homes. The same as what Lottie did with Walt. She brought in a nurse so he could die at home. They sent me the contract a few hours ago and I read through it. The salary's great, the benefits are good. The opportunity couldn't be more perfect."

Perfect for her.

As if she could read his mind, she continued, "This was what I was meant to do, Chris. You knew that. You knew this was only temporary. I was upfront about it."

He wanted to rail at her and ask her how she could just give them up and walk away. Not just from him but Dyna.

A fire now burned in his belly and soon those flames would become uncontrollable. Neither pot nor beer would douse them. He was afraid they'd grow to the point he would explode and say things he'd regret. So, he fought to remain silent.

"You know my memories here aren't good. In my profession, I can get hired anywhere. Since leaving Manning Grove, I've moved place to place because I didn't want to settle. For me, coming home is settling for the life my parents made. I don't want to live that life. I don't want to turn into Trixie. I don't want any man of mine to turn into Ox. I don't *ever* want to see a man use his child, or any child, as a shield. Not ever."

*Fuck.* They'd done that only yesterday. Used Shirley children as shields. But Dyna might not be home with them, or possibly even alive, if they hadn't.

They'd had no choice.

He couldn't hold his tongue anymore. "You'll never be Trixie, Jem. Not ever." That was the goddamn truth. He didn't understand why she couldn't see it. Maybe she just didn't want to.

"When Dyna was taken, I could've told that cop what happened and got the police involved. A normal person would've been screaming at the top of her lungs that her baby had been kidnapped. I didn't. I kept my mouth shut so the club could handle it. That's something Trixie would've done. Any of the ol' ladies, past and present. Afterward, that fact hit me harder than I ever thought it would. I could've put Dyna in danger by simply not letting the cops handle it right away. If something would've happened to your daughter, it would've been *my* fault, Chris. Mine."

"Nothin' happened to her. She's fine. She's home. And she's happy."

"This time. What about the next time?"

He gritted his teeth. "Ain't gonna be a next time." They'd make sure of it. Soon.

"There will always be a next time. This is what living this lifestyle entails. Constant threats. From law enforcement. From other clubs. Hell, from crazy fucking clans." She shook her head. "Don't you want better for her?"

"She's got the best right here. This ain't the Originals' club. This is *our* club. We haven't gone lookin' for trouble once. Not once. But we ain't gonna sit back and let someone fuckin' threaten or hurt our family. And that's what this is, Jem. The Fury *is* our family. Not just mine and Dyna's. Yours, too. Why can't you fuckin' see that?"

"That's not what I saw yesterday." Her voice was soft and filled with sadness. "Yesterday brought it all back. Reminded me of what I didn't want. And it did it in a way I couldn't ignore. We could've lost Dyna yesterday, Chris."

He slammed the now half-empty beer bottle on the plastic arm of the chair. "You hear yourself? *We.* You've raised her since she was just a few days old, Jem. She doesn't know any other mother but you. If you don't want to stay for me, stay for her. Don't desert her." His voice cracked on his last few words and he didn't fucking care.

"Don't you lay that guilt on me, Chris. Just don't. It's low. Jesus Christ, it's lower than low."

She couldn't abandon Dyna.

Not like Sarah did with his daughter.

Not like Bebe did with her sons.

He surged to his feet, his blood screaming in his ears.

"You, Jemma, *you* are her mother! Not Sarah. *You*. You can't leave!" he shouted.

She needed to see the truth, knock down the barrier of her past.

"I'm not her mother!" she yelled back, quickly getting to her feet, too. "I'm not. I..." She spun away, one hand clamped to her forehead, the other on her hip. She took two strides away from him before spinning back with her chest heaving.

Cage didn't like the expression on her face. It twisted his gut and caused a wider crack in his own chest.

Her voice shook as she shouted, "You want me to raise her? Be her mother? Let me take her with me. Let me keep her safe. I'll raise her and love her as my own."

"What?" tore from his throat on a raw whisper. His heart seized and he stared at her, the blood draining from his face and pooling like bubbling lava in his gut. "What the fuck, Jemma? *I'll* keep her fuckin' safe. I'm her goddamn father!" He couldn't stop the last part from becoming a roar.

He could feel himself breaking apart. He kept trying to gather the pieces and keep himself whole. Losing it wouldn't help.

"You didn't, though."

That accusation came so softly, so deadly, that Cage cringed as that fucking sharp knife of hers plunged deep into his chest. It caused him to strike out in defense. "Neither did you."

*Fuck!* He regretted those words the goddamn second they burst from him.

The wounded look on her face twisted the fucking blade stuck in his heart, turning it into mincemeat.

"I'm sorry it's come to this," she said in a choked whisper, the pain evident.

"It was always coming to this, Jemma, always. You always had one fuckin' foot out the door. Ready to escape.

'Cause you refuse to face your past. To move past it. You know damn well you could raise her here. With me. You just don't want to."

She said nothing. Her silence was killing him just as much as her words had.

"Bottom line is, you ain't takin' my fuckin' daughter. She's mine. And you know what? You're mine, too, Jemma. Take off your goddamn blinders and see what's right the fuck in front of you."

More fucking silence.

Her face had turned ghost white and she held one hand clamped over her mouth, probably to keep from verbally striking out at him. Either that or she realized what he said was true.

She was his.

She was his the second they kissed in the rain. That very goddamn second.

He knew none of this was temporary for him. That moment proved they were meant to be.

That they were meant to be a family.

That Jemma was supposed to be his ol' lady. To wear his cut. To stand by his side.

To raise his children.

To be the queen of his kingdom. Even if that kingdom consisted of a fucking single-wide trailer.

Even so, that trailer would contain two people who loved her.

Her daughter and her ol' man.

He had changed his life for them both.

But she wasn't willing to change her life for them.

So, fuck her.

Fuck Jemma for making him and his daughter fall in love with her.

Fuck her.

He'd been deserted before and survived. He'd survive it again.

"Fuck you, Jemma. You don't wanna be here, then go. Ain't stoppin' you. But I ain't leavin' my club, my family, and you ain't takin' my fuckin' daughter. You walk away from me, you walk away from her. This is a package fuckin' deal."

He grabbed his beer bottle and, instead of drinking from it, he threw it as hard as he could. It shattered—just like his life—when it struck the nearby metal shed.

This was Bebe all over again.

His daughter was going to lose her mother.

Because the club was too much for Jemma.

This life was too much for her to deal with.

But it was a life he wasn't willing to give up. No matter what Jemma thought, this life would be good for Dyna, he'd make sure of it. Even if Jemma didn't want to be a part of it.

"You have until Sunday night to get things in order for Dyna," she said flatly.

He squeezed his eyes shut, his clenched fingers pressed to his outer thighs and he said the hardest thing he'd ever said in his life. Every fucking word cracked off another piece of his crumbling heart.

"If you're goin', you go tonight. Pack your fuckin' shit and leave." He didn't look at her when he said, "I'll be back in thirty. Be gone in twenty-five."

He took long strides toward The Barn, not looking back once.

Not fucking once.

He'd known beer wouldn't be strong enough. He needed a shot or two—or, *hell*, a bottle—of fucking whiskey. But he doubted that would help, either.

Dutch raised him and Rook on his own. Cage could raise Dyna on his own, too.

Like father, like son.

Fuck Jemma and the goddamn Volvo she drove in on.

# Chapter Twenty-Three

JEMMA TALKED to Lottie on the phone once a week to check in, but she hadn't gone home.

She texted Judge a couple times a week, but she hadn't called. She was afraid if she did, she'd ask.

And he'd tell her they were doing great without her.

She had no idea if that was true.

She hoped it was. She hoped it wasn't.

Selfish, but true.

No matter what, if Dyna didn't need her, her patients did.

One took her last breath this morning, then faded away peacefully with her husband and her adult children at her side.

That was what her patient, Susan, wanted in the end. The love and support of her family. She wanted to spend every coherent moment with them. To share memories and stories, even if it caused tears and heartache. But they were memories Susan wanted them not to forget. Remembrances of happier times. Of healthier times.

Everyone died. The only difference was how and when. And, of course, where.

Susan chose to die in a house she built to be a home, where she raised her family with her husband.

Jemma was there to help ease her pain, ease Susan into the next chapter of her life, whatever it was.

Now, she sat on the tiny balcony off her tiny apartment above a garage on the outskirts of Williamsport. Her rental was smaller than the single-wide temporary trailer she'd lived in with Cage and Dyna.

She lifted the stemless wine glass to her lips and sipped at the semi-sweet red she'd filled to the very brim.

Honestly, after the day she had, she could use a hit off Cage's bowl.

A few hits, actually.

A week after she gathered her things and drove away from the farm, the trailer, the MC life, as well as Cage and Dyna, she got a text. From Reese of all people.

The text simply said, *I get it.*

A few minutes later Deacon's woman—it was difficult to think of Reese as an ol' lady—sent another. *We're here for you if you need us. Just call or text. Deacon and Judge love you no matter what. We all do.*

That text made her cry when she didn't think she had any tears left.

Cassie sent a text the next day. *Don't worry about Dyna, we have it figured out until Cage does.*

That text made her cry, too. She had to hide her tears behind an unsteady smile because she had been in the middle of dealing with a patient.

Stella sent one two days after Cassie's. Along with a picture of what looked like half of a modular home on an eighteen-wheeler's trailer, came the words: *The club's starting a new business. Renting out these homes on a corner of the farm. It's a really exclusive neighborhood. ;)*

Jemma could guess how "exclusive" it was. Somehow,

Trip knew how to make shit shine. Anything to help his brothers, but still help the club's coffers, he jumped on the opportunity.

The man was smart. He also had good people around him to help with his goals.

A few times a week, the Fury sisterhood would check in with her. The messages were short and she saw right through it all.

What they were doing and why they were doing it.

The ones that didn't make her cry made her smile. Even sometimes both.

Like a distant photo of Cage, wearing his cut and carrying Dyna.

Another picture of Cage propping up Dyna on the seat of his sled. Even with his disheveled hair falling in his face, she could see the wide smile he wore as he pretended the baby was riding his '75 Shovelhead. Her baby tee said *Ride or Cry*. Of course, accompanied with a little motorcycle graphic.

Next came a sixty-second video of Judge and Cassie's Daisy pushing Dyna's stroller as the six-year-old chattered a mile a minute. Jemma watched it over and over late one night until she fell asleep.

In all those texts no one judged her for leaving.

No one told her she was stupid to do so.

No one asked her to come home.

They only kept the connection going, kept open the avenues of communication.

Though, a two word text from her brother cracked open her heart and made it bleed all over again. It simply said: *Sorry, sis.*

That apology could be for so many different things.

Sorry for asking her to come home to help? For stirring up the memories?

Sorry for what happened to Dyna with the Shirleys?

Sorry she was so stupid to fall in love with a man and his daughter who lived a life she swore she never would?

*Sorry.*

She closed her eyes and simply breathed in the still very warm, early September air.

She was sorry, too.

For Cage not wanting to give up that life, even for Dyna.

For Jemma not wanting to live that life, even for Dyna.

Neither would give a fucking inch.

Because that was who they were...

Born from stubborn Fury blood. Built from unbreakable Fury bones.

Both stubborn as fuck and neither willing to compromise.

Each believed what they wanted was for the best.

In truth, that was what a solid relationship was. Full of compromise.

She had stayed for six weeks.

Now, she'd been gone for six weeks.

She had probably missed so much.

She didn't realize how badly she'd miss the photos and videos the ladies had sent her, Jemma was pretty sure without Cage knowing.

Didn't realize how badly she'd miss them. Not just Dyna, but Cage, too.

Didn't realize how much she'd miss snuggling with the baby or sleeping wrapped around Dyna's father. Simply hearing his voice.

Seeing his face.

Waiting for him to walk in the door at the end of his workday.

Watching him interact with his baby, one unplanned and unexpected.

But he did it.

To look at him, one wouldn't think he'd be the best father in the world. But he was. In the beginning by accident, now by determination.

Even raising her in an MC, he was.

*"She's got the best right here. This ain't the Originals' club. This is our club... The Fury is our family, Jem. Not just mine and Dyna's. Yours, too. Why can't you fuckin' see that?"*

He was right. The Blood Fury wasn't the same club as the Originals. They were a family. They had each other's back, they didn't stab each other in them.

The women weren't catty, they supported each other.

Even so...

It was new. Things could change.

Worse, the Shirleys still existed. Even if they didn't, something or someone else could come along to wreak havoc. To try to tear the club apart.

Who would be in the crossfire then?

Dyna, Daisy, the ol' ladies, future children.

The businesses they'd built. The homes they've made. The families they were creating.

All of it was at risk. Why?

The simple answer was because they were a motorcycle club.

No matter how clean the club remained, from the outside they were still looked upon the same. As a "gang" of rough, dirty bikers who broke the law, did drugs and were violent.

While some was still true, the Blood Fury Trip resurrected was not the same as their parents' club.

She shouldn't judge them like others did. She'd lived with them for six weeks, she knew the truth. The good, the bad, and even the ugly.

But she still worried...

She picked up her phone and scrolled through the latest texts.

They weren't from the ladies.

They weren't from Judge or Deacon.

No.

They came from Cage.

They started almost two weeks ago. About a month after she left.

The first one was a picture of what looked like a nursery. *Her own room* was the simple caption.

Two days later came a closeup photo of Dyna about to bawl. She had the red face, the trembly bottom lip and the big fat tear ready to spill over. That text read: *She needs you.*

That one tore out her heart.

A few minutes later: *I need you, too,* with a selfie of an unsmiling Cage attached.

The next day she got a picture of Dyna smiling.

The next day brought: *She had a whole conversation with me this morning.* He included a few seconds worth of video showing Dyna chitchatting away using nonsensical noises. The video was just long enough so Jemma wanted more.

A few minutes later came the following message: *Can't stop thinking about you.* A selfie of him holding his daughter, his expression serious.

The day after, she only received a photo of a fresh tattoo that included the words "Born to Ride" in a ribbon woven around the letters in Dyna's name. It was a closeup so she had no idea where he'd had it added to his body. She didn't know why that particular photo touched her so much. It simply did.

She wasn't sure if she looked forward to each text, or dreaded it. Each one tugged at her heart in a different way. When a text notification came in, her heartbeat would skip and her emotions would be like a roulette wheel. She wasn't sure where they would land.

Every damn day she warred with herself. Whether she was right for leaving. Or wrong.

*She misses you* had come in with a photo of Dyna crying again.

Those killed her. It made her want to reach into the phone, grab her baby and hold her close. To soothe her. To make things better.

The text a few minutes later simply said: *I miss you.*

Then, this morning as she was getting ready for work, steeling herself for what was to come, knowing today would most likely be Susan's last day...

Two texts lit up her phone, one right after the other.

*You're her world.*

*You're my world.*

No photos had been attached to his messages since the last one with Dyna crying.

She missed those photos. She needed to see them.

She was tempted to text him back and ask for a photo of Dyna happy. With a smile on her face.

She had needed it this morning to start her highly emotional day.

But she was afraid to respond. To ask anything of him.

So, she didn't.

But today, the tragic loss of a loving, beautiful and kind woman reminded her of something important...

Life could be cut short unexpectedly. The time spent with the ones you love was never enough.

Any time you had with them shouldn't be wasted.

She learned that when Walt died, but ignored it all of these years. When she shouldn't have. When she shouldn't have taken time with her family for granted.

Time with Lottie, with Judge, with Deacon. By avoiding coming home, by letting her past rule her life, shape her decisions, she'd been missing out on what some others only hoped to have.

Family. Love. Support. Devotion.

She was done with the texts.

She had a call to make.

She downed the rest of her wine for courage and did just that.

# Epilogue

## COMING HOME

With a frown, Cage jogged up the steps to his house and stopped at the landing, taking one last look at the empty stone driveway. Empty except for his sled.

Where the fuck did Tessa go?

Her Mazda was gone and she hadn't told him she'd be taking Dyna anywhere. Not that he cared if she did, he didn't, *if* he knew about it.

He had made sure her vehicle was safe before she began hauling his kid around. Her Protégé might be old but he'd worked on it until it was in tip-top running condition. The twenty-year-old couldn't afford anything nicer, especially with what Cage was paying her to be his house mouse and help with Dyna. Which was not a damn thing.

Not a week after Jemma left, Tessa had shown up. With dark brown hair in soft waves skimming along her jawline, big brown eyes and naturally pouty lips, everyone with a dick—except those with an ol' lady who wanted to keep theirs—had paid attention the day she walked into The Barn.

Until they found out who she was.

Suddenly that interest didn't remain so obvious. It turned more into his single brothers sneaking appreciative peeks when their prez wasn't looking.

Turned out most of his brothers, including Cage, had no fucking clue that Tammy—Buck's former ol' lady and Trip's mother—had remarried after fleeing Manning Grove all those years ago and popped out two more kids.

Trip's half-siblings—a brother and a sister—were unrelated to Sig since Sig and Trip shared the same father while Trip, Tessa and the prez's younger brother shared a mom.

Even so, while Tessa was hot, she was so damn young. And Cage needed her for Dyna, not for himself. Even if he was interested, he wasn't sticking his dick where it might risk getting severed off.

But truth was, he wasn't interested. Only one woman held his interest.

Even after her being gone for six weeks.

Even after she deserted him.

"Tessa!" he yelled as he flung open the front door after finding it unlocked.

The damn doors were always supposed to remain locked. For her safety and Dyna's. They weren't done dealing with the Shirleys and wouldn't be for a while. They were doing it slow and methodical, trying not to catch any heat from the PD.

He'd texted Tessa earlier to let her know he'd be home late, like normal, since he'd been working on a side project of restoring an old muscle car for a customer.

He needed all the extra scratch he could get. Dyna was outgrowing her clothes and going through diapers faster than he could keep up.

He stepped into the tiny foyer of the small three-bedroom ranch and yelled, "Tessa! You home?"

He froze with what he saw.

Furniture in the open-concept living room and dining area.

"What the fuck?" he muttered.

Did Dutch spring for furniture?

No fucking way. His old man was still grouching about what he'd shelled out for the temp trailer rent. When the single-wide was picked up, anything Cage didn't own went with it, including the rented furniture.

Maybe one of the ol' ladies came across an estate sale or something.

He had put off buying any furniture, even used, because he just didn't have the scratch. Another reason he was working his ass off for twelve fucking hours a day.

To provide for his family, which now included Tess. The same way Saylor had become a part of Judge's family.

He didn't need much—other than the basic furniture he already had—since he had Dyna.

He had his sled.

His Impala.

His club.

His family.

He was only missing one thing to make his life complete.

Eventually that gaping hole would fill, even though he wasn't in a rush to fill it.

Dyna was his priority. The most important person in his life.

Everything else could wait.

Then he heard it...

His daughter having a "conversation." Not that he ever knew what the fuck his little monkey was babbling about. Nope. Somehow, he needed to interpret cries and smiles. Facial expressions, too, like when she was taking a big shit. Or had to fart.

Or when she was pissed he wasn't picking her up as fast as she wanted him to.

Because she was stubborn as fuck.

Like her dad.

Like her...

He sighed.

He was going to kill Tessa, Trip's sister or not, if she left Dyna alone and not told him she was leaving. She was young, not stupid.

Well... She did stupid shit, too, as most twenty-year-olds did. One reason why she hunted down Trip and asked for his help.

So, here she was, helping out Cage and Dyna in exchange.

Sometimes fate timed shit just right. Tessa reaching out was one of those times.

*Thank fuck.*

But he was still going to kill her.

It was strange that furniture showed up unexpectedly at the same time Tessa disappeared.

He pulled his phone from inside his cut to text his house mouse to find out where the fuck she was, why she left his daughter and where the furniture came from. His head was down as he typed out the message while walking through the open door of the nursery.

His fingers and his feet froze at the same time, just like when he spotted the goddamn furniture.

Dyna wasn't alone.

His daughter had a perfectly good reason to be babbling.

Cage felt like if he tried to say anything, he'd be fucking babbling, too.

Jemma sat in the corner of the room in the used padded wood glider he'd bought at the consignment shop in town. Her eyes were closed, she wore a soft smile and held his daughter in a hug.

"Is that right?" she whispered in response to more of Dyna's gibberish. "That much, huh?"

Cage's eyes slowly closed, then, just as slowly, opened again to make sure he was seeing what he was.

Yeah, he wasn't imagining it.

He was afraid to walk across the small room. Afraid to say shit.

He was worried if he did, she might just evaporate into thin air. Then he and Dyna would be alone again. His daughter would be without her mother and Cage without his woman.

He almost missed what she asked him since his heart was thumping so loudly in his ears.

"Why didn't you tell me about Tessa? Why did everyone keep her a secret?"

Her green eyes met his and held.

*Goddamn*, he'd missed her. A million times more than his daughter had.

More than anyone had.

The air in the room crackled and popped with energy. That pull sucked him farther into the room.

The foot she'd been using to glide the wood chair back and forth stilled, and she adjusted his daughter in her arms and stood.

Six weeks. He hadn't seen or touched her in six weeks.

It had felt like fucking forever.

He moved closer and leaned in to brush a kiss over Dyna's dark hair. "Hey, monkey. Daddy missed you."

He didn't pull away immediately. Instead, he took that opportunity to inhale Jemma's scent and feel her warm breath stir his hair.

*Her daddy missed you, too.*

"Didn't want you to think we didn't need you," he admitted.

She lifted one dark brow. "We?"

He straightened and took a step back. He had no idea why she was here. Why she was back. And to remain that close he might not be able to resist taking her mouth and showing her just how much he had missed her. "Dyna. Me," he said instead.

"Took you a month to start texting me."

Did that upset her? Piss her off? If so, she shouldn't have left in the first place.

She shouldn't have just walked away.

Again, he kept that shit to himself and said, "Wanted to get my shit together first. Have somethin' to offer you. A reason for you to come home."

In truth, Dyna and Cage should've been reason enough for her to come home.

Maybe they were. Maybe they were why she was here now.

"Also had to convince your big-ass brother and your smart-ass cousin I was worthy of you. That was the hardest part." When she didn't say anything, he asked, "Where's Tessa?"

"She and Saylor took the night off. They're going out and having some fun."

"So, they're goin' to Crazy Pete's," he guessed. Where they could be watched and protected.

Jemma laughed ever so softly. "Yes."

It was one of the rules both Trip and Judge made for the girls. Even though they were too young to drink legally, they could play pool, darts and sing karaoke without anyone worrying. More often than not, Reilly joined them.

He didn't want to talk about Saylor or Tessa. He wanted to find out what the fuck was going on. What finding Jemma in Dyna's room meant. To him and to his baby girl. "Where'd the furniture come from?"

"Storage."

"It's yours."

She tipped her head. "It's mine."

"You don't need it?"

"I need it and plan on using it."

Thank fuck he was smart enough to read between the lines. He did his best to keep his next question calm and under control. "Why now?"

"When I lost a patient the other day, I was reminded of something important I'd forgotten."

"What's that?"

"How precious the time is with the people you love. You shouldn't waste the time you're given."

"So, you put your stuff in my place. Without askin' if it was okay."

"Did I need to ask?"

He smothered a grin. "Put Dyna down."

"Chris..."

"Put Dyna down, Jem."

Her gaze searched his face and with a single nod, she put Dyna in her crib and tucked the teddy bear that was propped in the corner next to her. The one he had clung to all those years ago.

Rook had found it hidden away in the garage a few weeks back.

"Got no idea how it got there," his brother had grumbled as he shoved the dirty stuffed animal into Cage's chest.

"You probably stole it and hid it to torture me, you fucker."

Rook had laughed. "Yeah, seems about right. But look, coulda burned the damn thing. Lucky I didn't, now you can give it to my niece."

That was exactly what Cage did. He cleaned up his bear, the most treasured possession of his childhood, and gave it to his daughter.

She loved it.

He loved her.

He loved Jemma, too.

He only hoped she loved him back.

He also hoped the furniture meant one thing.

She was home.

For good.

But he needed to hear it from her.

He also needed to touch her.

Actually, he needed more than that. But her telling him she was home for good was a good start.

The rest could come later.

Not too much later, though. Because by that time Tessa might be home. And what Cage wanted to do with Jemma was going to take time and a lot of noise.

He wasn't going to hold the fuck back. He didn't want her to hold back, either.

He'd fucking missed her.

They had a lot of lost time to make up for.

"Gonna kiss you," he murmured as he cupped her face and tipped it up to his. "Guessin' that's all right with you."

She looked serious when she said, "I'd be pissed if you didn't."

"I need to hear it, Jem."

"What?" she whispered, her eyelids getting heavy.

"Why you're here."

"I asked my director if she could move the area I cover closer to home."

"Home?"

"Here."

"You hate Manning Grove. You hate the club life." He needed to be sure this was what she wanted.

"You're right, I do. But I love you and Dyna more."

All the oxygen rushed from his lungs. "Love me?"

"Yes."

*Oh, thank fuck.* "Love my girl?"

"Yes. But she's not your girl."

"She ain't?"

"She's *our* girl."

Yeah, she was. "Gotta promise me, Jemma."

"Anything."

"That you won't leave. No matter what happens, no matter how hard life fuckin' gets. No matter how much this town reminds you of your past. You gotta stick. I need you to stick. Dyna needs you to stick. Six weeks was like a goddamn lifetime. Can't do it again."

"I'm not sure if I'll ever get over my past, but I hope building our future together will help with that."

"Make enough good memories to drown out the bad."

She nodded and the tip of her tongue swept over her bottom lip. "I need you to kiss me."

"Need to kiss you, baby. So need to fuckin' kiss you."

"Then stop talking and do it."

"Once I start, might not be able to stop."

The corners of her lips curled. "I'm okay with that."

"Got a daughter to worry about," he reminded her.

"We can make it quick," Jemma said, her eyes now crinkling at the corners, too.

"Fuck that. Ain't gonna be quick. Okay, maybe the first time. But right after that we're startin' again and makin' it last."

She sighed softly. "I've missed you, Chris. You and Dyna. I'm sorry I left."

He shook his head. "You never planned on stayin'. You only did what you said you were gonna do. You stuck with your plan." As much as he didn't like that she had, he also had to admire her for not wavering from it. But he still hated it.

"I know, but... Once I fell in love with you and Dyna... I shouldn't have been so damn stuck on that path."

One side of his mouth pulled up. "Stubborn."

"Yes."

"Our girl's stubborn, too. See it already."

"Like her Daddy."

"Like her Momma," he corrected.

"Now kiss me."

"If you fuckin' insist, woman."

"I do—"

He crushed his lips to hers, sweeping his tongue through her mouth, exploring every corner. He'd missed this, missed her. Missed her taste, missed the feel of her against him. Missed the noises she made when she came.

He couldn't wait to slide inside her, have her wet heat squeezing his dick. Feel her come. Fill her up.

Make her his all over again.

And that was what he did.

———

*When you find true love, home is no longer a place.*
*It's the people you love, wherever they are.*
*When you're with them, you know you're home.*
*~ Jeanne St. James*

———

**Keep up with my latest news by signing up for my newsletter here: https://www. authorjeannestjames.com/**

———

***A past that defined a future...***

Shade has a secret.
One he's hidden most of his life.
Secrets created in his past.
Of a broken family. A little boy lost.
Of broken dreams. With only nightmares left in their wake.

As a prospect, his MC nicknamed him Shady because he's quiet and keeps to himself.
As a patched member of the Blood Fury, he changed it to Shade, because that's what he prefers... to stick to the shadows.
To remain unseen.

Then he sees her. A flicker of light at the end of a long, dark tunnel.
The only problem is, he may never escape that darkness until he sheds the chains of his past that weigh him down.

**CONTENT WARNING: Some of the memories and flashbacks in this book involve a child. Those**

memories include sex trafficking, child trafficking, child abduction, child abuse, attempted suicide, and murder.

**Turn the page for a sneak peek of
Blood & Bones: Shade**

# Blood & Bones: Shade

BLOOD FURY MC, BOOK 6

### Prologue
### *Stolen*

THE SWEETNESS of the chocolate and vanilla swirl coated his tongue as soon as he took a lick.

He loved ice cream.

His mommy knew just how much, too. It was why every time she dragged him to the big building with all the busy stores, and the even bigger parking lot, she bought him an ice cream cone.

Because he'd been a good boy.

He hated this place, but sometimes it was worth going with her just to get his special treat. It had to be a swirl.

He followed his mommy out the doors and into the night, his sticky fingers leaving marks on the glass. His mommy had taught him to look both ways before stepping out into the street so he didn't get smashed by a car.

This wasn't really a street, but cars still drove on it. Sometimes really fast.

Most of the time she made him hold her hand so he'd

keep up. She told him it was because he got "distracted." He didn't understand what she meant.

Tonight her hands were so full with bags, she couldn't hold his.

One time when she wasn't holding his hand, he forgot to look. She grabbed his elbow, jerked him back onto the sidewalk, yanked his arm straight up and swatted his butt really hard.

He didn't like that.

It made him cry.

She cried, too, and tried to hide it. But he saw it and it made him cry more.

He didn't like when his mommy was sad.

When Daddy left, she cried all the time.

He'd climb into her lap and put his hand on her wet cheeks and ask why she was crying. Did she miss Daddy?

She'd hug him close and never answer him. But the hug felt good, because he missed his daddy, too.

Julian didn't know what he did wrong to make his daddy never come back. His mommy would tell him he didn't do anything, but Julian didn't believe her.

Maybe he'd been bad. Maybe Daddy was mad at him.

Now Daddy was gone, Mommy always brought him with her to this place.

The place with all the people and cars.

The place where he sometimes got spanked, but also got ice cream.

His favorite kind.

He looked both ways again because he couldn't remember if he already did. Maybe that was what Mommy meant by him being "distracted."

Sometimes he had to think really, really hard to follow what she said or remember what she taught him, so he wouldn't get a spanking.

She always said those spankings were for his own good. So, he guessed that was okay.

He wanted to be good for his mommy so she wouldn't leave, too.

Because if she left, he'd be all alone.

He didn't want to be alone. Being alone was scary.

If he was alone, no one would talk to him.

Without his mommy, he wouldn't get any more chocolate and vanilla swirled ice cream.

When he saw no cars coming, he jumped off the sidewalk onto the lane where the cars drove. Where he could be smashed.

He ran to catch up to his mommy.

She was talking on her phone and walking so fast! Why wasn't she waiting for him?

He couldn't run and lick his ice cream cone at the same time. He had to walk slowly and be careful.

The ice cream began to drip, so he stopped and licked his hand. When he looked up again, he knew he had to catch up. She'd be mad if he got too far behind.

"Julian, let's go! It's late." She was still walking and talking. She wasn't waiting for him.

With a last lick of his cone and another lick at another fat milky drop on his hand, he began to run again and his shoelace started to flap. Mommy needed to tie it for him.

"My sneaker—" He stumbled when he stepped on his lace. He almost fell but caught himself so he didn't skin his knees. It always burned when he did that.

When his arms went out like an airplane to stop from falling, his ice cream cone tumbled from his fingers. His mouth made an *O* as he watched it plop upside down onto the pavement.

He stared at the mess it made, and his ice cream began to make brown and white octopus legs around the cone as it melted.

His eyes began to sting just like when she spanked him. "I d-dropped my ice cream, M-mommy!"

"Julian! Hurry up!" She sounded mad now.

But he dropped his ice cream! He wasn't done with it.

With every step his mother took, she got farther and farther away.

She always spent way too long inside the big building. Way too long inside those stores.

Sometimes it wasn't worth the ice cream.

Like now.

Because he dropped it.

He squatted down and picked up the cone, but none of the ice cream came with it. It was almost all a muddy puddle now. The cone had broken, too.

"Mommy!" A sob bubbled up his chest and he let it out. He didn't care if anyone thought he was a baby. "Mommy!"

His heart was beating so fast and he had a hard time seeing Mommy since he was crying.

He stood up and, with one last look at his ruined treat, he began to walk again, trying not to trip. His lace whipped around like a snake he saw at the zoo. He watched as it flipped back and forth with each step.

*Flip. Flop.*

It was fun.

"Mommy!" he called. He couldn't remember where their car was. He could never remember. "Mommy!"

"Julian, come on!" she called out as she stepped back out from between two parked cars. She was no longer talking on her stupid phone and the bags were on the ground at her feet.

He tried to run again but almost tripped. "Mommy, tie my shoe," he shouted.

As he got closer, she disappeared again between what he finally remembered was their van and another big black van, a lot bigger than theirs.

He stopped and stared at it.

*Stranger danger.*

That was what Mommy taught him about big vans like that. To stay away from them. To never get in a car with a stranger. To scream if someone tried to get him inside a car or a van.

But their van was parked next to it. That was where Mommy was waiting for him. He didn't have to worry about the black one. It belonged to someone inside... He stopped and turned to look at the big building. The mall. That was what she called it. He had a hard time remembering.

He spotted his spilled ice cream again, even though the parking lot was full of shadows. He took a breath so big it sucked his belly in and then he pushed all the air back out so he wouldn't cry again. He rubbed the back of his hand over his eyes and his nose.

Mommy hadn't seen him crying yet. He didn't want her to know he wasn't a big boy. That he was a crybaby. If he told her what happened, maybe she'd stop on the way home and get him another one.

That was what she'd do! Because Mommy loved him. Not like Daddy.

He spun and ran, doing his best not to fall, to the spot where she disappeared.

He stumbled to a stop.

Two men were standing with his mommy.

She looked really scared.

She was crying and her eyes went wide when she spotted him.

Julian didn't like the way she looked.

He didn't like the way they were holding her.

She didn't look happy at all. She looked really upset.

She looked like this after Daddy left.

He couldn't understand what she was saying because of the man's hand covering her mouth.

"Mommy?"

The side of the black van was open, and they were trying to put her inside.

Her arms were moving and her feet were kicking. She didn't like what they were doing. *Stranger danger!*

She was fighting them so much, it took both of them to shove her into the van.

"Jul—"

A needle appeared in the one man's hand.

He hated needles! He hated going to the doctor to get shots.

They always gave him ouchies.

He ran over to them to stop them from giving his mommy an ouchie, too.

"Mommy!"

He was too late. The bigger man with the baseball cap and the bushy beard pushed it into Mommy. The other man who was short and fat turned toward Julian.

"What the fuck?" he shouted so loudly, Julian wanted to cover his ears.

"What are you doing to my mommy?"

"Fuck, asshole. She's got a kid."

Julian ran to the opening of the van and saw his mommy now lying on her stomach and not moving. There wasn't a seat in the back like in their own van, she was right on the floor.

Was his mommy sleeping?

Was she dead?

She wasn't moving. She wasn't crying. She wasn't screaming any more. She wasn't scared.

"Mommy!" He reached for her and the fat man grabbed his arm and yanked him away.

"What the fuck are we gonna do with this kid?"

The tall man shrugged. "Leave him here?"

"We leave him here, someone's gonna find him and this will be reported."

"Then we take him with us."

"And do what with him?"

"Who fucking cares, asshole! We can dump him somewhere, or let the boss deal with him."

"Don't think he was part of the deal."

"Just get the fuck in the van before someone sees us and calls the cops."

"You told me to take her car." He held up a set of keys and shook them, making them jingle.

"Then get in her minivan and shut the fuck up. Gonna call the boss and ask what he wants done with him."

"He's gonna be pissed."

"Maybe not. This kid's the right age. He's probably worth something."

"Maybe we can get money for him ourselves."

"Fuck that. I'm not risking that shit. We'll let the boss decide."

"Get in the van, kid," the tall one demanded.

"I don't wanna get in the van. I want my mommy!"

"Get in the damn van!" The fat man jerked on his arm. Julian winced. "Ow!"

*Stranger danger.*

What did mommy say he was supposed to do?

Yell!

Julian opened his mouth and let out a loud shriek.

A hand clamped over his mouth, stifling his yell. He bared his teeth and bit as hard as he could.

"Fuckin' A, you little asshole!"

Julian was struck alongside his head.

"Look, kid. We'll kill her if you don't cooperate. You need to be a good boy or you'll never see your mommy again."

*What?* He'd never see his mommy again?

Tears began to leak from his eyes.

"You think he understands any of that, asshole? He's what? Three?"

"He ain't three. Are ya, kid?"

No, he was four.

That was what his mommy told him when he blew out the candle on his birthday cake. It was ice cream, too. Chocolate and vanilla with chocolate crumbles in between.

But he couldn't answer, the man's hand was covering his mouth.

"Doesn't fucking matter how old he is. We got something to tie his ass up?"

"Need to keep him quiet, too. Can't be driving and hearing his ass screaming."

The fat man's big belly jiggled when he laughed. "Now I'm glad I'm driving her car. Wouldn't want to listen to that."

"Let's get him tied up and gagged then."

"We need to tie her up, too, in case that shit wears off."

"It won't."

"You wanna risk it?"

He tried getting loose, he tried biting the man's hand again. Nothing was working.

His mommy still wasn't moving.

She couldn't help him.

She couldn't.

He was supposed to fight and shout, "Stranger danger!"

But he couldn't.

He hated the mall.

He never wanted to come back here.

Mommy would have to get him ice cream somewhere else from now on.

He wasn't coming back here again.

He wasn't.

He needed to wipe his eyes so he could see. He needed

to wipe his nose so he could breathe. Snot was filling it and the man's hand was smearing it.

He was thrown onto the dirty floor of the van and before he could scream again as loud as possible, something was tied tightly around his mouth. It tasted yucky. He'd eaten dirt before and that was what it tasted like.

His arms began to hurt because they were yanked behind his back and his hands couldn't move anymore. He couldn't kick because the man tied his legs together.

The big side door slammed shut and the back of the van got darker.

He no longer heard the men talking.

He couldn't see the front of the van. He could only hear another door opening and slamming shut. Someone starting the van. The rumble of the floor beneath his wet cheek.

He stared at his mommy's face, making a wish just like he had with his birthday cake. He squeezed his eyes shut really, really hard and wished and wished and wished.

He wished Mommy would help him.

He wished she'd tell him what was happening.

He wished she'd open her eyes.

She didn't.

None of that happened.

Not until much later.

**Continue Shade's story here:
https://books2read.com/BFMC-Shade**

# If You Enjoyed This Book

Thank you for reading Blood & Bones: Cage. If you enjoyed Cage and Jemma's story, please consider leaving a review at your favorite retailer and/or Goodreads to let other readers know. Reviews are always appreciated and just a few words can help an independent author like me tremendously!

Want to read a sample of my work? Download a sampler book here: BookHip.com/MTQQKK

———

**Sign up for Jeanne's newsletter: http://www.jeannestjames.com/newslettersignup**
**Join her FB readers' group for the inside scoop: https://www.facebook.com/groups/JeannesReviewCrew/**

**Find my complete reading order here:**

**https://www.jeannestjames.com/reading-order**

### Standalone Books:

Made Maleen: A Modern Twist on a Fairy Tale

Damaged

Rip Cord: The Complete Trilogy

Everything About You (A Second Chance Gay Romance)

Reigniting Chase (An M/M Standalone)

### Brothers in Blue Series

A four-book series based around three brothers who are small-town cops and former Marines

### The Dare Ménage Series

A six-book MMF, interracial ménage series

### The Obsessed Novellas

A collection of five standalone BDSM novellas

### Down & Dirty: Dirty Angels MC®

A ten-book motorcycle club series

### Guts & Glory: In the Shadows Security

A six-book former special forces series

(A spin-off of the Dirty Angels MC)

### Blood & Bones: Blood Fury MC®

A twelve-book motorcycle club series

<u>**Motorcycle Club Crossovers:**</u>

<u>Crossing the Line: A DAMC/Blue Avengers MC Crossover</u>

<u>Magnum: A Dark Knights MC/Dirty Angels MC Crossover</u>

Crash: A Dirty Angels MC/Blood Fury MC Crossover

Romeo: A Dark Knights MC/Blood Fury MC Crossover

**Beyond the Badge: Blue Avengers MC™**

A six-book law enforcement/motorcycle club series

<u>**Double D Ranch**</u>

A six-book MMF ménage series

<u>**COMING SOON!**</u>

Property of Stone (Kings of Anarchy MC: Pennsylvania)

Dirty Angels MC®: The Next Generation

**WRITING AS J.J. MASTERS:**

**The Royal Alpha Series**

A five-book gay mpreg shifter series

# About the Author

JEANNE ST. JAMES is a USA Today, Amazon and international bestselling romance author who loves writing about strong women and alpha males. She was only thirteen when she first started writing and her first published piece was an erotic short story in Playgirl magazine. She then went on to publish her first romance novel in 2009. She is now an author of almost 70 contemporary romances. She writes M/F, M/M, and M/M/F ménages, including interracial romance. She also writes M/M paranormal romance under the name: J.J. Masters.

Want to read a sample of her work? Download a sampler book here: BookHip.com/MTQQKK

To keep up with her busy release schedule check her website at www.jeannestjames.com or sign up for her newsletter: https://www.authorjeannestjames.com/

**www.jeannestjames.com**

Newsletter: https://www.authorjeannestjames.com/
Jeanne's Down & Dirty Book Crew: https://www.facebook.com/groups/JeannesReviewCrew/

facebook.com/JeanneStJamesAuthor

instagram.com/JeanneStJames

bookbub.com/authors/jeanne-st-james

goodreads.com/JeanneStJames